VALLEY OF WOLVES

VALLEY OF WOLVES

A GYPSY SPY NOVEL

NIKOLAS LARUM

CARLISLE PUBLISHING, LLC
CHEASAPEAKE

Published by Carlisle Publishing, LLC
Chesapeake, Virginia 23321
Published 2022

ISBN-13: 978-0-9998850-4-8

Cover design by Devin Boyd
Front cover photograph by Clem Onojeghuo | www.stocksnap.io
Back cover photograph by Sebastian Picler | www.stocksnap.io

In memory of my brother Eric, who shared the original adventure with me and cheered me on to the finish line. This one's for you, Red.

Blessed be the LORD, *my rock,*
who trains my hands for war,
and my fingers for battle.
Psalm 144:1

PART ONE

Drom Reiziger

Chapter 1

The Wells Cemetery board lost its final appeal in its dispute with the National Park Service on Friday. At issue was a fence it had erected around the century-old community graveyard. The lawsuit alleged that elk introduced to the Buffalo National River Park had knocked over gravestones. The NPS claimed the fence was installed on Park land.

Craig Moore, the Park's superintendent, ordered the immediate removal of the fence.

Ferrisburg Daily Bugle, April 4, 1988

Ferrisburg, Arkansas – April 1, 1988

Buck couldn't stand Yankees. Always in a rush, even on a Friday night. "Iffin I gotta git her pulled out by another tractor, it's gonna cost you extra."

The man in charge just stared at him.

As darkness fell, light drizzle turned to hard rain. Buck maneuvered the backhoe off the lowboy and threaded his way down the slope. One of the agents stepped aside, pulling up the hood of his windbreaker. The agent in charge ignored the driving rain, his eyes fixed on the backhoe tracks. They kissed the stretched caution tape and he shot his hand up for Buck to stop.

Buck glared at him. "You best git out the way! Hate to see you git hit by this here claw."

The man slid over as Buck dug the bucket into the ground. He scooped back, swung left, and dumped the load, burying the tips of the agent's fancy shoes.

Digging fresh graves never bothered Buck much, digging up old ones made him plain onery.

Chapter 2

Spokane police, in coordination with the FBI, raided the home of a Gypsy family suspected of running an elaborate fencing operation. Officers confiscated $1.6 million in cash and an estimated $150,000 in jewelry. Five adults and ten minors were arrested. The family's patriarch, Karoly Bardu, denied all charges and promised a vigorous defense.

The Spokesman-Review, June 5, 1988

Penticton, British Columbia – June 12, 1988

The door brushed the carpet behind him, but Drom didn't turn from his task. Bending over the crib, he caressed the baby's cheek with the back of his fingers.

"Where have you been?" Her edgy whisper signaled trouble.

His shoulder blades drew together as he took a tight breath. "Climbing."

"Drom, it's two a.m. You were supposed to be home hours ago."

Turning, he faced the press of her gaze. Her beauty, etched in moonlight, overwhelmed his defenses. "It took longer than I expected, Shell." Shell, that's what he called her now, even in the stillness of the nursery. And though she was upset, she still called him Drom.

Her eyes softened. "You shouldn't climb after dark, it's not safe."

Safe. Was anything safe? Were they?

He willed his arms loose, his hands open. "It wasn't dark when I started."

She tucked a chestnut tress behind her ear. "Are you coming to bed? You're pitching tomorrow, remember?"

Church. Softball. Family Sunday normalcy. He needed it. She deserved it. "Soon as I check on the other two and shower."

"They're fine. And I'm awake now. Why don't you head straight to the shower?"

He breathed easier at her olive branch. "I'll be quick."

With a slight smile, she slid out of the room.

Afterward, he held her as she fell back to sleep. Burying his nose in her luxurious hair, he listened to her breathe. Praying, he reached for still waters, but the ripples in his mind refused to dissipate. Why hadn't Karoly contacted him? Her warm breath bathed his broad chest. He thought of the children, Amanda ten, Jakob three, and David fast approaching the terrible twos.

How long did they have?

He woke to sunlight scented with coffee and bacon. He sat up and his three-year-old flew into him. "Daddy!" Jakob clung to his neck. "Come on! Mommy's fixing breakfast."

Jakob's excitement was infectious. He carried him into the kitchen. Amanda was at the stove, David in his high chair. Shell gave him a kiss and ruffled Jakob's dark head of hair.

"How did you sleep?" she asked.

He gave her an easy grin. "Fast."

"Dreams?" Her eyes held his, probing.

"How many eggs do you want, Daddy?" Amanda asked.

He turned to her, glad for the distraction. "Better make it four, sweetheart. I'm famished."

"What did you climb yesterday?" Ever since he started taking her to the rock gym, Amanda loved hearing about his climbs in Skaha.

Setting Jakob down, he poured himself a cup of coffee. He blew across the mug, his eyes on his step-daughter. "The Replicant." He jumped at the crash of shattering ceramic, splashing his coffee on the floor.

Shell gaped at him, her hand slack from the dropped plate. "The Replicant? Are you out of your mind?"

The stove sizzled. Amanda turned to flip the eggs. Drom downed the remains in his cup and set it on the counter.

"It's not as bad as it looks from the ground." The Replicant—over ninety feet of sheer I-dare-you capped with a crux of climb-upside-down—truly wasn't as bad as it looked from the ground. It was worse.

"No gear and in the dark!" She threw her hands up. "You have responsibilities, Drom."

He followed her gaze as she eyed their boys. *I know, they are why I climb.* He grabbed a tea towel off the counter. "Stay put, I don't want you getting cut in that mess."

Kneeling down at her bare feet, he gave her ankle a gentle tug. She lifted it, placing her hand on his head. Drom swabbed her sole from heel to toe, then set her foot on the chair. He mopped the linoleum around her other foot, scooping the shards up with the towel.

The family ate in silence.

⊕

The drive to Grace Community Church was subdued, followed by morning pleasantries with parking lot friends and congregational greeters on their way into the sanctuary.

The bulletin advertised the sermon "Doing Difficult Things," with Psalm 144:1 as the central text—Blessed be the Lord, my rock, who trains my hands for war, and my fingers for battle.

Drom eyed his fingers, still raw from the climb, recalling a different verse. "You may not build a house for my name, for you are a man of war and have shed blood."

He scanned the sanctuary from his vantage point near front row center. The congregation of now nearly three hundred had tripled from two years ago. Too many new faces, almost. Relying more on instinct than insight, he identified a near dozen unfamiliar ones.

The musicians started to play, drawing the people to their feet. After the songs, the pastor challenged the congregation to embrace their talents and use them to further the kingdom of God. Drom had his doubts. Not all skills were redeemable.

Beside him, Shell kept pace with the sermon. One ear to the front, he scanned again, noting the new faces: a raised hand, an amen, an attractive couple working together to find the verses but turning pages in the wrong direction, a salt-and-pepper man in suit and tie perched on the edge of his seat like a hawk among sparrows.

Closing prayer.

Shell popped up to get the baby. He bolted to get the other two. They had a system.

Amanda and Jakob in tow, Drom spotted his wife talking with the page-turners. Amanda stepped past him and he restrained her with a firm hand on her arm. Her chin whipped over her shoulder. Nodding toward the wall, he positioned them within earshot of the nursery door.

The woman, blond and about Shell's height, put her hand on the man's arm. "We left our baby with the sitter. We weren't sure what the nursery would be like."

French accent?

Shell shifted David on her hip. "This church cares about its children. Parents take turns in here. Gives us all a chance to walk out the Golden Rule. Where y'all from?" Southern slipped out when she met new people. They needed to keep working on that.

"We are from Quebec," the man said.

Definitely French.

"Well, welcome to Penticton. My husband and I love it here. Be glad to give you a tour of the place." She invited them out for lunch after service next Sunday.

Drom had heard enough. He strode out to the station wagon with Amanda and Jakob. Unlocking it, he ordered the kids to get in. He cranked the engine to life, then stood next to the running vehicle, eyes fixed on the church doors.

As Shell approached with David in her arms, she slowed. Eyeing Drom, she locked David in his car seat between Amanda and Jakob. "Everything all right?"

He studied the stream of people pouring of the church. "What was her name?"

"Who?"

"The woman you were talking with by the nursery."

"She didn't say."

"Odd, don't you think?"

"You're being paranoid." Shell got in the car.

"Probably." He got behind the wheel and slammed the door. Making his way out of the parking lot, he glanced at his mirrors.

"Half the church is headed to the ballpark," Shell said. "We will be followed."

He was upsetting her. Relaxing into the seat, he eased his mirror checking. No need to fray her nerves any more than he already had in the past twelve hours.

You've frayed them for the past four years.

Minutes later, he pulled into the packed parking lot. He helped her get the kids out of the car and pulled his gear bag out of the trunk. "I need to change. You better hurry and get your seats. The stands are filling fast."

She took off with the kids, then doubled back and kissed him. "Don't fret over me. You know I worry enough for the both of us. Just get out there and have fun."

"This is fun."

"Go change!" With a playful shove, she was off to the kids. She spooked Amanda from behind and the boys squealed when their sister jumped. Twisting, Shell swooped David up. "Break a leg, Drom!"

"That's a good luck wish for actors, not ball players!"

"Whatever!"

Drom laughed despite himself. He lived for these happy morsels. Making his way to the restroom, he locked himself in the farthest stall and suited up, surprised at his eagerness to get on the mound. Have fun, she said. He wanted just that, to play a game for the sheer fun of it.

Grace Community's at bat in the top of the first inning ended in disappointment. Drom didn't make it off the bench, no one ran home. He trotted out with the team and took his place on the mound, reminding himself to allow the other team a couple of hits.

Drom let the first batter snag his second pitch. He drove it to the ground. The shortstop ran in on the bouncing ball, scooped it, and flung it to first.

"Safe!"

Drom struck out the second batter in short order. His slow pitch looked lackluster—the ball tracing a graceful arc—then veered at the last instant, leaving the batter to beat the wind.

The third batter took command of the box. Drom's forearms bristled. He checked the stands. Two rows above his family sat the woman from Quebec, childless. Scanning right, he found her counterpart near the stairs.

Snapping his head back to the batter, Drom took in the profile, the rigid readiness of his body. Tumblers moved. Click, click, click. The photo in *The Spokesman-Review*, another Gypsy humiliation captured in black and white. A face on the periphery of the police line. The hawk perched in church looking to feast on sparrows. The soldier in league uniform readying his aluminum club.

"Strike him out, Drom!"

The crowd's words faded beneath Shell's. *Break a leg.* Gripping the ball overhand, index and middle fingers riding the seams, he launched it in a gentle curve that concealed its violent spin.

The batter swung. The softball dove, slamming into his left leg just below the knee with a satisfying crack. He toppled, screaming and holding his leg above the sharp bone stabbing through the skin.

Drom was on him in an instant, pushing the man onto his back with his hand. "Call an ambulance!" He placed his cheek against the batter's ear. "Lie still."

Gasping, the man twisted his torso. Drom pinned him down and pressed his fingers against the man's carotids as if checking his pulse—but instead of counting beats, he cut them off. The man's eyes fluttered and his body relaxed.

"He's passed out. Where's that ambulance?" Drom glanced at the faces gathered around. No couple from Quebec. He slipped his belt off and cinched it around the leg to slow the bleeding. A siren wailed in the distance.

Shell burst into view. "Ga—"

"Where's that ambulance!"

The siren blared near and died. Red pulsed in sunlight. Drom faced Shell. "Take the kids, grab the bags. I'll meet up with you."

"Where are you going?" Shell asked.

"With the patient." The medics lifted the batter onto the gurney. "Go. Mind your mirrors."

Shell froze, locking eyes with him, then turned her gaze to the yawing back entrance of the ambulance.

Drom spotted the Quebec duo slicing their way through the crowd. Close, too close. He ripped off his cleats. "Go!"

Shell looked down at his hands, his cleats held like tomahawks. "Drom, don't."

Mr. and Mrs. Quebec were almost through the crowd.

"You have to move." It was a command, not a request.

Shell spun and darted off toward the parking lot. Mr. and Mrs. Quebec breached the crowd. The cleats flew from his hands.

Turning, he jumped into the ambulance and yanked the doors shut. The ambulance lurched forward in concert with its renewed wail. Drom peered from the back window at Mr. and Mrs. Quebec holding their faces, blood streaming through their fingers.

"You shouldn't be in here, Drom," the attending med tech said.

"Count it as one of my volunteer days, Mark." He pulled on a pair of latex gloves.

Mark stabilized the leg. "What happened?"

"Bad pitch." Drom slapped the patient.

The man came to, arms flailing. His left forearm caught the side of Mark's head slamming it into the compartment wall. The med tech crumpled to the floor, out cold. Drom blocked the right arm and shoved the patient back down onto the stretcher. Grabbing the chest strap and pulling it across, he locked it in and jerked the strap tight until it bit into the batter's biceps.

The driver stared at him from the rearview mirror. "What's going on back there?"

"Mind the road, Bill. I've got this." Drom pressed down on the knee of the broken leg. "Name."

The patient clenched his jaw. Drom pressed harder. The jaw turned loose with a stream of French profanities.

"Hey!" Bill barked from the front, "Get it together or I'm stopping this ride."

"Best not," Drom said. "Mark's down and I don't have time to check him. You need to push this beast as fast as it will go."

The engine roared with renewed anger, forcing Drom to grab the gurney rail to keep his balance. He bent over the batter. "Name."

More curses.

Snatching the key ring from Mark's belt, he opened the narcotics cabinet. He grabbed a vial and syringe, stabbed the needle into the morphine bottle, and drew the plunger back.

The Frenchman struggled against his restraints.

Hooking his thumb into the man's nostril, Drom jabbed his index and ring fingers under his eyebrow. He shook his head. Drom shoved his thumb in past the first knuckle and kept pressing with his fingers until the man stopped struggling. Bringing the needle to the stretched-open eye, he dangled the point over the pupil.

"I would lie still, were I you," Drom said in French. "Who are you working for?"

"*Qui de diable êtes-vous?*"

Drom pressed the point into the sclera. The man kept deathly still, tears streaming down into his ear. Drom was impressed. "Agency."

Clenched teeth.

Drom had enough. He needed fast answers and he wasn't going to get them. Shifting the needle from eye to thigh, he dumped the morphine into the injured leg, then tossed the syringe into the red sharps bin. The man passed out, nose bleeding.

He moved to Mark. The med tech had an egg-sized knot on the back of his head and the beginnings of a bruise on his cheekbone, but his breathing was regular and his pupils responsive. Drom strapped him into the side seat. "We're good back here."

Drom patted the Frenchman down. No concealed weapons. He dug through the back pockets. Nothing. No billfold, pocket litter, or even lint. Reaching in through the waistband, he checked inside the athletic cup. Standard equipment.

He scrambled into the passenger seat. "Mark should be fine."

"I know we owe you," Bill said, eyes riveted to road, "But this is over the top. How am I going to explain it all?"

"Tell them it was a rough ride."

"You know that won't do, especially once the patient comes to."

"He won't say a thing, trust me. I would appreciate it if you didn't either."

"You're crazy, you know that?"

"I wish I could still use that excuse." Drom checked the side view mirror. The nearest vehicle behind them was a hundred yards back and losing ground. The ambulance came around the curve of Martin Street as it became Main. "Slow it down a second."

"I'm gunning to Carmi then hooking it straight into Regional."

"Bill, please."

The driver glanced at him and then tapped the brakes.

Drom bailed out and hit the pavement rolling. Bouncing over the curb, he sprang to his feet and sprinted west through the neighborhood toward Fairview Road. Turning south, he hopped fences and cut through back yards, heading to the steeple of St. Gregory's. He needed a change of clothes and a pair of shoes.

Dressed in blue jeans, a T-shirt, and deck shoes from St. Gregory's donation closet, Drom made his way to the rendezvous, a supermarket in the middle of a strip mall. Slipping into the service alley, he scaled the utility ladder to the top of the first store. He crept across the flat roof to the façade and surveyed the parking lot. Their minivan wasn't there. He checked his watch. He had a half-hour before he could officially worry. He worried anyway.

Moments later, he spied their minivan heading west on Green Avenue. It drove past the entrance. Eight vehicles followed it across Skaha Lake Road. Five minutes later, the minivan appeared heading east on Brandon Avenue. It was alone. It turned south on Paris Street and crossed Green Avenue. It reappeared moments later, traveling northeast on Skaha without growing a tail. The minivan turned into the parking lot.

Drom padded to the north end of the mall and scaled down to the asphalt. He strolled past the shop windows, taking in the reflection of the parking lot with his peripheral vision and stopping occasionally to admire the displays. Popping into a card shop next to the supermarket, he browsed the aisles. A couple of other customers came in after him. One spoke with the cashier, the other made a beeline to the high-end fountain pen display.

Drom slipped out of the store, walked past the supermarket, and turned into the parking lot. Windows and waxed car bodies gave him eyes behind his head. He was clear. When he reached the minivan, Shell was in the passenger seat. Putting on his best smile, he got behind the wheel and twisted around to the back. "You kids ready for a road trip?" Jakob cheered. David chortled.

Amanda looked worried. "Where are we going, Daddy?"

"It's a surprise, sweetheart," he said, "but getting there will be as much fun as being there." Amanda didn't look convinced. Turning back to the front, he cut the radio on and faded the speakers to the back. Shell's silence weighed on him. He didn't expect she would keep it much longer.

He came out on Green Avenue and turned south on Channel Parkway. Any pursuit team would have difficulty following them without being spotted.

"The station wagon?" he asked.

"Wiped down and parked in the garage." Shell stared at the channel through the passenger window.

Drom checked his mirrors. "Did you light the candle in the window?"

She wiped the corners of her eyes and turned toward him. "Was it necessary?"

"The batter spoke French. The couple from church had French accents."

"They were from Quebec."

"So they said. That batter's French wasn't Canadian. It was Parisian."

Twisting in her seat, Shell squeezed David's foot, then turned back to the front. "They really loved that home."

Drom rode the right-hand lane at just below the speed limit. The southbound traffic behind him flowed around in the passing lane. He scanned the mirrors.

"It's was just a place," he said. "We can find another."

"Gavin," she said.

Gavin, that's what she called him when she was afraid. Turning to her, he wiped her cheek with his right hand. "We're going to be okay, Michelle."

Michelle, that's what he called her when she needed him the most.

Chapter 3

Romania, an ally of Nazi Germany in World War II, opened its files to the World Jewish Congress to aid them in tracking down pro-Nazi war criminals hiding in Western Europe.

Schenectady Gazette, June 22, 1988

Southern Manitoba, Canada – June 22, 1988

The zipper sounded, pulling Drom's eyes from the camp stove to their tent. Shell crawled out onto the dewy grass of the warm dawn. Yawning, she stretched her tall frame. Her hair was disheveled, her eyes puffy. She was adorable.

Drom took her in his arms before she could lower hers and kissed her forehead. Hints of bergamot and clove tickled his nose. "Morning, love."

"How long have you been up?"

He gave her a proper kiss, then poured them both some coffee. "A while."

"That's not an answer, Drom."

Drom. Even in an isolated camp ground, she uses his new identity. Gavin Leoppard died three years ago in the fires of his discovered and destroyed childhood. She only resurrected the name in moments of extreme duress.

He stared at her, weighing his options as he drank in her beauty. "A couple of hours."

Her brow softened, but her eyes probed. Her irises reminded him of the golden-hued burl wood border on the chess table his father gave him for his eighth birthday. He lost many games to the distraction of its swirling grain.

"A couple of hours as in two or a couple as in several?" Concern colored her tone.

"I went for a run, climbed an oak tree and then a spruce, rinsed off in the camp shower, and made coffee." He lifted his mug.

"A couple as in several, then." Her chide was salted with affectionate disapproval.

Drom gripped his mug tighter, bracing for the real question.

She sipped her coffee. "Dreams?"

And there it was. He knew her moods well enough. An I-don't-think-so answer wouldn't do. "One, at least."

She kept boring her brown eyes into his heart. Out with it, they said, letting them hide is toxic to us both. But her next question surprised him. "Isabela?"

Machine gun fire erupted in his head. He rubbed at the scar on his chest through his shirt. She hadn't mentioned Isabela in years. *Why now?* "No, just old scraps from the Warehouse."

And of flying into the smoke ring to do violence to men.

She squeezed his hand, pulling him present. "We need supplies. We're low on diapers and the go bags didn't have any coats."

He answered her maternal concern. "We won't be camping into winter."

Ten days out of Penticton, and he still worried he hadn't lost them. For the past several days, they had shadowed Lake Winnipeg's coastline, steering clear of developed areas. They could shop in one of the townships. Those would have fewer police. But strangers were more noticeable in small villages. Though Winnipeg had more watchers, it also contained more people to hide among.

"Would you like to sleep in a proper bed tonight?" Drom asked.

Jakob popped out of the tent. "I hafta go potty!"

Shell glanced at their son and turned back with a sly grin. "Two rooms, right?"

Doubts gnawed at him as he drove into the city. His Drom Reiziger alias was compromised. His new life was built around it. Jakob and David carried the only names they had ever known. For Amanda, Amy Lane was a distant dream of a bad memory. As far as their children were concerned, they weren't hiding out as the Reizigers. They were the Reizigers. Government inefficiency would hide them but for so long. He needed new papers from Karoly.

They checked into a cheap motel; reputable enough to be clean and have a set of connected rooms, far enough back from Main Street to take cash and not ask for identification. After the obligatory family run through the bathrooms, they headed out for a bite to eat.

They settled on burgers, the family diner type instead of franchised fare. Drom splurged on malted milkshakes, adding a festive flair to their meal. The kids dug in with gusto, even the baby.

After buying groceries and diapers, they searched for thrift stores. Secondhand stores saw their share of family shoppers and used clothing came with no trail. The first shop fit their bill with near perfection. They replaced their getaway clothes and current outfits, but didn't find coats.

The third store they entered was more factory retail outlet than middle-class castoff shop. Organized in distinguishable departments, it had wide aisles and was well lit, lending it an airy feel.

Drom caught the look in Shell's eye. "Remember, we're here just for coats."

Shell and Amanda picked through the coat racks while Drom watched the boys. Jakob was inching his way from a game of peek-a-boo into a full-blown hide-and-seek. David squirmed in the stroller, trying to get out. Picking him up, he bumped into a mannequin. Clutching David to his shoulder, he spun with leg extended and swept the mannequin off its feet. The dummy clattered to the floor and Drom kicked its head up the aisle.

"Easy, pal."

The green vest and white name tag registered in time for him to pull his punch. He glanced around. No fast movements. No brandished firearms. No law enforcement. No one staring at him. Almost no one. He lowered his fist from the wide eyes. "You startled me." The man didn't move. A warm hand touched the small of his back.

"Hey, it's me," Shell said.

Drom turned to her and she mouthed the word "water." Loosening his hold on David, he dropped his shoulders and took a breath, imagining a still pond.

"Sorry, sir," Shell said. "My husband's been working overtime at Stony Mountain and it makes him jumpy as all get out. You all right?"

"Yeah." The clerk tugged at his smock. "Had an uncle who worked at the penitentiary. Heard stories. Tough job." He eyed Drom. "Didn't mean to bump you, mister. I can't always see when I'm moving a mannequin."

I didn't see the mannequin move.

Drom scanned the store again, this time looking for ghosts. He set David down. "Fault's all mine." He picked up the mannequin. "Where do you want him?"

"Over by his head would be fine."

Drom walked the dummy over and put the head back on. Catching Shell's eye, he placed his fingertips below his lower lip and brought his hand down, signing "thank you."

Giving him a sad smile, she motioned Amanda to the registers. Corralling the boys, her daughter headed to the front of the store.

Drom paid in cash.

They rode back to the motel in silence. A child cried in Drom's mind—his much younger self, Carlos de Leon. *I didn't see the mannequin move.*

They worked together getting the boys to bed. Shell bathed them and brushed their teeth. Drom dressed them and tucked them in bed. He read them a Bible story while Amanda showered. Once she got situated in the other double bed, Drom prayed with them. He kissed their heads, cut the lights, and shut them in.

Stepping into the king suite, he spotted the stuffed trash bag at the foot of their bed. "We'll need to burn those at the next camp."

"I know," Shell said. "Clothes in the bag, Mr. Reiziger, it's shower time."

Afterward, they lay quietly in the dark, holding each other. He expected her to grill him about the store, but she fell asleep, leaving him with his thoughts. He listened to her breathe while he prayed the twenty-third Psalm. His eyes grew heavy and he drifted off.

⊕

His father stroked the wall, then jerked the handle at the click of the electronic lock. Stomach trembling, Carlos stepped through the doorway. His father pulled the power switch down, bathing the Warehouse in the harsh light of the mercury vapor flood lamps. He followed his father across the giant chess board, down the side of the Olympic-sized pool, and into the playground.

"*¿Que juego hoy, Papá?*" Carlos asked.

"English, boy," his father said. "Spanish at school and home. Here, English."

His mouth went dry. "Yes, sir."

"Today's game is Run the Mannequins."

"Mannequins?" Carlos tried to identify the word, but his mind refused to return a Spanish, French, or German equivalent.

"The target dummies." His father pointed. "You have to run past them."

Noting their placement, Carlos realized they weren't in their tracks. "Rules?"

"None."

He locked eyes with his father. Every game had rules. The base rule, the one Carlos called Rule #1, was time to completion. If he finished faster, he got rewarded. Overtime meant pain, needles from his father's fingers or darts from the air guns. It was why he made time Rule #1. Other rules ran the gamut from order of target to placement of projectiles. *No rules?*

Carlos studied the play area and noticed something else missing. "Ammunition?"

Waiting for the answer, he mapped the board. The mats were set for floor exercise, twelve meters to the side. *English, boy, English.* Forty feet to the side, four targets in play: left, right, center, and left again. All he had to do was run through, hitting them with …

"Ammunition?" he asked again.

The games always had ammunition, everyday items from home, school, or office. Anything Carlos could fit into his hand became a bullet in a gun.

"None."

Run the mannequins—no rules, no ammunition. "Weapons?"

"You," his father said. "Run!"

Carlos sprinted through the center, passing the first and second dummy, and was thrown onto his back. Kicking up onto his feet, he spun, looking for what tripped him. A needle pierced his biceps, cascading agony all the way to the bone. Negative biofeedback from his father's hand, a needle laced with synthetic bradykinin—liquid pain. Papá wasn't pleased.

"Run through the mannequins, Carlos!"

Turning toward the third and fourth targets, he moved despite the pain. Air stirred behind him. He ducked, but the blow caught the back of his head, sprawling him at the feet of the third mannequin.

"Why are you letting them hit you?"

Hit me? Getting on all fours, Carlos shook his head.

"I didn't see the mannequin move," he protested, as if a game with no rules still had a standard of fairness.

The mannequin kicked him in the face.

⊕

Springing out of bed, Shell stumbled to the connecting door. "What is it? What's wrong?"

"The kids are fine, Shell." Drom headed to the bathroom. He splashed his face with cold water and stared at his reflection. His lip was whole, his eye unswollen. His face carried only faint remains of his childhood. Shadows of Shane Leoppard played from brow to chin.

He punched the glass.

"What the—"

David's wail cut her off. Hinges squeaked. The baby whimpered. Shell cooed. Closing his eyes, Drom listened to her lullaby, letting it douse the fires of his rage.

His madness was gone, but anger remained, its coals banked on the ashes of his memory. He laid Carlos de Leon to rest in the dirt of Gavin Leoppard's grave. But Carlos kept clawing his way out, exposing Drom to memories denied and long forgotten.

"We'll need to get some hydrogen peroxide," Shell said, "and bleach."

Drom stared at his blood dripping into the sink. Three years now since he dragged her into the shadow life. She brought a murderer to justice once. Now, she stood ready to sanitize their room like an underworld cleaner. Leave no evidence. Her flat statement of tradecraft was a more stinging rebuke of his outburst than any tirade she could muster.

He shifted his eyes toward her without turning his head or letting go of the sink. She swayed with the baby at the bathroom door. She was a mother and a wife, adult to three children and one young man caught in between.

In moments like these, her aching beauty seemed phantasmal. He longed to hold and touch her, if only to be reassured of her tangibleness. But he dared not move. Instead, he focused on his raw knuckles. Pain was presence. It was a lesson learned from his grandmother, Hishoro, given with a sudden slap when he questioned his reality.

I hurt, therefore I am.

"Dreams?" Shell asked.

"Nightmare." He gazed at his shattered image, his arms shaking with the force of his grip on the basin's rim. Hinges squeaked. A mattress creaked. Closing his eyes, he held his breath. One heartbeat, two. He heard his children's slumbered breathing. He exhaled. One heartbeat, two.

He inspected the damage. The mirror was a loss, his knuckles skinned. He brushed the bits of glass scattered across the drainboard into the waste basket. Pulling the loose pieces of mirror out of the metal frame, he added them to the collection.

Reaching in from behind him, Shell folded her hands around his and pressed them under the flowing tap. Adding hot water and soap, she washed his hands in hers while gently kissing his shoulder. "Let's get you bandaged up."

She sat him on the edge of the bed and dug the first aid kit out of their bag. She swabbed his knuckles with alcohol wipes, then wrapped them in gauze. "Comfortable?"

He made a fist and opened his hand. Meeting her eyes, he gave a nod.

She knelt in front of him a moment longer, then sat beside him. "Tell me about it."

"I didn't see the mannequin move," Drom said.

⊕

The kick caught him on the chin and cut across his lower lip. He blinked the sparks away, tasting blood.

"I said run the mannequins, boy!"

His father's roar rallied him. He ran toward the end of the mats. The third mannequin caught him with a jab and he tumbled forward.

"Stop holding back, Luca," his father said. "I am not paying you and your men to hold back."

"You will get the lad killed if we go all out," the mannequin called Luca said.

"Do the job I hired you for."

Carlos was rattled, but not too rattled to do the math. His father had set an ambush. To complete the game without a severe beating or worse, he had to find a way to run the mannequins.

He reassessed, this time absent assumption. He was on his knees surrounded by four grown men dressed like his normal target dummies. As they closed in, he calculated target distances and time.

Luca lashed out with a roundhouse. Carlos rolled right, converting the vicious kick into a glancing blow that drove the needle deeper into his arm. The leg swung over him and he side-kicked Luca's supporting leg. As the man fell backward, Carlos pulled the needle out of his arm and flicked it up Luca's nostril. Luca hit the mat holding his face and howling like a wounded animal.

The three other men froze. Carlos ran toward the two nearest the end. If he could get one more down before they recovered, he had a chance of making it off the mats with nothing worse than a sore arm, a black eye, and a split lip.

He charged the target on the right. The man squared off in a fighter's crouch. Leaping up, Carlos landed his foot on the man's right thigh and hooking his fingers on the jaw just below the ear, sprang left.

Bone snapped and his feet hit the mat. Rocketing forward, he head-butted the next man's gut. The target doubled over and Carlos clipped his head with a knee. The man crashed to the mat and Carlos ran over him.

He crossed the finish line before the last man could reach him.

⊕

"Why would your father subject you to such abuse?" Shell asked.

"It wasn't abuse," Drom said. "It was necessity."

She turned toward him, her eyes probing. "Necessary for what?"

"You know what." He bent forward, clasping his hands between his legs, gaze fixed on the floor. It wasn't the crack of bone he heard in his head. It was the crash of glass and the thunder of the high-powered revolver. He remembered how she turned pale as death when she finally saw him for what he was. His chest caved under the weight of the memory.

Her finger tips pressed under his jaw, lifting his head to face her. "I know it hurts to say it, babe, but it was abuse. He could have done it differently or not at all. He could have let you be a child. I know you loved him. But you don't have to defend what he did to you."

He took her hand and kissed it. "He was who he was. Being his son was dangerous in and of itself, abuse or not."

"What made you scream?"

He gazed at the floor. "The snap."

"When you broke his jaw? Babe, don't let that give you nightmares. You were a child defending yourself against grown men."

"I've told myself that for years. Truth is, though, they never had much of a chance."

"I don't understand."

"The snap," he said. "It wasn't his jaw. It was his neck."

Chapter 4

A Reich citizen is a subject of the state who is of German or related blood, and proves by his conduct that he is willing and fit to faithfully serve the German people and the Reich. The Reich citizen is the sole bearer of full political rights in accordance with the law.

Reich Citizenship Law, September 15, 1935

Rosenheim, Germany – September 1935

Hishoro dumped her latest gleaning of branches near the kettles.

Her mother stirred the *jaxnija*, a hearty minced meat and red bean soup. She had two caldrons of it going, gently bubbling to the flickering flames of the fire. "You best add more wood now. By the looks of them, they'll be a while."

Hishoro followed her mother's gaze across the field to the corrals where German soldiers were busy bargaining with the horse traders.

The Reich's military escalation had dramatically increased the demand for draft animals. Hishoro's family brought their herd up from their traditional grazing grounds near the Tisza River in Hungary into southern Germany, hoping to get to top price for their horses.

But the Gypsies weren't the only ones at the horse fair. The army buyers gave preference to German sellers, followed by Czechs. The Slovaks were pressing for their chance with the quartermasters and the Romani men, who had been kept cooling their heels and herds for two days already, were cutting in where they could.

At the moment, her father and oldest brother were maneuvering some of their finer draft mares toward one of the officers. Even at this distance, Hishoro could tell her father's grip on the reigns was tighter than usual, an indication of his frustration and determination.

Smiles were scarce on the men's faces and the horses were skittish. Sensitive animals, they reflected the mood of their handlers. When men were tense, horses became jumpy. And a jumpy herd was a dangerous. Danger or not, Hishoro was glad they had come. With this many *kumpániya* gathered, someone was bound to make her father an offer.

At sixteen, Hishoro should be cooking her own family's meals instead of tending her mother's fires like a girl. But for her twin, Keti, she would have been married off years ago.

Hishoro stoked the coals and added wood. Through the dusty haze, she saw her father talking with a German officer. The man checked the mares' forelegs, hooves, and teeth. He waived a subordinate over. The enlisted man headed with her father toward the rest of their herd while her brother led the two mares to the purchased corral.

Maybe we can eat before sundown after all.

The meal was somber despite the sale. The women served, the men complained.

"Robbery," her father spat. The Germans paid the Gypsies half the rate they were giving everyone else. "We would have done better with the Magyars."

The Romani camped away from the *gazhe*, the non-Gypsies, at the fair. Hishoro heard music and revelry erupting from all points of the compass. Other families may have suffered disappointment in their selling price, but they weren't letting it dampen their spirits. She hoped her father wouldn't become so sullen that he avoided company.

Once their chores were done, Hishoro and Keti joined several other young women from their *kumpániya* and went exploring. They began with short visits to the camp fires nearest them, then widened their circuit to the other Kalderash Roma gathered. Lovari from Romania and Sinti from Germany had come to the fair as well, but the girls felt safer among their own tribe.

They wandered between the wagons, stopping here and there to chat and swap gossip, with no discussion of destination. But all shared the same goal, the two large bonfires blazing in the field away from the wagons and tents. Young men gathered there to dance to the fiddles and drink. The girls came to watch and be seen.

Their little band pressed through to the inside edge of the circle of people. Clapping to the lively music, they added their voices to the chorus. Young men challenged each other in dance; spinning, leaping, and slapping their kicking feet in complex rhythms.

"Enjoying the show?"

The baritone voice brushed across Hishoro's ear. Startled, she bumped into Keti, who would have fallen but for the man catching her. His back to Hishoro, he righted her sister. Keti's face came up and she stepped back, wide-eyed. Hand at her side, she made the sign to ward off *Beng*, the evil one.

He turned to Hishoro. "My apologies, I did not mean to startle you."

Hishoro froze. His right eye was warm, dark as burnt walnut. His left sat like a pale sapphire under his black hair, as silver as the moon above. Shaking herself to break the spell, she took Keti's good hand and stalked off without a word.

"What's wrong?" Keti asked.

Hishoro kept marching them away from the bonfires. "I didn't like his look."

"Me neither, but there was more to see besides him."

"It's late," Hishoro said. "Mother will have us up early to clean and pack."

"Pack? I thought we were here for the rest of the week?"

"The herd is sold. *Dáda* wants to leave before anyone changes their mind."

"Why should anyone change their mind? We sold them good horses."

"*Dáda* doesn't trust the Germans."

"*Dáda* doesn't trust anybody," Keti said.

Hishoro caught the undertone. Their father was suspicious by nature. His general demeanor had rebuffed the few bridal enquiries made since the girls came of age. Maybe Keti's withered arm wasn't the problem, Hishoro wondered for the first time. Maybe their father was unwilling to see them married and Keti was just the excuse.

Her mother rousted them out of their warm *plapóno* in the thin light of the breaking dawn. The girls folded the quilt in half, rolled it into a tight tube, and tied off both ends with short cords. Face pinched with pain, Keti stuffed it in the undercarriage compartment. The sisters headed to the water pump, Keti carrying one bucket, Hishoro two. Doing twice the work was her penance for Keti's arm.

Back with the water, they stoked the fires. Eyeing their fuel supply, Hishoro knew her next couple of hours would be spent scavenging for wood. Grabbing a hatchet, she set out toward the dark wall of the forest edge. No words need be spoken to Keti. They were used to the routine. Her sister would dump their buckets into the cleaning pots. While they came to a boil, she would make multiple trips to the pump. Meanwhile, Hishoro would chop and gather armload after armload of wood.

On her third trip back, she knew something was wrong. Instead of washing clothes or pots, Keti was cooking. Scanning the camp, she spotted her parents sitting cross-legged on the ground beside their wagon, deep in conversation.

Her mother waived her arms, her voice rising. Her father glared, his shoulders stiffening. It was the dance of their conversation. The louder her voice, the colder his stare. The more animated her arms, the more rigid his shoulders became with each measure of their private song.

Giving them wide berth, she dumped her load on the pile of wood. "What's with them?"

Keti scooped cornmeal porridge into a bowl and handed it to her. "It already has sugar, so don't add anymore." Her sister's authoritative tone wasn't lost on her. Older by only minutes, Keti still pulled rank now and again, but especially when she was troubled.

When Hishoro pressed her question again, Keti stuck a folded slice of bread in her open mouth. "I put fresh butter on it. Eat, then we'll get more water."

Hishoro knew better than to argue when Keti was in older sister mode. Resting on a low stool, she ate her breakfast in silence while her twin cooked. Keti had three caldrons going, more than was needed if they were breaking camp today. Looking at the piled branches soon to be ash, she wondered if she could talk her father into moving their camp closer to the tree line. Watching his face as her mother's arms waived, she doubted it.

Tossing her bowl into the wash basin, she grabbed a bucket in each hand and stomped off to the pump.

Catching up, Keti took a bucket from her hand. "No need to be cross. I didn't want you to hear it on an empty stomach."

"Hear what?" Hishoro asked.

Keti said nothing. There was a small crowd at the pump. Waiting patiently was not a Romani virtue. The girls jostled their way through more timid souls until they encountered more stalwart women. Words and insults were exchanged, but no blows. The twins weren't interested in starting a fight. They only wanted the others to know that they were a force to be reckoned with.

"His name is Tshuri," Keti said.

The piercing eye rose like a pale moon in Hishoro's mind. Goosebumps flared up her arms. She glanced at Keti's face. Stoic, it betrayed nothing beyond its usual etchings of pain.

"His father came by and had coffee with *Dáda* while you were gathering wood."

"*Dáda* doesn't like him." Hishoro had aimed for a flat, disinterested tone. But the disappointment in her voice surprised her own ears.

"*Dáda* doesn't like France," Keti said. "He and mother have been at it since the man left." They walked with a slow and steady pace, both to keep from sloshing water out of the buckets and to give them a few more precious moments of privacy.

"Which of us does he want?" Expectancy and fear churned Hishoro's breakfast into an uncomfortable weight in her stomach.

"Don't be silly," Keti said.

Chapter 5

In our continued efforts to revive the German nation and protect the purity of German blood, a national Gypsy law should be instituted. Such law should mandate the complete registration of the Gypsy population to facilitate their sterilization, restriction of movement, and removal from military units and civil jobs. A final solution for this Gypsy menace should be included in the law as well.

> General Memorandum – March 4, 1936
> Johannes Pfundtner
> Chief Secretary of State
> Reich Ministry of the Interior

Paris, France – July 1936

Hishoro placed a wet cloth on Keti's forehead. The heat in the wagon was stifling, the air outside dangerous. Keti's face, seamed by years of chronic pain, twisted itself into new masks of torment with each contraction. Hishoro's baby kicked up a storm inside her as if in protest of losing the race to see the light of day to its cousin.

Keti's marriage provided their release from their father's *vitsa*. He would not relent under her mother's badgering or Tshuri's father's increased bride price offerings. On the second day of negotiations, a cousin was presented to marry Keti. She went for half price, but she was married. Her father no longer faced the specter of a spinster daughter and further enhanced his standing through the additional tie to a prosperous Kalderash family in western Europe.

They married during the horse fair. The girls, now officially women, left their father's *vitsa* with their hair braided and heads covered in colorful scarves to signify their marital status. They were warmly welcomed into Tshuri's camp and put to work for the mother-in-laws the morning after their wedding sheets were displayed.

The wagon inched forward, then stopped again. The marchers' chants pounded into their *vôrdòn*, covering Keti's wail as another contraction took hold. As the baby pressed down the birth canal, workers in the tens of thousands marched for labor reform and increased wages. The throngs pressed past the vehicles and wagons clogged in the avenue. Police whistles and shouts broke across the rhythm of the crowd chant and strained Hishoro's already frayed nerves.

She had begged Tshuri to not take them back into Paris. Tensions were high and the strikes made peddling and begging beyond difficult. He measured her with his piercing gray eye, then smoothed her brow with a tenderness his calloused hand concealed.

"The delivery can't wait any longer," he said.

The gendarmerie had him spooked.

At a road block midway to Paris from Troyes, a squad of provincial police stopped their *kumpániya* and demanded papers. As the designated head of family, Tshuri was required to have a *carnet* listing all members of the band of travelers. Hishoro and Keti weren't in his paperwork. Once the officer in charge noticed the discrepancy, the sisters were hauled over to the large tent on the side of the road.

The *gazhikano* tent filled Hishoro with foreboding. Grasping Keti's hand, she let her sister pull her through the tent flap into the moldy gloom beyond.

An officer hunched behind a small desk piled with neat stacks of paper and a menagerie of rubber stamps. A metal contraption with lettered buttons held center stage. The policeman pinched a page from the pile, fed it into his machine, then assaulted Keti with a battery of questions. Name, date of birth, mother's name, father's name, grandparents, husband. His fingers hammered the buttons, the paper skittered left. He slapped a lever, sending the carriage right, and tapped the buttons again.

Pulling the paper out, he directed Keti to stand in front of the camera. It flashed. The sisters flinched.

Waiving Hishoro forward, the gendarme rattled his questions rapid fire. Page filled, he flicked his hand right. She stepped in front of the camera, gaze fixed on Keti, whose fingers were being pressed onto an ink pad.

"*Regardez l'appareil!*" The photographer's bark pulled Hishoro's head around. The light flashed, blinding her. Someone nudged her shoulder and she moved left. Her fingers were pressed into the inkpad one at a time and then pushed onto a white card. Through bright dancing spots, she spied Keti stepping behind a white curtain. A woman commanded her sister to unbutton her blouse. Hishoro eyed the exit. It was guarded.

The white curtain slid sideways. Keti shuffled out, head down, gripping the crook her withered arm with her left hand.

"*Sar san?*" Hishoro asked her, how are you?

"*Mishto.*" Keti kept her eyes down, her tone at odds with her response.

The nurse waved Hishoro in. She unbuttoned her blouse. The nurse lifted a rubber necklace up to her ears and placed its cold medallion on top of Hishoro's left breast. The nurse stared at her watch a minute, then jotted a note on her chart. She moved the medallion, warmer now, down to Hishoro's rib cage. "Take a deep breath." Moving the other side, she gave the same instruction.

Producing a tailor's tape from her pocket, the nurse took several head measurements, then had Hishoro stand. She checked leg and arm lengths, then wrapped the tape around her chest, waist, and hips. Last, she had her stand on a platform with a vertical board attached that had a sliding block.

"Stand straight." She pressed the block onto Hishoro's head and had her step away. "One hundred and sixty centimeters. You are a short one, even for your kind. I need you to sit back down on the stool and roll up your sleeve."

Her sleeve halfway up her, Hishoro stopped. "I am well. I don't need a shot." She rolled the sleeve back down.

The nurse faced her, syringe in hand. "It's not a shot. I need to take a blood sample. It's just a pin prick in your arm, then we're done."

Eyeing the needle, she thought of Keti holding her arm. "You hurt my sister."

"She didn't complain. Roll the sleeve up or I'll call an officer in here to help."

Hishoro glared at her, then pushed her sleeve up. The needle stabbed past her skin and into the vein. The nurse pulled back on the plunger, filling the syringe with blood. Placing a cotton ball over the venipuncture site, she extracted the needle.

"Hold the cotton ball down firmly for a few minutes. You won't bleed after that." She opened the curtain.

Hishoro stepped out of the tent. Keti was standing beside Tshuri at their wagon. The rest of the *kumpániya* were busy putting away the items the gendarmerie had tossed on the ground during their search of the caravan. She made her way over to her husband.

"They are updating our papers. Once I have the *carnet* back, we leave," Tshuri said.

Hishoro noted the good number of their company still queued in front of the tent. "Without them?"

"They can catch up. We need to get away from these roaches." Tshuri always referred to the police as roaches, soldiers he called rats.

Sensing his mood, she knew better than to argue. She and Keti gave their respective wagons the once over, making sure their men stowed the household items correctly. Satisfied, Hishoro climbed inside her *vôrdòn* to get away from the prying eyes of the *gazhe*.

Now, *gazhe* demonstrators threatened to push their way into her sanctuary as Keti's baby tried to find its way out. The wagon lurched forward and Hishoro struggled to keep on her feet as she braced Keti in her squat.

Keti grunted into her push and the baby's head appeared. "Breathe," Hishoro reminded her. "We're almost there." She knelt in front of Keti and her sister put her hands on her shoulders. "One more push." Keti bore down and baby came out. "A girl." Hishoro handed her up to Keti who immediately tucked her to her breast.

The wagon turned right and the horses quickened their pace. She watched as Keti's baby instinctively found her mother's breast and began to nurse. Keti's serene face shocked her. Pain's hold had loosened its grip for a moment, exposing the beauty beneath.

"What shall we call her?" Hishoro asked.

"Nadja." Keti kissed her baby's forehead. "I never thought I would see the day."

Her admission made Hishoro uncomfortable. Keti was reserved to a fault, limiting her conversation to the practical. Heart, hopes, and dreams were Hishoro's territory.

The wagon stopped and Hishoro welcomed the interruption. "I should get Mateo so he can meet his daughter." She retreated outside.

They were in the central courtyard of a group of tenements. Laundry hung on crisscrossed lines above. Hishoro stepped down, came around the rear of their wagon, and stopped short at the corner.

They were not alone.

Two black men stood at the tail of a truck. Tshuri and Mateo set a crate down beside the others in front of them. One pried the lid open with a crow bar. The other peered inside. "What's this?"

Tshuri reached inside and pulled out a rifle. Holding it in his right hand, he stretched out his left and a metal box appeared. It looked like a magic trick to

Hishoro. He clicked the box into the side of the rifle and pulled the bolt back. The black men stepped back, hands up. Tshuri rested the stock of the gun on his hip, barrel pointed to the sky.

"I brought fifty Erma EMPs, but since you are ungrateful, I'll be keeping this one."

The man removed his cap, exposing a wide brow. He mopped it with his sleeve, then turned his bright eyes on Tshuri. "We were only expecting pistols. How did you get your hands on submachine guns?"

"Not your concern, Andre. All I want to know is if you are buying or not."

Andre pulled one out, examined the frame, then put it back. He moved over to the next crate, extracted a pistol, and studied it closely. "You live dangerously, my friend."

"These are dangerous times."

"You've stolen these from the German army."

"As an honest businessman, I resent the accusation." The set of his jaw told Hishoro he was restraining a smile. She failed to find any humor in the situation. If the gendarmerie had discovered the crates, they would have been arrested as smugglers or, worse yet, spies.

"Erma EMPs and Lugers. What else did you bring?"

"A case of Mauser C96s along with several thousand rounds of nine millimeter ammunition. This haul is enough for you to start a small revolution."

"I am not interested in revolution." Andre scratched at his sharp jaw. "We need protection. These fascists worry me."

"This is France, Andre, not Germany."

"Too many here approve of Herr Hitler. Your skin isn't much lighter than mine. They'll need little encouragement to rid themselves of the likes of us."

"*Liberté, equalité, fraternité.*" Tshuri's smile bloomed with sardonic laughter. "You've enjoyed the deception of the sentiment and are disquieted when it is threatened. Lighter my skin may be, but it's no less a smudge on their society. I am Romani. No one has ever offered us liberty, equality, or fraternity. We do our best to make our own."

"Then you would do well to keep more than just one Erma."

"One is enough for now," Tshuri said.

"Forty-nine is less than I like. Can you get more?"

"If the price is right."

Andre reached into his jacket and handed Tshuri an envelope and a small, fabric pouch. "Cash and diamonds as agreed."

Tshuri inspected each, then deposited both in his trouser pocket. "It will take some time, but I can find you more."

"And pistols as well. We'll need more pistols."

Tshuri nodded. He and Mateo stood in the court while the men loaded the crates into the truck. When the transfer was done, he shook Andre's hand and walked back to their wagon.

Hishoro met him at the driver's bench. "It's a girl, Nadja."

"Are you staying with me or going back in with Keti?"

She scampered up beside him. Tshuri snapped the reins across the backs of his team and they lumbered out of the courtyard.

The demonstrators had moved several blocks north. The path now clear, the two wagons headed back the way they had come. Hishoro kept quiet, her gaze fixed forward. The hair on her nape stood on end and she knew he was staring at her. She turned and the sun glinted in his one gray eye, lighting it like an electric torch. She hugged herself against the shiver running down her spine in the July heat.

"How much did you hear?" he asked.

"All of it." She cast her eyes down and plucked at her skirt.

"And?"

She forced herself to meet his gaze. "Horse trading is legal."

"True," he said. "But no one is paying diamonds for horses."

Chapter 6

Officials blame drought conditions for the record number of forest fires in British Columbia. The Forest Service has banned all campfires in the Penticton and Princeton ranger districts.

North Island Gazette, June 27, 1988

Penticton, British Columbia – June 28, 1988

Special Agent Rick Cannon snagged his bag from the overhead compartment and made his way off the cramped airplane. The June heat assaulted him the moment he stepped onto the boarding stairs. Sweat cascaded down his sides, confirming the suit was a bad call.

A short walk took him across the tarmac into the terminal. Michael Blackmore was leaning against a column by the luggage carousel. He wasn't smiling.

"Michael," Rick said, "thank you for coming."

"Duffle bag all you bring?"

"Wasn't planning on staying long."

"Good." Spinning on his heel, Michael marched out to the parking lot. His government-issued blue sedan was unmarked. The Canadian Security Intelligence Agency felt no need to advertise.

Slipping into the passenger seat, Rick tossed his bag into the back. He loosened his tie to combat the heat. It didn't help. Instead of turning the air conditioning on, Michael toggled the windows down. Rick thought about taking his jacket off, but he didn't want Michael to see how much he was sweating. "I appreciate you doing this for me."

"You didn't leave me much choice," Michael said. "Besides, you know me. I keep my Nephites close, but my Lamanites closer."

The midday sun bounced on the chop of Lake Skaha, scattering bright arrows in all directions. Rick put on his sunglasses. "Two years we rode side by side in Paris and I'm your Laman now?"

"Paris was a long time ago, Rick."

"Not long enough to forgive?"

"Not long enough to trust. How's Adelaide?"

"Ada's fine." Rick shifted in his seat. "Were you able to get the records?"

"You tossed your bag on the file."

Reaching around, Rick dug the manila envelope from under his duffle. He pulled out the sheaf of legal-sized papers and several photographs spilled out into the footwell. He grabbed them up and shuffled through them. "How old are these?"

"The fire zone aerial was taken last week. You can see from the smoke that it still had some hot spots. The Mounties weren't able to get in there until a couple of days ago."

"Why are the Mounties investigating a forest fire?"

Michael glanced his way. "Why is FBI counterintelligence investigating a Canadian forest fire?"

"I'm not here about the fire. I'm here about the property." Rick buried himself in the papers, skimming through all the legalese of the land buy.

"You're going to have to do better than that."

"The property is connected to a human trafficking case."

"In what way?"

"How long before we get there?" Rick asked.

"Depends on how long you keep lying. You leaned on my uncle to make me your chauffer. That's a big favor for a human trafficking case. Why are you here?"

Rick studied his estranged friend, the man he completed his Mormon mission with a lifetime ago. He should offer an olive branch, but then Michael might just whip him with it. He decided to go with half-truths.

"My boss knows our history. He made it clear I should use our connection to move on the case."

"You always did need force feeding to swallow your pride. What happened, have a case go south that left egg on the Bureau's face?"

The problem with going to people you know, Rick thought, is that they knew you. "The case has national security implications. I'm tracking financials. I kept running into dead ends, then Bastien called me."

"Bastien Frabron? Son of a bishop! The more things change, the more—"

"He gave me a solid lead. The French have a stake in the case as well."

"Yeah, that's what he told me." Michael turned off the pavement and the sedan bounced down a dirt road. "What was the lead?"

"A name, Karoly Bardu. I checked into him. He was just a two-bit, Gypsy used car dealer. Bastien pressed me, though. I managed to pull a warrant and we busted his place in Spokane."

"When was this?"

"First of the month. Why did Bastien contact you?" Ten years of counterintelligence work had given Rick a fine-honed sense of suspicion.

"What did you find with the Gypsy, stolen children?"

"I wish. Would have made my job easier."

"What could be worse?" Michael asked.

"Deeper mysteries. The two-bit car dealer in last decade's clothes had over one and a half million dollars stashed in his house."

"Legit bills or forgeries?"

"Real money, along with equipment and supplies that could be used to forge papers. We could argue intent, but there were no smoking guns."

"This Bardu character talking?"

"Why did Bastien contact you?" Rick asked him again.

"He was following up on a lead from a case he was working in Spokane."

Rick shook his head. "He took the list."

"What list?"

"The client list. You know how forgers work, make false IDs and keep records of real ones as insurance or leverage. We tore his house apart. Bardu had cash stuffed everywhere, in dresser drawers, trunks, closets, mattresses even. But his safe was empty and there were no lists."

"So why come to Penticton?"

"Local law enforcement suspected Bardu of fencing, so I got a search warrant for stolen items. We arrested the family, confiscated cash and jewelry. Bardu lawyered up. District judge kicked the case within a week because we couldn't prove anything was stolen. Bardu was a no go, so I looked into the lawyer."

Michael shot him a glance. "The lawyer led you to Penticton?"

"The firm handles criminal and immigration cases. I found it odd that they brokered a land buy in Penticton. It was a corporate housing deal for a multinational conglomerate."

"Why didn't you just go back to Bastien?" Michael asked.

"What was he doing here?"

"Playing softball."

The air changed from muggy summer to smoke and ash. Michael turned off the dirt road onto a single-vehicle track. Within moments, the world turned from green and shade to harsh sun and cinders. The sudden shift made Rick glance over his shoulder. The fire had died at a green wall of pine.

Pulling the photos back out, Rick compared the most recent aerial shots with the real estate promotional ones taken two years before. The glossy pictures from the land agents showed a wooded parcel of fifty acres with a modest ranch house in the southern quadrant. The Forest Service photos showed a burned-out square. The surrounding forest was unscathed.

"The Mounties suspect arson."

"They're beyond suspicion," Michael said.

They came past a stand of scorched trunks into a small clearing. Two SUVs with the Royal Canadian Mounted Police insignia were parked near the remains of a house. Four uniformed officers, three men and a woman, were sifting through the burnt bones of the house. Michael pulled alongside one of the trucks and killed his engine.

The female officer walked over to them.

"Sergeant Rivers." Michael extended his hand.

"Officer Blackmore." She took off a glove and shook his hand. "I thought you finished up out here yesterday."

"I did. I need to tour my colleague through the site. Doing my bit for our southern cousins."

"Special Agent Rick Cannon." Rick displayed his credentials.

"Do me a favor and stay clear of the house. As you can see, we're still working the scene. Thankfully, we haven't found any bodies yet."

"Were you expecting to?" Rick asked.

"The residents haven't been heard from since the fire. Some of the locals were worried."

"Who were the residents?"

Sergeant Rivers eyed Michael, who nodded. "A young family, name of Reiziger. Husband, wife, three kids. We thought we had a real tragedy on our hands; but so far, no remains."

"Thank you, Sergeant," Michael said. "Don't let us hold you up. I'll take Agent Cannon over to the other spot."

"Suit yourself. Evidence team is on its way, so you will want to hustle through it."

Rick pulled his camera, tape measure, and a pair of latex gloves from his duffle. He snagged the photos for orientation and joined Michael at the edge of the foundation. It was a rectangle encompassing some nineteen hundred square feet, ample space for a family of five. The bare slab of what had been an attached garage extended from the house at ninety degrees.

The home sat on a flat clearing no more than an acre in size. The ground rose from this eastern edge of the property. Once surrounded in forest, burnt giants in fields of ash were all that remained. Rick studied the real estate photos and noted that trees had stood closer to the house in years past. The most recent occupants had enlarged the clearing, pushing the forest back an extra seventy-five feet with the exception of a narrow strand that appeared tethered to the northeast corner of the house.

"Did the forest light the house or the house the forest?" Rick asked.

"Fire started in the house," Michael said. "The trees nearest the house were the fuse that lit the plot."

"And none of the surrounding area caught fire?"

"Someone cut a firebreak around the entire property. Initial findings indicate that an opposing fire started at the property line about the same time."

"The property was prepped for arson?"

"The conclusion is inescapable. Whatever else this Reiziger fellow is, one thing is certain. He is a meticulous planner."

"What do you know about him?" Rick asked.

"Not much. He's from the Netherlands, naturalized in Toronto. Showed up in Penticton with his family a couple of years ago. No criminal record and nothing that explains what we've found. Let me show you."

Michael took a trail on the north side of the property. They climbed a couple hundred yards up a hillside to a ridge. Rick gazed into the defile below where several shipping containers lay scorched and scattered like the remains of a bad train wreck. He fired away with the camera. Hiking down into the gulley, Rick realized they weren't scattered, but laid against each other at odd angles.

Michael took him to the container at the top of the gulley. "They were all rigged with heat sensitive, mercury infused tape. The ones up here caught the brunt of the forest fire." He gloved up and Rick followed suit. Yanking the right door open, Michael waved him in.

Rick stepped through and stumbled forward.

"Easy, Grace." Michael took to calling him Grace in the early days of their Paris mission after Rick crashed his bicycle hopping a curb.

42

Rick glared at him. "Give us some light, would you?"

Michael clicked on a flashlight. The floorboards were all burned away, the walls scorched black. Michael led them down to an opening in the back left corner. He stepped through and Rick followed, minding where he set his feet.

This container ran at a thirty-degree angle from the one before. The floor was gone. The bottom frame hugged the downhill slope of the defile. Burnt items littered the ground, too damaged for Rick to make out what they had been.

Another doorway, another container. Halfway through, they stepped onto a metal floor. Michael reached down and opened a hatch. "Hold the flashlight. I'll go down first."

Michael lowered himself into the hole, hung from the lip by his fingers for a second, and let go. The thud of his landing echoed in the container below. Rick tossed him the flashlight and camera, then swung himself into position. He dropped to the floor, facing the forward bulkhead of the container. He turned around and instinctively reached for his gun. It wasn't there.

Michael laughed. "I know, freaky, right?" He panned the flashlight left to right. Mannequins stood in attack formation, silent sentinels guarding mysteries.

Rick stepped forward and his leg slid out from under him, crashing him to the floor. "Joseph Smith! What the heck was that?"

Michael shone the light across the floor and paused it on a small black ball tucked in the corner. "Must have missed that my last time through."

Rick picked it up. "Looks like a squash ball, except it doesn't squash."

"Let me see it." Michael rotated it in his fingertips. "How much film do you have left?"

"Ten shots left on this roll, plus two more rolls. Why?"

"Hand me your tape measure." Michael pulled a half foot out, locked the blade, and held the ball against tape. "About two inches in diameter." He bounced it off the floor and studied it again. He shone the light on the sheetrock wall. Dings and smudges showed between the crisscrossed incendiary tape.

Rick took a quick series of shots, sparking the flash into a miniature lightning storm.

"Goodness," Michael said. "Warn me next time!"

"Like you did?"

"And ruin the surprise? No way. You should have seen the look on your face when you reached for your piece." Michael's smile faltered. "You didn't bring it with you, right?"

"Into Canada? You guys are as bad as the British. God forbid a law enforcement officer should carry a weapon to enforce the law. No, I just reacted, that's all."

"Yeah," Michael said. "Look at them."

He played the light across the mannequins again. They were outfitted in tactical gear, posed for assault.

"The weapons are real," Michael said. "Submachine guns and pistols are locked and loaded, safeties off. The knives are steel and sharp. Battle uniforms and body armor are all current issue."

"For what, a creepy funhouse in the woods?"

"Beats me. But that handball has me thinking. Check this one out."

Rick stepped over to a mannequin holding an HK MP5 submachine gun. Michael trained the light on the back of the mannequin's hands. They were tattooed with round, black smudges reminiscent the dings and smudges on the walls. Michael brought the light up to the dummy's neck, revealing the same markings. They worked their way through all the mannequins and found similar evidence.

Rick finished his roll, reloaded the camera, and ran through another series of shots. "Seems a bit esoteric. If you want to practice taking out armed assailants, why use a rubber ball? Why not just shoot them?"

"Why practice at all?" Michael dropped the ball into an evidence bag. "The next group is more troubling." Michael picked his way to the rear of the container and slipped through an opening.

Rick followed him in. "Joseph, Mary, and Brigham!"

"I did warn you," Michael said. "You might as well use the rest of your film here. I haven't seen anything to top this."

Rick took his time, alternating from perspective shots to close ups. These dummies were a different type. None were clothed, all were anatomically correct. Rick had been in law enforcement too long for actual nakedness—male or female, living or dead—to shock his Mormon sensibilities. Normal, naked mannequins wouldn't have bothered him. These weren't normal.

Peppered with colored dots, they were grotesques—silent victims with their skin flayed from the side of the face down to the hip exposing muscles, nerves, and veins. The eyes were painted. Brilliant white sclerae, iridescent irises, and pitch-black pupils seemed to plead for justice in tortured patience.

"Have you tried pulling any of these things out?" Rick asked.

"A few."

"You mind?"

"No. You should try a couple to get a feel for it." Michael shined the light on one of the dummies. Its shadow looked like a spiked monster from a horror movie.

Rick marveled at the variety of objects impaling in it. Its skin bristled with pens, pencils, needles, glass shards, nails, toothpicks, and coins. Their distribution appeared random at first glance. Closer inspection revealed that each object was stuck in a colored dot with the exception of the metal button that cut across the mannequin's iris, turning it into a macabre cat's eye.

Rick pinched one of the toothpicks at its protrusion point and tugged. The buried half slid reluctantly away from the surrounding high-density foam.

"Try one of the pencils," Michael said.

Rick grabbed one sticking out of the dummy's chest. He pulled and the mannequin head butted his chin.

"Careful, Grace. They fight back."

"Unbelievable," Rick said. "Why stab someone with a pencil?"

The question brushed something in Rick's mind, déjà vu in half bloom. He tied to pin it down as he set the mannequin back on its feet. The memory wouldn't come. Bracing the mannequin with his left hand, he pulled the pencil out with his right and let out a low whistle. "Two inches. Can't see it killing someone, but it would hurt. You said this Reiziger was a meticulous planner. What do you suppose he was planning with all of this?"

"I hate to guess. Everything I come up with makes me queasy."

Bright light filled the space. They both turned to the doorway.

"Evidence team is here," Sergeant Rivers said. "You gentlemen done?"

Michael glanced at him.

Rick capped off his camera lens. "I'm good."

They climbed their way out and hiked back to Michael's car.

"What's your next move, Agent Cannon?" Michael Asked

"You said Bastien was here to play softball. Care to fill in the details for me?"

Chapter 7

PETA staged a demonstration during the Maximoff & Boromi Circus parade yesterday, claiming the circus abused its animals.

Owner László Boromi denies the allegation. "Our animals are treated better than most family pets. Why would we mistreat animals our livelihood depends on?"

Lion trainer Julia Mendez said their felines have all their claws, unlike many household cats. "Removing them would be degrading to the animal. Working with them is as dangerous as it looks." She offered the four parallel scars on her shoulder blade as proof.

Syracuse Herald-Journal, June 30, 1988

Johnstown, Ontario – June 30, 1988

Drom pulled into the gas station and gently shook Shell's shoulder.

She sat up straight and rubbed her eyes. "What time is it?"

"Just past three." Pulling his sunglasses off, he glanced over his shoulder at the kids buckled in on the back bench. They were all fast asleep, road drugged.

"Where are we?" Shell asked.

"Johnstown." He rolled the windows down and cut the engine. The summer heat poured into the minivan. "I need to fill up."

"I better check the restroom out before they wake up." She slid out.

Drom tracked her progress until she entered the station, then opened his door. He clicked it shut and moved toward the gas tank.

Amanda stirred, blinked a couple of times, then looked at him through the window. Drom tapped his lips and pointed at the sleeping boys. She nodded, opened her door, and wiggled out. "Where's Mom?"

"She went to the restroom. You might as well head that way too." He pumped the gas, keeping his eyes on her until she entered the convenience store. He scanned the lot and surrounding streets. No police. No government-issue sedans.

The cut off lever jumped against his fingers. He rattled the nozzle in the tank spout, and hooked it back on its cradle. He capped off the tank and leaned against the minivan, his gaze fixed on the store. Shell and Amanda came out together. His wife didn't look refreshed or relieved.

She marched straight to him, tight eyed and thin lipped. "We're on the Saint Lawrence River."

"I know."

"Why?"

"Get buckled in. I need to pay for the gas." He strode off before she could ask him any more questions. He had spent the past eight days trying to figure how to tell her what was coming next. Discarding one strategy after another, he defaulted to traveling slower, hoping to forestall the inevitable.

The inevitable had arrived.

Back in the minivan, he checked the rearview. Jakob and David were still asleep. Meeting his eyes in the mirror, Amanda gave him her small "mom's upset, but I'm not" smile. He pulled out of the station and got onto Highway 16 south. "We're heading to Syracuse."

"Through a regular border crossing? Do you think that's safe?"

He ventured a glance at her. "No. But we have to go across."

"You make me nervous when you grip the wheel like that. You think they'll have a problem with the passports?"

"The passports are good. I just wished we had different ones."

"What's in Syracuse?"

"Help. And information, I hope."

"Why risk a bridge? Couldn't we sneak across on land somewhere?"

Drom rubbed at the scar on his chest. "Sneaking across has its own risks."

She took his hand. "So does a border station."

He kissed her hand, then gripped the wheel. "It's a risk we have to take."

"Well, if we get stopped, at least we'll know it's official."

He had to agree. French mercenaries were one thing, official government manhunts another. Official hunts tended to end with an arrest, not an execution. Getting stopped would be small comfort. Making it through meant they kept running.

The Ogdensburg-Prescott International Bridge rose before them. The minivan climbed over the water. Under a clear sky, the Saint Lawrence River was a blue ribbon laced with green. Amanda pressed her nose to the glass. "It's so pretty."

Traffic was moderate. They made the opposite bank and four inspection lanes diffused the inflow, leaving Drom behind just two other vehicles. Border agents, relaxed and friendly, stamped passports and waved cars through. The lines moved.

He loosened his grip on the wheel. This was going to be easier than he expected.

"I hafta pee," Jakob said.

Drom glance at him in the rearview. "Hey, buddy! You have a good nap?"

"I hafta go, Daddy."

Shell reached back and patted his knee. "We'll stop somewhere soon."

The border agent returned the passport to the driver in front and the traffic gate lifted, letting the car through. He motioned for Drom to pull forward. Shell dug in her purse, pulled out their passports, and gave them to Drom. He stopped the van, rolled the window down, and handed the documents over.

The agent flipped through his passport. "Good afternoon, Mr. Reiziger. What is the purpose of your visit?"

"Vacation."

"I really gotta go." Jakob's whine woke up David, who started crying.

"You need to hold it, baby," Shell said. "We'll find a rest stop once we're across."

"We have restrooms inside, ma'am." He stamped their passports and handed them back. "Just pull through and park in front of the station. There is a small visitor's center inside with restrooms and vending machines."

"Hurry, Daddy!" Jakob's knees were pressed together, his face pinched.

Drom pulled through and parked in the visitor's lot. "Come on, buddy." Hauling him out over Amanda, he set him down and took his hand.

He marched into the station and eyed the lady behind the counter. "Restroom?"

"Take the hallway on our right. Restrooms will be on your left-hand side."

"Hurry, Daddy!" Jakob was holding himself with his free hand.

Drom scooped him up and shot down the hallway. He blew through the men's room door and rushed into the first stall. Lifting the lid with his foot, he pulled Jakob's pants down and pointed him in the right direction. Made it.

The door creaked. Putting a light hand over Jakob's mouth, he tilted the boy's head back. When they had eye contact, Drom tapped his lips with his index finger. Jakob's lips drew tight.

"The alerts come in yet, Chief?"

"Test fax came over the new machine a minute ago. We should have the full packet in time for the shift change."

48

Urinals flushed. Water splashed. Paper ripped. Hinges whined.

"Are you done, Jakob?"

"Almost." His flow trickled off and he pulled his pants up. "Can I flush it?"

"No. The handle is nasty." Drom pressed it down with the toe of his shoe. He picked Jakob up and headed for the door.

"I hafta wash my hands, Daddy!"

"We need to go, son."

"But I hafta wash my hands. Mommy says."

Drom took in the earnest expression on his son's face. Jakob didn't like missing steps. If they didn't wash his hands now, the boy would ask for it all the way to Syracuse. Drom held him up to the basin. Jakob soaped up, splashed, and soaped up some more.

"That's enough. Rinse off." He cut the taps, pulled paper towels out of the dispenser, and dried the boy's hands. Drom set him down and led him out to the lobby. They reached the front door. He pushed it open.

"Sir," the lady behind the counter said.

Drom glanced over his shoulder. She motioned him over to the counter. He looked past her to the officers at their desks behind her. No pistols drawn. No agents looking at him. He stepped to the counter.

"I found an extra one of these and thought your son might like it." She held up a small, plastic badge.

An electronic wail erupted behind her.

Drom lifted Jakob onto the counter. The lady handed him the toy U. S. Border Patrol badge.

"What do you say to the kind lady, son?"

"Thank you, ma'am."

She smiled at him. "Would you like me to pin it on you?"

Jakob looked up at his father. "Can I wear it, Daddy?"

"Sure, buddy."

As she pinned it on Jakob, Drom spied the fax machine on the table behind her. Paper stuttered out of its bottom. He caught his name on the third sheet as it cascaded down and scrolled back on itself in the catch basket.

A uniformed officer stepped away from his desk and retrieved the reports.

Thanking the lady again, Drom hauled Jakob off the counter and made for the door.

He kept his pace steady, resisting the urge to sprint to the van. Sliding the side door open, he handed Jakob off to Amanda. He jumped into the driver's seat and slammed the door.

The officer came out of the station, papers in hand.

Drom cranked the engine and put the van in reverse. "Buckle up, everyone."

He waited a beat to make sure they were all secure, then pulled out of the parking lot.

It was fifty miles before he relaxed his vigilance on the rearview.

⊕

The blue and white striped big top tent was impossible to miss. Drom navigated the van into the entrance of the New York State Fairgrounds on the shores of Onondaga Lake. He had opted for a straight shot to Syracuse via Interstate 81. The trip put a couple of hours between them and the border. If he could connect with László, he had a good chance of blurring their trail.

Amanda grabbed the back of the driver's seat. "Are we going to the circus, Daddy?"

He glanced at her reflection in the mirror. Her eyes were wide with excitement. "Yes, we are, sweetheart. This is the surprise I promised you."

Jakob bounced in his safety seat, clapping his hands. "A circus! We get to see clowns!"

It was just past six on a Thursday evening. Tonight's show started at seven and the parking attendants were already out in force. He followed the flow of traffic into the parking lot and backed the minivan in between a pickup truck with a camper and a conversion van with airbrushed artwork.

Shell and Amanda wrestled the boys out of their seats. Shell deposited David into the stroller and Amanda grabbed Jakob's hand. The family followed the growing crowd out of the parking lot, through the small carnival midway, and to the ticketing booth. Jakob hopped and David squirmed as the line crawled through the entrance.

"It's been years since I've been to a circus," Shell said. "This will be fun. Thanks, babe."

He squeezed her hand, but couldn't bring himself to mirror her smile. He scanned the crowd and looked over his shoulder after every step forward.

Shell kissed his cheek. "You mind holding David? He's about had it with the stroller."

Drom bent down, unbuckled David, and picked him up. The line moved forward and he found himself face to face with the dark eyes and meaty jowls of László Boromi.

"You fire your cashier again?" Drom asked.

László raised his ring-encrusted, sausage-fingered hands. "Leo, you *razbóinik*, where have you been?"

Drom bounced David on his hip and glanced over at Shell. Her eyes narrowed. He came back to the circus boss. "Here and there. I've been a bit busy."

"I can see that." László's hand came out of the booth window and swallowed David's foot. He gave it a tug.

David buried his face in Drom's shoulder.

"He's a bit shy around strangers," Drom said.

"Strangers, pha! Just because you ran away doesn't mean we're not family. You here to see the show or be the show?"

"You're incorrigible, you know that? I brought my family to see the show."

"Just the five of you or are some hiding behind your back?"

"Just the five."

László rolled out five tickets and handed them to Drom. "On the house. Come find me after the show."

"*Nayis túke*," Drom said, thanking him in Romani.

"*Khanchéste.*"

Drom led his family into the big top. László gave them good seats near the center ring. He let Amanda go into the aisle first, followed by Jakob. He handed David over to Shell as she passed him and sat beside her. He took in the audience around them, then focused on his children. Perched forward and eyes wide, they watched the elephants march out.

"How well do you know that man?" Shell asked.

"Well enough."

"What did he mean by 'be the show'?"

"You want popcorn? I think the kids would enjoy it." He signaled one of the concession hawkers. Drom bought three buckets of the buttery treat and handed the first two down the line for the kids. He held the third bucket up to Shell.

She cocked her eyebrow and took some.

The elephants lumbered out of the ring and the clowns blew in. During their slapstick antics, prop hands rolled in pedestals and built a cage inside the center ring. The clowns' game of musical tricycles turned into a shoving match. One fell face down into the saw dust. At that moment, a lion raced into the ring and jumped up onto a pedestal.

The clown troupe rode out of the ring at double-time, honking their tricycle horns as they exited. The downed clown rose to its knees and shook its head, scattering a cloud of sawdust and glitter. Children laughed. Gloved hands rubbed grease painted eyes in white face. The clown blinked, looked up, and spotted the lion. With a startled jump to its feet, the clown scrambled for the exit.

Leaping from the pedestal, the lion gave chase. His massive front paw swiped at the clown's back and tore off the entire outfit, revealing a shapely figure in a short, red dress.

A coiled whip flew into the ring. The clown caught it, spun, and snapped it out. The lion reared up, front claws extended, and backstepped to the center of the ring. Cheers and applause exploded from the audience.

"Did you see that, Daddy?" Amanda asked. "I thought that clown was going to be cat food!"

Amanda's excitement lightened Drom's mood some. She was a child enjoying childhood wonders. He took a moment to savor an innocence he had never known.

The clown's orange wig came off and brunette locks cascaded to her tan shoulders. She wiped her face with the wig, performing the makeover version of a quick-change artist. Bright eyes framed in olive skin scanned the audience. Smiling, she took a slow turn for the audience as the rest of the big cats loped into the arena and leapt onto their pedestals.

"What did the fat man mean when he asked you if you were here to be the show?" Shell asked.

Drom tore his gaze from the lion tamer and faced his wife. "He's going to ask me to perform."

"In what capacity?"

Wild applause made conversation impossible for a moment.

She slipped her arm under his and pulled him closer. "Drom, perform how?"

"I'm a juggler."

"*Were* a juggler."

Her emphasis on the past tense came through loud and clear. He had worked a short stint as a juggling dishwasher in a private club in Shell's hometown. It was how he had caught her full attention. She knew he was more than just a juggler, knew what his hands could make dancing plates and silverware do.

They watched the rest of the show in silence. Between judging the acts with a critical eye, Drom stole glances at his children, soaking in their wonder.

The announcer thanked the audience. The crowd filtered out. David snuggled into Shell's bosom. Amanda and Jakob stayed glued to their seats, eyes fixed on the ring as if the prop hands' closing work was part of the show.

Once the aisles were clear, Drom led his family to the main curtain behind center ring.

A prop hand placed himself in their path. He raised his hand with a smile. "Sorry folks. This area is for staff only. You need to exit out the arch."

"We're here as László's guests," Drom said. "He asked me to come see him after the show."

Keeping his smile, the young man hardened his stance. "Listen, I get wanting to give your kids an extra treat, get them close to the cages. But it's not allowed. Thanks for seeing the show. Tell all your friends about us."

Drom stepped into the man's personal space. "It was a good show. Could be better, but no real complaints from me. Julia was killer with the cats tonight. No surprise there, her timing has always been impeccable. I don't know why Quinn let Sheila perform tonight, though. I'm no elephant trainer, but even I could tell her front left foot was sore. If he loses another pachyderm, Max will red light him for sure."

The young man stood straighter. "You know Julia and Quinn?"

"And Max. And László, who asked to see me."

"What's your name, sir?"

"Moldovan."

The prop hand took a step back. "Moldovan? As in Leo Moldovan?"

"And family," Drom said.

The young man unclipped the walkie-talkie from his belt. "Gaffer, I've got an artist here, Leo Moldovan, who says you wanted to see him?" He held the radio to his ear for a moment then lowered it back to his mouth. "Yes, sir. No problem, sir." He hooked the radio back on his belt. "Mr. Boromi is tied up at the moment. The flag's up, he said you're welcome to it. He'll come find you once he's free."

"Thanks." Drom took a step.

The young man raised his hand. "Are the stories true?"

"What stories?"

"The Night of a Thousand Knives."

"No, they're not. It couldn't have been more than a hundred."

They crunched down the peat gravel lane between the trailers. Shell handed David to him. "The flag's up, what does that mean?"

"The cookhouse is open. László is feeding us dinner with his crew. My guess is he's still busy counting tonight's take."

"Leo Moldovan?"

He gave her a half smile. "Has a bit of a ring to it, don't you think?"

"I like Drom better," Shell said. "That stage hand didn't know you, but he sure knew about you."

"I used to be a thing here."

"A thing. What kind of thing?"

"A juggler, what else?"

He weaved through the hustling circus workers and past the animal cages, fried chicken pulling at his nose like a magnet. The cookhouse tent flaps were wide open. Drom took them straight to the serving line. No one challenged them. Dinner was fried chicken, mashed potatoes with gravy, string beans, and yeast rolls with butter. Trays full, they headed for an empty table.

"Leo!"

Drom looked over his shoulder. "Freida! I should have known this was your cooking."

A plump, middle-aged woman came out from behind the serving counter, wiping her hands on her apron. "Come here and give an old woman a hug."

Drom looked all around, eyes wide. "Old woman? Where?"

Laughing, Frieda pulled him into a hug. "Gone two years and you come back with this tribe?" She swept her gaze over Shell and the kids. "I should call you Jacob."

"I'm Jakob," his son said.

Freida bent down and squeezed his cheeks. "Are you, now?" She stood upright. "And these?"

"My wife, Shell," Drom said. "The lovely young lady is Amanda. And this little one here is David."

Freida ruffled David's hair, hugged Amanda, then kissed Shell on both cheeks. "You must be quite the woman to have slowed this wild thing down enough for a preacher to catch him at the altar." She gave Drom another hug. "Welcome back, dear. Will you be here for breakfast?"

"Not sure yet."

"Don't leave without saying goodbye." She headed back to her kitchen.

Drom picked a table near the far corner with a good view of the entrance. They took seats on either side—Amanda next to him and the boys with Shell—prayed, and dug into their supper. The mess hall filled in. He recognized many faces and saw a good number more that he didn't know. Hiding out a couple of days shouldn't be a problem. Any longer and questions were sure to arise.

He scanned the line, then stared at the entrance. Chestnut hair, tan shoulders, short red dress—prettier with each step closer.

"What is it?" Shell asked.

He swallowed a mouthful of green beans. "Nothing."

She glanced over her shoulder, then pulled David onto her lap. "How long were you a thing here?"

"I found them not long after I returned to the States. I wintered with them and was part of that year's spring and summer tour. All in all, about seven months."

She bit through a drumstick and tore the meat from the bone. Eyes fixed on him, she chewed through the bite and swallowed it down with a sip of sweet tea. "We weren't in a good place then. Anything happen I should know about?"

"Leo!" A tray clattered onto the table.

Drom was captured in an affectionate embrace. Soft hair tickled his nose with lemon grass and hints of fresh sawdust. Through the strands, he caught Shell's stare.

"Julia!" Rising to extricate himself, he inadvertently drew her closer. He gave her a gentle push at the waist. She let go of his neck, laying her hands on his shoulders. She beamed at him, her smile as broad as her face. "That was some show. The quick change was flawless. The crowd ate it up."

"Nothing beats a lion scratch for motivation. I've been working on that since you left. Where have you been?"

Momentarily lost in her red mahogany eyes, the heat of her waist brought him back to ground. Reaching up, he took her hands and turned her to Shell and the children. "This is my family. Our children, Amanda, Jakob, and David. And my wife, Shell. Everyone, this is Julia Mendez, lion trainer and sometimes clown."

"Nice to meet you," Julia said. "I may be a lion trainer, but it looks to me like you're the real lion tamer, Shell. Leo is the last man I expected to find with a family."

"Really? Do tell." Shell smiled at Julia, but kept a hard eye on Drom.

"Leo always reminded me of my leopards, restless and hard to tame. Not the kind of cat you turn your back on. And here you have him eating dinner with his family like a civilized human being. I hope we have time to get to know each other."

"That would be nice," Shell said.

To Drom, her face said otherwise. Behind her, he spotted the prop hand from earlier approaching. Thankful for the interruption, he waved him over.

"Mr. Moldovan," the young man said. "Mr. Boromi sends his apologies. He is still tied up, but asked me to show you to your quarters whenever you are ready."

Drom glanced at Shell. "We're ready."

"Amanda, gather up the trays, honey." Shell cleaned Jakob up, then rose with a sleepy David in her arms. She nodded to Julia and followed Amanda and Jakob to the dirty tray bins.

"Lovely family," Julia said.

"Look, Julia—"

"Don't trouble yourself." She laid a hand on his chest. "I always knew there was someone. I'm glad I got to meet her."

"Talk later?"

"Up to you." She gave him a peck on the cheek, grabbed her tray, and sauntered to a family of motorcycle stunt riders several tables over, her skirt swishing like a matador's cape.

The prop hand cleared his throat. "Mr. Moldovan?"

"Yeah, sorry. Lead the way."

He took them to the rear section of the back yard where the family RVs were parked. The man unlocked one of the motorhomes and reached his hand inside the door. Light spilled out of the windows. "Boss says this one's yours."

Drom took the keys from him. "Thank you."

He inspected the interior. Bleach and chemical pine perfumed the air. Vacuum tracks marked the carpet. Otherwise, the RV was much as he left it nearly three years before. He ushered his family in.

"Bathroom is that small door just past the galley. The back is our bedroom. Queen sized bed." He gave Shell a hopeful look. She didn't give him any promising signals. "The kids can all fit in the bunk over the driver's cab."

Amanda climbed up into the bunk. She kneeled on the foam mattress and bounced up and down. "This is way better than the tent!"

"Not exactly a hotel room," Shell said. "How long are we staying?"

"Not long. I need to get some things from László. It's a sure bet he'll want something in return."

"Like a performance from you?"

"More than likely."

She studied him for a moment. "I thought the whole idea was to hide?"

"Sometimes, it's best to hide in plain sight. I've done it before."

Her lips thinned. "They found you then, remember? One minute, I'm watching Amy's father bleed out—"

"Shell." He dropped her name like a knife, cutting her short. He glanced up to the bunk. Amanda and Jakob were frolicking in the tight space. His eyes came back to Shell.

She stood her ground, David clamped in her arms, his head on her shoulder. "You disappeared for a year. You came back to me with deeper scars and worse dreams. I can't handle more."

He wrapped his arms around them, careful not to wake the baby. "I don't know who, and I don't know why, but they're not looking for Leo Moldovan. They're hunting for Drom Reiziger, a lumberjack from Penticton. I need László's help to make their search as difficult as possible."

"What does the fat man have that we need?"

"Enough resources to get us to our other resources."

"I'm scared."

"I know." Stepping back, he caressed the tear from her cheek with his thumb. "Why don't you run the kids through the shower. Towels are in the pantry. I'll go get the car."

Keeping his head down, he legged it out of the back yard into the open fairgrounds. He joined the flow of stragglers moseying to the parking lot, matching pace with a small family. He walked behind them, close enough to look like he belonged but not so close that they took notice of him.

The lot had thinned out. He spotted the air-brushed van in the wash of the flood lights. Their minivan sat beside it. The pickup with the camper was gone. Drom tailed his cover family until they stopped at a station wagon. He ambled on for several parking slots, cut into another row, and stopped.

He did a slow turn, arms half raised; a befuddled man looking for his car. Moving on, he repeated the act a couple more times.

No one was following him.

He meandered to the minivan and checked his tells. A shoe lace dangled at the bottom of the sliding side door. The tab of clear adhesive tape remained stretched across the hinge gap of the driver's door. Satisfied, he peeled the tape, unlocked the door, and jumped in.

Back at the motorhome, he pulled their two largest suitcases from the van. He carried one in each hand to the door and knocked on it with his foot. It swung open, revealing the massive form of László Boromi.

"Leo, you're home." He spread his arms in welcome.

"So it seems." Drom lifted one of the suitcases to him. "Give us a hand, will you?"

László grabbed it and shifted out of his way.

Drom took the two steps up and set the other case on the floor. Shell was on the couch holding David. Jakob was asleep on the bunk. Running water put Amanda in the shower.

László lowered himself onto the three-seater couch, filling half of it. Shell pressed closer to the opposite arm. If László caught the move, he gave no indication. He gestured around the space with both hands. "I kept it for you just like you asked. But I have to be honest, kid, I thought of selling more than once."

"I paid you plenty to keep it for me," Drom said.

"Yes, you did. But I gave up on you ever coming back a long time ago."

"Well, here I am."

"In the flesh." With a speed his girth belied, László launched from the couch and caught Drom in a crushing hug, lifting him off his feet. "I feared you dead, boy!" He kissed both his cheeks and set him back down.

Drom parked himself on the end of the dinette booth opposite. "How was the take tonight?"

"Fair." László tilted his hand back and forth. "I'm hoping for better tomorrow. The fourth of July weekend kicks off in earnest then. We're booked here through Sunday, pulling out on Independence Day. No sense competing with the fireworks."

"No, no point in that."

Amanda slipped out of the bathroom and turned into the bedroom.

Shell rose from the couch. "The baby's asleep. If you will excuse me, I'll let you two catch up." Scooching sideways with David in one arm, she snagged her suitcase in the other and carried both to the bedroom, closing the door behind her.

The lock clicked.

"How long do you plan on staying with us?" László asked.

"Through Sunday, at least. A bit longer, maybe, if we're not in your way."

László leaned forward like a wave of flesh curling to the shore. "I don't know what wind blew you in and I won't pry. But you know you can't hide out as a circus performer and not perform."

Drom studied László's face. It gave nothing away. It never did. He had dealt with carnies and circus clowns far too long for that. Drom glanced at the locked bedroom door then over at his sleeping three-year-old.

Life was simpler when all he had to lose was his soul.

He got up, grabbed a glass from the cupboard, and filled it from the tap. Returning to the booth, he set the glass on the table and stared at it.

"Leo?"

Drom looked over at him. "Did you ever build the box?"

László's eyes brightened. "As a matter of fact, I did. Been dragging it with me like a fool ever since. I'm an optimist, I guess."

Chapter 8

The Italian ambassador in London has assured Great Britain that
Italy does not intend to send more volunteers to the Spanish civil war,
provided other nations refrain from doing so as well.

Ellensburg Daily Record, March 27, 1937

Vizcaya Province, Spain – Morning, April 26, 1937

Hishoro held nine-month-old Tshompi to her breast and he latched on. She
had come out to the driver's bench in hopes of sunning him. But they were
heading south. What morning light shone over the hills, Tshuri turned to shadow.

She had argued against the trip. "France is bad enough. Why risk worse?"

He snapped the reins and drove the team southwest toward Saint-Jean-de-
Luz. Hours later, he broke his silence. "Troubled times bring higher profits."

Part of her longed for the simpler days of her youth, before she had learned
to read under Tshuri's tutelage. Newspapers then were pottery packing or fire
starters. Now, they told her of *Gazhikaníya* troubles. France was a tinderbox.
Spain was in flames.

A military junta rebelled against the republican government six months previous. Spain was in the throes of a full-blown civil war between republican loy-
alists and fascist rebels. International volunteers and foreign mercenaries had
poured into the country to join the fracas.

Shifting Tshompi to her other breast, she eyed her husband. His fingers were
slack on the reins. Whenever the road straightened out, he closed his eyes and
his chin bobbed on his chest.

"I can manage the reins if you need to rest," she said.

"You nurse. I drive."

"He's almost finished. You can burp him and rest. I can drive for a while."

"Not my horses, you can't. What would Mateo say if he saw you driving and
me asleep holding the baby?"

She tossed one of her braids over her shoulder and slid closer to him. "It's not Mateo you're worried about."

Tshuri kissed her cheek. "You're right, mother would never let me hear the end of it."

The road uncurled onto a lengthy straightaway. She glanced over at Tshuri and caught him in a nod. "What do you think our chances are?"

Popping his chin up, and he turned his gaze on her. "Our chances with what?"

Each eye colored his question differently. She picked the warm tones of the walnut one. "The market. Will we find buyers? A day like this, the locals might take siesta early."

"I hear they've been selling cat meat for rabbit stew. They'll welcome what we bring even if we are late."

Hishoro craned her neck around the side of the wagon. The other two *vôrdòna* were keeping pace behind them. Most of their inventory gathered in France remained intact. They had let go of a few bottles of wine and small cheese wheels to ease their passage through the border.

She would have just as soon stayed in France.

They approached Guernica from the north against a steady stream of people leaving the city. With its whitewashed buildings in view, Tshuri steered the team off the pavement into the flat fields east of town. Hishoro steadied herself on the bench, riding out the unexpected jostle.

"What's wrong?" she asked.

"Roaches."

As they took a wide arc toward the east side of the city, Hishoro spotted a small company of police manning a checkpoint on the road. A line of trucks, cars, and wagons waited to get through.

She breathed easier once the wheels clattered onto cobblestones. Crossing the Renteria Bridge, they drove through a street lined with covered stalls. Turning south on Calle Ocho de Enero, past the Church of San Juan, and made their way into the market plaza. Tshuri stopped their *vôrdòn* at a gap between two stalls.

Holding Tshompi with one arm, Hishoro climbed down and grabbed a long scarf from inside the wagon. Bending forward, she placed Tshompi on her back facing away from her. Hooking the center of the scarf under his bottom, she wrapped it around her waist, crossed it over the back of her shoulders, and tied it off in front. She straightened up with a light bounce and Tshompi settled into his sling.

She opened the end compartment under the wagon and hauled out a full crate of medium sized wheels of Roquefort, Ossau-Iraty, and Comté vieux cheeses. She set these down on the table next to the crates of wine bottles Tshuri and Mateo had offloaded. An assortment of wooden spoons, copper pots, and reed baskets rounded out their wares. Hishoro's mother-in-law, Liliana, and Keti finished pitching the canvas over their stall.

The sun reached its zenith as Tshuri and Mateo maneuvered two of the wagons into an alley near their stall. Tshuri brought a couple of the young men from their *kumpániya* along to help. He left one guarding the wagons and told the other to stay with Hishoro. Liliana took Keti and Nadja with her to beg from the *gazhe* and sell fortunes to the unwary.

A woman in servant's dress came into their stall. She wanted cheese, but not at the asking price. Hishoro haggled with her, promising to sweeten the deal with cheaper wine.

"Rrómniorri," Tshuri called.

Hishoro spotted him back in the driver's bench "Where are you going?"

"To lunch. Is the special crate set?"

"Just as you asked."

"Mateo is staying here to keep an eye on things." He flashed his sideways grin at her and popped the reins across the horses' backs. The wagon lurched forward and cut its way through the shopping crowd.

The maid in gray demanded the Roquefort cheese at a cut rate. Hishoro glared at her, spat a Romani curse, and raised the price.

Tshuri followed his nose to the Taberna Vasca, Guernica's oldest restaurant. He brought the wagon around and retrieved the special crate of wares from the compartment beneath the bench. He walked up to the kitchen's screen door and knocked on the frame with his foot.

A stout man in an apron turned from the cauldron he was stirring and stared a Tshuri. "You want food, go around front with the rest of the paying customers. We're not running a charity here."

"I'm not begging, Señor Guezureya. I bring gifts."

The man stepped to the door, wiping his hands on his apron. Peering through the screen, he grinned. "Tshuri, you devil! I haven't seen you in years! What have you brought me?"

"Let me in and I'll show you."

Pedro Guezureya held the door open and Tshuri made his way into the center of the kitchen and set the crate down on the butcher block table.

A young man came out of the pantry, wiping his forehead with his shirtsleeve.

"Juan," Pedro waived him over "Come say hello, *hijo*."

"Juan?" Tshuri stepped around from the table for a closer look. "This *hombre* can't be Juan. Juan is just a boy, no taller than my waist."

"Señor Velveloz, *bien venido*." Juan stuck out his hand.

Grabbing his hand, Tshuri pulled him into a hug. "Pedro, what have you been feeding this son of yours? I swear, he's become a giant."

"Today, we all will feast on my *fabada*," Pedro said. "We picked up a sow and her entire litter a couple of days ago. This morning, one of the farmers came in with his cart full of beans. We shall all dine like peasant kings. Now, why don't you show me what you've brought to add to our fare."

Tshuri unloaded the contents of the crate onto the table, one item at a time. He brought the copper pans out first. Pedro picked the first one up and stroked the inside surface with his fingertips. He nodded in approval, then trained his button eyes on the crate to see what came next. Tshuri set out three wheels of cheese, one on top of the other. He followed these up with several bottles of French wine, which he set out in a line.

Pedro grabbed a wheel of the Comté vieux cheese along with two bottles of the best vintage and handed them to Juan. "These go in the wall."

Juan headed back into the pantry without comment.

Tshuri heard the scrape of heavy objects sliding across the stone floor followed by a slight creak. He smiled, glad that Pedro still had a black marketeer's heart. "Saving them for a special occasion?"

"Hiding them from soldiers," Pedro said. "General Mola's army shelled our troops into retreat. They've been showing up here in droves, disheartened and hungry. I fear it won't be long before they start confiscating the town's stores."

"Yet, in spite of the troubles, you still have a full house eating lunch."

"No one can resist my *fabada*."

"Not even Don José?"

Pedro's smile faltered. "Don José, as in José Rodriguez?"

"As I recall, the only thing he attended more faithfully than your lunch table was morning mass. Is he here?"

"Not just bringing gifts to an old man, I see. He came in ten minutes ago."

"I was hoping you could lure him back here for a special wine and cheese tasting."

Pedro leaned into the butcher block table, seeming suddenly weary. He studied Tshuri for a moment, then tilted his face to the ceiling. "A civil war wasn't enough for me to have to deal with?" His eyes came back to Tshuri. "I'm not pulling the good stuff out of the wall."

"No need. What's left is special enough to pique his interest."

When Juan came out of the pantry, Pedro told him how he to arrange the tray for Don José. He patted Tshuri's cheek with fatherly affection. "You are one of the reasons people are wary of Gypsies." He kissed both his cheeks. "Promise me you'll be cautious."

"You have my word."

Pedro checked on Juan's progress, then headed out to the dining room.

Tshuri paced between the stove and the sinks and then around the table. He fidgeted with Juan's arrangement until the young man's glare made him stop.

He shouldn't have worried. José Rodriguez, general manager of the Astra-Unceta factory, bustled into the kitchen and flew straight to the cheese platter. Slices of blue, soft, and hard cheeses spiraled a hollowed round loaf. The bread cradled a bowl of *boquerones*, marinated anchovies from the Bay of Biscay.

Don José tore a chunk of the bread away, spread a thick layer of the soft cheese on it, then topped it off with two anchovies. He popped it into his mouth and chewed with his eyes closed. Pedro opened a bottle of wine, poured a glass for his guest, and handed it to him. The man swallowed down his mouthful and chased it with a healthy swig of the prime vintage. "Heavenly, Don Pedro! Wherever do you find such delicacies?"

"He had help," Tshuri said.

Don José turned to him, noticing him for the first time. "Do I know you?"

"You might remember me. My name is Tshuri. I worked in your factory several years ago."

Don José stepped closer. "You're the Gypsy."

"I wasn't the only one you employed."

"You were the only one that mattered. The rest were laborers. You," the man pointed, "you were an artist. If you've come back looking for a job, I'm sad to say, you are too late. The army took over the factory and they're shipping all the machinery to Bilbao on tomorrow's train."

"Will you be moving with the factory?"

"I suppose, if it comes to that."

Tshuri glanced over at Pedro and the old man shook his head. He eyed the factory manager. "You are hoping Mola gets here first."

With a grunt, Don José turned back to the food. He chose the Roquefort this time and doubled down on the sardines. "I don't trust the government. If they move the machinery, Señor Unceta will lose ownership by default."

Tshuri refilled Don José's glass. "To your health, *señor*."

Nodding his thanks, he took a sip. "Look, I'm a business man, not a politician. Republican or Nationalist, I don't care, so long as whoever is ordering the guns pays."

"And the Republicans haven't been paying?"

"Not promptly or enough. And they shipped my stockpile off to Bilbao on the eleven o'clock train this morning. Lieutenant Gandaria promised payment, but at the rate his men are deserting, I doubt he can make good on it."

"So, you have no weapons and tomorrow you will have no factory." Tshuri scratched his head. "I had hoped we could do business, but if you have no weapons to sell…"

Don José fiddled with his empty glass. "I saw some colorful wagons come into the market. They yours?"

"*Sí, Señor.* I was afraid we came too late. But our wares were selling when I left."

"A merchant should always have a supply of what people want."

"Sound advice," Tshuri said. "Pedro, are you going to be chained to that stove all afternoon or will you have some time to come to the market?"

"We've been to market already, my dear boy. Your gift is all the cheese I need."

"You wound me, *señor*." Tshuri covered his heart with his right fist. "I was not suggesting you come to buy, but to visit. My wife is tending our stall. You could stop by and meet her and our son."

"Perhaps after three, I could come. The shepherds and cattlemen are in the dining room. They will be making deals and demanding food at least until then."

"I shall leave you to it." Tshuri hugged him.

Pedro patted Tshuri's cheek again, a little harder this time. "I'll come find you in the market later."

Tshuri made his way to the back door. He pushed on the screen, then glanced over his shoulder at Don José.

The man lifted his chin a fraction and brought it back down. Meeting accepted.

⊕

Tshuri entered their stall and found Hishoro sitting cross-legged on the cobblestones nursing the baby. Her helper was asleep on his side at the back of the stall.

"Little man sure has an appetite," Tshuri said.

"No different than his father. How was lunch?"

"Better than expected. Where is Mateo?"

Hishoro got up and stretched her back. With a deft finger, she detached the baby from her breast and handed him to Tshuri. "Your son could use your company for a bit. I'm going for a walk."

Tshuri kissed his sleeping son's cheek, then kissed the top of Hishoro's head. "Don't be long. And if you see Mateo, send him to me. I'll need his help to load the inventory."

She glanced around the near empty stall. "What inventory?" Church bells tolled three o'clock. "Dinner shoppers will be coming to market soon. I expect to sell out."

"I told you, it went better at the Taberna than I expected. Take care of your needs, find Mateo, and send him to me."

She left the stall without further comment.

Tshuri held the baby against his shoulder. Tshompi nuzzled into his neck and Tshuri wallowed in his peaceful breathing.

Before Hishoro, love was just a word abused by singers. It couldn't buy clothes, food, or wine. He never expected it could warm his heart, fill his soul, and intoxicate him all at once. Hishoro stretched his heart to bursting, leaving room for nothing else.

Then came Tshompi.

From the first moment he held his son, he understood what his parents couldn't tell him. Growing up, it puzzled him why the elders struggled so. They bore child after child, bringing them into a world that would just as soon see all Gypsies dead. His baby's breath whispered the only sensical answer. Life was precious, love all that was ever of worth.

Mateo's appearance broke his reverie. "Where's Hishoro?"

"Two stalls down arguing with an *habichuela* farmer. We loading up?"

"Not here."

Hishoro came into the stall with a large bag of beans on each hip.

Mateo's eyes widened. "I thought he said the lot was sold already?"

"He did," she said. "I pressed him, but he wouldn't budge. So I spit in one of the bags."

"He didn't chase you out?" Tshuri asked

"No, he cursed at me, said I had to buy the bag. I told him it was two bags or none."

Shaking his head, Tshuri handed her the baby and gave her a lingering kiss.

He stepped to the back of the stall and tapped the young man with his toe. "Get up and look lively. We leave as soon as I get back."

He gave Hishoro another kiss and got onto the wagon with Mateo. They turned south out of the market plaza and headed toward the Astra-Unceta factory.

Tshuri hoped Don José had enough time to set the plan in motion. They worked the details out in an alley two blocks down from the tavern. Tshuri had waited for the man to leave the restaurant, then cut ahead of him on the sidewalk. He led him into the alleyway and they got straight to business.

Lieutenant Gandaria had shipped out all the firearms reported in factory's inventory. Don José confided that while Gandaria was surprisingly astute for such a young man, he was not familiar enough with the factory's production capabilities to spot the inconsistencies in the inventory reports. The factory still had two thousand weapons stashed away in parts crates.

Tshuri ordered four hundred of them.

He drove the wagon to Calle Iparragirre, which ran parallel with the rail line on the west side of the factory. Tshuri pointed to the rail cars parked along the line of Astra-Unceta. Soldiers guarded the dock while laborers moved crates and machinery to the train.

Mateo brought his hand up, shielding his eyes from the western sun. "You have a plan for not getting shot, *véro*? I'm thinking those soldiers will not take kindly to competition."

"We'll be offloading from the other side, farther down the line." Tshuri eyed the windows on the second floor. The first two had their shutters rolled down. Don José was ready for them. Santa Maria's bell tolled four o'clock.

Tshuri took the wagon along the tree line, screening it from the railbed, and parked it in line with the third boxcar. The loading dock chatter diffused through the tress. He motioned to Mateo and they climbed down from the driver's bench.

Carved panels, painted in bright reds and greens, decorated the sideboards of the *vôrdòn*, hiding the secret compartments in its false floor. Tshuri brushed the hidden latches as he walked down the side. Mateo slipped through the tree line. Tshuri followed him a moment later.

At the top of the railbed, they laid flat on their bellies and waited. Distant droning tickled the back of Tshuri's brain. The boxcar door rolled open a half meter and a man in machinist coveralls leaned against the frame. He took a final drag from his cigarette and flicked it to the ground.

"I estimate twenty to twenty-five crates," Tshuri said. "We'll grab the first two. One of the workers will bring a third. When we get back to the wagon, you stay and load. The worker and I will keep hauling crates over."

They scrambled up the bed and crossed the first set of tracks. When they reached the open boxcar, a wooden crate was waiting for them. Tshuri grabbed the rough rope handle and turning, pulled the crate onto his shoulder. He hustled to the wagon with Mateo close behind.

They had the first crate loaded by the time the factory hand arrived with the third. Tshuri told him to leave it on the ground, then led him back to the train.

Tshuri's misgivings grew with each crate he carried. He should have brought more help. Sweat soaked and sore, he braced himself for the pain of another twenty-kilo load on his shoulder. Wincing, he shuffled down the grade and set the crate at Mateo's feet.

He grabbed his fifth crate, tenth of the haul, and carried it at his waist, a handle in each hand. He navigated the tracks and started down the grade. The droning grew louder. The bell of Santa Maria sounded out, disorienting him. It couldn't be five o'clock already. Distant peals joined the clanging from the nearby church and droning rumbled into roar.

Tshuri ran. Dropping the crate near the wagon, he followed Mateo's gaze to the northern skyline. The shape of the bomber was unmistakable. Black dots dropped from its belly, a giant monster relieving itself on the hapless city below. The plane nosed up and the beast climbed. Whistling cut through the jangle of the factory's fire alarm. Both men stared up, mouths agape, as the plane roared over their position.

Seconds later, explosions drowned out all else.

Chapter 9

Starting at once: A/88 and J/88 for free fighter bomber mission on the streets near Marquina-Guernica-Guerriciaz. K/88 (after returning from Guerriciaz), VB/88 and Italians for the streets and the bridge (including suburb) east of Guernica.

Initiation Order for Operation Rügen
Oberstleutnant von Richthofen
Commanding Office, Condor Legion
26 April 1937

Guernica, Spain – Afternoon, April 26, 1937

Tshuri threw himself to the ground. The earth beneath him trembled. He covered his ears and waited. A minute passed, then two. He stood. His horses were rearing up, trying to tear away from their harnesses. Grabbing the halter of his lead horse, he coaxed his head down with a firm hand and gentle words. The horse settled. His harness mate followed suit.

"Tshuri!" Mateo pointed north. Over the tiled rooftops of the city, a dark column of smoke rose into the cloudless sky. "That's near the center of town."

Tshuri glanced at the crates. "We're almost done here." He hustled back to the train. The laborer was at the base of the grade, lying face down with his hands over his head, his dropped crate beside him.

Tshuri crawled up the grade and peered over the edge. The soldiers were gone. The man in the boxcar waved him on. Tshuri ran over to him.

The machinist slid a crate out. "Grab this one. We'll help you with the rest."

"How many left?"

"Ten crates after yours."

Tshuri pulled the crate free of the floorboards, catching the second handle in his other hand. Scrambling down to the prone helper, he tapped him in the ribs with the toe of his boot. When the man didn't move, he gave him a light kick in the thigh. "Get up! We need to hurry. Grab that crate and get it to the wagon."

The man got to his knees and looked around, dazed.

"*Ayi.*" Tshuri pointed at the crate.

The man gained his feet, hefted the crate, and trudged toward the wagon.

Mateo was frozen, his gaze fixed on the column of smoke filling the sky.

Tshuri bumped him. "Keep loading. We have ten more crates to go."

Mateo faced him, eyes wide with concern. "We need to get them."

Setting the crate down, he grabbed Mateo by the shoulders and pinned him with his stare. "We will. After we load. Hurry."

Mateo shrugged out of Tshuri's grip. He maintained eye contact for a beat, then bent to the crate and shoved it into the wagon's hold.

Four men broke through the tree line in fast succession, each hauling a box of the precious cargo. A fifth, younger than the rest and dressed in a suit, followed them. He carried two carboard boxes to the driver's bench and slipped them underneath.

Like Don Pedro's son, he had grown in Tshuri absence. "Luis, I'm surprised to see you."

"It's a family business," Luis Unceta said, raising his voice over the factory's fire alarm. "Father is moving all the workers into the bomb shelter. My men will grab the rest of the load while you and I settle up."

"What's in the cardboard boxes?"

"Compact pistols. You asked for four hundred weapons. We had a cache of our F Model machine pistols. You should have seven crates of those, fifteen guns per crate."

"With holsters and stocks?"

"Of course, and all with twenty-round magazines. The bulk of the merchandise is the fourteen crates of our Model 400 semi-automatic pistols."

"The *mange-tout*," Tshuri said, using its French nickname, eats anything. Chambered for the nine millimeter Largo, the pistol could fire multiple types of nine millimeter and .38 caliber rounds.

"The very ones. We packed them twenty to a crate."

"And the final fifteen?"

"Under your bench. Model 200s with a supply of 6.35 millimeter rounds."

Tshuri climbed into his living quarters and came out moments later with a small leather pouch in hand. He opened it for Luis to inspect. Even in the recesses of the purse, the cut diamonds caught the light of day and sparkled with cold wealth.

Taking the pouch, the Unceta scion pulled it shut with the drawstrings. "These will come in handy regardless who wins this war." He supervised the final loading of the crates, shook Tshuri's hand, and led his men back up the grade.

Tshuri and Mateo double-checked the closures on their hidden compartments, then climbed up into the bench. As he turned the wagon north, three bombers broke over the horizon. Both men jumped down and scrambled under the wagon.

Whistling cut the air, then all was rumble, horror, and roar.

⊕

Hishoro crouched in the school hallway, her back against the wall. Keti and Liliana sat facing her. They were all in their stall when the alarm bells sounded. "Air raid!" someone cried. The shout was echoed throughout the market. Panic ensued, people screaming and running in all directions. The women followed a group to the school.

People crammed into the hallway. High-pitched whistling pierced through the din of the terrified civilians. The rumble of explosions shook the concrete beneath them. Classroom windows shattered under the assault of the sonic waves. Keti clutched Nadja. Tshompi wailed. Hishoro tried nursing him, but it was no use. Struggling in her arms, he cried louder. Liliana held her hands over her ears and rocked back and forth, screaming.

The explosions stopped.

Tshompi's mouth was open, his eyes shut, his face red. Hishoro couldn't hear his wailing over her own howling. A stinging slap rocked her face and her baby's crying filled her ears. She blinked against the dust and smoke.

Keti glared at her. "We have children. You cannot lose yourself to fear."

Hishoro rubbed her cheek. People were leaving the school. She shook Liliana's shoulder until her mother-in-law stopped screaming and opened her eyes.

"T'aves mansa," she said, come with me. She helped her up and the women made their way out of the hall. Outside, people milled in confusion.

They walked to Calle Andullende Salazar. Hishoro looked east. The market was in flames, the surrounding buildings turned to rubble. They moved north along the cratered, smoldering road. Cries for help sounded from every quarter.

"We should get our wagons," Liliana said.

"Look, mother." Hishoro pointed to the market plaza. "Our wagons are gone."

"Where's Tshuri?"

"South," Hishoro said.

Liliana turned north and marched off.

Hishoro glanced at Keti, then ran after Liliana. *"Dey!"*

Liliana didn't slow her pace. The sisters caught up and walked on either side of her, babies on hips. *"Kaj dzas?"* Hishoro asked, where are you going?

"To find my son."

"Dey, you are going the wrong way. Tshuri is south." She turned Liliana around. "This way." With a tug, she headed her in the right direction.

Moments later, she checked over her shoulder for Keti. Her sister stood in the middle of the road, pointing her mishappen arm at the northern horizon. Hishoro spotted a cluster of black marks in the blue sky swooping toward the town like a murder of crows, their engines buzzing with malevolence. Past the crater in the road, dust kicked up and people ran.

The fighter planes mowed them down.

Keti spun on her heel and launched toward Hishoro and Liliana. "Run!" Tucking Nadja to her chest, she broke into an all-out sprint.

Hishoro stood dumbfounded. Keti breezed past her. Machine gun fire split the air and cut into the road beside her. She dropped to the ground, curled over Tshompi.

Fighter after fighter flew over, close enough to the ground that Hishoro could make out the pilots in the cockpits. Their wings obscured the sun and for a moment, Hishoro was transfixed by the roundels on their undersides, black circles quartered with white exes. They seemed omens of worse things yet to come. Making the sign against *beng*, she buried her face in her arms.

The buzz of engines faded. Hishoro rose to her knees and inspected her baby. He was full of life and crying with displeasure. She got to her feet and looked south. Her sister wasn't on the road. Looking north, she spotted Liliana sprawled on the street, her floral print blouse stained with blood.

Hishoro raced to her side and rolled her over. Liliana's body flopped onto its back and stared at her with dead eyes. The air rumbled. Planes, larger than the last, filled the northern skyline. Springing to her feet, child clutched to her bosom, she dashed south in search of Keti.

⊕

Tshuri and Mateo sheltered under the wagon. Bombs pounded down for an eternity. Through miracle or shock, the horses stood their ground. It was dusk before the men crawled out from under the *vôrdòn*.

After three hours of explosions, the quiet was unsettling. The burning remains of Guernica lit the evening sky.

Tshuri checked on his horses. Unscathed, they neighed under his affirming caresses. The factory peeked above the railbed, its roof intact. A column of smoke rose just north of it.

He climbed up into the driver's bench and found Mateo already there.

"We have to look for them," Mateo said.

"No, cousin, we have to find them." Tshuri gave a short whistle and his team trudged forward.

They reached the destruction zone within minutes. Dismembered bodies of horses, cattle, and people littered the cratered roadway and lay atop the piles of rubble. Burning flesh and ash choked the air. Tshuri tied a kerchief over his nose and mouth. He glanced over at Mateo. His cousin scanned the destruction, tears cutting tracks through the dirt on his sun-seamed face.

They rode into the bedlam of the market plaza. The carnage was stupefying. Puddles of blood reflected the flames above and smoke choked the air. He maneuvered the wagon close to where their stall had been and joined the others clawing at the piled stones in search of survivors.

Mateo appeared beside him. When he pulled a crushed copper pot from the bricks and crumbled mortar, the cousins redoubled their efforts. Tshuri uncovered a boot and recognized it as belonging to the young man he had left behind to help Hishoro. He dug the hole wider, exposing the calf. Grabbing it by the ankle, he pulled. It came away from the hole, its shattered bones poking out of its torn flesh.

Tshuri threw it to the ground next to Mateo. "Let's go." His cousin kept digging. Tshuri hauled him to his feet. "Let's go."

"We have to dig them out."

"They're not here. If they were, they'd be dead. We need to look among the living."

Mateo gave him a dumb stare for a moment, then scrambled back to the wagon. A group of men were unharnessing their team. Tshuri slammed into the one unbuckling his lead horse and followed up with a right hook to his accomplice, dropping him to the ground. Mateo tangled with the third man. Tshuri moved to help him when someone grabbed his arm and pulled him up short.

"*Señor, por favor*," the man said, "we need the horses to dig them out."

Tshuri glanced around. All was pain and desperation, an entire town in need of rescue. His own wife and son were missing along with his mother, sister-in-law, and niece. But this man was here, pleading for help.

"*Donde?*" Tshuri asked.

"La Taberna Vasca."

The tavern's front was peeled away and piled in a burning heap that ran from the standing remains to the middle of the street. The man who had pleaded for help climbed on top of the rubble and slapped a beam protruding from the surrounding stone. "We need to get your team harnessed to this beam so we can pull it out."

Tshuri scanned the remains of the restaurant to get his bearings. "Why there?"

"My son is under there."

"He was near the animal pens?"

"No, he was in the dining room with me. We ran out when the alarm sounded. I was in the shelter before I realized he wasn't with us."

Tshuri climbed down and paced out the front of the pile. "Mateo, unhitch the team." He studied the broken roof line, working out the geometry. "Where was Don Pedro?" he asked the man.

He scrambled down next to Tshuri. "In the dining room, telling us we had to finish up."

"Did he run out with you?"

"He wasn't in our shelter."

"I see." Tshuri took them to the rubble mound on the west side of the restaurant. "Anyone alive will be in there."

The men set to work under Tshuri's direction, using the horses to drag out any debris too heavy for them to lift. An hour later they exposed the pantry doorway. It had collapsed inward with frame and door intact.

"Almost there," Tshuri said.

They cleared the rubble away from all but the bottom third of the door and stepped back to catch their breath.

Tshuri pounded on the door with his fist. *"Hola! ¡Hay algien ahi?"* Putting his ear to the door, he heard tapping, light but persistent. He sprang to his feet. "Someone is in there. We need shovels."

"We only have our hands," one of the men said.

"Not true." Tshuri pulled on a square post that had been a support beam in the kitchen. It didn't budge. "Mateo, rope." His cousin threw him a line and he rigged it around the post. Mateo urged the team forward and the beam came free of the pile. Tshuri loosed the line and leveraged the beam off the ground. "Battering ram."

The other men grabbed hold and together they charged the pantry door. The paneling splintered under their assault. Mateo brought a lantern over from the wagon and Tshuri shined it into the interior. Food tins and collapsed shelving were scattered at the bottom of the hole.

Tshuri crawled through the opening and stood in the space. Holding the lantern up, he inspected the ceiling. Aside from cracked plaster, it appeared sound. He moved to the back of the pantry and listened. Faint tapping reached him through the wall. "Need help down here."

The distressed father was first in, followed by the man Tshuri had punched. Tshuri handed cans and sacks back without looking. He quickly cleared the rear wall, then ran his rough hands across its plastered face until he detected a variation in texture.

Whenever Don Pedro referred to it, he called it "the wall." A portion of the hill behind the restaurant had been carved away to accommodate this corner of the building. The back wall of the pantry stood against the bedrock of the hill. Don Pedro's grandfather had dug the smuggler's hold. Don Pedro had hidden it with the secret door.

Tshuri ran his fingers up and down, looking for the actuating spot. Sensing a slight dimple in the wall, he pushed against it. With a click, a section of wall popped out. Pressing down on the top edge with his fingertips, he pried the door to him.

Tshuri reached inside and grabbed a hand. Don Pedro's wife crawled out, kissed his cheek, and scrambled past. Two men clambered out in short succession, neither of which Tshuri knew. A small hand grabbed his and he tugged. A young boy wearing a dusty black beret came out of the hole and crawled by. Tshuri leaned into the opening and held the lantern up.

Don Pedro was seated on the floor, his back against the far wall of the modest cavern. Clutched in his arms were a bottle of wine and a wheel of the finest aged cheese France had to offer. "Tshuri, you devil! What took you so long?"

"Hand me the contraband and come out of there."

Don Pedro hesitated a moment, then moved toward him. Tshuri took the wine and cheese from his hands and cleared out of the opening. Don Pedro crawled through, then up and out onto the street. Tshuri handed up the luxury items to his grasping hands, then climbed out.

In the glow of the fires, the survivors took stock of one another. Don Pedro embraced Tshuri, then stepped away. "Have you seen Juan?"

"No." Tshuri's momentary sense of victory evaporated. "I am sorry. I must search for my wife." He marched toward the wagon and was intercepted by the rescued boy and his father.

"*Señor*, I can't thank you enough for saving my son. Tell me your name. I will light a candle and say a prayer for you every morning mass."

"Tshuri Velveloz." He extended his hand.

The man shook it with a firm grip. "Gorka Colón *a su servicio*. This is my son, Alvarez." Gorka pushed his son forward.

Tshuri crouched eye level to lad. The size of a six-year-old, his looked older. "Your father is a brave man and your people resilient. The day will come when you will make the fascist pigs who did this pay." He patted the boy's head and tilted the beret to a military angle. He stood and eyed the father. "Señor Colón, I now need your help. Mateo and I have to find our family."

"Dead and wounded are being taken to the school plaza," Gorka said.

Gorka led the way. Tshuri pointed his team at the man's back and kept them moving, refusing any appeal to commandeer his horses. As the demands became more belligerent, he handed the reins to Mateo and reached under the bench for one of the cardboard boxes.

Setting it on his lap, he broke it open. Inside were the Astra 200s, each in its own case, along with packages of the .25 caliber ammunition. He opened one of the pistol cases, palmed the gun, and ejected the magazine. He loaded it with six rounds and slapped it into the grip. He chambered a round, ejected the magazine, pushed in another round, and returned it to the receiver.

Pocketing the pistol, he repeated the process with another. He handed it to Mateo and took the reins.

The dead in the plaza were stacking up faster than the wounded. Tshuri left Mateo to guard the wagon while he searched for their loved ones among the injured and those tending them. After a half hour of frantic searching, Tshuri succumbed to looking among the dead.

He found her in the third row. Kneeling beside her, he closed her eyes and kissed her cold forehead.

Back at the wagon, Mateo had scrounged up a tub to water the horses. "Did you find them?"

"Not the wives." Tshuri climbed inside the *vôrdòn* and grabbed a rolled canvass. He took it to his mother's body and wrapped her in it. He carried her over his shoulder to the wagon and laid her inside. Coming around to the front, he found Gorka talking to Mateo.

"We should go there next," Gorka said.

"Where?" Tshuri asked.

"The Convent of Santa Clara. People came out of the school after the first raid and ran there when the second one started."

Tshuri climbed up onto the bench. "Lead the way."

They found the survivors sitting in the lawn outside the convent. The grounds were quiet. The nuns moved among the people, serving bread and water. Spotting a bright calico skirt, Tshuri jumped from the bench and ran towards it. Mateo charged past him.

"Keti!" Mateo scooped his wife and daughter into his arms.

Tshuri's gate faltered, then stopped. He stared at Mateo and Keti for a beat, then spun around searching for Hishoro. He didn't see her. He broke into the family reunion and faced his sister-in-law. "Where is she?"

Keti lifted her chin, pointing over his shoulder.

Tshuri turned and Hishoro buried her face in his chest.

She cried. Tshompi wailed. Tshuri laughed, tears streaming down his cheeks.

The men took a short respite and had some of the bread and water offered by the nuns. Introductions were made and both Hishoro and Keti made a fuss over Alvarez.

"Liliana," Hishoro said.

Tshuri took her hand. "I found her. I won't bury her in Spain."

"Where will you go?" Gorka asked.

"We need to get back to France. If possible, I would like to avoid scrutiny."

"I've herded sheep through the Pyrenees since I could walk," Gorka said. "I can get you into France without any officials being the wiser."

Chapter 10

The Maximoff & Boromi Circus opened last night to a near-capacity crowd. The star of the show was Julia Mendez. This reporter has never seen a lion trainer work as close to the wild instincts of the big cast as Ms. Mendez. "They are predators, born to hunt and kill. Showcasing those instincts in the ring has its risks," Mendez said.

Syracuse Herald-Journal, July 1, 1988

Syracuse, New York – July 1, 1988

The house lights dimmed. A spot light shone on the announcer in the center ring. "Ladies and gentlemen, the Maximoff & Boromi Circus is pleased to announce the return, for a limited engagement, of Leo Moldovan, Romania's juggler extraordinaire and Nicolea Ceauşescu's most wanted defector. Tonight, for the first time and exclusively for Maximoff & Boromi, he performs The Box. Give Leo a warm, capitalist welcome."

Anemic clapping sputtered in the stands. The tent went dark for a second, then two amber beams lit the air nine feet above the saw dust of the center ring. The band's percussion section broke into a military tattoo and one of the lights swooped to the back curtain. Out flipped a dark-skinned man in a close fitting, purple top and white sirwal trousers.

The spotlight tracked him as his back handsprings brought him over the wooden curb of the center ring. He landed on his feet in the thin air, nine feet above the floor. The crowd gasped. He flipped in mid-air across the diameter of the ring, then came to ground in a crouch facing the audience as the drummers' dance ended with a crash of cymbals. Exuberant applause and whistling sounded from all quarters of the big top.

Drom bowed his head. Guitars strummed a Flamenco beat. He winged his arms, displaying orange balls wedged between his splayed digits, four to a hand.

The applause trailed off. Rhythmic clapping and castanets joined the strumming guitars in increasing volume. Stretching to his feet, Drom launched the balls overhead with a flourish. They came back down in turn to each hand. He tossed them up the center, juggling them into flowing circles on either side of him.

After several rounds, he changed the pattern into a cascade, the balls crossing overhead as they circled left-to-right and right-to-left. He spun, capturing ball after ball behind his back. The music stopped. The crowd cheered. He bowed and turned his back to the spectators.

The spotlights played across the ring as the houselights came up, showcasing his entry platform.

Drom stared at the Box, an acrylic cuboid the size of a standard maritime shipping container, and repressed a shudder. He had had memories become dreams, both coherent and jumbled. He also had dreams that were neither memories nor logical. This dream—the one he never told Shell about—was in a class of its own.

It began with an explosion.

A rumble in crescendo, like an approaching thunderstorm, stirred his stomach and vibrated his bones. It climaxed in an ear-splitting boom with a flash of fire and billow of smoke. The floor beneath him lurched and he ran instead of standing his ground. Launching his body, he flew through the air into a dark smoke ring and landed hard on concrete.

He rolled, absorbing the shock, then sprang to his feet. He couldn't see, but knew where to go. Straight ahead stood the door to the stairs. He was through it in two bounds, turned right, and jumped. His boots hit the landing below, sounding it off like a giant drum echoing in the stairwell. He spun left, flexed his knees, and jumped again. Jump, land, and repeat; three turns pers story.

He was five floors down when the klaxons wailed. Emergency strobes flashed, revealing the smoke from the explosion pouring down the stairwell.

Ten floors to go.

Quickening his pace, he made eight more floors before the door on the target floor banged open. Boots hammered in the well. Vaulting over the rail, he dropped past the guards charging up the stairs. Catching the landing of the floor below with his fingers, he swung himself through the open doorway.

Roll, spring, run.

He kept his shoulder a whisper from the wall. Twenty feet ahead, lasers cut across his path from a lit hallway. Unzipping his pouches halfway, he loaded both hands with four balls each. Five feet from the hallway's mouth, he launched a curve ball. It arced into the passageway and thumped against the facing wall. The light winked out with a shattering of glass.

Men shouted. Machine gun fire erupted.
He charged toward it.

Drom was as familiar with visions as he was with dreams, both demonic and holy. This one didn't smell demonic and played out more like a vision than a fanciful imagination. It disturbed him nonetheless. He had charged armed men before. They didn't survive the encounter.

He tried to forget the dream.

It refused to leave him. Night after night, it came in crystal detail. He started picturing the moves in his waking hours, then practicing them. He ran the exercise over a thousand times until he was sure he could do it with his eyes closed. Then he practiced it blindfolded.

Guitars strummed, breaking his reverie. Drom spun left in an aggressive ballet, arching his arms overhead. His feet stopped, his torso twisted, his left arm whipped out. A ball slammed into the side wall of the acrylic container, ricocheted to the ceiling, and bounced down to the opposing wall.

Drom charged the opening, sending two balls in the path of the first. Before the first hit the floor, he kicked it with his right foot, bouncing it off the left wall halfway down the container. He struck the next two with spinning kicks, launching an additional ball from his right hand with each spin.

Six balls were now in play bouncing against the walls, ceiling, and floor of his see-through container. Just as the balls farthest from him threatened to lose energy, he fired off the last two with full-force *pelota* serves.

The guitars faded away. Drom's dance with the balls provided its own music. Running up the sides, flipping off the walls, and spinning on the floor, he swooped his hands and feet into the path of the bouncing balls. Their rhythm intensified, each collision adding energy to the mix.

He altered the angle of his drives. The melee of balls halted their forward progress and coalesced their angular bounces around him in the center of the container. He spun, bent at the waist and arms outstretched. As he helicoptered, the balls changed trajectory and described a circle in a parallel plane to the opening. He pivoted the circle as he spun, jumping back and forth through it like a lasso trick.

The crowd roared.

Working the circle parallel to the floor, Drom spun faster. Scooping the balls, he fired them in a line at back wall, shattering it. He turned, took three leaps, landed on his knees, and slid out of the Box with arms outstretched.

The applause thundered on and on. Ponies rode in with acrobats standing on their backs and circled the ring. Drom stole a glance into the grandstand. There, four rows up, was his family. Amanda and Jakob were jumping up and down, cheering. Shell stood with David in her arms, tears running down her cheeks.

Head bowed, he slipped through the curtain.

⊕

Sweat soaked, Drom marched back to the trailer, avoiding eye contact and playing deaf to all greetings. László put his act near the end, which gave him enough time to wash up before he faced Shell.

She wasn't the only one he had to worry about. He had fulfilled László's request, which was good. It entertained beyond expectation, which was bad. Seeing dollar signs, he would press Drom for more performances.

One problem at a time.

He rinsed off, resisting the temptation to soak in the hot water. Dressed in a green T-shirt, blue jeans, and loafers, he headed back out to find Shell and the kids.

Cookhouse smells grabbed his nose. He veered toward the food. The staff filled his tray with generous portions of meatloaf, new potatoes, and steamed broccoli. He claimed a table in the back of the tent and ate, his eyes fixed on the entrance. Let them find him.

You're delaying the inevitable. Again.

His meal was nearly finished when Shell got in line with the kids. Amanda looked around. He waved, smiling. She pulled on her mother's arm. Shell shifted David to her other hip and kept her eyes forward.

Amanda led the family to his table, carrying her tray and a small plate for David. Drom took the baby from Shell and kissed her cheek. She didn't turn away, but she didn't look at him either. He put David in the highchair and prayed over the food.

"Daddy, that was amazing," Amanda said.

"It was just a simple prayer, sweetheart."

"You know what I mean," Amanda said. "Are you going to do it again?"

"Only time will tell." The dream flashed though his mind—the explosion, the jump, the guards.

The cell.

"Drom." Shell's voice was low, her tone brittle.

He turned to her. Her lips were drawn tight, her knuckles pale from the death grip on her napkin.

"Shell—"

"Were you ever going to tell me?" Her burlwood eyes burrowed into him.

"Leo!" Julia sideswiped him with a head hug, nearly knocking him out of his seat. "Where have you been hiding that?"

"Julia!" He patted her arm. "You better get in line before all those animals leave you hungry."

She pulled him around to face her. "Food can wait. When did you came up with that act? I thought the Night of a Thousand Knives was something until tonight. Wow! I mean, wow!"

"Get some food, Julia."

"Nonsense," Shell said. "Amanda, slide over and let Ms. Mendez sit next to your father."

"Please, call me Julia. Ms. Mendez sounds too formal for friends."

Moving over, Amanda turned her back on the adults and cut up Jakob's broccoli.

"Hudson had to send the ponies in to get you out of there," Julia said. "That crowd, my goodness! You were all anyone was talking about on the way out."

"Get real," Drom said. "It was just a bounce juggle. Those folks came to the circus to see trapeze artists, lions, tigers, and—"

"Leopards," Shell said.

Julia shot her a glance. "I didn't use the leopards tonight. Henry had indigestion and Cleopatra gets cranky when he's not feeling well."

They were all quiet for an uncomfortable moment, then Shell broke the silence. "That's the second time I've heard of this Night of a Thousand Knives. It must have been some event."

"It wasn't even close to a thousand knives." Drom bent to his tray, but it was empty. No hiding there.

Julia slapped his shoulder. "Oh, shut up, Leo." She faced Shell. "I hate it when he acts all modest."

"Modesty, that's our boy," Shell said. "What was this Night?"

"A piece of marketing genius from the wizard behind the curtain," Julia said. "Leo?"

"No, Leo couldn't stay behind the curtain if his life depended on it. I'm talking about László. Our agent messed up, had us booked in Minneapolis the same week two other circuses and a carnival were in town. Most of our artists were for blowing the engagement off and heading to the next gig. László would have none of it. He pulls Leo into the Red Wagon and a couple of hours later, rest of us are out papering the town with advertisements for the Night of a Thousand Knives."

"The name was László's idea. He said anything less than a thousand wouldn't sound dramatic enough," Drom said.

"Well," Julia said, "the night proved him right. We were standing room only. People were taking bets on whether Leo would survive the night."

"Come on, Julia, it wasn't like that," Drom said.

"It most certainly was! I bet a week's pay on you."

"You took a chance on him," Shell said. "Sounds dangerous."

"Crazy, more like," Julia said. "László knew the other circuses had knife throwing acts. The carnival had one too, as a side show to get people to try their luck, win a teddy bear, that kind of thing. But László was sure we had the only artist talented enough to catch the knives."

Shell slid her chair back and stared at him. "You volunteered to be a knife catcher."

Julia eyed them for a beat. "I should get dinner. We can catch up later if you like."

"Please stay," Shell said. "I want to hear the rest of the story. Amanda, be a dear and get some food for Ms. Mendez."

"But I want to hear the story," Amanda said.

"Go ahead, honey," Drom said. "I'll fill you in on any part you miss."

Amanda gave him a puppy dog look, then shuffled off to the serving line.

Julia leaned on the table with her elbows, closing some of the distance Shell put between them. "László challenged the other outfits to a knife throwing contest in our big top. They would each show off their skills with a short act, then take a shot at hitting Leo with a knife. If any of them succeeded, they kept that night's take and László would move on, leaving Leo behind to do his regular act gratis for the winning outfit. If we won, the town was ours."

Shell's eyes dove into him. "And you agreed to this?"

He met her glare head on. They were apart when it happened, their future uncertain. She had reason to be mad about the Box, but she had no claim on the knives. "It was my idea."

Her eyes flared and he regretted the admission. He wasn't helping his cause.

"I should have guessed," Julia said.

Amanda came back with Julia's dinner. "What did I miss?"

"Not much, sweetie," Julia said. "All the knife throwers, ours included, did their acts. The lights came down and the hands rolled out the new set up. When spots came on, there stood Leo dressed in white with a big bull's eye on his chest. Two boards stood on either side of him at an angle making a u-shape, like this." She arranged the salt and pepper shakers to demonstrate.

"What were the boards for?" Amanda asked.

"László knows how to plan a show, let me tell you," Julia said. "After the announcer explained the challenge, the clowns ran in. I clowned up and joined in for the fun of it. Working in pairs, we put the knife throwers against the boards in ridiculous poses. We drew their outlines with huge black markers and wrote their names over it."

"I take it Leo didn't leave it at catching knives," Shell said.

Julia glanced at him. "You know your man. At the time, I thought the clown act was just a gag to throw the others off their game."

"That was part of it," Drom said.

"We set them in a line facing Leo and ran into the grandstand to watch the show. The knife throwers were each given thirty knives—"

"One hundred and twenty total, way less than a thousand," Drom said.

"Shush," Julia said. "I'm telling this. The knives were color coded so that if one got through, everyone would know who won. The announcer blew the whistle and the daggers started flying."

Drom remembered the thrill of it. Juggling was the foundation of his particular skill, but nothing compared to catching lethal danger. That night was like a morning drill in the Warehouse with his father.

"Did you catch them all, Daddy?" Amanda asked.

"If he had only done that, it would have been amazing," Julia said. "But your father was spectacular. He danced in front of the flying steel. I don't know if anyone breathed. All you could hear were grunting throwers and knives thudding into the side targets."

Amanda faced him, wide-eyed. "Can you teach me that too, Daddy?"

"It took me years to learn, sweetheart."

"Did any of them come close?" Shell asked.

"Who could tell? The knives were a blur and Leo was spinning like a top. When it was all done, the stage hands turned the boards to the audience. Our guy said that it wasn't until then that he realized what Leo had done. He caught every knife and spun them into each thrower's board, nailing their outlines in perfect color code. The audience exploded. Until tonight, I'd never heard louder applause."

"Incredible," Shell said. "I'll make sure not to throw any plates at him when I get mad."

Julia laughed, then stopped when they didn't join in. "Yeah, no kidding." She took her last bite. "Freida outdid herself on this meatloaf. Did you kids like the dinner?"

"It was yummy." Jakob rubbed his belly. "I like meatwoaf."

Julia glanced at Drom. "I would die of cuteness overload if I had to live with him."

"Trust me," Shell said, "he's not always cute."

Julia turned to Shell. "I'll have to take your word for it. Thanks for having me at your table." She slid her chair out and Drom stood with her. "You did great out there tonight, Leo." She gave him a quick hug and picked up her tray. "Thank you for getting dinner for me, Amanda. If your folks agree, maybe you can stop by the cages tomorrow and I can give you a proper introduction to my cats?"

"Oh, could I, Mommy?"

"Let's play it by ear, okay," Shell said.

They finished their goodbyes to Julia and headed out to the motorhome. Drom couldn't avoid the glad handing and back slapping from the other performers and fell behind Shell and the kids. Entering the trailer, he found Amanda sitting on the edge of the bunk. The shower was running. Shell and the boys were nowhere to be seen. He closed the door and Amanda jumped on him.

"Easy, girl," he said. "You're liable to knock me over."

She held him tighter and he wrapped his arms around her. "What's the matter, honey?"

"I don't want you to leave."

He sat on the couch and put her beside him. "What makes you think I would leave?"

"Mommy's really upset." Her tears tumbled out. "Last time she got this mad at you, you left for a long time."

Drom bit his own tears back. He could buy her a new identity, give her a different life, maybe even secure her future. He was powerless to change her past. Or his.

He wanted to tell her he wasn't leaving, that he would never disappear again. It would be a lie. Only ten, his step-daughter was perceptive beyond her years. She would see through his subterfuge. Any attempt at false comfort would only insult her emotional intelligence.

He kissed the top of her head. "I love you, you know."

She hugged him. "I know."

"And I love your mother. We'll work it out."

"When?" Shell asked.

Shell herded the boys through the galley. Her eyes were red and puffy.

"Get ready for bed, okay, sweetie." He kissed her head again.

Amanda grabbed her towel and pajamas off the bunk and trudged to the bathroom.

Drom worked with Shell tucking the boys in. He prayed with them, then kissed them both on the cheek. "You two stay in bed. Daddy and Mommy are going to sit outside for a bit."

"You can smooch on the couch," Jakob said. "I'll keep my eyes closed, promise."

"Go to sleep, Jakob," Shell said.

Jakob frowned, then closed his eyes and rolled deeper into the bunk.

They stepped out to the lawn chairs under the camper's awning and each took a seat, neither shifting to face the other.

"How long?" she asked.

He wondered how much of his conversation with Amanda she had heard. "How long for what?"

"I'm in no mood for games, Drom. How long have you been practicing?"

"My whole life."

She launched out of her chair and stormed off.

He chased after her. "Babe, stop. Just stop, please."

She turned and faced him. "What I saw tonight was no circus act. Are you going to tell me what's going on or not? I can handle it, Gavin, whatever it is. What I can't handle is you shutting me out."

Gavin—she was more upset than he thought. "Come back to the camper, love. Come back and I'll do my best to explain."

She stared at him a moment, arms crossed as if the July night had grown cold. With a slight dip of her head, she plodded past him. She turned her lawn so it faced his.

He sank into the nylon webbing. "I wanted to tell you. I just didn't know how."

"I'm listening."

"I had an idea for a bounce juggle act when I joined this circus. I gave László the plans for the Box. By the time he agreed to it, I had to go. I needed to find out if we had a chance."

"You're stalling."

"I'm trying to explain. Anyway, the act I imagined never happened. Last year, the dream came." He leaned forward, elbows on knees, and rubbed his face. He blew his breath out and sat back. "I've had it every night since."

"More memories?"

"Not memories. Premonitions."

She leaned forward. "Premonitions?"

"It wasn't anything like the act I planned or a replaying of past events. I fought it for weeks, wouldn't sleep for days. Didn't matter. In the little sleep I got, it came, clear and persistent. I started sketching it out. It helped, but it wasn't enough. I built a space to work on it."

"Where?"

"In our north woods." He walked her through it, the lay of the land, the placing and outfitting of the containers. "I knew every move I had to make, but I didn't know how to make every move. In the dream, the balls hit the targets and the targets fell. It was counterintuitive. I would have hit them differently. I couldn't figure out why they were falling."

"You talk like it's real. Are you sure it isn't a memory or just a bunch of them jumbled together?" Concern colored her tone.

"There are days when it's the realest thing I know."

"I wish you had said something before. We could have talked it over with Pastor Chen."

Drom stared up at the awning for a moment, wondering how to proceed. Chen was an assistant pastor at Grace Community. While the senior pastor excelled in teaching and administration, Chen was the church's go-to counselor, gifted in walking people past their soul hurts and seeing them delivered from demonic oppression.

He brought his head back down. "Babe, I know what it's like to be insane. I've had demons chase me to the brink of the grave. This isn't that."

"You think this dream is from God?"

"Pastor Chen agreed."

"You talked with him about it? How much did you tell him?"

"Only as much as I could." He paused. "Did I ever tell you about Chimo?"

"I don't recall the name."

"He betrayed my father."

"What does that have to do with this dream or the Box?"

Drom rubbed his eyes again. *Hand, wall, floor, hand. Slap, boom, bounce, slap.* "I questioned him at his racquetball club." He stared at his hands, afraid to go on.

Taking them, she tugged him toward her and kissed his knuckles. "Worse than the frisbees?"

"Worse than Sam." Sam, Amanda's father—another body to his count. "At least with him, I was rescuing you and Amanda. Chimo was spiteful vengeance."

"What happened?"

Hand, wall, floor. Slap, boom, bounce. "I pummeled him to death with handballs."

"And you thought honing that skill made sense?"

He pulled his hands away and slumped back in his chair. "That's why I went to Pastor Chen. The moves in the dream told me it wasn't a memory. If I had hit targets like that in real life, my father would have reprimanded me."

"Hurt you, you mean."

"I prefer to call it negative biofeedback."

"I prefer to call it abuse," Shell said.

"We've been over this."

"We've been through it, but we're far from over it."

Drom nodded, granting her the point. "Like I said, I couldn't figure out why the targets were falling. None of the shots were kill shots. One day, I mapped out the strike spots on a couple of Jakob's G. I. Joes."

"That was you? I scolded him for painting tattoos on his action figures."

"I remember," Drom said. "I shouldn't have let him hang for my crime. Truth is, I was too scared to own up to what I was dealing with."

"I only fussed, Drom. He didn't get a spanking for it."

"No, he didn't, thank God. Anyway, when I drew the dots on the action figures, the pattern reminded me of the chart in Chen's exam room." Pastoring wasn't Chen's only occupation. He was also a chiropractor who practiced acupuncture. "I made an appointment and took the G. I. Joes with me."

"He ask to pray for you right away?"

"He was concerned, no doubt. But when I explained the situation to him, he asked the sequence I hit the strike points in. I numbered each series for him. He took his time looking them over, then asked me where I had studied it."

"Studied what?"

"Acupuncture. All the dots the dolls corresponded to acupuncture sites. The sequences produced paralysis or unconsciousness. None were lethal."

She scooped a stray lock with her thumb and tucked it behind her ear. "Didn't your father teach you pressure points?"

"He did." He understood her implication. "But only ones pertaining to pain compliance. He never taught me anything as sophisticated as what I saw myself doing in the dream."

"What was Pastor Chen's take on all of it?"

"Not what I expected. He said sometimes God revealed things to us that we could use immediately. He had a Ghanaian friend who wanted to go to a Bible college in Accra, but couldn't get admitted because he didn't speak English. His friend prayed, hoping they would change the admission policy. Instead, he woke up the next morning and could speak English."

"Just like that?"

"Just like that. He said the Lord also worked with what a person already knew and supercharged their skill with the Spirit, like He did with the workmen who built the tabernacle of Moses. Then he added that sometimes God showed us things we needed to learn."

"Like immobilizing targets with handballs without killing them?"

"He didn't say it that way, but yeah."

She threw her hands up. "Come on, Drom! Why would God want you to do that? I mean, what kind of facility are you breaking into, some drug lord's house?"

"No. It's a prison. I think I'm supposed to break someone out."

"Who?" she asked.

"I don't know," he said. "The dream always ends when I unlock the cell door. I never see inside."

Chapter 11

Law enforcement has a new tool to bring criminals to justice. Using radiation, scientists are able to produce distinct images, similar to bar codes, from sequences of deoxyribonucleic acid (DNA). Called "genetic fingerprinting," the process can positively identify people from the smallest traces of bodily tissues or fluids. Experts state the technique has proven effective even with five-year-old dried blood.

The New York Times, March 3, 1987

Syracuse, New York – July 4, 1988

Drom spent his morning wrenching on the motorhome.

"It's almost noon," Shell said. "Did you ever get breakfast?"

He came out from under the hood. "Forgot all about it. Kids leave me any pancakes?"

"A couple. I can fix you some eggs."

"I'll take a break in a minute." He ducked back under the hood and gave the water pump bolt another crank with his socket wrench. "Do me a favor and start it up." Seconds later, the engine kicked to life. He watched the belts spin for a minute, listening to the motor, then dropped the hood. Pocketing the socket wrench, he climbed into the passenger seat. "Think you can handle driving it?"

Her hands came off the wheel like it was on fire. "Me, drive? Why?"

"The circus is heading to Philadelphia today."

"You drive me crazy when you do this."

"Do what?"

"Give me answers without answering me. Why do you need me to drive this beast?"

He twisted around and peeked between the seats. The kids were still in their pajamas. Jakob was tickling David. Amanda was clearing the dinette table.

Drom pulled the cab curtain shut and faced her. "I need to stay in Syracuse one more day. It's better for you all to go with the circus than hang back with me."

"What's here that you can't get today?"

"Reach under your seat and feel along the left side of the base."

David chortled and screeched.

Shell stuck her head through the curtain. "Jakob, let your brother breathe." The giggling tapered off. Bending forward, she reached under the seat and pulled out a hide-a-key tin. "Spare key?"

"Open it."

She took the key out. "You have a post office box in Syracuse?"

"I'm hoping I have mail in Syracuse."

"From who?"

"One of Karoly's people."

"Considering the raid on his house and the arrests, do you think it's safe to go looking for mail from him?"

"No, I don't. That's why I want you on the road when I check it. The box is downtown. Noon hour on a Tuesday after a holiday Monday is sure to be bedlam in that post office. There will be plenty of people to blend in with."

"So what? Karoly is on their radar. If he's sent you mail, even to a dead drop, the Feds have probably read it. They could be waiting for you."

"You know I've been running dead drops since I was thirteen, right?"

"And I had to burn our house down because our cover got blown."

They eyed each other. David's chortle came back full throttle. Amanda must have joined the fray because Jakob's uncontrolled laughter followed soon after. Drom poked his head through the curtain. "You kids better cheer up or I'm coming back there!"

The children broke apart and ran to the cab.

"Get Daddy!" Amanda said.

Drom let them pull him into the tiny living room. They fell in a pile on the bit of open floor in front of the couch, the children tickling him mercilessly.

"Okay, okay, you win. I give." Rolling out from under them, Drom got to his feet and helped them up one by one.

"Let's do it again, Daddy," Jakob said. "That was fun."

"Maybe later. You all have to get ready for the day. Amanda, keep your eye on the boys. Your mother and I are going for a quick walk."

"Come on boys, let's get your teeth brushed." She herded her brothers to the bathroom.

Ducking back into the cab, he kissed Shell's cheek and cut the ignition. He slipped out, ran around the front, and opened her door. "Take a walk with me."

She slid out and shoved the door shut. When he took her hand, she didn't resist. They strolled to a small rise with a good view of big top's final disassembly. He sat on the grass and Shell joined him. Sheila, the circus's matriarch elephant, trumpeted as her trainer, Quinn, adjusted her harness and tied the rigging ropes to it.

Drom kept his gaze on the elephant. "I'm done running."

"What's that supposed to mean?"

He pulled at the grass in front of him. "Hiding I can do. I've done it all my life. But running …" He turned his head and her profile sent his heart into his throat. "The other player determines all the moves. I don't like the odds. Better to be predator than prey."

Shell watched the crew lower the giant tent top down its two supporting steel strut frames. The main guy rope was tied to Sheila's harness. She took measured steps at Quinn's direction and the canvass billowed to the ground. The circus hands swarmed the cloth and separated the sections. They folded the segments and stacked them beside a forty-eight-foot trailer hooked to a spotless tractor.

Shell wrapped her arms over her knees. "You're saying there's a chance you won't make Philadelphia." Her tone was flat, almost despondent.

"That tractor trailer is László's pride and joy." Drom pointed at the rig beside the canvass stacks. "He bought it right after I came aboard, said he was tired of his best billboard sitting on the side of the road broken down. He replaced the old Freightliner with a sparkling new Mack. When he hooked it to the old trailer, that one there parked beside it, he knew it wouldn't do. So, he sprang for the fancy custom trailer with updated artwork."

"You're doing it again." Shell stood up and brushed off the seat of her pants. "I'm going to check on the kids."

He got to his feet beside her. "Don't go yet. I want to show you the trailer first."

She spun on him. "I don't care about the trailer! I care that you are sending us away while you go prowling after whoever it is you think is chasing us."

He took hold of her shoulders. "Come with me, please." She didn't leave. She didn't move, either. "I need something from that trailer and I need your help to get it."

She tucked a lock behind her ear, bumping his hand off her shoulder in the process, and headed toward the rig.

Catching her hand, he led her to the rear of the trailer and pointed at it like a tour guide. "The interior is partitioned to idiot proof the loading. Each part of the big top has its own slot. The last things down are the first things to go in. Sounds a bit backwards, I know. The crew has to stack everything on the ground, not load as they go. But this way, when it gets to the next venue, the tent goes up as it's unloaded. Plus, it makes for an impressive show all on its own."

She cocked an eyebrow at him, then put her hands on her cheeks and opened her eyes wide. "Wow! I never realized how much planning and work went into just getting the circus on the road."

Her sarcastic hamming tickled him. He knew better than to laugh. "Amazing, right?" He gave the loaders a big smile and two thumbs up. The second they disappeared inside, he pulled her between the trailers and stopped at the center line of the rear tandems.

"Warn me if you see anyone coming." He took five steps, dropped to the ground, and rolled under the new trailer, his feet facing its rear. Laying on his back with eyes closed, he counted to twenty, letting his eyes adjust.

He opened his eyes and scanned the chassis all the way down to the rear tandem. It wasn't there. He rolled onto his stomach and checked all the way up to the fifth wheel. He didn't see it.

"You better hurry," Shell said. "The other tractor just started up."

Shutting his eyes, he dug through his memory. It had to be here. He crawled forward a couple of yards, rolled onto his back, and inspected the frame again. There it was, a lump of mud stuck on the inside of a cross member near the slide rail.

Sitting up, he rubbed the lump with his fingertips. Road grime gave way, revealing the putty-colored fake mud beneath. He pulled the socket wrench out of his back pocket and hammered off the brittle plastic shell. Behind it sat a metal box bolted to the steel cross member. He ratcheted out the bolts, dropped the box onto his lap, and peeled out the plastic pouch taped inside.

The other trailer lurched forward and Shell yelped.

Drom froze. The other trailer stayed put. He stuffed the pouch in his waistband, then bolted the metal box back in place. He rolled out and got to his feet.

Shell threw herself at him, kissing him with such passion that he closed his eyes. His lids brightened as the truck rumbled out. She pulled away and smoothed her shirt down.

László stood several yards behind Shell. "Don't you two love birds have a camper you can go to?" He mopped his brow with a kerchief and waved them over.

Taking Shell's hand, Drom gave it a slight squeeze. Genuine or not, her kiss was a welcome cover move. He stepped over to the circus owner. "What you figure, a couple more hours before we hit the road?"

"Not if I have anything to say about it. And since I'm the boss, I've got plenty of say. Forty-five minutes or less. You folks ready to go? My advance team is already hanging paper in Philly advertising the great Leo Moldovan."

"Forty-five minutes is cutting it a bit short," Shell said. "The kids weren't dressed when Leo dragged me out here and I still need to make sure everything in the camper gets stowed correctly."

"You still have gear to pack up?" László eyed Drom. "You must be slipping, Leo. You used to have half the world conquered by noon and only took a break to think through how you were going to tackle the other half. I swore you never slept."

"Family life," Drom said. "It changes a man."

"I've noticed." László winked at Shell. "You two have a fine brood. I don't think you'll have a problem meeting the roll out time. Amanda has your caravan spic and span."

Shell's grip tightened on Drom's hand.

"Glad to hear it." He wrapped his arm around her waist. "We better head back before the boys mess it up again."

"Why don't you let the lady of the house take care of that? I need to square up with you at the Red Wagon before we go."

Drom glanced at her.

"You boys run along," she said. "I'll make sure we're ready to go."

Drom swung her from his left arm to his right, dipped her back, and gave her a kiss. "You're the best wife a man could ask for." He slipped the plastic-wrapped packet into her waistband at the small of her back and brought her back up.

Flush-faced, she gave him a playful push. "Go on, now."

Laughing, Drom put his arm across László's shoulders and propelled them both forward. "Come on, old man, let's take care of business."

⊕

Shell was wiping down the counters when he entered the motorhome. She dropped the towel in the sink and faced him. "I don't like that man."

"Where are the kids?" Drom asked.

"I told Amanda to take the boys and run them as hard as she could. I'll have my hands full enough driving this beast. I don't need them bouncing off the walls while I'm doing it. Did you tell the fat man you were hanging back?"

"I did."

"And that didn't worry him any?"

"It would have if you weren't going with them. He knows I wouldn't abandon you to the circus."

"How can he know something I'm not sure of?"

"Michelle—"

"Gavin Leoppard, don't you patronize me. I opened the package."

"You think I would have handed it off if I meant to keep it from you?"

"For better or worse," Shell said, "I'm Mrs. Drom Reiziger. I don't want to be Michelle Lane ever again."

"Shelley Reiziger isn't safe in the United States. And she doesn't own this motor home, Michelle Lane does."

"Michelle Lane doesn't want it. She wants you."

"You have me."

"Do I?" She crossed her arms. "Have I ever?"

He took in her bloodshot eyes, set jaw, red nose, and rigid stance. He longed to close the distance between them and pull her into his arms. But the pain in her face reminded him that more than space stood between them.

"Sweetheart, I went through hell and heaven to find my way back to you. I don't want to be away from you and the kids. Ever. But I have to do this. No one should be looking for us, except they are. Maybe they're just tugging on thread from Karoly. That's not good, but I'll take it over the alternative."

"Which alternative, that someone figured out you're not dead?"

"Yeah, that one. Either way, I need to find them before they catch us."

She eyed him for a long moment, then leaned forward and peered through the windshield. "The kids are back. I packed you a bag. It's on the bed along with your stash." She came away from the counter and brushed past him on her way out the door.

Drom watched her through the windshield as she scooped David up and swung him around a couple of times, her hair flying. Jakob jumped up and down, begging for a turn. Shell tickled him instead and ran off. The kids gave her chase, their laughter audible in the closed camper.

He tore away from the windshield and shut himself in their room.

He sat between the duffle and the pouch, flipping a coin in his head. He opened the duffle first. Just a change of clothes and a toothbrush. Hurry back, they said. He dumped the plastic pouch out on the bed and picked up the

Missouri driver's license. He stared at her photo. Even the DMV couldn't make her look bad.

Shell had made a couple of attempts at a life in St. Louis before they married. No one would question her having a Missouri driver's license. As an added bonus, it was good for two more years.

He grabbed the other license, issued by the state of New York to Leo Moldovan and expiring in a month, and slid it into his wallet. He contemplated the four bank bundles of twenty-dollar bills for a moment, then tossed one in the duffle and two up on the pillows. Moving to the cabinets overhead, he twisted one of the recessed light fixtures out and slid the money into the small cubby in the cabinet's false bottom. He was twisting the fixture back in when the kids thundered into the motorhome.

"Shell, can you give me a hand?"

"Mommy, Daddy needs you," Amanda said.

A moment later, Shell came in the room and closed the door behind her.

Drom handed her the license and the last stack of twenties. "That's two thousand dollars. Break it up. Give a couple hundred to Amanda in case you get separated. Keep a thousand on you and stash the rest wherever you see fit. László is holding my earnings on account. Let him pay for the gas when the convoy fuels up."

"What are we telling the kids?"

"That I'm staying behind to take care of the van. I need to show you a couple more things." He pulled her toward the bed.

She pulled back. "We don't have time for that."

"I like your train of thought," he said. "But I had something else in mind."

He tugged on her arm again and she crawled up onto their queen-sized bed. The head of their love nest rested against the rear of the motorhome. Cabinets on either side and overhead framed an alcove around it. He plopped down on the right side of the bed and patted the comforter beside him.

"No funny business," she said.

"Enter at your own risk."

"Drom."

"Lay down, honey. I'll behave."

She joined him and he nudged her over onto her right side. Spooning her, he reached over her shoulder and pushed in on the bottom trim of the decorative half-round column beside the bed. It slid over a half inch and popped back. He swung the column out and showed her the narrow safe behind it.

"Put our Reiziger passports in there." He clicked the column shut and rolled onto his back, pulling Shell over with him. "If you twist that light fixture to the right, it will come out of its housing. Two more stacks of bills are hidden in a small space to the right."

They sat up and she kissed him. "Be careful."

"Bank on it."

Drom picked up the last two items from the pouch, a key and a notebook. Pocketing the small notebook, he handed her the key. "That's to the safe. David's left boot has a hollow heel. If you work a dime into the seam between the top of the heel and the sole, you should be able to pry it away. Hide the key in there."

"You're scaring me."

"You told me to be careful. I'm helping you do the same."

"When will you get to Philadelphia?"

"Wednesday is opening night."

"What if you don't make it?"

"I'll be there, Michelle."

"But what if you aren't?"

"If I'm not back in time for the Box, then things went horribly sideways. You'll need to get away from the circus as fast as possible. Head to Denver and find Robert."

"Your brother? Are you crazy?"

"No. If I get detained, he's your best bet. I'll reach out through the classifieds like we discussed. But don't worry. I'll be there."

"You better be."

He pulled her close and bergamot and clove infused his brain. He kissed her. "Don't fret. It's just a dead drop."

They came out of the room and he said his goodbyes to the children. He stood by their minivan waving as Shell maneuvered the motorhome into the convoy. He waited until the last circus vehicle was out of sight, then climbed into the minivan and went in search of the dark side of Syracuse.

Chapter 12

Yugoslav and Italian police have arrested seven Yugoslavs and charged them with smuggling Gypsy children, boys and girls ages eight to fifteen, into another country for the purpose of prostitution or slavery. The scale of child slave traffic between East and West Europe is estimated to be 1,000 children per year. Sold as high as $700 each, the children are forced into the sex trade or made to steal and beg.

The Citizen, June 2, 1987

Syracuse, New York – July 5, 1988

Drom sanitized the van at a self-serve car wash. Slipping on a fresh pair of latex gloves, he gathered up all his used cleaning supplies and dumped them in the trash barrel.

He reconnoitered neighborhoods south of Armory Square the night before, searching for crime, decay, and poverty. He drove to one of the festering pockets and pulled behind a dying strip mall, a liquor store and a flea market its only open businesses.

He backed down the depressed loading dock of the end unit, keeping the passenger side close to the concrete sidewall. Turning the wheel a degree to the right, he put it in drive and stomped the accelerator. The side panels screeched against the concrete as he shot out of the dock.

He barreled across the asphalt service lane into the dirt lot on the other side. Locking the brakes, he gunned the engine, kicking up a cloud of dust with the back tires.

Drom threw it in park and got out. The dirt cloud settled on the wet van, giving it a neglected look. The right side bore the fresh scars of a major sideswipe.

He strolled around the vehicle, kicking at patches of gravel imbedded in the dirt and gathering the larger stones. Stepping back several yards, he threw the stones, peppering the top and hood with dents. He sent the last two rocks through the passenger side windows, shattering them into the interior.

He drove deeper into the crime-infested neighborhood and parked in front of a boarded up, two story house. He cut the engine and dropped the key on the floor board. Reaching behind him, he snagged his bag and slid out of the driver's seat. He kicked the door shut, leaving a sizeable dent in its center.

He removed the license plates, stowed them in the duffle bag, and checked his watch. The lunch hour was half gone. He was a twenty-minute walk from the post office. He snapped the long strap onto the duffle, slung it onto his shoulder, and headed to the dead drop.

Drom glanced across the street at the post office as he walked past. People bustled up and down the uncrowded sidewalk. Crossing the street at the end of the block, he cut down to the next corner, turned left, walked a block, and turned left again. He crouched down and retied his shoe. No one made any sudden stops.

He strolled to a book store and window shopped. Everyone else in its reflection was on the move. He set off again, slowing his pace when he turned left on Salina. Up ahead, a steady trickle of people entered and exited the post office. There were no coffee shops or diners with a commanding view of the entrance. The cars parked on the street were unoccupied.

Drom stepped inside.

A dozen people stood in line for the lone postal clerk in the service area to his right. He checked the walls for surveillance cameras and didn't see any. He walked past the service wing into the mailbox lobby.

He loitered until the other patrons cleared out, then stepped over to his box on the left wall. He slipped his key into the lock and opened the ornate brass door. Inside was a standard mail pickup notice on yellow cardstock with the "there is too much mail to fit into your box" option marked.

A key was taped to it.

He locked his box and studied the second key. It belonged to a large box on the bottom row of the back wall near the right-hand corner. Opening it would put him out of sight of the service line, close to the floor, and with his back to the door—precisely the type of box he had avoided renting in the first place.

Why that box and not the service counter?

He glanced over his shoulder through the glass front. A police cruiser pulled up to the curb and two officers popped out. They entered the post office. He stood, key in hand, wondering if it was the cheese on the trap catch.

"Good to know I'm not the only one," a lady said.

She was on his left, middle-aged and dressed more like a fashionable house-wife than a business woman. *Where did she come from?* "Pardon me?"

"The big box key." She pointed to the key in his hand. "The postmaster here started the practice a while back to expedite the over-mail resolution with self-service. If your regular box gets too stuffed, they move it into one of the bigger ones and stick the key in your regular box. Second time they've put mine there this month. I really need to get down here more often."

His eyes followed the officers as they joined the service queue. "Could just keep the big box key."

"Wouldn't be honest. Besides, no guarantee they'd put your over-mail in the same box next time."

He held the key up. "First offender. Mind showing me how it's done?"

"You poor man," she said. "Give me the key."

He handed it to her. She checked it, then panned down the line of larger boxes. She squatted, unlocked the box, and dug out the contents. "My, you must have gotten on somebody's list." She handed him the stack of envelopes. "Shame all those trees had to die just for junk mail."

"Never know, might be a good offer in there somewhere."

"Don't hold your breath. After all, how many records does anyone need anyway?"

He lifted out the colored envelope from a major record label. "At a dollar an album, who could resist?"

She laughed. "Seriously, hun, you shouldn't wait so long before getting your mail. The postmaster is a peach, but he doesn't let us abuse the system."

Drom lost some lift to his smile. "I'll bear that in mind." He studied her for a beat, making sure he wasn't missing something.

She shifted back. "Sorry, young man. Didn't mean to tell you how to run your business. Force of habit, I suppose. Once a mom, always a mom."

"Oh, I don't mind." He turned the wattage up on his smile. "Didn't realize it could mount up like that. Thanks for the help." He stuffed the mail into his duffle bag, nodded goodbye, and strolled out of the post office.

Turning left, he walked north on Salina, then crossed over to the Galleries of Syracuse, a sprawling shopping mall, office complex, and host of the new Syracuse Central Library.

He opened the door and the cool air of the shopping cathedral washed across him in welcome. He walked through the crystal-roofed atrium into the open architecture of the retail space. He took a slow spin, a summer shopper deciding where to spend first. He spotted the library's mall entrance on the second floor, tucked in a corner to his left.

He puttered to the escalator and let it carry him up. He turned right, strolled several yards, then leaned against the railing and watched the shoppers below. Gawking like a tourist, he counted down from one hundred and twenty.

Everything looked normal.

He strolled around to the library entrance and paused at the railing again. Down below, people traversed the atrium and disappeared into various shops. Some made a straight line for the escalator and rode it up. Nobody glanced his way. A security guard walked his beat. Drom turned his back on the scene and rested his buttocks against the rail. Mothers with young children and college-aged men and women drifted in and out of the library.

He followed in on the heels of a couple with book bags on their shoulders. He kept close to them, making himself part of the study group, until he was out of sight of the information desk. Ducking into an aisle, he navigated toward the array of study carrels in the back. He sat down in the end one and set his bag on the desk top.

He pulled out the stack of mail and a graph ruled notebook. He flipped through the junk mail addressed to John Smith, tossing into a pile the various offers for credit cards, book club memberships, record clubs, and sweepstakes. Near the end of the stack was a marketing letter from the Texarkana Land Agency.

His law firm had information for him.

He opened the envelope and pulled out the sales pitch. It informed John Smith that when it came to real estate investment, no company could match the Texarkana Land Agency. As evidence of their reach, a listing of zip codes in six columns was attached to the letter. The top code of the left-hand column was 72601.

Drom dug out the small notepad he had retrieved from his stash under László's trailer. Each page was filled with five-digit numbers arranged in six columns. He thumbed through the pages until he found the one with 72601 as the last number in the sixth column. He tore the page out and set it down next to the Texarkana listing. Grabbing pen and graph paper, he set to work deciphering the message.

He transcribed the bottom row of numbers from the letter, arranging them in pairs and leaving a blank block between each pair. Under this, he wrote the first row of numbers from the page he had torn out of the notepad, using the same paired pattern. He subtracted his second row from his first using non-carrying math. He converted the two-digit results into letters, using 01 for A as his starting point. He worked his way up the rows until he encountered a double-x, which signified the end of the message.

He read the communique.

The application for the Karoly search warrant had been filed with the United States District Court for the Eastern District of Washington. The applicant was Special Agent Richard Cannon with the Federal Bureau of Investigation. Chief Judge Robert J. McNichols had signed off on it. The basis of the search was the "contraband, fruits of crime, or other illegally possessed" rationale of the federal code.

Because the search was carried out on the suspicion of stolen items and ill-gotten gains and no evidence of such was found, the judge in Karoly's case dismissed the charges and mandated that all confiscated property be returned.

All this was a matter of public record. What followed wasn't. The defendant stated in a privileged conversation that all confiscated items were not returned. Said items weren't on the official inventory of items taken. The defendant believed the government's theft amounted to "a loss of identity." The cryptic notice confirmed that their Reiziger alias was burned. It offered no clue regarding the FBI's motivation or how the French fit in.

The last bit of intelligence regarded Special Agent Cannon. He was assigned to a task force working with the Inspector General investigating past Central Intelligence Agency operations in the wake of several high-profile scandals that had rocked the intelligence community.

Cannon was the thread Drom needed to pull.

He gathered up the Texarkana letter and envelope, the sheet from his one-time pad, and the decoded message. He stuffed the lot into his front pocket. He tossed the rest of the mail and his supplies back into the duffle bag.

Exiting the library, he took the stairs to the first level. He ducked into the men's room near the main entrance, entered the stall farthest from the door, and closed himself in. While relieving himself, he shredded the papers he had stuffed in his pocket and tossed them in the bowl. His business finished, he flushed, entrusting the communique's destruction to the city's sewage treatment system.

Back out on Salina Street, he headed north to West Fayette. The intersection served as the hub of Syracuse's public transportation system. Drom stepped into a small convenience store. He picked up a couple of dollars' worth of savory snacks, paid the cashier with a twenty-dollar bill, and requested all his change in quarters.

The store clerk eyed his drawer, then gave Drom a quizzical look. "Are you sure, man? That's a lot of quarters."

"I don't have a bus pass and want to have a look around the city, you know?"

Pawing the quarters out of his drawer, he stacked them out by fours on the counter. He lifted the tray and pulled out a ten-dollar roll. "That's all the quarters I got, man. Still owe you twenty-nine cents. Dimes, nickels, and pennies okay, or do you want it all in pennies?"

"Keep the change." Drom pocketed the coins, snagged his treats, and headed back out onto the street.

He found a bank of pay phones half a block up from the intersection. They were installed at standing height along the building face, each partitioned with steel side panels that did nothing to dampen the street noise and little in offering privacy. Moving to the one on the far end, he pulled the phone book out of its cubby shelf and found the number for long distance information. He picked up the handset, loaded the phone with quarters, and tapped the number out on the metal keys.

Five rings in, a woman's voice came on the line. "Long distance information, how may I help you?"

"I need the number for the FBI regional office in Spokane, Washington, please."

"Please hold." Dead space followed for a beat, then the woman came back on the line and gave him the number.

Drom hung up.

He jumped on a northbound bus and got off near the university campus. He walked until all the passengers who exited with him were out of sight, then stopped a moment to get his bearings. Catching whiffs of frying food and whispers of amplified music, he chased them to their source. The pub had a couple of occupied four-tops out on the sidewalk under the awning. Speakers above piped out an upbeat ambiance. He stepped inside.

A waiter in black slacks and t-shirt with a tan apron approached him. "Lunch or liquor?"

"Lunch." Drom eyed the chalkboard advertising the specials. "I'll take the Italian hero with chips. And a pay phone, if you have one."

The waiter jotted his order down. "Drink?"

"Water's fine."

He led him to a table and Drom took a seat. The waiter served him his water. "Food shouldn't take long. Phone's in the back by the restrooms."

Drom drained half the glass in one gulp, then headed to the payphone. It was in a small booth trimmed out in wood paneling that matched the dark maple wainscotting of the hallway. He opened the two-section accordion glass door, settled into the tiny bench, and closed himself in. He picked up the receiver and fed eight quarters into the slot.

He dialed the Spokane office.

Three rings later, a woman answered. "Federal Bureau of Investigation, how may I direct your call?"

"Special Agent Richard Cannon."

"Please hold."

An instrumental version of a popular easy-listening tune filled his ear. He kept an eye on his watch as the second hand ticked its way around its face. He was close to hanging up when the lady came back on line.

"Sir, I'm sorry, but Special Agent Cannon is not assigned to the Spokane Office. May I ask what this is in reference to? Perhaps I can get another agent to help you."

"No. It's imperative that I speak with him. Do you have a number where I can reach him?"

"I'd be glad to take your information, sir, and have the agent contact you."

Drom held his breath for a beat. "I don't have much time. My life is in danger. I need to keep moving. Tell a supervisor that I have information on Karoly Bardu. I will only give it to Special Agent Cannon. I know what he was looking for and can help him find it, but I need assurances."

"Sir, please—"

"What is your name?"

"Ms. Claridge. Sir, if you feel you are in danger, let me know your location and I can—"

"I'll call in thirty minutes. Have a number for me." He hung up.

Drom's lunch was waiting for him when he returned to his table. He picked up one half of the hero and took a healthy bite. Oil and vinegar dripped down his chin. He wiped it with his napkin as he chewed through the mouthful. The textures and flavors of the vegetables and cold cuts hit the right notes for him, but left him longing for the hard crust pub sandwiches of his Spanish youth.

He made short work of the hero, then devoured the chips. He tucked a twenty under the edge of the plate, shouldered the duffle bag, and pushed out onto the street.

He backtracked along the bus route. Spotting a public trash receptacle, he quickened his pace as he nonchalantly unzipped the duffle and palmed the stack of mail. Brushing past the trash can, he slipped the stack through the lid flap.

He hustled to Fayette Street, found another bank of pay phones, and dialed Spokane. A man answered.

"Ms. Claridge, please," Drom said.

"Hold while I transfer you."

Five seconds later, she came on the line. "This is Ms. Claridge, how may I help you?"

"It's me. Do you have Special Agent Cannon's number?"

"May I have your name and number, sir, in case we get disconnected?"

"Listen, I need—" Drom hung up.

He slid two phones down and let ten minutes go by. He broke open the ten dollar roll and fed quarters into the phone. He tapped out the number. A woman answered.

"I need to ..." Drom sucked in several sharp breaths. "I need to talk to Ms. Claridge. It's urgent."

"This is she. Sir, you sound distressed. Please, give me your location. We can have law enforcement to you in a matter of minutes. We can get you safe."

"You ... don't ... understand." He panted, a man catching his breath. "No one is safe from them. Cannon's my only chance. I'm running out of time. The number, I need his number."

"Do you have something to write with?"

"Hold on." He patted his pockets like she could see him. "Okay, I'm ready."

She gave him the number. He repeated it back to her. She confirmed.

He hung up.

Drom scanned the intersection. The only visible police presence was a parking enforcement officer ticketing a rusty Jeep. No dark suits cased the hub. He turned back to the phone and drew out the directory chained beneath it. He checked the area code map. Cannon's number belonged to Washington, D.C.

✦

A thirty-minute stroll brought him to a single-bay mechanic's shop on Fabius street. It commanded the foot of an L-shaped lot littered with cars in various stages of disrepair. A bell jingled when Drom pulled the office door open. Stepping inside, he found the interior much as he remembered it, if a bit more worn. A threadbare couch sagged against the right wall. Two bar stools with blistered vinyl upholstery beckoned the unwary to take a perch at the raw plywood service counter. Blue paint flaked from the cinder block walls, exposing patches of old primer and gray stone.

A sixtyish woman he didn't recognize came through a side door behind the counter and glared at him. The set of her dark eyes reminded him of the look his grandmother Hishoro would give him when she was displeased. It took him back to his life with the *kumpániya* and he found himself choked with nostalgia.

"Young man! You want help or no?" Her accent was thick, her tone brusque.

Drom cleared his throat and blinked the memories clear. "Is Mitko here?"

"Who asking?"

"Someone who wants to buy a car."

Her lip twitched. Keeping her eyes on him, she picked up the phone receiver with her left hand. Her blouse sleeve pooled at her elbow, exposing a faded blue tattoo on her forearm, Z·10814. She thumbed a button at the base of the handset. "Mitko, you have customer." Her voice echoed out of the intercom speakers in the bay.

Drom pointed at her forearm. "You were in Auschwitz. Sinti or Roma?"

"Mind you business." Jerking her shirtsleeve down, she darted through the side door and slammed it shut.

He should have known better than to ask. His own grandmother wouldn't talk about it. When he had asked her about her tattoo, she said it was proof of ugliness. It was all he ever got out of her on the subject.

Mitko Zajda barreled through the double swinging doors directly behind the counter. He hadn't aged much. Built like a fire plug and dressed in short-sleeved coveralls smeared with grease, his close-shorn hair had gone gray. His dark eyes retained their intelligent spark. "Leo, as I live and breathe!"

Mitko came around the counter and clamped him in a bear hug. Drom returned the affection and the men kissed each other's cheeks.

Drom gave Mitko's belly a friendly pat. "Looks like Antonia's cooking is as good as ever."

"Stay for dinner and see for yourself."

"I would love to, but I can't, old friend. I have to be on the road before the afternoon rush."

"You wish me dead? If Antonia find that Leo Moldovan was in my shop and I no bring him home, she kill me."

"Really, Mitko, I can't. I came to buy a car from you so I can hit the road."

"That settles it, then. You come outside, pick car, my boys have ready for you in morning. Tonight, you stay with Mitko and make Antonia happy." Mitko pinched his ribs. "She make feast when she see you. You too skinny."

Drom eyed him a moment. "A clean ride?"

"Spotless. I take care of you, the great Leo Moldovan."

Drom lifted his hands in acquiescence. "*Te den, xa*," he said in Romani, when you are given, eat.

Mitko completed the proverb. "*Te marren, de-nash.*" When you are beaten, run away. "And if you don't eat, Antonia will beat me." They both had a good laugh, then Mitko slapped his shoulder. "Come, let's find your car."

Drom held his hands up. "Antonia, I couldn't possibly. You've fed me three plates of food already."

"Young men need to eat," she said. She placed the *guzvara*, a peach and apple strudel, in front of him. "I make just for you."

The oldest son stuck his head between them. "If I eat it for you, will you teach me a juggling trick?"

Mitko waved him back. "Johnny, let Leo eat in peace." Like many immigrants, the Zajda's had given their sons common American first names to help them fit in.

"What is this 'juggle'? It's all boys talk since he come." The sixtyish woman with the Auschwitz tattoo, Antonia's aunt, pointed at him with her fork.

"Auntie, you should have seen him at the circus the other night," Tommy, the youngest boy said. "He was spinning in this plastic box and all these orange balls were BOOM! BANG! and then—"

"He kicked them so hard, they shattered the back wall," Greg, the middle boy said.

The woman glanced at both of her grandnephews then stared across the table at him.

Drom snagged five forks off the table cloth and scooched his chair back. He tossed the forks up from right-to-left and left-to-right and they flew in a sideways figure eight that crossed at his forehead. After four rotations, he flicked the forks back to their perspective places and they slid in beside their plates.

"Sim shuditóri," he said, I am a juggler.

Her eyes narrowed. She took her returned fork and pointed at him. "Eat."

Drom knew better than to argue with Romani women. He pushed his way through two servings of the dessert, then gave a resounding belch of appreciation. "After this much food, young men need to sleep, Antonia."

Antonia motioned to her fourteen-year-old. "Johnny, show Leo to your room."

"Yes, mama." The boy rose from the table.

Drom stepped over to his hostess and kissed her cheek. "It was wonderful, Antonia. Thank you."

She patted his hand, then dabbed her eye with a napkin. "Get rest. Tomorrow, Mitko will have car."

Drom followed Johnny upstairs and found his bed decked out with fresh linens and a mint candy on the pillow like he would find in a hotel. A towel and washcloth were folded at the foot of the bed and they had set his duffle beside it. He took a shower, thankful to wash off the day's grime.

He put on a pair of shorts and a T-shirt, then laid on his back in the bed. He stared at the ceiling, soaking in the sounds of a family settling in for the night.

He kept turning over the information from Spokane deep into the night. An agent with the D.C. office filed for a search warrant in the state of Washington. A chief judge signed off on it, not one of the district court magistrates. The raid on Karoly had high level attention. Agent Cannon would know why.

He recited the hundred and nineteenth Psalm to quell his churning mind and drifted off near the end of *rësh.*

Breakfast lasted until mid-morning. Every time Drom made to get up from the table, Antonia produced another treat. It was Mitko who finally called an end to the repast.

"Enough, woman!" Mitko said. "He eat plenty. I promise him car, we get car now."

Antonia stood with the coffee cake fresh from the oven held in her hands. "He'll need food for the road. I wrap some up."

Back at Mitko's shop, Drom realized skipping Antonia's morning feast wouldn't have gained him any time. The blue Chevrolet Cavalier wagon he had picked out was up on jacks and missing its windshield.

"Almost done," Mitko said. "They wait on glass. Be here soon. Meanwhile, they double-check brakes."

The glass truck showed up moments later. Mitko's men swarmed the car like a pit crew.

"How clean are the plates?" Drom asked.

"Fresh off press. Insurance say car dead. Papers say car is Leo's."

"You want to settle up in the office?"

"Settle? Settle what? You see Johnny. My boy's alive and healthy. If not for you—"

"You would have figured something out."

"No, you find him, make sure he get best doctors. We move here, safe now. The car is yours."

"Let me give you something for the labor, at least. Your guys worked hard to get it ready."

"It's no problem, I tell you. You get on road, meet circus. Make others happy like my boys."

Drom thought of his talent, the base skill of his deadly art. Any happiness it had brought was drowned in an ocean of blood. He embraced Mitko. "Until next time, my friend."

"*Le petúte sáma,*" Mitko said, look after yourself.

Drom gave him the customary Romani goodbye *"Devlésa."* Stay with God.

Despite the late start, Drom still had enough time to reach the circus before the first act with an hour to spare. His buffer evaporated in the road construction outside of Scranton that brought highway speeds down to city crawls. Twenty miles south of the city, the lanes opened back up. He kept to the right and resisted the urge to speed. He couldn't afford a traffic stop.

He checked his watch as he entered the north side of Philadelphia. The first clown antics would be underway in the big top, warming up the crowd. He wondered if Shell and the kids would be in the grandstand as usual or in the wings for a different view of the action.

Twenty minutes away from the venue, he hit a traffic jam. The vehicles in front came to a dead stop and cars packed in beside and behind him. He threw the shifter into park and killed the ignition. Sirens wailed in the distance. He climbed onto the roof of the Cavalier and peered north. A mile or so back, red lights flashed. The ambulance pushed through the stalled traffic like an artic ice breaker. He spun south and noted the traffic trickling out a half mile ahead. He jumped down and got back behind the wheel.

Time bled away.

The cars in front inched forward. The siren blared closer, insistent and pushing. Vehicles trickled onto the emergency lanes. The ambulance plowed its way through the middle. Minutes later, he joined the others creeping down the side lane and passed the mangled cars that clogged the center of the highway.

He glanced at his watch. If the announcer had kept everyone on pace, the lion was tearing Julia's clown costume off.

Pressing the accelerator, he ramped back up to speed.

He pulled into the back yard lot with only ten minutes left to get in costume and warm up for the Box. Tossing his keys to one of the hands, he asked him to park the car by his motorhome.

He ran into wardrobe, changed his clothes, and grabbed his props. He hustled to the curtain and took a breath.

"Give Leo a warm, capitalist welcome."

He flipped into the cheers.

⊕

He came through the shattered back wall of the Box wrung out. The tension of clearing the dead drop, the wear of the drive, and the demands of the performance all stacked up and seemed to land on him at once. He was exhausted. He needed Shell, a shower, and sleep. He navigated through the back yard and trudged into the camper area. Every venue was different, but the circus organized itself in the same way. Drom had a good idea of where his motorhome should be.

He was wrong.

The blue Cavalier sat by itself next to an empty slip.

Adrenaline dumped in his veins, pushing his exhaustion back. In his second circuit of the camper area, he ran across the hand who parked his car. He got the keys back, but no information on his family. It unnerved him. What happened? Why did Shell bolt?

You're overreacting.

He headed into the cookhouse and scanned the tables. They weren't there. He slipped behind the serving line and found Freida in the kitchen.

She pulled a banquet pan of lasagna out of the industrial oven and set it down on the counter. "Leo, I know you need to fill both those legs after that act, but you should get your food from the serving line like everyone else."

"I'm not here for food, Freida. I'm looking for my family."

"They wouldn't be eating yet, silly boy." She tossed her oven mitts onto the counter. "The big top is still emptying out. Why don't you get a table and let them find you?"

"So they're still here?"

"Far as I know. Shell helped me with breakfast this morning."

"Our motorhome isn't in the camper area."

She frowned, stepped over to the stove, and gave her pot a stir. "You should check again. It was parked next to the Belyankov's rig. You know László, he likes keeping you eastern Europeans together."

"It's not there, Freida."

She called one of the kitchen staff over carry the lasagna to the line. She took him by the arm and led him outside away from other ears. "I hate to pry, but have you two been fighting?"

"What? No."

"Leo, Mama Freida is no fool. I know you two love each other, but don't pretend nothing's wrong."

Drom shifted on his feet and stared at the ground. "She didn't want to move."

"And you brought her here, to Julia? You're a juggler, Leo. Playing the fool you should leave to the clowns."

"Julia and I never—"

Freida flashed her palm. "Whether you did or didn't doesn't matter. What matters is that the attraction is mutual and apparent to anyone who cares to look. You were not wise to bring your family here. If your wife has pulled out, you should talk to Julia."

He studied her face a moment. "What aren't you telling me?"

"Not my story to tell. Find Julia. Her cats aren't the only ones with claws."

Drom's gut twisted on itself. He had foiled the French team in Penticton. He had gotten them safely across the border. He'd remained vigilant against surveillance and tapped into hidden resources. He had protected his family from everything except an assault on the heart. "For goodness' sake, Freida, don't send me to her in the blind. What do you know?"

"I needed help this afternoon." She wiped her hands on her apron, then smoothed it down. "Went looking for Shell. Your woman knows her way around a kitchen and she's good company. Anyway, I didn't find her in your camper. I figured she was taking the boys for a walk. I found them all at Julia's cages. I couldn't hear what they were saying, but it ended abruptly."

"How do you mean?"

"Amanda was standing next to Julia. Shell was in front of them, holding the boys' hands. Julia said something, then Amanda chimed in. Shell said something and they all marched off. Julia just stood there looking pale."

"Did you talk with either of them?"

"Put my nose in someone else's fight? We're circus folk, Leo. Can't live this life and be a busybody."

Drom gave her a hug and kissed her cheek.

"I hope you two work it out," Freida said.

He squeezed her again, then strode off to find Julia. He spotted her in one of the cage trailers brushing Cleopatra, her female leopard. She was still in her red dress.

He stepped up to the cage. "What did you do?"

"Pushed her too hard." She didn't turn from her task. "I knew she wasn't ready yet. But László pumped your act so high, I figured I had to up my game."

"By lying to my wife?"

She glanced over her shoulder at him. "What are you talking about?"

"You said you pushed her." He pressed closer and grabbed the bars. "What happened?"

A low rumble erupted from Cleopatra. She curled her upper lip, exposing her fangs.

Julia rubbed the bridge of Cleopatra's nose. "Easy girl, it's just Leo. You know him." The rumble turned into a purr.

"Julia, what happened?"

"I don't know what your problem is, but if you upset Cleopatra again, I'll open the cage and let you deal with her attitude."

Drom pushed away from the cage. "We need to talk. Shell and the kids are gone."

"Gone? What do you mean gone?"

"They left. Freida said you and Shell got into it this afternoon."

"You think … Oh, forget it! How about you keep your mouth shut until I get out of here?" She turned back to Cleopatra and finished brushing her. She backstepped to the opposite side of Drom, reached behind her through the bars, and opened the gate. She came down the ladder and shut the gate without once taking her eyes off the cat.

Drom charged around the trailer. "I need to know what you two argued about."

Julia pushed her arms into his chest, stopping his forward march. "Slow down."

The heat of her hands radiated through his shirt. A lock of hair fell across her eye and he resisted the urge to comb it back in place with his fingers. He lowered her arms. "What happened?"

"You're all worked up over nothing. Shell's sister showed up. They're probably out to dinner somewhere."

"Shell told you her sister showed up?"

"No. A lady came through during the pre-show tour. She showed me a picture of Shell, said she was her sister, and asked where she could find her."

"And you told her?"

"Almost, but Amanda called for me before I could."

"Where was she?"

"Behind my camper getting the lions' lunch dished out. I asked your sister-in-law to give me a second. I got to Amanda and told her her aunt was here to see them. She put her hand on my mouth and shook her head."

"Shell has several sisters and we don't get along with all of them," Drom said. It wasn't a lie. It wasn't the entire truth, either. "What did this woman look like?"

"Shorter than Shell, taller than me. Dirty blond, hazel eyes."

Drom nodded like he knew the woman she was describing. "Did Amanda say anything?"

"She asked me to send her aunt off to the cookhouse to wait for them, said she wanted to surprise her mom. I let Amanda finish dishing out the meat for the lions while I gave the lady directions to the cookhouse."

"She have anyone with her?"

"Not that I saw. Anyway, Shell showed up before I had to go looking for her. I guess Amanda couldn't wait to surprise her. She ran out and told her mom about the aunt. Shell didn't look too happy. She practically threw David to Amanda, grabbed Jakob, and took off."

"I'm an idiot." He ran his hands through his hair. "I thought you had goaded—"

"Leo Moldovan!" She slapped his arm. "You think too much of yourself, or too little of me. You're a married man now. I've never denied how I feel about you, but I always knew there was someone else. I would never try to get in the middle of what you two have."

"You're a better friend than I deserve."

"Friendship isn't about deserves," she said.

He kept quiet for a moment, soaking in the sight of her. He owed her an explanation and a proper goodbye. He could give her neither. Again. "I have to go."

"Shell's not out to dinner, is she?"

"No."

"What's going on, Leo? If you're in trouble, I can help."

"Trust me, the less you know the better. Tell László he can keep my take as compensation for not finishing the run."

"Are you coming back?"

"I don't know."

Her arms were around him before he could stop her. She held him tight for a moment, her head against his chest. Lemon grass and fresh sawdust tugged at his heart. She broke the embrace and brushed the tears from her face. "Come back, Leo. Whenever you can, come back. I need to know you're okay."

"I have to go." He spun on his heel and marched away without a backward glance.

He climbed in behind the wheel of the Cavalier and several minutes later, he was heading south on Interstate 95.

The Reizigers were burned. Shell was on her way to Denver. It was time to have a chat with Special Agent Richard Cannon.

Chapter 13

Germans have imposed increasing control in occupied France, restricting foreign press and outlawing criticism of the Reich. A German firing squad executed eight men yesterday for espionage and activities against Germans.

In Bordeaux, German authorities condemned a twenty-one-year-old Frenchman to ten years' imprisonment at hard labor for having a loaded revolver in his possession.

New York Times, August 31, 1941

Nantes, France – October 19, 1941

Thsuri had been tailing the Paris team for two days and they hadn't made him yet.

It worried him.

The men were either Gestapo pretending not to notice him; or worse, were amateurish enough not to know they were being followed. Amateurs could get one killed. Gestapo got one tortured, then killed.

The older man—small, ragged, and sporting a worn Basque beret—split off from the other two. Tshuri let him go and heeled the young pair. They ducked into the same bistro they had lunched in the day before. He walked past the restaurant's glass front, glancing inside to be sure they were seated.

Times of turmoil expanded black market economies, spawning traders and thieves scratching out a living and chasing fortune. More trader than thief, Tshuri possessed skills in both departments. His current customers wanted explosives. In occupied France, the order placed procurement directly in his thieves' camp.

Despite the theater of intimidation deployed by the Nazis through their marching columns, ornate unforms, oversized swastikas fluttering on fields of red, and public notices posted in thick, Germanic font, Tshuri was aware of their sensible insecurity in occupied territory. Soldiers stuck together. Officers had bodyguards. Garrisons built bunkers.

Gypsies caught in the labor draft were digging through the bedrock below Colonel Karl Hotz's headquarters in the Hotel d'Aux, driving a shaft toward the Saint-Félix canal as get-away tunnel for the *Feldkommandant* of Nantes. Tshuri paid the Roma workers to divert some of the dynamite crates his way.

The Paris commando was in Nantes to take them off his hands. And fill his pockets.

Or get him hung.

Tshuri ambled through the streets two blocks behind the bistro, making sharp turns and sudden stops. He loitered against buildings. Once he was confident that no one was trailing him, he made his way back to the bistro. He purchased a newspaper from a stand across the street and pretended to read it.

His marks left the restaurant. He gave them a comfortable lead, then set off behind them. They kept to their regular route to their flat. Turning from his quarry at a cross street, he charged around the block. Cutting through an alley, he tucked against the wall and waited for them to catch up to him.

He let the taller one pass, then hooked his arm around the neck of his comrade and hauled him into the alley. The youth managed a short cry before Tshuri choked off his airway. His partner spun around and stepped toward them.

Tshuri pressed the muzzle of his pistol against his captive's temple and backed up. "Come slowly, or I shoot him, then you."

The man raised his hands. "What do you want?"

"I want you to step into the alley, slow and steady." Tshuri continued backing up, drawing the other man in. Once in deeper shadows, he stopped.

"Now what?" the tall one asked.

Releasing his chokehold, Tshuri pushed the youth toward his companion. Stumbling forward, he sprawled onto the cobblestones gasping for breath. Tshuri aimed at the other man's head. "What day is the day that brings fair weather?"

The man's eyes narrowed. "The eleventh." It came out more question than response.

Tshuri kept the pistol trained on him. "Do you have the money?"

"Do you have the explosives?"

Tshuri motioned to the boy on the ground. The other man helped him up.

"I have what Paris asked for," Tshuri said. "The money?"

"Spartaco has it. I am Gilbert and this is Marcel. You are?"

"The man who can shoot you. Head back to your flat. I'll be right behind you. You won't see me, but trust me, I'll be there. I see anything I don't like and I'll finish what I started here, understood?"

They glanced at each other, then stared at him and nodded.

"Good." Tshuri pointed the pistol at them. "Go."

They backstepped to the sidewalk, spun, and ran away.

⊕

Tshuri was seated in the lone easy chair of the apartment's small parlor when Gilbert and Marcel stepped through the door. "When is Spartaco supposed to be back?"

"How did you get in?" Gilbert asked.

"Wrong question. What should worry you is that I know where you've been staying. At the rate you two are going, the only objective you're going to reach is the wrong side of a German barrel."

Gilbert stared at him, looking more like a rattled youth than the field-tempered operative he was reported to be.

Marcel's eyes darted between them. "You're Gestapo." His voice was raspy from Tshuri's abuse.

"Relax, boy. If I were Gestapo, we'd be having this conversation in the basement while you hung from your wrists on piano wire. Spartaco?"

"Soon," Gilbert said.

Tshuri kept his eyes on Gilbert and chin-pointed toward Marcel. "What's the boy's story? I doubt he's started shaving yet."

"I don't need a razor to resist the Nazis," Marcel said.

"Your country needs your seed more than your blood. You should keep your head down, find a girl, and raise a family in free France."

"My seed would only give the Nazis more slaves," Marcel said. "My blood might help future workers get their just due."

"I like this one," Tshuri said to Gilbert.

The door opened and a man stepped through—small, ragged, and sporting a worn Basque beret. He stiffened, wide-eyed, then shifted back toward the hallway.

"Leave now and you'll be alone with no explosives," Tshuri said.

Spartaco came in. He eyed the other two. "Get some chairs."

Tshuri's seat gave him a commanding view of the flat. Set in a corner, he could see into the kitchen and the bedroom without taking his eyes off Spartaco.

The young commandos each grabbed a chair from the dinette table in the kitchen. Marcel spun his chair, straddled it, and crossed his arms atop its back. Gilbert placed his to Tshuri's right and perched on its edge like a guest at a formal dinner.

Spartaco stayed on his feet near the door. He removed his beret and ran his hand through the mop of brown hair, pushing it back from his high forehead. Heavy-lidded, deep-set eyes examined Tshuri, waiting.

"Andre told me Remy was buying," Tshuri said. "These boys call you Spartaco. Last time I heard that name, the Marseillaise Brigade was getting pounded near the Ebro River."

"You were there?"

"Only when I had to be."

"For the Republic or the Nationalists?"

"You mean for the Communists or the Fascists. Both sides needed supplies. I was there for my wallet and my family."

Marcel glowered at him. "Capitalist."

"I'm a merchant," Tshuri said, "with the supplies you need. I'll take half the money now. Meet me in front of the Saint Nicolas Basilica in an hour and I will lead you to the cache. Once you inspect the merchandise, you pay me the other half."

"What's to stop you from disappearing with the down payment?" Spartaco asked.

Tshuri reached inside his coat and flicked a brown cylinder to Spartaco. The man caught it between his palms. He pinched each end and turned it with his fingertips. The Reich's eagle swastika scrolled into view beside the word "DYNAMIT." "GEFÄRLICHER EXPLOSIVSTOFF" followed in finer print.

"I risked my life getting the product for you," Tshuri said. "I have every intention of receiving full payment."

Spartaco dug into his jacket pocket, pulled out a roll of bills, and tossed it to Tshuri. He caught it in his left hand, the pistol in his right trained on Spartaco's chest.

"That's three thousand francs," Spartaco said. "You get the rest on delivery."

Tshuri rose, pocketing the money. He checked his wrist watch. "I have three twenty. Saint Nicholas, one hour." He backed his way to the door and let himself out. He eased up the central stairwell to the next floor and watched their door. Ten minutes passed. No one came out. He pressed up to the top floor, located the roof maintenance hatch, and climbed out. He inched across the slate shingles, keeping the roof peak between him and the street. Near the corner of the building, he scaled down the gutter spout. Back on the ground, he scanned his surroundings. There were no bystanders in sight, no faces pressed to windows.

Taking a tortuous route to the basilica to lose any pursuers, he reached the rendezvous with minutes to spare. The Paris commando loitered on the wide church steps. He marched past them, his feet carrying him north on Rue Affre. He turned left on Rue de Feltre and kept to the street until he reached a wide boulevard with trees down its center. He glanced over his shoulder. The three men were half a block behind him.

He turned south on the tree-lined boulevard and led his tail to a narrow street with decaying tenements on either side. He opened the green metal door to the courtyard of the second building and dipped through. He strode to the building entrance and waited. Marcel and Gilbert filed into the courtyard. Spartaco brought up the rear and shut the gate.

Tshuri pushed into the building and launched down the hallway. He paused at apartment number three and took a moment to study the neighboring doorways. No one came out. He glanced down the hinge-side crack of his door. A centimeter above the floor, the point of a toothpick peeked out of the crack. No one had entered since he left. He turned his key in the lock, swung the door open, and motioned for the others to enter.

Spartaco nodded to his companions. The two men slipped past Tshuri.

A moment later, Gilbert poked his head out. *"Rien à signaler."*

Spartaco went in. Tshuri scanned the corridor again, then stepped into the apartment and locked the door.

The flat was bare of furnishings save for a single bed in the corner and wooden chair by the window. Three crates sat in the middle of the floor.

Spartaco's bright eyes scrutinized him for a beat. "Some call me reckless. Anyone barging in here would have found these."

"They would have to find the flat first," Tshuri said. "Unlike you three, no one's been tailing me for days."

The man gave a short grunt, then turned to the other two. "Open them."

Gilbert and Marcel produced pocket knives and set to work prying the lids up. They dug through the crates, talking to each other in hushed tones. Inspection complete, they closed the boxes up.

"It's all here," Gilbert said, "dynamite, caps, fuse line, and detonator."

"Satisfied?" Tshuri asked.

"What about pistols?" Spartico responded.

"One transaction at a time." Tshuri put his hand out.

Spartaco pulled out another bill roll and handed it to him.

"Fabien ordered us to travel unarmed," Gilbert said. "We need pistols."

Tshuri glanced at him, then faced Spartaco. "Your man sounds worried."

"Can you get us guns or not?"

"I can outfit you with Astra Model 200s in 6.35mm like this one." He raised his pistol.

"You have them here or do we have to shadow you someplace else?" Spartaco asked.

"Seven hundred francs buys you an answer."

Spartaco brought out another wad of bills and counted out Tshuri's price.

Tshuri tucked the money into his shirt pocket. "I took the liberty of putting some luggage together for you. It's under the bed. You should change your wardrobe up a bit. Trapsing about in the same clothes every day makes you easy to identify." He slid back to the door.

"Wait, the pistols," Gilbert said.

"Black valise." Tshuri waved the gun toward the bed.

Marcel scrambled over and slid the valise from under the bed. He thumbed the latches and came up with the pistols. "They're not loaded."

"You'll find the ammunition in one of the other suitcases." Tshuri tossed his key to Spartaco. "Flat's yours. Landlord will be collecting rent tomorrow. You'll want all this gone by then."

"Keep your head down for the next couple of days," Spartaco said. "If we're successful, the Nazi's will go on high alert."

Tshuri reached behind him and turned the deadbolt. "Hope you hurt the bastards." He slipped into the corridor and closed the door on them.

Chapter 14

Cowardly criminals in the pay of England and Moscow have killed, by shooting in the back, the Feldkommandant of Nantes on the morning of 20 October 1941. Up to now, the assassins have not been arrested.

As atonement for this crime, I have ordered that 50 hostages be shot, to begin with. Because of the gravity of the crime, 50 more hostages will be shot in the case of the guilty not being arrested between now and midnight of 23 October 1941.

Notice from General von Stülpnagel
Military Commander of the Frankreich
Paris, France, 21 October 1941

Region of Nantes, France – October 21, 1941

Tshuri scrambled through the cobwebs of sleep and sat upright.

"*Öffne die Tür, schnell!*" Banging followed the order. "*Auf! Auf! Auf!*"

He shook his wife's shoulder. "Hishoro, rats."

Hishoro patted her five-year-old's cheek. "Tshompi, get up." The boy rubbed his eyes, sat up, and yawned. She reached past him to the twins. "Alfonso, Pierre, get up."

More banging. "*Ich komme, ich komme.*" He unlocked the wagon door.

It flew open.

Hands gripped his arm and jerked him to the ground. He got to his knees and held his hands up. "*Wir arbeinten zusammen.*"

"*Stille, schwein!*" The soldier's boot slammed into Tshuri's ribcage, knocking him over. Through blurry eyes, he saw Hishoro emerge from the wagon, her dark face gray in the moonlight.

"*Schnell! Schnell! Schnell!*" The soldiers' shouts matched the cadence of the dogs' barking.

Hishoro jumped to the ground and lifted the boys out one by one. The twins latched onto her skirt. Setting Tshompi down, she grabbed his hand. A soldier prodded her away from the *vurdon* with his rifle barrel.

Tshuri rolled onto his knees and elbows and forced air into his lungs. His ribcage howled at every expansion and wailed with his exhale. Two soldiers hauled him up by his arms and threw him against the wagon wheel.

A third man stepped into view. He held his hand out. "Papers."

Tshuri noted his sergeant's rank and the double lightning bolt of the Waffen-SS on his collar. "In the wagon."

"Go with him," the sergeant said.

The soldier on his right pulled him around to the back of the wagon. Mateo's protests and Keti's pleading joined the dog barks and soldier shouts. Tshuri climbed inside and shuffled to the bed at the front. He shoved his hand under the thin mattress. His fingertips brushed the pistol grip. Cold steel pressed into the back of his neck. He slid his hand left, grabbed his pack of papers, and pulled them out.

The soldier took them, then waved his barrel toward the door. *"Auf!"*

Tshuri scrambled out, his left arm pressed against his injured ribs. The soldier pushed him back to the wagon wheel.

Tshuri surveyed the scene. Keti and Hishoro were huddled with the children. Soldiers tossed household wares out of the wagons. Mateo was on his knees by the remains of their central camp fire. An officer stood in front of him, an Astra Model 200 in his hand.

"Where did you get this?"

"Guernica," Mateo said.

The officer backhanded him with the pistol. Mateo's head snapped right and he fell onto his side. *"Zigeuner schwein."* The officer swung his jack-booted leg and his foot struck Mateo's face with a sickening thud.

Tshuri's guard shoved him toward the officer. He pulled him up short by the collar and slammed the back of Tshuri's knee with his rifle butt, forcing him to kneel.

"How is it that you are still traveling?" the officer asked.

Tshuri swept his gaze up the man, from his blood-splattered toe boot, up his trim form, to his collar patch with the silver stripe and three silver pips. "Your man has our *carnet*, *Obersturmführer*, and my peddler's permit."

"For a *Zigeuner*, your German is impeccable." He took the papers from his underling and examined them in the light of the troop truck's headlamps.

Splintering wood and shattering glass vied for Tshuri's attention, but he kept his eyes on the officer. Faint echoes of Keti's voice wafted through, her tone the one she employed when calming Hishoro down. Not for the first time, he sensed that in marrying Hishoro he had somehow married them both. The sisters were a unit, each incomplete without the other. He and Mateo were fortunate observers of a relationship deeper than marital intimacy.

"Tshuri Velveloz, this is you?" the officer asked.

"Yes."

"And that man?"

His cousin sat cross-legged, arms behind his back and head slumped forward. Blood dripped from a cut below his left eye. "Mateo Landaru. We are peddlers."

"My men aren't finding any merchandise."

"We are good salesmen."

Crouching eye level with him, the officer displayed the Astra. "Bad liars, more like. We found this pistol on your man. It's a 6.35 millimeter, the same size used to murder Feldkommandant Hotz yesterday."

"Mateo didn't shoot your colonel."

"It doesn't matter to me who shot him. In my book, he's guilty enough, as are you. I need no other reason aside from you being Gypsies. The pistol is a bonus." He stood. "Load them up!"

The soldiers cuffed his hands behind his back. He struggled onto his feet as they dragged him to the troop transport. They pushed him up the rung ladder onto the bed of the truck. A soldier followed him in and shoved him down onto one of the side benches.

Mateo landed on the floorboards like a sack of potatoes. He spat a curse, blood spattering the wood. Two more soldiers clambered in. They grabbed Mateo by the elbows and flung him onto the bench opposite Tshuri.

"*San sar?*" Tshuri asked, how are you?

"*Mishto.*" Mateo licked his split lip. "*Te lel lêm o bêng.*"

"I'm afraid the devil has us, cousin."

A sharp hit to Tshuri's face slammed his head into one of the canopy's supporting steel struts. He tasted blood and his nose drained over his mustache.

"No talking." The guard glared at him.

Tshuri leaned his head against the strut and blinked his eyes clear. Mateo said he was fine. His face said different. And Tshuri's body disagreed. Adamantly.

He kept to short breaths and weighed his options. The two of them were unarmed, battered, and cuffed in the company of three fully armed soldiers. He had to add the driver into the equation and the possibility of another passenger. And then there were escort vehicles to consider.

They were far from fine.

The truck struck a pothole, bouncing them up. Tshuri slammed down on the bench, jarring his spine. The road degraded. The soldiers braced their rifle butts on the benches for additional support. He and Mateo had no such luxury. Denied even their hands to help keep balance, the rough road jostled them mercilessly.

Tshuri stared out the half-open flap at the rear of the truck and saw no headlights. Moonlight shone on familiar farm houses, telling him they were headed north. Châteaubriant was north, home of the Choisel internment camp. Hopeless as their situation was in the truck, it would become impossible once inside those gates.

He eyed the corporal. He held the rifle limb in his left hand. His right wrapped around the grip, his finger inside the trigger guard. *Bad discipline, that.*

"Pashuno grápa," he said to Mateo, next hole.

The front of the truck shook. Tshuri braced his feet against the truck bed. The rear axle struck the pothole. He sprang up with the bounce and kicked back at the stock of the corporal's Mauser. Tshuri's face slapped the floorboards. The rifle round exploded above him. Glass shattered and the truck swerved left. He rolled under the bench on the other side of the truck as two more shots rang out.

The truck bounced, banging Tshuri against the underside of the wooden bench and back down on the bed. The vehicle shook and careened over. Tshuri landed on his back on the underside of the bench. Groans and coughs came from below. He shifted onto his side, biting his lip against the pain. Peering over the edge, he spotted darker shapes piled on the canvass below.

Flopping onto his back, he pressed his knees into his chest. He forced his manacled wrists past his buttocks and over his legs. A soldier cried out, begging the others to get him free. Tshuri scooched backward along the bench until he was directly above the screaming and glanced over the side. The corporal's legs were pinned under the sidewall.

"Hol mich hier raus," the corporal said, get me out of here.

Tshuri pounced.

Hands clasped together, he rained blow after blow on the corporal's head, the steel handcuffs cutting into his wrists as they destroyed the soldier's face.

Tshuri hammered away until the man lay still. He rolled off the limp form, his heart pounding. His world was pain.

"Mateo," he hissed, then louder, "Mateo!"

No response.

He could make out more crumpled shapes near the rear of the truck. Searching through the corporal's pockets and belt pouches, he found the handcuff keys. He released his hands and shook his arms out. He pulled the corporal's bayonet out of its scabbard and crawled forward.

His hand landed on a wool tunic. The soldiers stirred. Tshuri plunged the knife into his throat. A warm spray splashed his face. The man shuttered with a gurgling hiss, then was still.

"Mateo?"

No one stirred.

Tshuri tore down a side flap at the back of the truck. Moonlight spilled in. The last soldier was on top of Mateo, a metal pipe protruding from his back. Tshuri pulled him up and his body came off the broken strut with a sucking sound.

Mateo's eyes opened. He coughed, then managed a broken smile. "The devil did take them."

"I have to get you out of here."

"Don't be foolish, cousin. I'm skewered like a pig for roasting." Another coughing fit seized him and blood oozed around the pole sticking out of his belly.

"I'll get you lose. We can get you patched up."

"You'll get ... yourself ... killed. Keti ... Hishoro ... the children."

"Mateo, come on."

"Devlésa." His breath wheezed out. His jaw went slack and his eyes glazed over.

Tshuri stared at him for a long moment, hoping for a sign of life from his cousin's corpse. When none came, he lowered Mateo's lids and kissed his forehead. *"Devlésa."*

He searched the soldiers. None of them had a sidearm. He unbuckled the corporal's tunic belt and slipped the scabbard free. He wiped the bayonet on the man's coat, sheathed it, and stuck into his boot. He found a clean kerchief on one of the soldiers and tore it in half. He poured water over his wrists and swaddled them with the pieces of cloth.

He crawled out of the overturned truck, crept up to the cab, and peered inside. The driver was crumpled on the ceiling, a black pool surrounding him. Tshuri spotted the dark leather of the holster. He pried the door open, reached into the holster, and pulled out a Luger. He ejected the magazine and checked it. It was fully loaded. He slapped the magazine back into the grip and tucked the gun into his waistband at the small of his back. He climbed up the side of the deep ditch and took to the road.

He sprinted south. The pain in his ribs became unbearable. Unable to run, he marched through the fields alongside the road. From the familiar terrain, he guessed he was at least fifteen kilometers from his campsite. Whenever headlights appeared on the road, he hugged the ground.

Dawn found him breaking through the hedgerow that bordered the field of his campsite. Smoke drifted up from the scrub. He shuffled on. Presently, he stood among their scattered belongings surrounding the burning remains of their wagons. The horses were gone.

Kicking around the debris, he found a latrine shovel. With it, he panned through the cinders and burning planks searching for bodies. There were none.

He backtracked north looking for any trace he might have missed in the dark. After two kilometers, he reversed direction. He traveled south past the camp site, scanning both sides of the road for *patrin*—signs for the *wúrma*, the trail the Roma blazed for each other so they could be followed. A cold gust bit through his clothes. A flash of red in the trees caught his eye.

He quickened his pace. The wind cut into his side again and red fluttered like a flag from a birch tree branch. Tshuri stood under it and watched the riot of flowers on a field of red wave in the wind like a distress signal. Hishoro's headscarf marked her passage. He paced around the trunk, studying the limbs. He stopped under the lowest one, jumped, and grabbed it with both hands. He pulled himself onto the limb, then climbed up to the kerchief. He teased it free from the grasping twigs and brought it his face.

Her scent quelled his pain. He eyed the road south.

I'm coming, beloved.

Chapter 15

In order to augment Congressional oversight capabilities, the Committee established an Audit and Investigations Staff in January 1988. This initiative was undertaken to strengthen the Committee's ability to conduct the detailed and independent audits and inspections of highly classified intelligence activities. It was also a carefully crafted response to Congressional concerns regarding the ability of the Intelligence Community to adequately audit its own programs.

Report 101-219
Select Committee on Intelligence
United States Senate

Alexandria, Virginia – August 10, 1988

It took Drom a week to pin down a service company that suited his needs, another two to settle on a mark. More days slid past as he followed his target, learning the man's haunts, habits, and mannerisms.

Intelligence takes time, his Uncle Alfonso said. It was the first lesson of the game he hammered into him after his father's death. *Patience pays.*

He pushed into his mark's favorite watering hole and stepped across the hardwood floor of the pub over to the central bar of the tap room. Moving to the far side of the three-section square bar, he parked on a stool with a clear view of the door.

"What can I get you?" the bartender asked.

"It's early yet. I'll have tonic water with lime."

"Waiting on friends?"

"Something like that."

The man set his drink on a pulp board coaster. Ambient light from the gold leaf ceiling enriched the warm hues of the glossy mahogany bar top. Drom swirled his fingertip on the grain, thinking of Shell. He was hunting and she was running. Knowing where she was headed did little to ease his sense of abandonment.

More suits and business dresses filtered in, nuts and bolts of the Beltway machinery looking to take some pressure off their torque. His man breezed through the wood-framed, beveled glass door during Drom's second tonic water with a twist. True to habit, he chose a seat just shy of center of the bar's front. He was dressed to fit in and had lost the five o'clock shadow he sported when leaving work.

Everyone plays in the masquerade.

One of the bartenders slid a coaster to the man, plunked down a shot glass, and filled it from the green-labeled Canario bottle without being asked.

The man raised his glass in salute. *"Obrigado."*

"De nada," the bartender said.

Brazilian. The language helped Drom put the man's dark complexion in context. Their hair matched, as did their skin tone. his eyes were brown, but Drom had a fix for that.

More patrons poured in. As the number of voices colliding in the close quarters of the pub increased, the pop music from the house speakers amplified, making eavesdropping difficult. People leaned into each other, their body language converting idle chatter into intimate conversation. Servers weaved through the throng and kept the mini-buffet topped off with single-bite tacos, chicken wings, miniature quiches, fried clams, shrimp, and cut vegetables.

His stomach grumbled. He sipped the carbonated water and waited.

Twenty minutes later, a tall brunette sauntered in, the hem of her pink summer skirt swaying just above her knees. Her sleeveless, white blouse showcased toned, sun-kissed arms. She circuited the hors d'oeuvres without grabbing any, then waltzed to the bar and slid into one of the last empty stools, her bare shoulder whispering past Drom's. As she hung her handbag on the brass hook beneath the bar, the bartender placed a flute of champagne in front of her.

"Compliments of the gentleman." He pointed at the smiling Brazilian, who lifted his half-empty shot glass of Canario.

"Impressive," Drom said.

She faced him, eyes flaring like she just noticed his presence. "What's impressive?"

"You've been inside for less than five minutes and you already have a free drink."

"What can I say?" She shrugged her tan shoulders. "It's bad form for a single lady to buy her first round."

He took a sip of his tonic water. "Interested in a second?"

"You in a hurry?" She gave him a wistful smile. "I haven't even tasted this one yet."

Turning his knees toward her, he leaned against the bar and tugged at his tie knot. He scanned her profile, taking in the costume pearl necklace gracing her slender neck, her simple silver earrings, and the class ring from Towson State University devoid of any gem stones. He guessed her to be a few years older than Shell—thirty maybe—with eyes as captivating. Every line of her was stunning.

He played a smile across his lips, aiming for sly and tired. It usually added a bit of age to his twenty-year-old face, not that anyone ever pegged him that young.

"You haven't tasted the champagne yet because, truth be told, you don't much like it," he said. "You'd rather have a beer from the tap with a good head on it. But a single lady takes the first round that's offered. You're here to see who's here more than to be seen, though you paint a beautiful picture without looking like you tried too hard. You're tired, but chose to stay out and face the inconvenience of being hit on by strangers over the loneliness of pulling a beer from your fridge to unwind while you decide what takeout to dial."

She stared at him, neck flushed and mouth slightly agape. She lifted the champagne and for a moment, Drom wondered if he was going to wear it. She took a deep breath, her bosom rising, and downed half the glass. She grimaced, then dabbed her painted lips with a cocktail napkin. "I hate champagne."

Drom signaled the bartender over and ordered a full-bodied, draft ale for her. "I wasn't sure how that would play."

She gave a nervous laugh. "You almost got drenched. No one's ever pinned me down like that. It's a bit scary, if I'm honest."

"You're safe," he said. "I don't bite."

"Alisson." She offered her hand.

Drom kissed it, holding on to it for a beat. Her hand was warm, dry, and soft. "Javier." He released it and turned his gaze back onto his glass.

"Well, Javier," she said, "you seem to know a bit about me. What's your story?"

"This is the part where I should try hard to surprise and impress you with a song and dance about how I am a professional juggler of international renown." He looked up at her and played the tired, sly smile back across his lips. "While I admit it would be fun, I honestly don't have time for that."

"You are an odd one. Professional juggler of international renown? Why not something more believable like, say, a junior attorney at some fancy law firm?"

"Junior," he said. "Ouch. Anyway, you're proving my point. Here we are dancing around each other. Meanwhile, the guy who bought you champagne is getting antsy."

Alisson glanced at the Brazilian. He lifted his glass and smiled at her. "You worried about him?"

"Handsome guy, buys you champagne. Shouldn't I be worried?"

"Good looking, like you. You two could be brothers. But you bought me ale." She took a drink, her eyes closing as she swallowed the amber brew. Glass back on coaster, she placed her hand on his. "You're not, uh, you know?"

Sandwiching her hand with his other one, he leaned into her, bringing his lips close to her silver-jeweled ear. Sweet floral musk with an earthy, woody edge tickled his nose. He savored it a moment and watched the gooseflesh bloom down her arm. "Not by a long shot, but I do need your help with him."

"You read me well, but I think you've wandered onto a wrong page."

"You see?" He drew back, slipping his hands away. "That's why I told you the juggler bit. I knew you wouldn't buy the truth. And now I've spooked you."

"I haven't run off yet. How about you tell me the truth and we see where this goes?"

Intelligence was a confidence game. This was the second lesson his uncle drilled into him. Cut outs, informants, and agents all had to believe you—your promises and your threats. And they needed to believe in the objective. It helped them justify their questionable actions and betrayals. *The spy and the carny*, Alfonso said, *both are conmen*. Near truths worked better for their trade than outright lies.

He looked her in the eye. "I am working on a federal case with national security implications."

Alisson snickered. "What are you, FBI? I liked juggler better."

"Take your pick. Either way, our handsome friend is my only lead and you can help me reel him in."

She seemed to consider this as she sipped her ale. "You're serious, aren't you?"

"Dead."

"What do you need me to do?"

"Wave."

Her left eyebrow curled down. "You want me to wave him over?"

"No," Drom said. "We'll sit here chatting it up like old friends for a few more minutes. Feel free to flash him a smile now and then. Once he's paying us enough attention, I'll go over and join him. At some point, I'll wave at you and

130

point at his face. All you need to do then is wave back and nod like you're agreeing with me."

"That's it?" she said. "You don't want me to lure him out of the bar so you can knock him over the head and throw him in the back of your black sedan?"

"You would do that?"

"Could be fun."

"If only I had a black sedan." He drained his glass. "No, just smile and wave, nod your head. I'll take it from there."

She took another sip, then leaned into him, her forehead touching his. "I'm in, though it sounds like I'll be eating that take out alone after all."

They chatted and drank. She laughed at his stories. He pointed at the Brazilian and she beamed her radiant smile at him. Caught in the act of staring at them, the man looked away.

"Time to go." Taking her hand, he palmed her a hundred-dollar bill. "Please don't take it the wrong way, but do take it. My way of saying thanks. If I could, I wouldn't let you eat alone."

She curled her fingers over the bill. "Pleasure meeting you, Javier. Good luck."

Drom rose and stood a moment with one hand on the bar and the other on the stool as if steadying himself. He burst out laughing, then rested his forehead on her crown. He pressed his lips into her hair, breathed in her perfume one last time, then straightened up. He patted her smooth shoulder and strolled over to his mark.

He squeezed up to the bar between the Brazilian and the man on his left. "They say every man has a doppelgänger. I never believed it until my lady pointed you out."

The Brazilian tilted his head. "Dupelganger? What is dupelganger?"

The man behind Drom vacated his seat. He slid onto it, still facing the Brazilian. "Doppelgänger, a double."

The man frowned. "I no understand."

"Oh, what is the word in Portuguese?" Drom stared up at the ceiling, tapping his chin with his fingertips. "Got it!" He snapped his fingers and faced his mark. "*Gêmeo*. Everyone has a *gêmeo*. That's what they say." He waved to Alisson, pointed at the Brazilian's face and then his own. She smiled, nodded, and waved back. "See that? Alisson agrees. You and I could be twins."

The man eyed him a moment. "Brothers, maybe. *Gêmeo? Acho que não.*"

"Javier." Drom extended his hand.

The man shook it. "Breno. Breno Costa."

"Muito prazer em conhecê-lo," Drom said. "What are you drinking?"

"Canario cachaça."

"Straight?" Drom wrinkled his nose. "To each his own. Humor me, though." He motioned the bartender over and slapped a twenty on the bar. "Pour my brother here a double shot of Ypióca Ouro."

Breno smiled as the golden liquor filled the glass. He raised it, glanced across at Alisson, then faced Drom. *"Saúde!"* He sipped it, then drained it.

"Better, right?"

"Muito."

"Bartender," Drom said, "pour my friend another."

Drom held him against the wall and smacked his cheek a couple of times. "Breno! Breno! Which key?"

Breno fish-eyed him like a man trying to figure out where he was. "Keji? Keji, jes." He grabbed his set of keys from Drom's hand and brought them close to his face. "Dis won."

Drom unlocked the door, holding Breno up against the wall with his other hand. He pulled Breno's arm over his shoulders, wrapped his around the man's waist, and stumble-dragged the Brazilian into the apartment, kicking the door shut behind them.

"What bar dis is?" Breno asked.

"Home." Drom's eyes adjusted to the dark. Slim tendrils of light wisping through the window blinds gave shape to the living room furniture. "Let's get you in bed."

Drom moved toward a darker shadow on the back wall and pulled Breno with him down the hallway. They passed the kitchenette on the left, then a bathroom on the right, and made it into his bedroom in the back. He dumped Breno on the queen-sized bed and hustled back to the front room.

He locked the door, then fumbled around until he found a lamp. He switched it on and checked his watch. 4:10 a.m. He had less than two hours to transform himself into Breno Costa and report for work at Superior Custodial Services.

Drom feigned sleep in the back of the van as it pulled through the service entrance of the Harkins Building on T Street Southwest. He climbed out of the vehicle and mingled in with the crew from the other van as they filed into the ground floor of the eleven-story, block-sized building. He approached the supervisor and volunteered for rest room duty.

"Start on Eleven and work your way down," she said.

"Always."

"Last time you started on the ground floor."

"I learn." According to his pay stubs, Breno was a recent hire. Drom played his role with equal parts eagerness and ignorance.

"Get to it."

He loaded up his cleaning trolley and trailed the others to the elevators. He pushed into the first one that opened and two of the others joined him. One pressed the button for eleven. The doors slid shut and the car lifted. They rode in silence.

The doors opened onto a gray-carpeted hallway with flat cream walls. They spilled out of the elevator. Glass fronts closed off each end of the lobby. His companions turned left. Drom pushed right. He backed through the swinging glass door, then spun around with the cart. Six quads of desks sat in a row in the open space. Agents in business dress shuffled through folders and spoke in hushed tones into the receivers tucked between shoulder and cheek. Behind them stood a line of private offices. Senior agent territory, Drom figured.

Turning right, he pushed the cart down along the interior wall until he encountered the first set of restrooms. He propped the ladies' room door open and set out his "Closed for Cleaning" sign. He had eight hours to clean eleven floors while spying around for a glimpse of Special Agent Richard Cannon with nothing more to guide him than the name and a hunch that the *Spokesman-Review* photographer had captured him in the photo along with the Frenchman.

"Custodial service! Anyone in here?"

Noon found him on the sixth floor, still scrubbing toilets and none the wiser. The cleaning crew was most likely heading to the basement cafeteria for lunch. Drom kept working, His brown contact lenses, adjusted hair style, janitor's uniform, and Brazilian accent had fooled them in the bleary-eyed hours of the morning. They were sure to be more alert now and his façade would fail under deeper scrutiny.

He spotted the name plate on the fourth floor two hours later. It hung on the wall beside the door of a near-corner office on the south side of the building. Donning a fresh pair of latex gloves, he entered the corner office, a janitor doing his authorized work. He dumped the waste bin, dusted the surfaces, and moved on. He breezed through the next office in similar fashion, then rolled into Cannon's, leaving the door slightly ajar behind him.

Drom grabbed his dust wand and started with the diplomas and pictures hanging on the wall. Cannon earned his Bachelor of Science from Brigham Young University in 1972. His master's degree in forensic accounting, earned from the same institution in 1976, hung next to it. He waved his wand across the glass covering a photo of the President shaking hands with a young man. The agent, perhaps. Beside him stood a man Drom recognized as the senior senator from Utah. An oil painting of a trellised garden path full of gardenias in bloom added a balancing soft touch to the business décor of diplomas and the power photo.

Drom turned his attention to the credenza against the wall behind the desk. He dusted the top of the hutch, then opened the overhead cabinets one by one. He scanned the book and binder spines as he brushed his wand over their tops. None of the titles stood out to him.

He dusted the chrome picture frame on the credenza top. The man in the photo was an older version of the man shaking the President's hand. Closing his eyes, Drom brought the newspaper photo of the Karoly bust into his visual cortex. He panned across the image, starting with the Frenchman then moving in circuit to those around him. There, caught in profile as he made to enter the front door, was the older Richard Cannon.

Opening his eyes, he studied the color photo. He memorized the man's long face with its meaty cheeks and clear, blue eyes that sat astride a thick nose and under light-brown eyebrows. Clean shaven and sporting a thick head of hair, he stood a good half-foot taller than the woman next to him. The wife, no doubt. Four children stood in front of the couple, three girls and a boy.

Drom reviewed the information, getting a better handle on his subject. Cannon had spent at least six years of his life in higher education. He had a hardwall office in the Bureau's most prestigious field office. These two data points alone put him at least in his mid-thirties. The oldest child in the picture, a girl, looked to be no more than ten. Taking in Brigham Young and Utah, Drom doubted she was illegitimate. He must have married sometime after his undergrad studies.

The wife was a looker, narrow-faced and fine-featured. Her brows were wisps of blond over luminescent brown eyes. Her cheekbones were defined without being prominent. Her petite nose accented the perfect symmetry of her face. Her shoulder-length, blond hair was tucked behind her ear on the right side of the middle part. He traced her ear with his eye, from its slight point on top around to its dainty, detached lobe and the boho-chic earring dangling from it.

He picked the picture up for a closer look. The top stone of the earring was an oval topaz set in antiqued silver. From it hung a teardrop red garnet cradled in a loose nest of silver wire. Drom recognized the work of the Paris jewelry maker. It wasn't a luxury piece, but it wasn't cheap or easy to come by. Cannon, his wife, or both had spent enough time in Paris to come across the Dierx Boutique.

He tuned his ears to the office noises outside. Scraps of conversation, phone rings, and fax squeals filtered through the cracked door. He couldn't linger much longer without raising suspicion.

He made quick work of the credenza drawers and undercabinet, then moved on to the desktop. A calendar blotter commanded its center. He scanned the dates. The morning of August thirteenth was blocked out with the word "SOCCER." "Case Briefing" was penciled in on the thirty-first. Aside from those two notations, the blotter was clean. The phone sat on the right side with a blank notepad next to it. Drom tore off the top page and pocketed it.

He opened the top drawer of the desk's left pedestal and found an assortment of paper clips, push pins, correction fluid, and clear tape along with several pens and worn pencils. He snagged one of the pencil stubs and slid it into his pocket. The bottom file drawer had folders with take-out menus, internal memos, and one filled with various comic strips clipped from the newspaper. The agent had a sense of humor.

The right pedestal was locked.

He pinched two paper clips from the left pedestal drawer, one large and one small. He straightened the small one out to use as a pick and bent the first leg of the large one for a makeshift tensioning tool.

Voices—one baritone, the other tenor—approached and faded.

Squeezing into the desk knee hole, Drom set to work on the lock. He lodged the straight leg of the large paper clip in the bottom of the key slot. He turned the clip, tensioning the cylinder, and jiggled the wire of the small paper clip against the spring tumblers. The cylinder rotated and he pulled the bottom drawer open. He crawled around to the front of the drawer and thumbed through the folder tabs, looking for any references to Karoly, Spokane, Penticton, or anything French printed on the white labels.

Near the back of the drawer, he stopped.

SL/OMEGA

Hand trembling, he pulled the red folder out. He backed into the knee hole and sat cross-legged, the file in front of him. He opened it.

"Rick, you in here?"

Drom froze.

"Rick?" The door creaked. "Must still be on the conference call. We'll catch him up later."

Another man responded. The voices moved away.

Drom took a deep breath, then bent to read the file.

The first page was a summary of the SL/OMEGA operation, its officers and objectives. Drom read the familiar names: Charles Drake, Marco Tichell, and John Swenson. Swenson's destroyed face flared in his mind's eye and he pushed it down. Next came a listing of the casualties: Alvarez Colón, Ahmed Jamal, Michel Jugaro, Alexandro Martelli, Herman Morgan. Near the bottom of the page, under the heading "Targets," was his father's name: Shane Leoppard.

The stench of smoke and burning hair infused his brain and blurred his vision. A teardrop splashed onto the page and smeared the ink beneath it before Drom regained control of himself. He breezed through other target names and slowed down when he came upon the financial report for the operation. He focused on the names of the institutions the CIA used to move its black bag money. The funds sprang from American banking institutions, flowed into several Swiss banks, spilled back out to dozens of Western European businesses, and eventually landed in the hands of the agents on the casualty list.

Near the end of the report, there was mention of the ten million dollars missing from a Bank of France account. Scrawled in the margin was the note "Gold Card stolen."

Drom had used the card to drain the account four years' previous. Despite all the financial maneuvering he had done since, Cannon had still found his way to Karoly Bardu. He respected the man's investigative skill, taking note that an accountant could be a dangerous foe.

He put the file back, locked the pedestal, and pocketed the paper clips. He dumped the waste basket, put in a fresh liner, and exited the suite. The next two offices were occupied. The men inside, deep in telephone conversations, waved him on. He cleaned the next office in line, then headed to the elevator lobby. He stabbed the down call button, lighting it up. Moments later, the central elevator doors swished open. Agents and support staff spilled out of the car and flowed left and right of his cleaning cart.

Drom kept his head down.

He rolled into the elevator and pushed the first-floor button. Back on the ground, he pushed the cart to the supply cage and abandoned it. He retraced his steps from the morning and exited out the service entrance. Crossing the back lot, he slipped through the gate as an electrical contractor drove in.

He hiked ten blocks before looking for a bus stop. He chose one with people waiting and mingled in. A bus pulled up minutes later. He boarded and navigated to a back bench. Sliding into the window seat, he closed his eyes.

The names in the SL/OMEGA file swam in his head. The casualties were a small portion of his substantial body count. He had been an enraged and grieving teenager with lethal skills and no governor. People died. Many people. He was blood stained.

And blood washed.

In the eternal court of justice, he knew his sins were forgiven. The court of man, however, held a different verdict. If Special Agent Richard Cannon was any indication of its commitment to hold him accountable, his day of reckoning was fast approaching.

He rubbed his eyes, then blinked them open, letting the light in.

He dug the piece of note paper out of his pocket and spread it against the window. The afternoon sun glowed through the white paper, highlighting the flowing indentions on the blank page. He set the paper on his thigh, pulled the pencil stub out of his other pocket, and rubbed the sheet with the lead using a light touch. White lines stood out in the gray field. "Fairfax Police Youth Club, Saturday, August 13th, 8:00 a.m."

The tired smile came unbidden this time.

Chapter 16

Police suspect a group of Romani Gypsies in a recent spate of burglaries in affluent neighborhoods. Over $25,000 worth of jewelry has been reported stolen. Detective Robert Brown stated that Gypsies were notoriously difficult to bring to justice. He said that though he has had his share of investigations of criminal activities by Gypsies, both in Baltimore and formerly in New York City when he was a detective there, he has never seen a Gypsy criminal suspect in court.

The Baltimore Sun, July 28, 1988

Washington, D.C. – August 19, 1988

Rick Cannon glanced at his watch. 6:12 p.m. on a Friday. *At this rate, I won't get home before eight.*

"Agent Cannon?"

He looked up. The senator from Nevada was staring at him. "My apologies, Senator. Could you repeat the question?"

The senator pushed his aviator glasses up on his hawk nose. He leaned into his microphone. "The French funds, the ten million, where did they go?"

"Near the end of the operation, a small amount was transferred to a bank in New York. It was withdrawn a couple of months later."

"The New York account was set up in the name of one of the SL/OMEGA operatives. Your investigation exonerated this individual?" The senator's nasal tone increased with the question.

"No evidence connected the officer to the funds."

"What about the rest of the money?"

"As stated on page thirty-four, five million moved out into the investment markets. We traced the initial exit, but the trail disappears after that. The remaining 4.8 million found its way to hundreds of orphanages scattered across Europe. The State Department advised against a seizure of assets."

The senator jotted something on his notepad. He opened a folder and flipped through the pages. "Did you personally supervise the exhumation?"

"Yes, sir."

"I don't see any updates from Walter Reed in the report."

The press presented the junior senator from Nevada as a man out of his depth and reveled in publishing his frequent verbal slips. For the first time, Rick began to suspect the press was wrong about the man. "I received the result just prior to coming to the Hill, Senator."

"And?"

"The genetic fingerprint is identical."

The senator's attention returned to his file. He wrote on one of the pages. "Thank you, Agent Cannon. Mr. Chairman, I have no further questions."

The Chairman glanced left and right. The others leaned back in their chairs or shook their heads. "The meeting is adjourned."

⊕

Traffic was park and go. Mostly park. Rick spent the first hour of his commute home on the 14th Street Bridge. He should have jumped on Interstate 66 and paid the toll. Or swam the Potomac.

Cheaper doesn't mean smarter.

Horns blared. He jumped. The vehicles ahead had a two-car lead. He put it in drive and pressed the accelerator. He shook his head like a wet dog and smacked his cheek. "Wake up!"

Rounding past Annandale, he finally reached highway speed. He checked the time. 8:20. Cold dinner and questions were all that waited for him now. Ada understood the demands of his job. Understanding didn't mean she liked it. "It will be different. Once I wrap this one up, it will be different." He wanted to believe his own voice.

Only the porch light and one glowing window gave evidence of life in the raised ranch house. He nosed into the driveway and parked beside the family minivan. He cut the engine and stared at the remote control clipped to his sun visor. He had installed an automatic door opener for the garage the previous Christmas. It seemed a good idea at the time, an incentive to gain control over their mounds of junk and actually use the space for their vehicles. He underestimated his wife's sentimentality.

One day. First the garage, then the attic.

He trudged to the front door, the three steps onto the stoop a needless reminder of the depth of his exhaustion. He slipped the key into the top lock and rolled back the full two-inch throw of the dead bolt.

Maybe this Christmas I'll buy the alarm system.

He unlocked the knob and stepped inside. Nails clicked against linoleum. His golden retriever rounded the corner from the kitchen with a deep-throated woof and scrambled up the steps to him.

"Max, boy, Daddy's home." Kneeling, he caught the dog in a hug on the landing and scratched behind his ears. "Good boy, Max!" He petted the rich coat on the dog's flanks and stood up. The dog looked up at him, tongue hanging and body wagging.

He locked the door.

He sunk onto the wooden bench in the entry and pulled off his shoes. Leaning back against the wall, he closed his eyes and breathed in the mélange of oranges, crayons, dog, garlic, and a hint of cinnamon. Home, no other place smelled like it.

Max whined.

Rick opened his eyes. The dog's earnest stare made him smile. "Okay, boy." He padded down the carpeted stairs to the family room. He opened the sliding glass door and Max rushed out to the fenced backyard.

He turned and looked past the bar-height serving counter into the kitchen. The stove hood light shone on a plate covered with a pot lid. Ada was a superb cook. Whatever was underneath the lid would be good even cold. He was too tired to eat.

He checked on the dog. Max was snuffling his way through every nook and cranny of the back yard. Lifting his leg, he marked the fence.

"Come on, Max." Rick swatted his thigh. "Inside!" The dog galloped to him. He rubbed his ears. "Good boy, Max, good boy." He slid the door shut and locked it.

He lumbered up the stairs to the bedrooms on the top floor. To his right, in the space above his cluttered garage, was the master bedroom. Their shower was running. He eased down to the first door on the left. Five-year-old Dalan, his only son, was sprawled on top of his Star Wars comforter, his Spider-man pajamas offering a clash of imaginary universes. He kissed the boy's towhead.

He moved down the hall to the girl's room. He visited the bunk beds first. His baby, three-year-old Jewel, was asleep on her side on the bottom bunk, sucking her thumb. He tugged it out and kissed her cheek. She didn't stir.

He stood up and Emelie's eyes met him.

"You missed dinner," the seven-year-old said.

"I know, sweetie. You should be asleep."

"I waited for you." She wrapped her arms around his neck and squeezed.

He hugged her and kissed the top of her head. "I love you, Emelie."

"I love you too, Daddy." She let go and rolled onto her side, facing the wall.

He patted her head, then turned to the bed on the right side of the room. Their eldest, ten-year-old Solaine, lay on her back, snoring softly. Her soccer uniform was set out on the small bench at the foot of her bed.

No sleeping in tomorrow.

He sighed, kissed her head, and slipped down the hallway into his room.

Ada looked up from the book in her lap. Her dark-rimmed reading glasses added another dimension of adorableness to her elven face. "You're home."

"Long day." He tossed his suit jacket onto the bergère chair opposite the foot of their bed. He sat on the edge of the mattress next to her and gave her a kiss.

"Everything okay?" she asked.

"Yeah. The senators went long. The Committee seldom convenes on a Friday, and when they have, it's never gone past two. I had no idea they were going to keep me that late."

"You couldn't call?"

"We were in chambers, honey."

Her eyes dropped to her book. "I left dinner for you on the stove."

"Will it keep till morning? I'd rather get in bed than eat alone."

"It's polenta. It will keep. Come to bed."

"You're a saint. I need to wash up. You'll be awake?"

She closed the book and gave him a lingering kiss. "Don't be long."

A stinging slap woke Rick out of a dead sleep.

Sitting up, he wiped his wet eyes clear. In the gloom, he could make out a darker shadow in the bergère chair. "What the—"

Another stinging slap filled his mouth with water.

His wife stirred at his side. *"Mon Dieu, que se passe-t-il?"*

Rick lunged for the shadow. Wet slaps drove him back to the headboard, leaving him dazed and soaked.

"What is going on, *madame*," a French voice, male, "is that your husband threatened my family. I'm here to find out why and for who."

I threatened his family?

The man's French was flawless, native. The only Frenchman he had been in recent contact with was … He pulled the chain on the bedside lamp. It lit for an instant, then shattered to darkness with an explosion of water.

"Woof!" Max's bass rumble filled the room.

"Easy, boy, we're just having some fun." Same voice, English now—newscaster American. "Sit. That's a good boy."

The dog's panting filled the silence.

"Who are you?" Latex slapped his face, showering him with cold water.

Ada screamed.

"Adelaide, silencieuse," the man hissed. "The children are sleeping."

Dear God, the children! He called her Adelaide. How does he know her name?

Rick inched a hand to his bedside table. Sliding the drawer open, he reached inside and gripped the pistol. "You've made a serious mistake. I advise you to leave now." His hand was halfway out when the drawer slammed shut with a spray of water.

"You're welcome to try again, if you like," the man said.

Rick did. Tightening his sore hand around the pistol grip, he pulled the firearm out. Something smacked his hand and the pistol clunked on the floor.

Ada gripped his left forearm. *"Les enfants."*

Rick pressed into the headboard and stared at the shadow. "What do you want?"

"I'll ask the questions. You will answer them. Simple, really. What is the name of Solaine's teacher?"

"Mrs. Smith," Rick said.

Something thumped against the padded headboard between his and Ada's heads. Sharp bits scratched across his face. He smelled gasoline.

"Shame," the man said. "Nineteen sixty-nine Meisenthal glass Christmas ornaments are rare and truly beautiful. Your collection is exquisite. Keep lying to me and, if you make it to Christmas, your tree will be sporting K-mart decorations. Solaine's teacher?"

Rick hesitated.

"Need me to take a smoke break while you think about it?" There was a click, followed by a rasp. A flame bloomed, lighting a hand and leaving the face in shadow.

"Mon Dieu, mon Dieu, mon Dieu—"

"The name. Now."

"Margeret Johanssen," Rick said.

"Family man. Saving Christmas. I'm proud of you, Agent Cannon. Tell me, what is the name of Jewel's pediatrician?"

The intruder knew his name, his wife's full first name, the names of his daughter's, and Solaine's teacher's name. It meant the man also knew where his children went to school. All of it was disturbing, but not too difficult for a motivated individual to find out. Medical records were different. Doctor-patient confidentiality and a host of laws kept them out of easy reach. For whatever reason, this was the real question, the information the intruder didn't have and wanted.

He's not going to get it from me. "Dr. Terry Cornetti."

Glass shattered on his face, cutting his cheek. Gasoline burned in the wound, heating and chilling it all at once. Fumes and fear overwhelmed him with nausea.

"We are running out of time. Solaine's alarm will ring before long. Disciplined girl, your daughter. You won't want her finding this mess when she gets up. Let me help speed this along. Jewel's pediatrician is Dr. Lina Salvessen. Her office is at 3563 Broadcast Drive. She is one of the best pediatric cardiologists on the east coast, which is fortunate for you because Jewel was born with an atrial septal defect. You've been praying she grows out of it, but are seriously considering the surgery. She wants to be as active as her siblings, but can't. It breaks your heart. The surgery worries you, though, as it would any parent. Isn't that true, Adelaide?"

"Don't answer him, Ada." Tortured mannequins, their dead eyes in quilled faces, filled his mind and froze his limbs.

"She doesn't like it, you know."

"Doesn't like what?"

"The name. Ada. She answers to it, puts up with it. But she doesn't like it. Never has. Adelaide. It's the name her mother chose for her and the one she calls herself. I'm certainly not here as a marriage counselor; but if you want to improve yours, I suggest you start calling her by the name that makes her heart sing."

Enough! I can't let him keep the upper hand.

"You seem overly concerned about names. You go by Drom Reiziger. But it's not your real name. How about you leave my wife out of this and tell me why you're here?"

"Don't change the subject, Agent. You have a life construct that needs adjustment. Ask your wife. Afraid of the answer? Afraid you've been offending her all these years and have been too dense to notice?"

He turned toward her. Her eyes shone in the darkness. "Ada?"

"It's the truth," she said. "I don't know how he knows, but it's the truth."

"Agent Cannon, what is the Frenchman's name?"

"Frenchman? What Frenchman?" Rick's head slammed into the headboard. A barrage of strikes held it there, each forcing more and more water into his mouth and nose, making it impossible to breathe. He twisted to find air, but the water punches followed him. Consciousness started slipping away. At the edge of panic-soaked oblivion, the battering stopped.

He sputtered, coughed, then vomited the bile remains of his lunch into his lap.

"Once I run out of water balloons," the man said, "all that's left are gasoline filled ornaments. The Frenchman."

"Bastien Frabron."

"Bastien?" Ada asked.

"Your wife knows him. Interesting. Bonus round, Agent. Who does he work for?"

"The DGSE," Rick said.

"The French General Directorate for External Security," the man said. "It would explain his discipline under questioning. It doesn't tell me his purpose. Why did he and his team come after my family?"

"What's the deal with the mannequins?" Rick's question earned him another barrage of balloons. He tried counting the blows in an effort to stave off panic. It was useless. He couldn't breathe.

He heard Ada screaming. It was abruptly replaced with coughing and gagging. He fought air into his lungs.

"Adelaide, another outburst like that and your children will be at the door. You've upset Max enough already. No need for you to burden the children as well. Sit, Max. Good boy. Now, Agent Cannon, what interest does the DGSE have in me?"

"Please," Rick said, "no more. You have to believe me, Bastien never mentioned you. He sent me to Karoly Bardu."

"Why?"

"Bastien knew I was tracking SL/OMEGA black bag funds."

"You found no evidence of such in Spokane. Even so, Frabron and you both made your way to Penticton. Why?"

"I was following a hunch. I didn't know you existed until I saw the property."

"And Frabron?"

Rick slumped against the soaked headboard. "You're in a better position to know that than me. You were just an arson victim in an odd land deal to me until I toured your burnt-out containers. What's with the mannequins? What are you planning?"

"I ask, you answer. Why investigate SL/OMEGA? Its scope and failure are an embarrassment to your government. What purpose could bringing it into the light serve?"

"I investigate as ordered."

"The Bureau looking to hack a couple more chinks into CIA's armor?"

"No one is above the law."

"True, but the lawless don't play by your rules. SL/OMEGA has buried its share of good men. Keep digging and you're in danger of joining them."

"Is that a threat?"

"Rest assured, Agent Cannon, I am a dangerous man. But I am only one man. What I have done here tonight is nothing compared to what they can do to you. I left your children sleeping and your wife unharmed. If you think they'll be as kind, you're more naïve than I gave you credit for."

"Who are 'they'?"

"Oh, you're in a better position than me to know that." The shadow rose. Max whined. "It's okay, boy." The dog panted, his tail beating the floor. "I will take my leave now. Solaine wakes in ten minutes. You have enough time to get cleaned up so you don't distress her. Please use the time I am giving you wisely. I know what you will feel compelled to do. Don't. It won't end well." The shadow glided toward the door.

Rick dove off the bed and landed on the floor, his hand on the gun. He rolled onto his back and popped his torso up, pistol trained on the intruder. He squeezed the trigger and the resulting click sounded louder to him than the expected boom. Glass exploded across his hands and gasoline showered his face. Pain seared through his fingers and he dropped the pistol.

The shadow slipped out the door.

Scrambling to his feet, Rick chased after him. The hallway was empty. He rushed to Dalan's room. His son was still asleep. He barged into the girls' room. "Solaine, get up! Get up, honey, quick!"

She jumped out of her bed. "Oh no, did I oversleep?"

"Get dressed. Help your sisters." He ran out of the room and checked the hall bathroom. Empty. He raced down the stairs. The front door was wide open. He charged out into the street. The intruder was gone.

Chapter 17

Over half of Europe's 5 million Gypsies live in Romania, Hungary, the Soviet Union, Czechoslovakia, and Bulgaria. Most of these Gypsies live in poverty and resist assimilation. Many still live in ragged camps on the fringes of cities, looking as if their great migrations from India began last week instead of a millennia ago.

Nomadic Gypsy clans survive in settled society through odd jobs and artful foraging. Gypsy stews pots are as likely to be supplied with butcher meats as wild game, and wild mushrooms and roots as market vegetables.

Associated Press, July 29, 1988

Fairfax, Virginia – August 20, 1988

Drom ran. Cannon would check on his children, then sound the alarm despite his threats. He set his pace to chew a mile every eight minutes and kept to it like a runner training for a marathon.

His legs cramped in protest before he made it out of the neighborhood. Three days of hiding in the Cannon's attic had left his muscles congested. He pushed past the discomfort, mopping the sweat off his brow with the sleeve of his black sweatshirt but keeping the hood up.

His route took him through the George Mason University campus. Spotting a cluster of runners heading south, he trotted up behind them. He matched their pace, staying twenty feet back from the last man. Two miles later, the lead runner checked over her shoulder, darted across the road, and ran north. Her entourage followed suit, heading back the way they had come.

Drom continued on, turned right at the cross street, and kicked into high gear. Turning left at the next intersection, he sprinted deep into the neighborhood, then slowed down.

The street ended in a cul-de-sac.

He slipped between the houses into the woods beyond. Five hundred yards later, he was back on asphalt, heading east. Another mile brought him to a strip mall. The parking lot lights made the gray dawn seem farther away than it was. He jogged around to the back and stopped at the dumpster behind the army surplus store. He slid the side hatch open, sparked his lighter to life, and peered inside. Flattened boxes, several trash bags, and discarded clothes covered the metal floor. Empty as it was, it wouldn't be serviced for days.

He climbed through the hatch and slid the door shut. He made a bed with the cardboard and old clothes. It would do for the next couple of hours. He curled up on his side and pulled the hood down to cover his eyes. Usually, sleep was something he had to chase. His days of hypervigilance in the Cannon's home capped by his run weighted his lids down without prompting. Within minutes, he drifted away.

He flew through the air into a dark smoke ring and landed hard on concrete.

He rolled, absorbing the shock, then sprang to his feet. He couldn't see, but knew where to go. Straight ahead stood the door to the stairs. He was through it in two bounds, turned right, and jumped.

His boots hit the cobblestones below, throwing him off balance. He rose, hand on wall for support. The dim, yellow-hued light reflected on the wet stones.

Something is wrong.

Pressing his back against the wall, he eyed the stairs behind him.

Where are the guards?

The stones swirled in arcs beneath him. Tamping down his rising vertigo, he chased the swirls. Like waves, the arcs of stone brought him to the shores of a manhole, its lid bolted shut. He drew the bolt and gripped the cold iron handle. He heaved. The iron hatch creaked on its hinges. He hooked his forearm into the opening and lifted. Pain shot up his arm and punched his head. He pressed through it, his breathing ragged. The weight transferred from his lifting forearm to his pulling hand and he let go.

The hatch hit the floor with a clang that bounced off the walls and echoed down into the darkness below. Kneeling, he bent over the manhole. "Hello?" His call reverberated in the void.

He sparked his lighter to life. A girl's face, acorn shaped and smeared with dirt, appeared in the dark circle. Spacious brown eyes stared up at him under dark brows and ringlets of black hair. Her broad nose pointed down to trembling lips astride a sharp chin.

"Adjutati-ne," she pleaded. "Adjutati-ne, va rog!"

The vertigo bloomed, tipping him forward. He tried to catch himself, but his hands refused to move. He fell into the darkness.

⊕

His leg cramped and he kicked out. Thundering metal jerked him awake. Putrid air pressed in on him. He sat up, sweat-soaked and disoriented. Sunlight pierced through the crack of the divided plastic lid above. He placed his hand against the metal side of the dumpster and jerked it back.

The metal was stove hot.

He cracked the side hatch and peered out. The back lot was quiet. He climbed out. The fresh air cleared his head a bit. He pumped his legs into a fast walk to speed his return to waking reality.

The dream of a thousand nights took him somewhere else.

"Adjutati-ne, adjutati-ne, va rog!" Help us, help us, please. He understood the words. He couldn't place the language.

He came around to the front of the strip mall. The parking lot was packed. He scanned it for patrol cars or sedans that screamed "Government Issue" and didn't spot any. He pulled off his hoodie and ditched it in the first trash barrel he passed as he marched down the awning-covered sidewalk in front of the shops. He checked his watch. Ten o'clock. He had slept for four hours, a rare occurrence for him.

He entered the army surplus store and headed directly for the racks of camouflage fatigues. He grabbed three pairs of pants with matching overshirts. A pack of tan T-shirts, socks, underwear, sleeping bag, tent, canteen, and a small backpack rounded out his purchases. He piled them up on the cashier's counter. "You have a dressing room?"

"Back corner of the store, on your right," the man said.

Drom opened the pack of T-shirts and pulled one out. He snagged a pair of trousers, underwear, and shocks out of the pile. "Be right back to settle up." He beelined to the dressing room and changed.

He paid for the purchases, then loaded the backpack, securing the sleeping bag to the bottom. Shouldering the pack, he headed out.

He stuffed his old clothes into the Goodwill box in the parking lot and marched south along the road. The homeless camp in Woodbridge was twelve miles away. If he kept a good pace, he would be there in time to cook dinner.

A mile past Butts Corner, Drom pushed into the woods, shadowing the line of the divided highway. A mile later, he encountered a wide power line clearing.

Hovering at its edge, he inspected the slice of sky east to west. He spotted a jet liner high above, but no prop planes or helicopters buzzing about. He quick marched across the cut and didn't slow down until he was twenty yards past it.

He pulled a swallow from his canteen, last filled at a public fountain in a play park outside of Fairfax. He still had at least four hours of hiking ahead of him. He needed to ration his water. He took another sip and pressed on.

Near a drain field, he spotted a patch of stinging nettles, uncommonly green for the season. Inspired, he unshouldered his pack and dug out a pair of socks. Using them as gloves, he picked the youngest leaves. He piled his harvest beside his pack and pulled out one of the T-shirts. He laid the leaves in it, folded the arms and edges over them, then rolled the shirt up. He stowed it back in the pack along with the socks and shouldered the load. He set back out, paying closer attention to his immediate surroundings.

Not long after, a hint of garlic settled into his nostrils. The scent took him back to the first time he had met his *Mami*, his grandmother Hishoro. His Uncle Alfonso brought him into an abandoned garage. Hishoro rose like a vision out of a savory cloud of steam billowing up from her makeshift kitchen in the mechanic's pit. Her nettle soup became one of his favorite dishes that day.

He studied the ground around his feet. Round, short stalks of wild onions were scattered about. "Thank you, Lord," he said aloud. He slid his pack off once again and spent the next half hour foraging. "You keep this up," he said, continuing his impromptu prayer, "and I can skip the stop at the grocery store."

His next find came miles later. Clinging to the side of ancient oak tree like giant orange and cream cockles was a cluster of shelf mushrooms, the chicken of the woods. He broke them away and added to the weight of his pack. He had enough to make stew for at least a dozen people. It had been a long time since his last visit. There may be more now.

He kicked around in the dirt and picked up a handful of walnut-sized stones. A couple squirrels or rabbits could only improve the feast.

Drom ducked down the dirt path on the west side of the factory outlet mall. Tarp lean-tos, carboard huts, and tents seeded the open ground between the trees. A scarecrow made from a scavenged stop sign and old brooms marked the spot where many of the residents piled their trash. The scarecrow's red prom dress had faded past the warning color of the stop sign. The residents called her Madonna.

He strolled to the orange-topped, green-sided canvas tent set in the trees at ten o'clock from the fire pit clearing. "Manush! Manush, you here? I need to borrow your kettle."

The tent flapped open. A dark-skinned man with shoulder-length, raven hair shot through with gray stepped out of the zippered opening. His dark eyes peered at Drom over weather creased cheeks. He pointed his sharp nose at him. "What business have you with the Old Man's kettle?"

Manush—old man—was the only name Drom knew him by. "When was the last time you tasted *cignidaki zumi*, Manush?"

Manush tilted his head and stroked the sides of his mustache with his ring-encrusted thumb and forefinger. *"Cignidaki zumi?"*

"Your grandfather's copper kettle was hammered out for just such a dish. And I have *shoshoiya*." He held up three rabbits tied by their hind legs.

He shuffled a few feet closer to Drom. "Shavarro, is that you?"

Shavarro—young man—is what Manush had always called him. "It's me, Manush. Do you want to feast tonight or not?"

"Shavarro!" With a couple quick strides, the old man had Drom in his arms. He kissed both his cheeks. "Forgive me, friend. My eyes are not what they used to be."

"Your hug is still as strong." He kissed the old man's cheek. "I'm hoping you have some lard tucked away in your tent?"

"I have better than that." Manush rummaged through the plastic cooler beside his tent and came up with a butcher paper packet. "Bacon. I picked it up yesterday."

Drom sniffed it. "Yesterday?"

"Or the day before. I can't remember." He waved his hand at Drom dismissively. "You start the fire, I'll get the kettle."

In short order, Drom was in full chef mode. He procured a smaller pot from a young woman new to the camp. He rinsed all the wild plants at the pump, then set the nettles to boil in the small pot. He skinned and cleaned the rabbits as the cut bacon sizzled and melted in the bottom of the kettle. The smell of food pulled more residents out of their hiding holes.

Someone set up a metal card table beside the fire pit. Salt and pepper shakers, flour, wilted celery, vinegar, a few wilted carrots, and packets of red pepper flakes like they gave with takeout pizza found their way onto it. Drom cut the rabbits up and laid the meat in the bubbling bacon grease to sear it. Manush brought over two coffee mugs and Drom filled them with water from the nettle pot. He handed one to the old man and took a sip from the other. The nettles were progressing nicely. He set the mug down, then tore the leaves in the pot apart with two cooking spoons and tossed in chopped celery.

He turned the meat over, then chopped up the wild onion shoots and carrots. He tossed these into the cauldron and stirred them around. He worked with the shelf mushrooms next. He cut away the fleshy outsides from the fibrous centers, then tore the flat mushrooms into bite-sized chunks and tossed them into the grease.

The camp residents gathered around the fire and sat on dilapidated lawn chairs, overturned buckets, and patches of ground. Drom scanned their faces.

He hadn't come out yet.

Once the vegetables softened, Drom poured a cup of the apple cider vinegar into the kettle to deglaze the bottom. He scraped the charred bits of bacon free with Manush's hand carved wooden spoon, then poured the boiled nettles and celery into the fond. He added in generous amounts of salt and black pepper as he stirred the pot. His ingredients differed a bit from Hishoro's traditional recipe, but he was determined to make it just as spicy. If the flavor was strong enough, Manush would declare the meal *baxtalo*, lucky by Romani standards. Drom tore open the packets of red pepper flakes and shook them into the stew.

When the rabbit meat started falling off the bone, he thickened the broth with some flour. He drained his cup of nettle tea, then ladled some of the dark green stew into it. He grabbed one of the plastic spoons from the card table contributions and tasted his wild version of his grandmother's *cignidaki zumi*, nettle soup.

The spinach taste of the nettles blended perfectly with the trinity of celery, carrots, and wild onions. The mushrooms' meaty texture and poultry taste balanced the rabbit's dark richness and hint of gaminess. The red and black pepper bloomed in his mouth, loosening his sinuses. He grabbed the salt saker, twisted off the top, and measured a tablespoon with his folded palm. He dumped it into the soup and gave it a stir. He ladled another bite into his mug and tasted it.

Perfect.

"Everybody hungry?" he asked.

The residents shuffled over to the eclectic stack of bowls on the card table.

"God provided this meal from the ground. Let's give Him thanks." He swept his eyes around and the folks bowed their heads. Drom raised his face to heaven. "Lord, we thank you for your provision and the meal we are about to share. By your grace, Lord Jesus, let this meal bring health to the feasters. Amen."

Mumbled amens echoed around the fire. The young woman with the small pot came to him first. Drom filled the bowl and looked down the line.

He was still hiding.

✧

Manush sat back in the lawn chair and patted his pot belly. "Shavarro, I haven't eaten like that since my wife died."

Drom stared into the remains of the fire. "You flatter me, Manush."

"To say you're good at women's work is no flattery, my friend. But your secret is safe with me. No Roma will hear it from my lips."

Drom laughed at the good-natured jab. "I didn't see Miles at supper. He still here?"

"Miles of Smiles? He's here. Lives in that blue tent." Manush pointed to a tent south of his and deeper in the woods. "Hasn't been out in a couple of days."

"You check on him?"

"This morning. He yelled me away. You remember how he is, few good days among many bad ones."

Drom remembered more than he cared to. "I still send the money. The nurses still come?"

"Every couple of weeks. He's not always here when they show, though. And when he is, he doesn't always let them in."

"I need to talk to him."

"Help yourself, but tread lightly. Many bad days and some worse."

Drom grabbed a bowl from the card table. The remains of the stew simmered on the coals of the dying fire. He scooped a bowl full, snagged a spoon, and traipsed to the blue tent. A breeze flowed in from the west through the fading daylight and brought with it the sour stench of Gregory Miles.

Drom peered through the tent screen into the shadows beyond. "Miles, I've brought you dinner."

"Go away!"

"I walked a long way to get here, Miles. I'm not going away."

"Take your food and shove it up your—"

"Stop it, Miles! You need nourishment. Manush says you haven't been out in days. I made stew. It's full of protein, vitamins, and flavor. Come on out and let me feed you." Silence. "Come on, Greg, don't make me beg."

A shadow shifted from the gloom around it. The bottom zipper walked to the right corner, then the vertical one climbed to the peak. Squalid fingers curled around the flap and pulled it in. A disheveled head of dark blond hair poked through the opening followed by Miles's lanky form. He stood up and stared down at Drom for a moment.

"Shavarro, where have you been?" Miles asked.

"Travelling," Drom said. "Take a whiff of this stew." He brought the bowl up under the man's nose and stirred it with the spoon. Miles's nostrils flared and his eyes widened a bit. "Come, join me and Manush by the fire. You won't have to touch the bowl or spoon. I'll feed you."

Miles smiled one of his rare smiles. "Sure."

Drom led him over to his empty seat. Crouching in front of him, he offered him a spoonful of soup. Miles wiped the spoon clean with his lips and chewed, eyes closed.

"Good?" Drom asked.

Miles nodded.

He got two bowls into the man before Miles waved him off. He set the bowl onto the card table and stoked the fire. Snagging one of the five-gallon buckets, he set it upside down in front of the homeless man. He perched on his stool and caught the man's eyes. "I need to check your feet."

Miles slid them under his seat. "They're fine."

"I can smell them through the boots. Come on, I'll be gentle."

"It hurts."

Gregory Miles lay before him, strapped naked to a metal desk. He stood in the dark, a syringe of bradykinin in his hand. "How familiar are you with pain?"

Drom shoved the memory down. "I know. It always hurts. But if you let me take care of them, they'll feel better after."

Tears welled up in the sea-blue eyes. "Promise?"

"Promise. Will you slide them to me?"

Miles glanced over at Manush. The old man tipped his head. Miles turned his haggard gaze back on Drom. With a shuddering breath, he brought his feet forward within Drom's reach.

Drom untied the left boot. The stench of putrid puss with undertones of rancid corn assaulted him as he loosened the laces. Stifling a retch, he cupped the heel in his right hand and gently lifted the leg with his left on the lower calf. The boot slid off. The athletic tube sock, once white, was gray with yellow splotches on the instep and dark brown stains on the sole. The striped, elastic band at the top was cut, leaving the sock sagging around the ankle.

"Manush, heat up some water in the small pot, would you?"

Drom rolled the sock off Miles's foot. "This has to go." He tossed the sock into the fire, then inspected the foot. A weeping, red wound in a bed of grimy skin glared at him from its stronghold on the outer quadrant of the instep. He looked up at Miles. "I need to turn the ankle to see the bottom."

Miles gripped the arms of the lawn chair and gave a sharp nod, bouncing his matted beard against his chest.

Drom rolled the foot in and leaned over to examine the sole. An ulcer the size of a fifty-cent piece oozed yellowish-green puss. The first time he had held this foot, it was smooth and smelled of talcum powder.

"Who is Pegasus?" No reply came. He grasped the foot and plunged the needle into the tender flesh between the big and long toe. He pushed the plunger down and bradykinin—pure, liquid pain—shot into foot. The man's howls broke past the decibels of his previous screams. Still, no answer came.

"Miles, you know I have to clean this up, right?"

"I don't like taking my boots off."

"I know, but we have to bandage you up. Can't have you losing your feet."

Manush reappeared with the pot and set it on the coals at the edge of the fire. He stepped into his tent and came back carrying a white enameled basin in his hands and a small bundle tucked under his arm. He set the basin beside Drom, then handed him the bundle. "I've kept supplies for him like you asked. But he's stubborn. Hasn't let me check his feet in weeks."

Drom worked in silence. Miles's right foot was no better off than his left. Drom bathed them with a feather touch. He added Epson salts to the third basin of water and let Miles soak his feet in it while he tossed more wood on the fire.

Manush brought out a kerosene lantern and hung it on a wrought iron plant hanger he speared into the ground beside Miles. The lamp's dual mantles washed the former CIA intelligence officer in a warm, yellow glow.

Drom took one of the towels from the bundle of supplies and laid it across his thighs. Lifting Miles's left leg, he set the foot in his lap. He padded it dry, checking to make sure all the grime and puss were washed away. He applied a generous layer of antibacterial ointment on the wounds, then wound the foot in gauze. Over this, he pulled one of his army surplus socks. He left the elastic intact even though he knew Miles didn't like the constriction. He needed the socks to stay on at least overnight.

He treated the right foot and sheathed it in a sock. "Better?"

"Better." The shadow of a smile played across Miles's lips.

Manush rose from his chair. "You need anything else before I turn in, Shavarro?"

"No. I think we're good for now."

"Don't worry about the dishes. I'll get it all cleaned up in the morning." The old man trudged back to his tent. Drom watched until he had zipped himself in.

"Miles," he said, "I need to ask you about Madrid."

The man stared at him, slack-jawed. The sea-blue eyes narrowed and he leaned forward, pressing his heels into Drom's thighs. Gasping, he sprawled back in his seat. "Madrid?"

Drom pointed at the boots. "Are these your only shoes?"

"No. There's another pair in the tent."

Drom cupped his ankles and slid off the bucket. He lowered Miles's feet onto it.

He grabbed the lantern and headed off to the blue tent. He dug around, found the other pair of boots, and gave them a quick sniff. They smelled of old leather and sweat. He returned to the fire. He laced the boots onto his patient and set his feet back on the ground.

"I dumped Epson salts into the other pair. You'll want to shake them out before you wear them again," Drom said.

"Madrid." The sea-blue eyes glinted in the lantern light.

"What about Madrid?" Drom asked, tap dancing with Miles's awareness. He needed him to open up without resurrecting nightmares.

"You said you wanted to ask me about Madrid."

Drom snapped his fingers. "Madrid, that's right. You told me you used to work there."

Folding his arms, Miles gazed at the dying fire. "I wouldn't have told you that."

"If you didn't tell me, then how would I know it?"

Miles slid his elbows off the lawn chair arms and tucked them against his ribs. His fingers pulled against each other in his lap. "Have you ever been to Madrid?"

"As a child. My father took me there. We looked at a lot of statues, but what I remember most was a glass building in a park."

"The Crystal Palace," Miles said. "Beautiful place."

"When you told me about Madrid, you said it wasn't your station. You were doing a favor for a colleague."

Miles tugged at his beard. He shifted in his seat, his knees turning away from Drom. "I need to go to bed."

"Look, I only mentioned Madrid to see if you up to talking some more. What I really need to know about is Paris. You were assigned to Paris station, right?"

The eyes burrowed into him. "They sent you, didn't they? I told them. I told them when I left. I'm not coming back. You tell them. Tell them to leave me alone. He didn't get it from me, you hear? I didn't break." He rocked back and forth, his left arm tight to his chest, his right hand twisting his beard into knots.

"Nobody sent me, Miles. I came on my own. I need your help."

Miles glanced at him, then turned away. "You take care of me. I can't help you."

"I spoke with a man the other night. He mentioned a name I thought you might know."

The eyes stayed on the fire. The rocking slowed. "What name?"

"Bastien Frabron."

Miles locked eyes with him. His hand trembled away from his beard and he stuffed it under his arm. *"L'Egorgeur d'Abéché."* His French was a whisper.

"L'Egrogeur?" Drom said. "The throat slitter? What happened in Abéché?"

"They sent me to Chad to assist covert ops once Hissène Habré took N'Djamena in August of 1982. Chatter indicated that Gaddafi was exerting influence in the conflict. France remained aloof until the following summer when the Libyans invaded northern Chad in support of the opposition forces. They sent DGSE operatives in ahead of their troops."

Drom let the briefing soak in for a minute. North African civil wars and French projection of power in the region were not his areas of expertise. He knew of France's troubles in Algeria, but Chad was new to him. "Did you work with them?"

"The French? No. We are allies politically, rivals when it comes to intelligence."

"But you knew Frabron."

"Of him. He had a reputation in Paris and abroad."

"So, what happened in Abéché?"

"France wasn't interested in an all-out war with Libya. They wanted to push Gaddafi and the rebels north of the fifteenth parallel. Abéché was to be the eastern anchor of their line in the sand. Frabron went in with his team to deal with some prominent rebel sympathizers." Miles paused. His brows pressed down, darkening the shade around his deep-set eyes. Crow's feet spread across his temples. "I need a drink."

Drom handed him his canteen. "Have some water."

Miles swallowed several gulps, then mopped his mustache and beard with his sleeve. "We shadowed them. We had poured tens of millions of dollars into Habré to prop him up. Africa desk wanted to make sure the French could set and hold the line to protect our investment. We got there after Frabron was done."

"What did he do?"

"Hassan Djabou and Kandamaye Ibaka were big men in Abéché. Both were sympathetic to the rebel cause and on Gaddafi's payroll. Frabron moved on Djabou first, then Ibaka. In both instances, he invaded their family compounds. He and his team herded the wives and children together. They made the men watch while L'Egorgeur slaughtered their families. Then he slit the men's throats. After that, Gaddafi's money couldn't buy any more support."

Drom thought of Michelle driving the children to Denver with the French team on their trail. If Frabron tracked them to his brother's house, Robert wouldn't be able to protect them. Drom had to find Frabron's control to pull the plug on the operation before it was too late. "Did you have any dealings with him back in France?"

"No," Miles said. "We didn't cross paths again until Madrid."

"Madrid? What was he doing in Madrid?"

"I was at a bar enjoying some tapas while waiting for my contact. He strolled in and sat beside me like we were old friends. My appetite vanished. I pushed my plate away and pointed at him. *'L'Egorgeur d'Abéché,'* I said, putting as much disgust in the title as I could muster. He laughed and ordered a pint."

"He tell you what he was after?"

"Not exactly. He said he knew we were looking for a weapon. As a professional courtesy, he wanted me to know he thought we were hunting for the wrong one."

The weapon CIA was after was the one his father and Velhoussen had developed that threatened to make nuclear war obsolete. It was the one he had destroyed, the one that let him bury Gavin Leoppard. What sort of weapon did the Frenchman think was more important?

"Any idea what he meant by that?" Drom asked.

"None. I thought at first that he did it just to rile me. Not his style, though. He sat next to me in a city I wasn't supposed to be in, one he didn't usually haunt. He'd been sent to give a message. I couldn't figure it out and I was in no position to report the contact. After that, I was in no position to report anything."

After that, you walked into a Madrid garage where I cracked your mind with unrelenting agony.

"You look tired. How about we get you to bed?"

"Bed would be good. I need a drink."

"Have some water." He handed him the canteen again. Liquor and Miles would never do.

Miles eyed the canteen for a beat, then gave in. He tilted it back for a full swig and handed it over. He stretched out of the chair. "You ever been to Madrid?"

"As a child. My father took me there. The Crystal Palace."

"Beautiful place."

"Yes, it is."

Drom lifted the lantern and lit their path to the blue tent. He held the flap open and Miles settled in on the sleeping bag. Drom slipped the boots off and set them to the side.

"Shavarro?"

"Yeah, Miles."

"You coming back?"

"Soon as I can. Sleep well, friend."

Drom zipped the tent up and returned to the camp fire. He slipped the lantern handle onto the plant hanger, then dumped the basin on the fire. He shouldered his pack and cut the fuel supply to the lantern.

Drom filled his canteen from the pump and marched back out onto the highway. He pushed his feet forward, hating where they had to take him.

PART TWO

Gavin Leoppard

Chapter 18

The practice of executing scores of hostages in reprisal for isolated attacks on Germans in countries temporarily under the Nazi heel revolts a world already inured to suffering and brutality... These are the acts of desperate men who know in their hearts that they cannot win. Frightfulness can never bring peace to Europe. It only sows the seeds of hatred which will one day bring fearful retribution.

Declaration Regarding the Execution of Hostages in France
President Franklin D. Roosevelt
The White House, Washington, D.C. – October 25, 1941

Southeastern France – May 14, 1942

Tshuri spied the column as it broke out of the woods into the scrub grass of the bowl below him. He counted eleven, nine men with two women in the lead. After following them through the woods for the better part of the day with his ears alone, he was relieved to finally see their number. Hugging the crest at the edge of the trees, he marked the cadence of their single-file march. Scrub grass gave way to beanfields of dark green on the far side of the bowl. The troop climbed the rise and cut into the fields without a backward glance.

Tshuri scrambled down on their trail. Halfway up the bowl, he crouched into a bear crawl and made his way to the lip. Peering over the rim, he spotted a lone stone cottage two fields to the east. The commando was heading straight for it.

The café was easy to find. And easy to ambush. Just because he paid for a meeting didn't mean he agreed to the rendezvous. Having avoided a potential trap in the village, the current situation didn't leave him with much better options. The bowl was too exposed, the bean vines too low. He could wait for nightfall and get shot knocking on the door.

That would be a waste of diamonds.

The marchers fanned into the cottage yard. A brown scar cut north through the green grass. Risking another meter of altitude, Tshuri eyed the topography the dirt path intersected. He detected a shift in the windbreak trees, the hint of a uniform bank.

Roadbed.

Tracing the formation with his eyes carried his chin over his shoulder, back the way he had come. He slid into the bowl, climbed the other side, and melted into the trees. He hiked over the ridge he had paralleled following the commando and kept north on an interception course with the manmade rise. He came to a dirt road with an overgrown berm. Breaking cover, he ambled east down the track.

Passing the bowl and beanfields on his right, he caught flashes of the cottage between the trunks. A man rested on the stoop, rifle slung on his back. The windbreak thinned. With a slight pause, Tshuri shaded his eyes with his hand, staring at the sentry. Quickening his pace, he turned onto the path.

The man rose, stance relaxed, eyes vigilant.

"Peppin?" Tshuri cut the distance between them in half. "Peppin Montblanc?" His stride amped into a run. "Praise heaven, it cannot be!" The man tried to unsling his rifle. Tshuri spun him off his feet in a bear hug. "I thought you dead, Peppin!" Tshuri was in full bellow, wanting those inside to hear.

The man thrashed in his arms. Tshuri slammed his forehead down on the man's nose, stunning him. The cottage door banged open. Spinning his hostage around, he whipped the bayonet out of his boot and he held it against the man's throat. With his right hand, he pointed the Luger at the commandos crowding the stoop.

"Get this madman off me!" his captive said.

"Quiet," Tshuri hissed in his hear, "or I'll slice your wind pipe open." He pressed the honed metal into the notch above the Adam's apple hard enough to draw blood. He glared at the men on the porch. "Weapons down, hands up."

Rifle stocks pressed into shoulders; heads leaned down to the sights.

"Four of you will be dead before any one of you gets a shot off. If you hear me out, we can all walk away from this alive. Your choice." He increased the pressure on the blade.

"Do as he says." A woman pressed through the knot of men. "No need to lose Anton just yet."

"Anton?" Tshuri trained his Luger on the woman. "He looked more like a Peppin to me."

The riflemen held him in their sights a moment longer, then slowly laid their weapons down at their feet. They rose, hands up.

"So talk," the woman said.

"Six of you on the stoop and one with me leaves at least four inside."

"And they'll stay inside. State your business before I have one of them shoot you through Anton."

"I've come to buy tulips," Tshuri said.

Her eyes narrowed. "Stay still, boys." She backstepped into the house and reappeared a minute later. "We only sell tulips on Fridays. Come back tomorrow."

Tshuri released Anton. The man spun, fist raised. Tshuri pressed the muzzle of the Luger against his forehead. "Time for that later."

"Let it go, Anton," the woman said. "He's the one we hiked to the village for only to hike back and be followed."

Lowering his fist, Anton backed off. "Next time."

"Normand," the woman said, "you're on watch. The rest of you, inside."

Tshuri slipped the bayonet back into the scabbard tucked in his boot. He stuck the Luger into his front waistband. Normand posted himself forward and right of the door. The woman held her spot to its left. She swooped her arm toward the opening in mock welcome. He crossed the yard, moved up the steps, and entered the cottage.

Hardwood echoed under his heels in the central hallway. To his left, the setting sun spent its fading light through two long windows into a small dining room. A worn, cherry wood table sat beneath them. Four wood spindle chairs, each a different style, surrounded the distressed table like miserable comforters. Four of the men pulled these out and took a seat.

To his right was an alcove sitting room. An arched fireplace, its hearth stones reaching out into the room, dominated the main wall. A threadbare sofa sat perpendicular to it against the front wall of the house. In the shadows of the opposite corner, Tshuri could make out the side of a highbacked chair.

Stairs spilled down into the hallway, leaving a narrower corridor that led to the back of the cottage. Through the opening at the back of the hallway, he caught a gleam of white porcelain, the edge of a deep basin. A man leaned against the counter beside the sink. The arm of another moved behind him.

Anton leaned against the wall at the foot of the stairs with his head tilted back, a kerchief pressed to his neck and his nose pinched. Both hands were bloody. One of the other men took him by the elbow and helped him upstairs.

One out front, four in the dining room, two upstairs, two in the kitchen, and the woman barring my path makes ten. Where's the other woman?

A form rose from the shadows of the highbacked chair and stepped into the fading daylight dusting the corridor. Tshuri turned toward her. Bright eyes beneath chestnut bangs peered up at him and popped wide. Her full lips blossomed into a dazzling smile.

"Tshuri!" She flung her arms around his neck with a suddenness that unbalanced him. "If they had told me it was you, I wouldn't have believed them."

Her voice, a husky alto that transformed her mountain French into a cabaret come-on, jarred something in his mind. He pressed his hands against her waist, easing her back. He took in the chestnut waves spilling out of her beret, the wide amber eyes, turned-up nose, and heart-shaped face. Hardness sculpted her temples despite her smile. A thin scar, like a wisp of red ink, cut across her right cheek. The fighting girl he had known was now a grown woman. And still fighting.

"Eglantine, had I known it was you, I would have dispensed with the theatrics."

"Tshuri?" the other woman said. "*The* Tshuri?"

Eglantine's hand came up to her scarred cheek. "Yes, Raison, *the* Tshuri."

Murmuring broke out in the dining room.

Raison pushed a blond lock behind her ear and examined him with renewed intensity. "From all the stories, I thought you would be taller."

"And lighter skinned, no doubt," Tshuri said.

Raison broke eye contact and leaned against the stairs.

"Marcel," Eglantine called into the kitchen, "put a pot of coffee on. Make it stronger than your usual. No need for my favorite Gypsy to get testier than he already is." She took him by the arm and led him to the sofa.

He planted himself on the seat farthest from the alcove opening. It put him in a corner with a commanding view of the entry and the dining room. Eglantine settled in next to him, her right arm laid across the back of the sofa. She reached toward him with her left and for a moment, he feared another embrace. Her hand passed his shoulder and with a click, soft light diffused into the shadows of the sitting room. She remained sideways, facing him.

"Has it only been four years?" she asked.

Four years, the Battle of the Ebro. "After Amposta, any sensible girl would have given up getting shot at by Fascists."

"We have left the Spanish trenches to fight the Fascists where we find them." Her sultry alto turned the partisan song intimate. Untold thousands had died singing it.

"These Nazis aren't Franco's Moroccans."

"All the more reason to resist."

He eyed her for a quiet moment, then traced her scar with his finger. "It healed well, the cheek."

Her ears flushed. She pulled his hand away from her face and held it in her lap. "I would have no cheek at all were it not for you."

"I only did what any man would."

"You did what plenty couldn't. One minute, that beast was on me while the others held me down. The next …" She glanced at their hands, then cleared her throat. "But it wasn't just me. You got us all back across the river through that hailstorm of destruction."

"You should have never crossed in the first place. I told Lister the Nationalists were dug in near Amposta. He didn't have artillery, never mind air cover. He had no business pushing across the Ebro."

"We were winning."

"You were marching into a meatgrinder. Franco had no interest in quick victories. All the *Generalísimo* cared about was slaughtering as many of his enemies as he could."

A tired smile played across her lips. "Same old Tshuri."

"Old, perhaps. The same? No. These evil times change us all."

"We are here on your diamonds. If you are not fighting this war, why come to us?"

"To help get my family back." Tshuri briefed her on the night of their arrest, his escape from the soldiers, and his months of searching since. He left out his involvement with other resistance cells. The less she knew about that, the better for everybody. "When I learned of a *maquis* operating in the area, I paid for the meeting to see if we could get it done."

"Where are they being held?"

"Gurs." He took his hand back and stared at the cold fireplace. "I think."

Eglantine rose. "Marcel, bring the coffee into the dining room." She marched across the hallway, pulling Raison in her wake.

Tshuri followed them to the table. Marcel set the coffee service down on the distressed wood, the single bulb dangling above highlighting the scars in the cherry.

Eglantine poured a cup, dropped three cubes of sugar into it, and handed it to Tshuri. "Strong, dark, and sweet, if memory serves."

Tshuri gave it a stir and took a sip. "Memory serves well."

"Marcel," she said. "Fetch Anton. We need him for this."

"*Oui, m'dame.*"

She poured herself a cup and took a drink without bothering with the sugar. "You *think* they are in Gurs."

"Gurs?" The single word was laced with nasal irritation.

Tshuri checked over his shoulder and spotted Anton. The man's neck was wrapped with strips of white linen. Some type of fabric peeked out of the nostrils of his swollen nose. Above his stubbled cheeks, bruising eyes darkened his glare.

"No permanent damage, I hope," Tshuri said.

Anton shifted his gaze to Eglantine. "What's this about Gurs?"

"Tshuri believes his family is being held there."

Anton's glare shone back on him. "*The* Tshuri? He's nothing like I imagined."

"And you're not what he remembers," Eglantine said. "No wonder, last time he had you in his grasp, you were unconscious and slung over his shoulder."

Anton turned back to her. "It's pointless to go to Gurs."

"Why?" Tshuri asked.

"The camp is too open. We couldn't get in unobserved." Anton faced Eglantine. "What he did for us was a long time ago in a different war. We may owe him, but not this. I have no love for the Vichy, but I'm in this to fight the Nazis, not to shoot Frenchmen."

"You're wrong, Anton," she said. "It is the same war. If more had fought for the Spanish Republic, we wouldn't be battling the same evil on our own soil."

"Does our battle include setting Gypsies loose to traipse the country?" Raison made no attempt to hide the contempt on her face.

"A Gypsy's diamonds were bright enough to set you on the march," Tshuri said. "You need not worry about my family spoiling your precious France. Once I have them out, we'll head south. There is no safety for the Roma under the swastika."

"How many?" Eglantine asked.

"Six. My wife with our three boys, my sister-in-law, and my niece."

"Six out of fifteen thousand and you're not even sure they are there." Anton's hands shot up. "I don't know what you thought we could do, but your case is hopeless."

Tshuri eyed him a moment, then turned to Eglantine. "We'll need regular papers designating us as French."

"A white pass won't change the color of your skin," Raison said.

"No," Eglantine said, "but it could buy them a little time. Anton, Raison, join me at the table with Tshuri. We need to map this out. The rest of you can go see what magic Marcel performed with our scant stores."

The men rose with a scraping of chairs. One of them set paper and pencils beside the coffee service. Eglantine took the head of the table. Anton moved to the window side with Raison opposite. Tshuri took a seat at the other end.

Anton slid one of the sheets in front of him and grabbed a pencil. "They housed thousands of us there after the fall of Catalonia. It is a miserable place, especially when the winds and rain come down from the mountains." He turned the paper lengthwise and drew two parallel lines close together near the bottom edge. "This is the highway on the east side of the camp. Navarrenx is about nine kilometers north. The pavement is good and wide enough for military convoys. The highway has an unobstructed view of the camp."

"How frequent are the convoys?" Tshuri asked.

"Sporadic. There are farms all along the western edge of the camp." Anton outlined another road near the center of the page running parallel to the one at the bottom. He sketched in patches with rows. "Some of the produce makes its way into the camp, but the bread, bedding, and other supplies come in from Navarrenx or Oloron."

"Do you have any contacts with the suppliers?"

"Are you trying to get in the camp, or get people out?" Eglantine asked.

"If I could ride in with one of the suppliers, I might be able to find out what part of the camp they're in."

"No, you won't." Anton tugged his neck bandage. "Pretending you know the guard won't work either." He drew in two roads, each a couple of centimeters in from either end of the page and cutting across the first two at seventy degrees. He tapped the left one with the pencil point. "This one leads to the hospital in Saint Blaise, about five kilometers due west."

"What if they were thought ill?" Tshuri asked. "The hospital has to be an easier target than the camp."

Anton laughed. "If they were suspected of disease, they'd be quarantined. The officials would see if they recovered or died. What they won't do is take them to the hospital."

"There was an infirmary in the camp when we were there," Eglantine said.

Anton outlined another road parallel to the one at the bottom and connecting the two on the sides. "This is the camp midway. Seven islets of barracks are situated between it and the highway. Six more blocks sit along its western side. The infirmary is here." He drew in a small, vertical rectangle to the right of the Saint Blaise road. "During our internment, they provided minimal care for the sick. It's rumored now that they are making some inmates ill so they can test the new medicines from the Reich."

Tshuri gave Anton the full intensity of his gray eye. "You have contacts inside."

Eglantine flashed her palm. "Our last informant was released a month ago."

"If the camp is exposed, what's to stop me from walking along the fence line to see if I can spot them?"

Anton's pencil came back to life. A dashed line framed a horizontal rectangle between the main road and the camp midway, filling most of the space between the crossroads. Above the midway, his dashes outlined the shape of a chef's knife pointing south with a handle as long as the blade, its blunt side lying along the midway. "Both sides of the camp are surrounded with a double line of webbed barbed wire. There are guards' quarters on all four sides of the camp." Solid lines formed more rectangles. "They can see everything in the camp and around it. They would see you at the wire and you would still be thirty meters from the inside line."

"People came to the wire when we were there," Eglantine said.

Raison scoffed. "They weren't allowed to stay long. What you are proposing is idiotic. You think they'll let you march up and down the perimeter calling your wife's name?"

Tshuri glared at her, but said nothing.

Anton roughed out the long blocks of the cabins. "Each block of thirty cabins is surrounded with its own wire. There are up to sixty people crammed into each cabin. Eighteen hundred people per block, Tshuri. You're looking for straw in a hayfield." He tossed the pencil onto his map and crossed his arms. "Like I said, it's hopeless."

Tshuri rubbed his face. Leaning back in the chair, he stretched his legs out under the table. He clasped his hands behind his head and stared at the ceiling. "Hopeless is an attitude, Anton, not an analysis." He whistled out a tune, one of the jaunty fighting songs of the International Brigades. Images of carnage from Spain's killing fields unfurled in his mind and the tune turned into a dirge. It stopped in mid-measure. Tshuri popped up and leaned on the table. "People are dying in there." It wasn't a question.

"By the hundreds," Anton said. "When our man left, typhoid fever was burning through the camp."

Tshuri bent over the map. "Where do they bury them?"

Chapter 19

The Committee has no more important responsibility than the oversight of Covert Action programs. Since the formation of the Committee in 1976, no area has produced more tension between the Executive and Legislative branches of Government than the planning and implementation of these programs.

Report 101-219
Select Committee on Intelligence
United States Senate

Washington, D.C. – September 6, 1988

Rick Cannon sprang out of his seat and stood in front of the secretary's desk, his throbbing fingers a reminder of the urgency of his errand. "How much longer?"

She peered at him over the computer monitor, her fingers clicking away on the keyboard. "Have a seat, Agent Cannon. Be patient. He's a busy man." Her head bent down. The clicking accelerated.

He stepped back, his heart mercilessly hammering pain through his broken fingers. Gasoline and bile painted the back of his throat like malevolent ghosts. *Holy Moses! Two weeks! He invades my home, terrorizes my wife, threatens my children, and I'm supposed to sit?*

He stared at the secretary—her gaze fixed on the document hanging beside her monitor, her fingers playing the keyboard in staccato bursts. He was invisible, the same non-entity she turned him into the minute after his arrival. Anger boiled up from his gut, balling his hands into fists.

"Son of a bishop!"

The clicking stopped. "Agent Cannon?"

He relaxed his hand. His fingers throbbed. He sucked air through clenched teeth and exhaled against pursed lips. Gasoline hung in his nostrils like bad cologne.

"Agent Cannon, are you okay?"

He blinked. "To heck with it." Charging past her desk, he barged through his boss's door.

Special Agent-in-Charge Dale Pritchett glanced up from the papers on is desk. The secretary's heels clicked behind him. "Agent Cannon, I will call security."

"No need, Carol," Pritchett said. "It appears Agent Cannon is ready to talk now."

"Ready to talk *now*?" He glanced between the secretary and his boss. "I requested this meeting a week ago. I've been sitting outside of your office for two hours."

"Carol, if you will excuse us."

"Sorry, sir," she said. "I told him—"

"That will be all, Carol. Thank you."

She left, closing the door behind her.

He faced Pritchett. "Sir—"

"Sit."

Rick perched on the seat in front of the SAC's desk, cradling his right hand in his lap. "You know what this is about."

Pritchett leaned back in his chair, resting his elbows on its leather arms. Steepling his fingers, he tilted his head. "Let me tell you what I know, Rick. I know I'm looking at a talented investigator who has given good years to the FBI and I'm wondering how much longer his career is going to last."

"He invaded my home."

"We've been through this."

"And through my house and my entire background and all the work I've done on this case. Justice has chewed up the overtime of at least twenty agents carving through my life. How many do you have looking for this psycho?"

"You should have waited for the process to work itself through."

"How long? School started today, but my kids aren't in classes. They're doing puzzles in a safehouse. My youngest needs surgery, but can't see her doctor. My wife is terrified and I can't tell her anything. How long do you expect me to just sit and wait?"

"How long of a career do you want with the FBI?"

Rick bit the inside of his lower lip. Wet iron washed his tongue. It didn't mix well with the bile and gasoline. He spied the papers on Pritchett's desk. Even upside down, he could make out the form on top. "I can't do my job without full access."

"You jump the line like that again, you won't have a job."

"Sir—"

"No, Rick. You don't go over my head to the Chairman of the Select Committee on Intelligence and have him lean on the Director, who then orders me to cow tow to my subordinate and still get to call me 'Sir' like you think I believe you mean it."

"Look, Dale, I didn't—"

"Save it. It will be a long time before I meet with you again, if ever. And when we do, I'm Special Agent in Charge Pritchett to you, got it?"

"Understood."

"Good." Pritchett signed the form and handed it over. "Langley is expecting you."

Rick scanned the document. SCI had been added to his Top Secret clearance. He now had access to Sensitive Compartmented Information. "Thank you, Dale."

"Get out of my office before I change my mind."

Rick was almost through the door when Pritchett called his name.

He turned. "Yes?"

"Once you see it, remember you're the one who asked for it. You've stepped into a world of pain and it can only get worse from here if you don't back off."

"He terrorized my family." He gave Pritchett his back and walked out.

Rick pulled up to the gate of the CIA headquarters and rolled his window down as the sentry approached. "Morning, Frank. Your wife have that baby yet?"

The guard took his credentials wallet, glanced at it, and handed it back. "Sir, if you would pull through and park in the security office lot on the left, your escort will be along momentarily."

"What's going on, Frank? You guys have never made me wait for an escort before."

"Pull forward and park your vehicle in the security lot."

Rick stared at him. Frank stared back. He shook his head and drove through as instructed.

World of pain is right, pain in my...

He let it go and parked the car. Squinting against the defused glare of the louring sky, he loosened his tie. Sweat cascaded down his sides. Rumbles in the distance promised rain.

A black sedan with tinted windows pulled in behind him and disgorged two T-framed men in tight suits. Rick grabbed his briefcase and got out.

"Best leave that in the car, sir," the taller one said.

"I need my briefcase."

"Sorry, not allowed. It and your vehicle stay here. We'll escort you to the meeting."

Rick faced them for a long moment, his knuckles white on the briefcase handle. Neither man stirred, their faces impassive behind their mirrored sunglasses. He tossed the case in the car and slammed it shut.

They put him in front. The tall one drove. The shorter one sat behind Rick.

He walked through the main doors of the headquarters building, his escorts flanking him. Rick's heels tapped across the marbled lobby. Glancing down at the agency's emblem, he noted his escorts' combat boots. His eyes came up to the familiar, if unofficial, motto of the CIA engraved in the wall.

> "AND YE SHALL KNOW THE TRUTH AND
> THE TRUTH SHALL MAKE YOU FREE."
> JOHN VIII - XXXII

He hoped he found enough truth here to free his family from fear.

At the elevator bank, the taller escort pressed his badge against the card reader. It winked green. The man stabbed the down call button with a cigar thumb.

Moments later, the elevator dinged open. The three men stepped in. His escort formed a wall in front of him, their personal space squeezing him into the back wall of the car. Tired of their intimidation tactics, Rick deployed countermeasures, christening the shorter one Tweedledee and the taller one Tweedledum. He imagined propeller caps on their heads and his diaphragm loosened a fraction.

The doors hissed shut. Tweedledum hit the single button below G. Rick's stomach leapt against his loosened diaphragm. A slight breeze filtered through the car as they plummeted below ground. He sensed the cable brakes grabbing. The car came to rest and the stainless-steel doors slid open onto a concrete hallway bathed in harsh florescent light.

Tweedledum took lead. Rick stepped in behind him. Tweedledee brought up the rear. Near the end of the corridor, a uniformed officer manned a metal detector.

The guard nudged a gray plastic tub across the table to him. "Empty all of your pockets. Remove your jacket, shoes, and belt. Place your belongings in the tub."

Rick eyed his escorts, shook his head, and complied. He stepped through the metal detector. It remained quiet.

"I need to pat you down." The guard came around from behind his table. "Arms out at shoulder height and spread your feet." He combed his latex-gloved fingers through Rick's head of thick hair, worked his way around the collar, then stroked down his tie. He patted down his sides, pressing the wet undershirt against his rib cage. Rick repressed a shiver.

He ran the back of his fingers around Rick's waistband, then patted his way up both legs. "He's clear, gentlemen."

Tweedledee and Tweedledum marched through the metal detector. It screeched, blinking red. The officer hit a switch, silencing it. He pressed his badge against a reader and pulled the metal door open. "You can pick up your items on the way back out."

The corridor led into a wider passageway with several doors along the right-hand wall. Tweedledum opened the fourth door with his key card. He waved Rick inside.

Rick stepped through and the door shut behind him. In front of him in the otherwise bare room were two men seated at the end of a wide table. One was a complete stranger. The other he knew from news reports.

"Special Agent Cannon, have a seat." The silver-haired man pointed to the lone chair at the other end of the table.

Rick plunked himself down. Cold concrete soaked through his socks. He laid his right arm on the table and examined the two impeccably dressed men at the other end. Weariness washed over him. He rubbed his face with his left hand, his fingertips skipping across the stitches and scabs.

"You know who I am," the silver-haired man said, "this gentleman is from the Office of General Counsel. He's here to help you through all the jargon of the non-disclosure agreement."

Rick studied the man's face. In his career, he had come across prominent people before. They generally looked different in person than on screen. Not so, the Deputy Director of Central Intelligence. His stout frame and round, generous face were perfect compliments to his frank and direct speech. "I have no issue with signing the NDA."

The Deputy Director leaned back in his chair. "Counsel will handle that in short order. I am here to make CIA's position crystal clear. Before I proceed, I must know if you still wish to move forward. Say the word, and I'll summon the escort. You can call it a day and return to your regular life."

Rick scooched closer to the table. "Sir, we all bear the responsibility of keeping our nation safe from enemies both foreign and domestic. We are all bound to do so within the framework of the Constitution. I can't imagine you are unaware of my record. I am devoted to our country. I cannot give her my full duty and not be read into all parts of SL/OMEGA."

"So, you wish to go forward?"

"Yes."

"Then read in you shall be. The files will be brought here. Take as long as you like to examine them. Note taking is forbidden. All case items will remain in this room. When you are done, press the buzzer by the door. Make the most of your opportunity. Due to the sensitivity of the information, setting up access takes time. Once you leave this room, I cannot say when you will be allowed to return."

"Sir, I've been tasked with tracking lost government funds to help CIA improve its processes. It may take me several days to work through the material."

"Take all week, if that's what you need. What you can't do is leave and come back in. Once you press the buzzer, the files go back to the vault."

Rick straightened in his seat. "Your house, your rules. Hand me the NDA so I can get to work."

"Let me give you my version of it first. All the information you've accessed already is flagged blue. It remains governed under your original non-disclosure agreement. The rest of it is subject to the new NDA. Under it, you many only discuss the information with me or the Committee Chairman. Breach that and I will throw you in a black site. You will stand before no judge, plead with no jury. For all practical purposes, your wife will be a widow and your children orphans." He rose. "I leave you in counsel's able hands."

The Deputy headed for the door. It opened before he reached it. He strode out like a king leaving his castle.

The lawyer skated the document across the table to Rick. A pen followed it a second later. "Please read through the agreement, sign and date where indicated."

Rick signed it. Reaching across the table, he slapped it down. "Tell your goons to get the files in here. I have work to do."

The lawyer picked up the non-disclosure and turned to page two. Satisfied, he moved to the buzzer and tapped it. The door swung in and he walked out.

Tweedledee and Tweedledum rolled in with banker's boxes stacked five high on hand trucks. They unloaded them against the left-hand wall. A third man entered pulling a flat cart loaded down with eighteen more. He was still unloading it when the other two returned with an additional ten.

"A couple more rounds should get it," Tweedledee said.

The floor's chill clawed up Rick's legs and his back stiffened. The room filled with boxes, forcing him to push the table against the other side wall to make more floor space.

Flat cart man rolled out and didn't return. Tweedledee dumped off his last five boxes. Tweedledum came in with a gallon jug of water and an empty two-liter bottle. He set them on the table. "Contrary to popular belief, CIA isn't into wet floors." When he left, the clack of the electromagnetic lock echoed in the room like the dropped lid of a crypt.

Rick stood, hands on hips, and surveyed the chest-high stack of boxes that filled two thirds of the cramped cell. Using his thumb and the two good fingers of his right hand, he rolled up his left shirt sleeve. His right sleeve rolled up painlessly. Bending down, he gripped the plastic handle of a bottom box and dragged the stack across the polished concrete floor to the table.

Hugging the top box, he turned and set it on the tabletop. He unwound the closure thread on both sides and lifted the lid. He pulled out the top file, set it on the wood, and flipped through its contents page by page.

Rick shivered awake. He pushed up from the table and sat upright. His hand throbbed, his back ached. He shook uncontrollably, his teeth clattering. He scanned the room. His Oxford button down was wadded up on the floor by the door. His tank-top undershirt sagged with sweat against his skin. He pulled it off and draped it over the back of the chair the Deputy Director had sat in two liters and ninety-five boxes ago.

He snatched up the jug of water and drank the last mouthful down a sandpaper throat. He unzipped and gave the jug twice as much back. He stumbled over to the door and picked up his shirt. It was still wet, but drier than his undershirt. He threw it on and rolled the sleeves down.

Box ninety-six slammed onto the table. Hooking his fingers under the lid, he yanked up. The plastic buttons on either side shot across the room and bounced off the walls. He clawed out a handful of folders and tossed them on his work surface. Their contents skated out across the table. Numb and tired as he was, the pictures still wrenched his gut. He clamped the bile down at the back of his throat, refusing to vomit the few ounces of fluid he had left.

Turning from the images, he pulled out more folders. His right arm hung useless at his side, his fingers wailing with every heartbeat. He flipped through the files. Reports and photos blurred by. He couldn't unsee the pictures he didn't want to look at.

He grabbed his undershirt and swabbed his face. He bit a hole into the bottom hem with his eye teeth, then wormed his fingers into the tear and ripped the shirt open. He improvised a sling from the torn fabric and slid his right arm into it. His wailing hand whimpered.

Rick sighed.

He turned back to the horror scattered on the table. They belonged to the John Swenson file. The report included the man's official head shot. His post mortem portrait was a grotesque of a marionette—twisted and broken with a pulverized face. He retched and swallowed hard.

According to the files, the body exhumed from the Ferrisburg graveyard had caused the violence before him and in the boxes around him. He finished reading through the report and set it aside.

Examining the rest of the box, he came across the first set of blue-flagged photos. He thumbed through them, memory slowly returning. Pictures of a murder scene reviewed in the early days of the investigation. The victim, Andres Pablo Hernandez Palco, was an off-book recruit turned from the Leoppard's organization by one of CIA's most successful deep cover intelligence officers. Whatever they paid the man wasn't documented. The black bag might as well have been a black hole. He hadn't given the incident a second thought.

Now, the red pock marks on the wall of the racquetball court held him riveted. It itched his brain like a word unremembered. He rubbed his eyes, then studied it some more. Nothing. He set the pictures down by the Swenson file.

He sped through boxes ninety-seven through one hundred and three. They contained much of the segregated information he had analyzed over the past two years.

Box one hundred and four contained files that stood directly before box ninety-six in the SL/OMEGA chronology. In it, he discovered names and money trails previously kept from him. The primary file regarded one Juaquin Morreno Zapato. Sick of pictures, Rick read through the reports first.

Morreno was an agent on the CIA dole, part of their grand plan to strangle European unification in its cradle through the funding of subversive groups. He was in a safe house with a security detail when the wheels came off the operation. Morreno died from gunshot wounds. One intelligence officer had his neck broken; another fell seventeen floors to his death. Two others died from "deep punctures to the cerebellum causing long lacerations in the cerebellar artery."

Deep punctures to the cerebellum…

He turned back to the photos—skipping past the pre-operation surveillance shots, the dead officer on the rooftop, and the one splattered at the bottom of the atrium—and found a shot of three bodies on a sidewalk. The front one belonged to Morreno. The other two were the officers with base-of-brain punctures.

Punctures…

He brought it to his nose. He squinted. He couldn't make out the wounds. He thumbed through more photos. He came across shots of their post mortem CT scans. Beyond what they were, he couldn't make out much.

The last picture took his knees out.

His tail bone slammed into the concrete floor. He stifled a cry as tears of pain streamed down his cheeks. They cracked the dam. Pain, trauma, terror, and exhaustion washed over him. He wept, curling into a fetal position.

He came to, unsure if he'd blacked out for a moment or been asleep for hours.

He pushed up onto his knees. Pictures lay scattered around him. Grabbing the one that put him down, he struggled to his feet. He stared at the photo. He cleared a space on the table and set it down.

Pulling out the stack of images from the Hernandez file, he shuffled through them until he found the one with the red pockmarks on the wall—macabre dots of death peppered above a broken form on a polished wooden floor. He set it next to the one from the Morreno file—four pencils in a steel tray, bloody from their tips to their eraser bands.

Why stab a pencil that far into something?

Two more uses of the jug later, Rick hit the buzzer. He waited. He paced the room. He straightened the front stacks of boxes. He hit the buzzer again. He counted. At thirty-Mississippi, he hit the buzzer again. Ten-Mississippi. Buzz. Five-Mississippi. Buzz. One-Mississippi. Buzz. Buzz. Buzz. Buzz. Buzz. Buzz. Buzz.

Click.

Tweedledee filled the doorway. "You finished?"

"What day is it?"

"Friday."

"Friday. Friday." Rick glanced at the ceiling. "The ninth? September ninth?"

"Yeah. You done?"

"For now. Your floor is dry, mostly."

Rick checked into the first hotel he encountered. After a long shower and several glasses of water, he sat down at the small round table and wrote on his legal pad. Thirty pages later, he crawled into bed and faded off into a dreamscape filled with tortured mannequins.

Chapter 20

The defendants in this case are charged with murders, tortures, and
other atrocities committed in the name of medical science. The victims
of these crimes are numbered in the hundreds of thousands. A handful
only are still alive; a few of the survivors will appear in this courtroom.
But most of these miserable victims … are nameless dead. To their
murderers, these wretched people were not individuals at all. They
came in wholesale lots and were treated worse than animals.

Opening Statement in the Doctors Trial
Brigadier General Telford Taylor
Nuremberg, Germany – December 9, 1949

Harman, West Virginia – September 12, 1988

Drom stirred the pot as he sprinkled in more cayenne pepper followed by a
generous helping of salt. He glanced at the clock. Two thirty. Dinner service,
officially on menu at four, didn't get a real head of steam until six. Grabbing a
tablespoon from the stainless steel counter next to the stove, he dipped it into
the chili and blew.

"You think one pot will be enough?" Paulette Arwood, owner of the Cheat
River Family Restaurant, leaned against the sinks drying her hands on a bar
towel. He had met her three weeks' previous, shortly after his arrival in Harman.

Harm man.

He shook his head, but his personal epithet for the town kept ringing in his
mind. He tasted the chili, then reached for the shaker of herbes de Provence.
"Wouldn't you know it!"

"What?"

He waved the shaker at her. "Mind getting me more? Gotta keep stirring."

Paulette gave him her who's-the-boss-around-here look, then headed to the
pantry. She made a show of opening the shaker for him and handed it over.

Herbes de Provence—along with the honey and extra garlic cloves—elevated Drom's venison chili from a wild version of the American classic into something reminiscent of the French Pyrenes. He shook in the herb mixture of rosemary, thyme, fennel, and summer savory.

"You think one pot will be enough?" she asked again.

"Twenty-five gallons? No way. But just in case, I only made fifteen for tonight."

"We can't keep up with demand as it is, and your solution is to make less?"

"Twenty years on the French circuit and they never taught you that scarcity builds mystique?"

Drom knew the restaurant and Paulette's reputation, a Michelin starred chef who had turned the quintessential family restaurant into a foodie destination by reimagining classic Americana table fare through the lens of French cuisine. Finding a help wanted sign in her window after a hundred-and-seventy-mile hike in under four days seemed providential. He had plucked it from the window and handed it to her.

Can you cook? she asked.

Do you have any venison?

His first pot sold out that night and went on the menu the next day.

The back door bell rang. She pointed over her shoulder. "You want me to get that?"

"You want the chili to burn?"

"And to think only a couple of weeks ago, you worked for me."

Drom gave her his best smile.

The grip on her serious face slipped, turning it into the look of an indulgent parent. The bell rang again and she headed down the back corridor. "Jimmy, what a surprise."

Jimmy? Who's Jimmy? Lowering the flame, he slipped a paring knife into his back pocket and crept to the rear of the kitchen.

Paulette held the walk-in refrigerator open for a white-haired man in overalls carrying a short stack of crates. The box logos looked like stemmed brains—if brains were football shaped. "Just set them on the floor in the back. I'll take care of them from there."

"You can't forget 'em. They don't take a cotton to bein' on the floor." Jimmy's voice held no trace of old age tremble. Exiting the cooler, he spotted Drom and froze.

Paulette closed the walk-in. "Jimmy, meet my newest cook."

Drom offered his hand. "Hunter."

Jimmy's grip shallowed it, his palm smooth as a farrier's rasp. "They named ya right. Never tasted better venison."

"Hunter," Paulette said, "this is Jimmy, mycologist extraordinaire."

Drom squeezed back on the grip. Muscle, bone, and sinew remained impassive as stone. "Not every day I get to meet a mushroom hunter."

"You flatter me, chef. You and me both know Paulette don't hire cooks. I imagine you met yer fair share of fungi foragers." He set Drom's hand free.

"Were those morels?"

"Still are." His voice held humor even if his face didn't.

"Late in the year for morels," Drom said.

"They ain't late. God just put the good stuff where lazy people can't have any."

"Well, I hope plenty of the idle rich come in to buy what the working folk found."

Jimmy clapped him on the shoulder. "Can't wait to see what you do with 'em." He held his arm out to Paulette. "Walk me to my truck, darlin'. It's the least you can do for an old man."

She took his arm and the pair disappeared out the back door.

Drom darted into the industrial chiller. He grabbed a handful of morels from each of the four flat crates, dumping them down his shirt. He leveled out the boxes and stacked them on the shelves. He was at the stove when Paulette returned.

"Jimmy likes you."

"You sure? I've counted my fingers twice since that shake. Still can't believe he didn't take one with him."

"If they aren't broken, then he's definitely taken a shine to you."

"You want to lead with the chili tonight or are we starting on those morels?"

"Let's do both, make it a special night." Paulette left the kitchen for her daily wait staff meeting in the top dining floor.

Drom checked the clock. He had at least twenty minutes before anyone else was scheduled to be in the kitchen. Pulling a blender onto the central prep table, he scanned the kitchen. He was alone. He took off his apron and untucked his shirt front over the table. Morels tumbled out into a pile. He stared at them a moment, calculating.

"You fixin' morels tonight, Hunter?"

He spun, knocking the blender off the edge and catching it near the floor. Rising, he eyed the busboy. "Just prepping."

The teenager filled his tub from the front ice machine. "Well, don't stop there. Everyone loves your cooking." He pushed through the dining room doors and they sashayed close.

Drom took a deep breath and exhaled slowly. He estimated the revenue loss from his misappropriation of supplies and added twenty dollars on top. He dropped the mushrooms into the blender and pulsed several times. He spread a cheese cloth on the table and dumped the chopped morels on it. Pulling the cloth into a bundle, he tied it shut with kitchen string.

Grabbing a glass gallon jar, he placed a rimmed mesh strainer in its mouth and set the mushroom bundle inside. He retrieved the customized lid from the utensil drawer and screwed it down tight on the jar. He hustled over to the wine chiller and selected a bottle of Hermitage Blanc.

Best add thirty to the tab.

He uncorked it and let it breathe while he dug out a modified cap hidden between two stacked pots on a shelf by the stove. Back at the table, he rolled the rubber sleeve over the wine bottle neck until the flange of the short drip feeder sat flush on the bottle neck rim. He turned the bottle upside down. Five seconds later, a small drop of wine hit the stainless steel top.

Drom plugged the wine bottle into the receiver hole in the center of the gallon jar lid. Like an hourglass in slow motion, wine dripped onto the filter affixed to the underside of the lid, soaking it. The filter spritzed the cheese cloth with a misty wine shower.

He buried the contraption in a dark corner of the pantry and let the chemistry do its work.

On the fourth night of the morels' planned ten-day run, Drom strolled through the upper dining room to get a read on the guests. He spotted the pair downstairs at a table near the edge of the atrium opening. Dressed in near business casual, they conversed like old friends as they picked through their appetizers and sipped tonic waters on ice with lemon twists. He knew the trick. Have fun, look like you're drinking. Stay sober. Stay vigilant.

He hovered at the atrium, spying. One sat on the edge of his seat, the swell at the back of his blazer a tell of the iron he was carrying. The other talked with his left elbow on the table, his right hand flat in front of his plate, ready to draw a pistol from a shoulder holster at a moment's notice. They ate, talked, and smiled. Their eyes stayed hard, scanning.

The recon team had arrived.

"They came up here first."

Drom turned to the pouting waitress. "They who, Karen?"

"Those two down there." She pointed at the men. "Nice shoes, expensive watches, no wedding bands. Could have been my best tip of the night. Guess it's Jordan's lucky day."

The upper dining room catered more to date-night couples and parties of four than to mid-level managers out for an early dinner. Four-tops surrounded the atrium in two staggered rows. The glass roof bathed the space with sky, its mood playing on the Italian marble below and teasing out a thousand shades of nuance from its veins. Every table had a good view of both. Considering how full the reservation calendar stayed for the space, Drom was surprised the hostess had even taken them upstairs.

Unless they had requested it, and couldn't be denied.

"You can't measure generosity from clothing, Karen. I'm sure you'll get plenty of tippers tonight. Cheer up! It's Morel Fest at Cheat River, for goodness' sake."

Morel Fest came every year to Cheat River. Exactly when depended on the harvest. Word of this year's run spread quickly. Dinner service went to near capacity on the second day. Tonight promised to have them waiting at the door.

She smiled. "Maybe they'll leave enough of your chili for me to have a bite."

"Not likely. I only made half a pot."

The pout returned. She slapped his shoulder. "You shouldn't make the women in your life sad. You'll die lonely that way."

Dropping his gaze, he swallowed past the knot in his throat. "I know."

Back in the kitchen, the other cooks were holding their own. In the end, Paulette hadn't trusted her morels to anyone else but Drom. He came up with two standard appetizers, morels in spicy butter sauce and sautéed morels in white wine sauce, along with five new entrees featuring the flavorful mushrooms. He patrolled the stations, ensuring the other chefs kept to his recipes. The order rate increased. The kitchen hummed.

Drom hung his apron on a peg by the lockers and stepped out the back door. The mountain breeze made the air feel colder than it was. He unlocked one of the side sheds, grabbed an overstuffed gunny sack of potatoes, and heaved it onto his shoulder. He scrambled to the bottom of the hill, spun right, and sprinted the seventy feet to the creek.

He sidestepped down the bank into water much colder than the wind. He waded upriver, the current gripping his calves to spasm and splashing his thighs.

The air seared his lungs. Pushing fifty yards past the bridge, he blinked sweat out of his eyes and climbed up the north bank.

Half mile to go.

He pumped his legs uphill through the claustrophobic forest, forcing each breath into the bottom of his lungs. At the blind, he laid all one hundred and thirty pounds of potatoes on the ground with the gentleness of a father putting his child to bed.

Leaning over, hands on thighs, he chased his breath and checked his watch.

Five minutes later, he lifted the sack and ran back to the restaurant.

⊕

Day five, Friday night. Only six thirty, and Drom was hard pressed to keep up with the orders. Table wait time was at an hour and climbing. He reviewed the layout, probing his plan for faults. Cheat River hugged a hilltop and hid its elegant dining rooms under a plain wrapper of red clapboards and a magic hat of a single-story store front promising a hole-in-the-wall greasy spoon. The street level entrance brought patrons to a mid-level waiting area with a bar sandwiched between the date deck above and marbled dining below.

They would eat downstairs.

If they showed.

Plating entrees and sliding them on the line, he updated his mental map of both dining rooms, flipping the table colors from yellow to green as they turned over. He weaved around the other chefs. Wait staff waltzed in and out. Drom had all their stations memorized, could picture where every appetizer and entrée landed.

Paulette, furrows like fangs dipping down from her widow's peak, approached the ready line. "How's the supply holding up?"

"It's only day five, Boss Lady." His tone said *Relax, lady.*

"Don't cut them off. I can't have folks waiting for over an hour and not get any morels."

"Fine by me, but we won't make the ten-day run."

"We can worry about that later. Just make sure everyone gets served tonight." She fidgeted with a bar towel, eyes fixed on him but focused elsewhere.

He twisted back to the grill, plated the butterflied chicken breast, and slid it onto the ready line. She hadn't moved. "Everything okay out there?" Thousand-mile stare. "Paulette?"

She focused. "Sorry, what was that?"

"Never mind. You should mingle with your guests. I've got this."

She studied the cooking line for a moment, then tossed the towel onto the counter. She smoothed out her corduroy skirt, combed her fingers through her hair, and headed toward the swinging doors. The maître d' blew in before she made it out. He whispered in her ear and she shot a glance back at Drom. "I don't care if we run out tonight. Generous portions and better than your best."

"Yes, ma'am." He gave her a salute.

He tasked one of the kitchen porters to clean the last two crates of morels. He assigned prep to the pantry chef. Handing off his current orders to the two grill chefs, he spoke to the sous-chef. "Service is yours. I'm on mushrooms for the rest of the night."

Coming away from the grill, Drom supervised the pantry chef as he set to work. "Make the cuts larger." The chef nodded, his knife never slowing.

Drom shed his apron and grabbed a ball cap out of his locker. He glided out into the upper dining room and circuited the atrium, keeping to the low lighting between the table rows of chatting couples. Down below, twice-lucky Jordan set drinks down. The recon team was now the security detail. He watched as she handed menus to the two bodyguards and their ward.

The man's grace of motion was noticeable even in the simple act of receiving a menu. Restrained poetry. Entranced, Drom absorbed his refined face, petite frame, and the long black fingers turning the leather-bound parchment pages. His men looked like hulking bears guarding a rabbit—a regal rabbit with gravitas. It pulled at Drom even at this distance.

"Shouldn't you be in the kitchen?" Karen said. "Folks are lined up all the way down to South Main."

"Just checking on the guests." He glanced at her. "Customers treating you right?"

"I dumped my pockets out twice already." She smiled provocatively.

"Good for you." He marched back into the kitchen. Concentration painted every face.

He ducked into the pantry.

The wine bottle was on its last turn at bottom in his asymmetrical hourglass. He popped the gallon jar off and unscrewed the lid. He donned a pair of clear plastic gloves and strangled the cheese cloth. Hermitage Blanc, now stained to a weak tea, spilled through the strainer and puddled at the bottom of the jar. He tapped the strainer against the jar rim, releasing the final drops of fluid, and set it aside. He pulled the drip feeder off the wine bottle and poured the wine from the jar into the bottle. He dug the spout out of his pocket and corked the bottle with it.

He needed to dispose of the jar, strainer, and marinated morels in their own trash dumpsters miles apart. No time. He settled for stuffing strainer and mushrooms back in the jar and hiding the whole works in the empty slot of a four-jar pickle case. He grabbed the wine bottle and returned to his station.

"In the best cons," Uncle Alfonso *said a lifetime ago, "a mark never knows he's the mark because he's not alone in his misfortune."*

Scanning the tickets, he flipped greens to yellows on his mind map. Painting the target table red, he moved two tables over and pinned it as the strike's epicenter. Calculating cook times, he shuffled the tickets into necessary order.

Drom lined out the small appetizer bowls, five for spicy butter morels and six for morels in white wine sauce. He plated the mushrooms, then splashed Hermitage Blanc into all the wine dishes. The Hermitage flavored all the entrees and the next round of appetizers. He eyed the clock, used up the rest of his wine, and motioned to the sous-chef. "Take over, I need to see how it's going out there."

She slipped into his station, picking up where he had left off. He strode over to his locker in the back corridor, grabbed his pack, and headed out the back door.

The waxing moon gave little light. Slipping into a side shed, he changed into the all-black gear from his locker. Hands gloved in thin leather; he pulled the ski mask over his head and rolled it up to make it look like a stocking cap.

He crept up the side of the restaurant and stopped beneath the men's smoked-glass restroom window. He lifted it an inch and peered inside. Empty. He opened it all the way and climbed in. He cracked the door. Noise from the dining room rushed in like a rogue wave. He spotted two men running for the door and stepped aside. Barreling past him, they dove into the stalls. Their retching echoed behind him as he stalked out to the braker boxes near the second-floor waitress station.

Voices from the dining room below roiled up to the glass ceiling in drunken waves of slurred speech punctuated with retches and moans. Drom scooped up a bunch of dinner knives. He studied the reflections in the ceiling, marking the targets. A siren wailed through the din below. He drew the ski mask over his face and cut the lights.

He sprinted through the pitch-black dining room, following the map in his head. Dividing the knives between both hands, he leapt onto the railing, turned five degrees right, and front flipped into the atrium. His right arm whipped out. Flatware clanged against steel. Water hissed from the first-floor ceiling and splashed below.

His body tumbled over, his left hand flicked down, sending the knives into wine glasses on the target table and the tables on either side. Landing on the balls of his toes, he coiled into a crouch, absorbing the fall. He shielded his face with his forearm, blocking the shrapnel wave of crystal shards that had been wine glasses a heartbeat before.

He stayed on his haunches, tuning out the shouts and cries.

A large body smacked the floor to his left. Bear number one down.

"Sir, I need to get you—" Violent retching erupted from bear number two.

Drom sprang, whipping his knee around to the sound. It struck body armor, shooting pain up his thigh, into his hip, and across his loins. China shattered. Wood splintered. A body slapped the floor.

The emergency exit lights kicked on. The target remained seated, head lolled back and drool trickling out of the corner of his mouth. The light upstairs brightened. "Please remain calm." A man's voice, confident and commanding. "We need everyone to lie face down on the floor."

Slinging the target over his shoulder, Drom ran for the back door.

He scrambled down the bank, splashed into the center of the stream, and charged upriver. Past the bridge, up the north bank, his arm a vice around his captive's thighs. Distant sirens singing. Legs pumping, dead-weight head bouncing against his back. Inhale. Exhale. Press, press. *Push!*

He reached the blind and laid his captive down. The whites of his eyes beamed from a face darker than the pale-moon night. Drom checked the pulse at the carotid. Strong and regular. He opened the blind and dragged the man in. He wrapped duct tape around his wrists and ankles, then waited. Tendrils of noise from the restaurant wormed through the dense forest. Soft snoring filled the brush igloo. Drom taped the man's mouth shut.

He crawled out of the blind and retraced his steps to the creek. He found a fallen branch with leaves and swept away his trail as he backtracked up the hill. Dogs barked in the distance. He scooched into the blind, drawing the makeshift door closed.

His captive was sitting up, taped arms hooked over bent knees. The eyes blinked. Drom reached over and ripped the tape off his mouth.

The man cleared his throat, turned his head, and spat. The eyes beamed at him. White teeth broke out in the darkness.

"Well, Gavin," the man said, "took you long enough."

Chapter 21

After two years of examining the moral implications of modern biotechnology, an interdenominational commission of twenty-five prominent religious leaders released their report yesterday. In it, the commission stated that the new technologies offer "exciting possibilities and devastating uncertainties." The report questions the ability of scientists to self-regulate in the face of such powerful technologies and warned against the nascent industry playing God. "No individual should be compelled to undergo genetic treatment in the name of improving the human species," the report said.

Associated Press, November 6, 1982

Harman, West Virginia – September 16, 1988

Drom slipped off his ski mask and studied his captive. Trussed up, eyes floating in a bobbing head suffering from morel poisoning, he still looked much more the spider than the fly.

"You don't seem too surprised," Drom said.

"I've never held much confidence in a grave's ability to keep a man dead." The same voice, its calming timber sluggish on the intoxicated tongue.

"I suppose not." For all his precautions, Drom knew from the day he left Spain there was a chance Stockton Wilson would see through his elaborate ruse. "How long have you known?"

"For sure?" The eyes wandered. "Not until you took off the mask. You've matured."

"You haven't aged a bit."

"I should hope not. It's only been four years."

"Four for you. A lifetime for me." Drom had tried to kill Stockton in his own office during their first meeting at the Foundation for Controlled Anarchy headquarters. He had his hands around the man's throat, but Stockton's guards got the drop on him.

He pricked up his ears. Oaks and maples rattled their branches against the pine. Mountain breezes rustled leaves to ground. The sirens were gone, the barking hounds fading eastward. He guessed they had another mile to go before they hit the hot scent on the decoy trail.

"You going to tell me what we're doing here?" Stockton's face was placid as ever. A master of serenity, he hadn't even flinched those many years ago when Drom tried to choke the life out of him. Once released, he'd coughed it off like a wrong swallow.

"I need your help," Drom said.

"You have an odd way of asking for it."

"I didn't think strolling onto the Foundation's campus was my best course of action."

"You could have reached out without kidnapping me."

"Like you did?"

Stockton blinked. His hands trembled. "My hands are freezing."

Pulling off a glove, he felt Stockton's fingers. They were cold, but not stiff. "You'll live."

"I hear the dogs. My team will be here soon, so you might as well speak your peace."

"We have longer than you think." Drom shuffled over to the stash of supplies, dug out a hand warmer, and shook it. Chemical heat bloomed and he slipped the packet between Stockton's hands. "If it gets too hot for you, just drop it. How are your feet?"

"Cold, but bearable. They would feel better loose."

"I imagine so." Drom uncapped a water bottle. "Drink as much you can. It will help flush your system." Putting the bottle to Stockton's lips, he tipped it up.

Stockton drank half of it, then he turned his head away. "Morel poisoning."

"You always had a weakness for them."

"Everyone has a weakness." The eyes narrowed. "Your father would have been proud."

"I don't know. I missed one of the sprinkler heads. He would have darted me for that."

"What happened to you in Spain?"

"You had your plans. Somebody more powerful had different ones." He locked eyes with Stockton as the memories of his final days of madness washed through him. He searched for the bitter edge of revenge he had honed for the man who had promised help and then sent him on a path of sure destruction. It was worn flat and polished smooth.

"Is this a new interrogation technique where you kidnap the subject and they badger the questions out of you?"

"Think it will work?"

"Hasn't so far."

"We'll talk later. You need to sleep your dinner off."

"I'm awake enough to hear you out."

"You're a toxin drunk who thinks he's doing a good job of acting sober. You are slurring words, trembling, and by the look of your eyes, having a hard time focusing. Do us both a favor and close them. If I intended to kill you, I wouldn't do it in your sleep."

He grunted. "You've killed me in my sleep more times than you could imagine."

"The nightmare is always worse than the reality. Lay down, Stockton. Trust me, you need it." Drom turned back to the supplies and retrieved a sleeping bag. He unrolled it, ran the zipper down and around, then wrapped Stockton in it.

Stockton shifted sideways. Drom helped him lay down and zipped him in. Within minutes, he was snoring.

⊕

Drom chewed through another bite of oatcake. Gray shafts of dawn pierced through the gaps in the blind and dappled Stockton's shiny black pate with light. Moaning, he stirred and tried to sit up. "Easy does it. Even with a bed of leaves, the ground is still pretty hard. You're bound to be a bit stiff. And if you get your head up too quickly, it will make you pay."

Stockton coughed and gave a low groan. "What did you put on me?"

"Sleeping bag. Didn't want you freezing to death on me."

"No, not that. I have on different pants and—"

"Adult diaper. Sorry for the indignity, but I didn't catch you in time last night. Had to get you changed and take precautions."

"Help me up, will you."

Drom eased him into a sitting position. "Better?"

"For now." Stockton brought his knees up and hooked his arms over them. Drom lifted the oatcake. "Hungry?"

"No, thank you. Your cooking is exquisite, but it doesn't settle well."

"Suit yourself." He took another bite and bought himself a moment as he worked his jaw through it. "I paid Gregory Miles a visit."

Stockton's eyebrow twitched. "How is Miles?"

"Fractured."

"But alive?"

"Living. We talked about Madrid."

"So he knows you're not dead."

"He doesn't know what I am any more than you do."

Stockton tilted his head. "You said you needed help. Is your problem in Madrid?"

"Miles told me that when he was there, a French operative approached him, said he knew the Americans were looking for a weapon. This Frenchman thought they were looking for the wrong one."

"This Frenchman have a name?"

"Bastien Frabron."

"The Butcher."

"You're familiar with him."

"His work."

"Who does he work for?"

"That's a matter of debate. Officially, he's DGSE, French Foreign Intelligence Service."

"Unofficially?"

"Miles wouldn't volunteer Frabron unless you shattered him worse than I thought. Why are you interested in him?"

"What weapon would the French be hunting?"

Stockton stretched his arms overhead, arching his back. He lowered them and rubbed his jawline with a knuckle. "I asked first."

"I'm not the one tied up with duct tape."

"No, but you crawled out of the grave to ask me about Frabron. Looks like you've abandoned torture and I'm still breathing. So how about some quid pro quo. Why are you hunting the Butcher?"

Running his hands through his hair, Drom drew a deep breath. He was on the slope's edge, could see the dirt dusting down the cliff. *Everyone has a weakness.* His gaze drifted left of Stockton's shoulder. The woven branches of the blind faded to a gray blur. "He led a team in against my family."

"Dear God! How bad was it?"

"Bad."

Stockton was silent for a minute. Yawning, he rubbed his jawline again. "You want my help tracking him down so you can avenge your family?"

Drom focused on Stockton's eyes. "Vengeance is a fool's errand. I need to know what the French are after."

"Why come to me? You have contacts in France."

"I'm dead, remember?"

"Seems the French don't think so."

"Can you help or not?"

Stockton held out his bound wrists. "Not like this."

Drom dug his lock blade out of his pocket and flicked it open. Leaning forward on his knees, he pointed the knife at the hollow of Stockton's throat. "You're the most dangerous man I know. Setting you free goes against my instincts." He slashed down, cutting the tape between the wrists without breaking skin.

Stockton peeled the tape off and shook his arms out. "A German Romeo spy has secured an agent in a sensitive facility in Boston. Said facility has something I want and may be of interest to you. I need to get it before the German does."

"You don't need me to stall a DDR operative. Sick the Feds on him. I'm sure you have enough documentation to get him deported."

"He's not East German. He's BND."

"And exposing West Germany is of no value to you at the moment. I get it, but how is this relevant to the French?"

"Whatever they're after, the Germans want it too. If you retrieve the item before Romeo convinces his Juliet to grant him access, we can get a step ahead of them."

"You want me to do the job for you."

"You came to me. Fortunately, this quid pro quo can help us both."

"I assume you have a complete intelligence packet on the facility?"

"Personnel schedule, architectural plans, and item location. Standard brief. All you need to do is get in and get out."

Drom knew this venture would cost him before he took his first step from Woodbridge. He cut Stockton's ankles loose. "I'll need help with something else as well."

Stockton rubbed his feet and ankles. "Name it."

"I had enough to reimburse Paulette for the morels and wine I used, but not for the water damage or the cost of the bad publicity."

Stockton shrugged his shoulders and a slight smile played across his lips. He slipped a finger into his mouth and swabbed it along his jawline inside his cheek. He brought it out and pincered his thumb to it. Pinched between fingertip and thumb was an electronic device the size of a shirt button.

"No need to worry about Paulette," Stockton said. "You should know by now that I always take care of my people."

Drom caught the thump, thump, thump of the rotors rushing down from the mountain's north ridge. Their blade wash smashed through the blind, scattering it down the slope, exposing both men to the morning sun. Drom rose to face the security force in full tactical gear charging down the hill, their Heckler and Koch MP5s trained on him.

He lifted his head to the windstorm above as more of them repelled to the ground from the two helicopters. He lowered his gaze to his former captive, the Director of the Foundation for Controlled Anarchy.

"Welcome home, Gavin," Stockton said, his feral grin shattering all rabbit illusions.

Chapter 22

The stronger must dominate and not blend with the weaker, thus sacrificing his own greatness. Only the born weakling can view this as cruel, but he after all is only a weak and limited man; for if this law did not prevail, any conceivable higher development of organic living beings would be unthinkable.

"Nation and Race," *Mein Kampf*, Adolf Hitler, 1925

Gurs, France – May 22, 1942

Tshuri crouched lower at the knocking of the diesel engine. He nodded to Eglantine. She crept backward from the brush into the tree line. He followed her with his eyes as she reached the large oak and slipped behind it. Her boots pounded the forest floor, their sound angling toward Raison's position.

Turning his gaze back to the cemetery, he peered past the festering trench to the gravel road east of him. Squinting against the mid-morning sun, he spotted the Citroën stake body truck rattling into the graveyard. Behind its dust trail came two guards in an open top patrol car.

The two-ton diesel charged straight toward him. Tshuri held his ground. The driver cut the wheel hard right, crashing the front left tire into the brush less than a meter from Tshuri's head. The turn straightened out and the truck skidded to a stop, parking parallel to the trench. The patrol car stopped several meters behind it and the two guards stepped out, submachine guns held low.

The Citroën driver climbed out and walked the length of the truck, banging the side with his fist. *"Déscendez! Déscendez!"*

Six men in tattered clothes spilled out of the back, their faces grim and gaunt, their body odor palpable despite the cargo's stench. Working in two-man teams, they hauled corpses out of the truck by legs and arms and tossed them into the pit.

Sliding to the edge of the brush, he spied across the cemetery's downward slope. Raison, red roses on white skirts flapping like flags, peddled up the gravel path, offering tantalizing glimpses of her shapely calves. Tshuri checked to his left. Anton, tucked in beside a tree, trained his carbine on the truck driver. To Tshuri's right, Normand hid prostrate behind a log, rifle pointed toward the two guards.

Raison wobbled on her bicycle then sprawled into the gravel with a cry, her dress bunching up to mid-thigh. The driver turned to the sound. The two guards rushed downhill to assist the blonde.

Tshuri sprang out of the brush and scrabbled up the side of the stake body. Flipping over the top, he thudded into flesh. The dead breathed out their stench, slamming his stomach into his throat. Clamping his mouth shut, he rolled down the pile and came to rest nose to nose with a skeletal old woman, her blank amber eyes staring at him.

She slid away. He tumbled down. He rasped across the floorboards, wrists and ankles viced in skin and bone. Rough wood gave way to air. Hard earth slammed into his back. His head bounced against the ground. Sky moved above.

They lifted. They swung. They released.

He latched on.

He smacked a wetter patch of death and a man landed on top of him. Clamping his hand over the man's mouth and his arm around his throat, Tshuri hissed in his ear. "Stay still. Say nothing and you will soon be free." The man went limp. Tshuri slid out from under and took the man's cap. Snugging it on his head, he pulled the visor low on his brow.

He clawed up the side of the trench and came eye-to-eye with the one who moments before had him by the ankles. He gripped Tshuri's forearm and pulled. "Jaques, you clumsy fool! Fall like that again and they'll leave you in the pit."

Keeping eye contact, Tshuri climbed out onto level ground. The man slapped his shoulder. Tshuri glanced down into the body-strewn pit. The real Jaques lay still as a corpse. He followed the other man to the rear of the truck and started hauling bodies to the mass grave.

Deeper into the truck, children's bodies mixed in with larger forms. Relief washed over him with the last body's thud. He wanted to find his family, but not here. Climbing up into the truck with the rest of the burial squad, he spotted Raison downfield playing the two guards with musical laughter and a flip of blonde hair.

The driver called down to the guards. They tipped their hats to Raison and marched uphill. She swung her leg over the bicycle and peddled off, disappearing into a trail that cut into the woods.

The truck lurched forward and Tshuri grabbed a rail of the stake body to steady himself. His new partner leaned into him, offering a hand. "René." Tshuri shook it. "Whatever you're up to, you need my help. All I ask in return is that you get me out too."

"What section of the camp is Jaques supposed to be in?"

"We're in Block C, Barracks 19."

The truck slowed and turned right. Tshuri moved to the front of the stake body and climbed up to see over the cab. The main gate lay dead ahead. Guards swung the right gate in. Tshuri jumped over to the right side as they rolled into camp on the midway. He took in the heavy beams, bolts, and iron bands of the gate webbed with barbed wire and discarded the idea of barreling a truck through it.

They passed a lone barracks centered in its dusty block surrounded with its own wire. The massive incarceration blocks slid past. People milled in the alleys between the barn-like, a-framed barracks. Inmates bunched and separated at the wire like flies on a screen door. L, J, H—Tshuri ticked off the blocks from his memory of Anton's map. They turned right onto the narrow path between H and F blocks and rolled through a miniature version of the front gate. Pulling past the barracks rows, they turned left into a long, rectangular field that sat at the blade's edge of the camp's knife layout.

Tshuri eyed the black cloud swarming over the pile of bodies at the fence line.

"Second load," René said.

The truck backed to the pile and the burial squad jumped out. Tshuri waved his arms against the flies, then stopped when he realized the others ignored them. Bodies piled up on the tail. René climbed onto the bed and Tshuri followed him. They dragged the corpses to the front of the truck. The other men tossed. Tshuri and René hauled and stacked.

"Are they dying of starvation or typhoid fever?" Tshuri asked.

"Yes," René said.

Back at the cemetery, Tshuri found no trace of the real Jaques or the commando. When they pitched the last body into the trench, the chase vehicle pulled forward. The burial squad grabbed pick axes and shovels and set to work cutting a new trench parallel to the first one, casting the dirt over the discarded bodies. Once the mass grave was mounded with fresh dirt, they kept digging until they were three meters below ground.

The guards stepped to the edge of the pit and aimed their rifles at the prisoners.

"Throw the tools up," the truck driver commanded.

Tshuri tightened his grip on the pick ax. René bumped his shoulder and heaved his shovel out. Tshuri hesitated a moment, then complied. The guards waved them out of the pit at rifle point. The men clawed their way up the loose earth, crawled out onto the grass, and marched back to the truck.

They carried lye with them on the third load. After layering the bottom of the new trench with corpses, they dusted the lot down. Sunset found them rolling back into camp.

Hunger kneaded Tshuri's stomach in tandem with death's stench strangling his appetite. The barracks blurred past, the camp lights letting day shadows turn to darkness. Head swimming, he grabbed a rail to steady himself. Two men got off at G block, the next two at E. René and Tshuri jumped off at C and the truck rumbled away.

A guard escorted them through the outer wire, across the open buffer zone, and inside the inner security fence. Tshuri resisted the urge to drop where he stood and followed René to a queue in front of Barracks 15. "What's the line for?"

"Breakfast," René said.

Tshuri took his bowl of thin soup and hunk of stale bread and sat on the ground next to René. The man swilled his bread in the lukewarm water dotted with potato cubes and leeks, took a bite, and chewed long before swallowing.

René eyed him. "Eat, Jaques. It's not much, but you will need all you can get."

Tshuri followed René's example. His fetid hands turned the soup putrid. He swallowed and forced another bite in. Somewhere in the distance, a guitar strummed. Small groups broke away and flowed to the block's center. He chewed. The strumming resonated with the rhythms of southern Spain's Cale flamenco. A voice broke above it in words neither Spanish nor French.

"Le cha dodi likrat kala, p'nei Shabbat n'kabelah!"

Other voices flooded in.

"Shamor v'zachor b'dibur echad,
Hishmi'anu el ha'meyuchad.
Adonai echad u'shmo echad;
L'shem ul'tiferet v'l'tehila."

Tshuri turned to René. "What are they singing?"

"A song welcoming the Sabbath. The chorus is 'come, my friend, to meet the bride; let us welcome the Sabbath."

Tshuri grunted. "Sabbath in a prison camp. Anyone let the gendarmerie know you plan on taking the day off?"

"Scoff all you want, the Sabbath is ours. They can't lock us away from it. It reaches us wherever we are."

The song rose, its urgency pulling at Tshuri's heart even as it pushed his exhaustion back a step. "And now? What are they saying now?"

"Shake off your dust, arise!

Put on your glorious garments, my people, and pray:

Be near to my soul, and redeem it

Through the son of Jesse, the Bethlehemite."

The chorus came and René joined it. Tshuri hummed along around a mouthful of stale bread and it somehow made it more palatable. They deposited their spoons and bowls in the common washtub and plodded toward the singing. Tshuri paused at the edge of the worshipers, baffled by their devotion. He believed in spirits, most of them malevolent. The day's work had deepened his doubts about the existence of any benevolent god.

René led him away. Barracks 19 was no different than the rest. A-framed, long, and flared at the sides, it looked more like a giant chicken coop than a housing cabin. Square wind holes lined the top of the tar-paper walls. Its single entrance had no door.

He followed René's path through the inmates laying on the floor. René stopped and kicked the foot of a man sleeping on a pallet of straw. The man sat up, then shuffled off without comment.

"We can both fit here if you don't jostle about in your sleep," René said.

"I'm too tired to jostle, but I have questions."

"The questions will have to wait until morning. Pray not too many die tonight." René laid down on his side.

Tshuri joined him on the filthy pile of straw, his back to the man. He closed his eyes and all was black

⊕

Whistles, insistent and sharp. Tshuri sat up, back screaming. All about him in the shadows of the barracks, men got to their feet. He spotted René kneeling over an inmate curled up on the straw. "What's wrong with him?"

"He's dead." René dug through the man's pockets and came up with a crust of bread. He popped it into his mouth and spoke around the morsel. "Help me get him out to roll call."

"Why? You said he's dead."

"Doesn't matter. Hook his arm over your shoulder. I'll get the other side."

They carried the man upright, his lifeless feet scrapping the dirt. They swung into the assembly square and joined their barracks' formation. The dead man dropped at Tshuri's feet. René stood behind him. Officers and guards marched out, clipboards in hand, and the name calling began.

Tshuri rubbed his arms to ward off the pre-dawn chill. As the names droned on, he studied the arrangement of the camp lights and power lines.

A well-placed rock or two would put a piece of the wire in the dark.

"Jaques Grenier!"

Or I could cut one of the power lines.

"Jaques Grenier!"

"That's you," René hissed behind him.

"Present!"

"René Grenier!"

"Present!"

Sunlight splayed across the Pyrenees as the roll call dragged on. They remained in formation—six ten-men columns per barracks—while the officers reviewed the guards' reports. The sun climbed higher. The whistles sounded and the men dispersed.

René kicked the dead man's foot. "We need to load him up."

Tshuri followed his gaze to the two-wheeled wooden pushcarts at the edge of the assembly yard. He trudged over to one and rolled it back to the corpse. They hefted it onto the flat planks of the wagon. "Jaques is your brother?"

"Yes."

"You could have mentioned it."

"You didn't ask."

"I might have, if you had talked last night. Where are you two from?"

"Nantes. We were arrested in October after Colonel Hotz was assassinated."

Tshuri worked in silence until they grabbed the second cart. "They arrested me too."

René eyed him over the glassy stare of another typhoid casualty. "Nantes?"

"Near Châteaubriant."

Second cart full, Tshuri followed René through the gate and joined the burial squad train pushing their carts up the midway. They reached the end of the exercise field sweat-soaked and out of breath.

René led him out of earshot of the others and started unloading. "Why are you here?"

"I escaped and made my way back to our camp. The Germans had burned our wagons and taken my family. I've been searching for them ever since."

Carts empty, they rolled into Block H and René parked his near the midway wire. "We troll the alleys first, then collect the dead left from roll call." The dead of Block H didn't fill the second cart. René commandeered it, leaving the heavier load for Tshuri. "They put all the Gypsies in Block J with the rest of the asocials."

Tshuri hefted his load behind the Frenchman. "Do we go to J next?"

René didn't answer.

Tshuri strained the cart through the barbed alley and over to the growing pile of bodies. He released the handles and the stabilizer struts stabbed into the earth. He shook his arms out, pressed on the small of his back, and flexed backward. René grabbed a set of ankles. Tshuri scooped his hands under the dead man's shoulders and lifted.

"We go to Block A next," René said.

"Block A? That's next to our block. Why not have us start there instead of H? It doesn't make sense."

"What about any of this does?"

They dropped the body on the pile. "How do I get into Block J?"

"You don't."

One of the guards stepped closer. Tshuri picked up the pace, forcing René to follow suit. Carts unloaded, they pushed out behind the two men from Block E. René got alongside them and exchanged words. He dropped back to Tshuri. "Those men collect in J next. They can look for your wife and deliver a message. But it will cost you."

Tshuri slowed his pace, allowing the Block E crew to get well ahead. "I have money."

"Reichsmarks?"

"Francs."

"How much?"

"Two hundred."

"Might not be enough."

"Let me talk with them."

René gave a short whistle. Then men stopped at the end of the alley. "Make it fast."

Tshuri trotted his cart to them and tipped it on its side across the path. "Help me with this wheel."

"What's wrong with the cart?" the larger of the two asked.

"It's not going to Block J," Tshuri said. "I need you to find someone for me."

The big man's eyes narrowed. "You have money?"

A whistle trilled behind him. Peering over the cart, Tshuri eyed the approaching guard and held his hand up. *"Une minute, la roue est coincée."* Gripping the wheel with both hands, he hunched over it and rocked it left and right like it was stuck.

The guard pulled his truncheon from his belt loop, his step turning into a march.

Tshuri turned to the big man. "One hundred francs now, another hundred when you have found her."

"Two hundred now."

"Take what I offer or have nothing."

"Who am I looking for?"

The guard passed René and was fast approaching.

"A Gypsy woman named Hishoro. She has three young boys with her."

"And when I find her?"

Tshuri pulled Hishoro's headscarf out of his back pocket and pressed it into the man's hand with the franc notes. "Tell her it needs washing."

He tipped the cart upright as the gendarme reached him. *"Réparée."*

The guard swung.

Pain shot into his shoulder, numbing his hand. He lifted his arms to protect his head and the truncheon struck his ribcage, dropping him to his knees. The guard yelled at him, the scar cleaving the left side of his mustache jumping like a lightning bolt.

René lifted him to his feet. "Move."

He fumbled for the cart handles, grit his teeth, and pushed. Blinking against the blur, he willed his left arm to work as each breath shot a hot knife through his side. Hours, miles, or minutes later, the guard waved them through the Block A gate and locked it behind them.

Tshuri soldiered on to the first street and turned up the alley. As soon as he was out of sight of the guard shack, he lifted his shirt and inspected his side. He pressed his fingertips along the angry welt.

Hurt, but not broken. Maybe.

"I'll push my cart through first," René said.

They cleared the block, René hefting trunks and leaving the legs for Tshuri. Somehow, he made it to the dead pile with his cart.

The Citroën pulled into the exercise field as they dumped the last body off the cart. The burial squad loaded the two-ton diesel, then climbed up on the corpses for the ride to the cemetery. Tshuri made eye contact with the man from Block E. The man shook his head and looked away.

"They will continue looking?" René asked.

"Yes."

"And if they find them?"

"We'll begin stage two."

Tshuri dug his small notepad and pencil out of his pants' pocket and scratched a note to Eglantine without bothering to code it. Any gendarme dedicated enough to find it where he intended to hide it was bound to foil his plans anyway. He tore the page out, folded it into a small square, and slipped it up his sleeve.

The lye was losing the battle against the rot in the pit. Tshuri eyed the woods as they moved the bodies into the common grave. Near the end of the load, he caught a flash in the trees. Single dot, "e." Eglantine was there.

A woman's body dropped at his feet at the tail of the truck. He stared at her legs, surprised at the sheer stocking covering one of them. He seized her ankles, René clasped her wrists, and they lifted. They shuffled over to the pit, René walking backwards and Tshuri struggling to keep hold of the silk-encased ankle in his right hand. He pulled it toward him and the stocking slipped free. His left hand lost its grip and René fell backward with a curse.

A gendarme with corporal insignias headed toward them. Tshuri noticed the scarred lip and mishappen mustache. "Get up, quick." Pocketing the stocking, he lifted the body with René and they were on the move before the corporal reached them. He glared at them, hand on truncheon, as they tossed her in.

Their dead barracks mate hit the dirt. Tshuri hooked his hands through the arm holes, leveraging up with his right. The body tipped, its face rolling into Tshuri's left hand. He stuffed the note into its gaping mouth and lifted.

René glanced toward the guard. "Let me get that end."

"I can manage. Grab the legs."

They dropped the body on top of the others, then scattered lye on the new layer.

They climbed up into the bed of the truck with the rest of the squad. As the Citroën rolled out of the graveyard, Tshuri caught another flash from the forest.

Chapter 23

At present there exists one State which manifests at least some modest attempts that show a better appreciation of how things ought to be done in this matter. It is not, however, in our model German Republic but in the U.S.A. ... By refusing immigrants to enter there if they are in bad health, and by excluding certain races from the right to be naturalized as citizens, they have begun to introduce principles similar to those on which we wish to ground the People's State.

"Subjects and Citizens," *Mein Kampf*, Adolf Hitler, 1925

Gurs, France – May 27, 1942

Whistles, insistent and sharp. Scrubbing his eyes, Tshuri counted the days. This marked his fifth roll call. Uncoiling stiff muscles, he rose in the shadows. Up and down the barracks, all were moving. He faced René. "No snacks for you this morning. Looks like everyone survived."

"Less for us to carry."

They stood for roll call. Names barked out. Responses echoed. "Present!" "Present!" "Dead!" "Present!" Black sky shifted to gray. Clouds appeared with darker forms beneath them. Sunlight painted the southern range, giving texture to the looming mountains. Tshuri kept his ears tuned to the roll call as his mind crawled through the ditches in the fields south of the camp, wormed its way to a game trail in the woods, walked over the Pyrenees foothills, hiked through the pass, and made its way down to the Spanish Basque country.

"Jaques Grenier!"

"Present!"

Tshuri set the collection pace. René struggled to keep up. Halfway through their rounds in Block C, René plunked down beside a barracks and leaned against it. Tshuri dragged a body past him and fought it onto the cart. He lifted the handles and rolled forward.

René planted his palm against Tshuri's chest, checking him. "Faster won't help."

"I'll need extra time when we get to Block H."

Sweat rolled down René's sallow cheeks and dripped off the sharp line of his jaw. He lowered his hand. "It doesn't matter what the searchers said or what you might see of Block J during our rounds in H. We will have to dig before this day is done. If we lack the strength to climb out of the pit once it's dug, the guards will make sure we stay there."

"I'll have the strength, trust me."

"You might," René said. "But at this rate, I will not."

Stepping closer, Tshuri squeezed the man's shoulder. "I'll make sure you do."

They emptied their carts in the exercise field and proceeded to Block H. Tshuri was eager to head straight for the wire facing Block J, but they had to keep to their regular route. The camp's rectangular blocks sat lengthwise against the midway, the barracks oriented in the same fashion. Block H had thirty barracks laid out in five columns, each six barracks deep. They worked their way up the first row, turned right down the long side of the last barracks, then turned right again heading down the short alley toward the midway.

As they wove through the milling people in the alleys, Tshuri peered northeast down the long lanes for any glimpse of red fluttering in Block J. The closer they got, the heavier his disappointment grew to carry. He stopped, winded and needing rest.

René caught up to him, leaned against a light pole and slid down to its base. He wiped his face with his shirt tail. "If Block A's death toll is higher, I won't make it to the dig. You'll be carting me there."

Tshuri eyed him a moment, tempted to join him on the ground. Only the second block of the morning and he was already more tired than his first night.

What if she's not there? She must be there! But will I see her?

"Be near my soul," he whispered.

"What?" René asked.

"Be near my soul and redeem it. Will you sing it for me?"

René raised an eyebrow. "The *Lecha Dodi*, you want me to sing this now?"

"Please."

"But today is ..." He tapped his thumb down his fingers. "Wednesday. That's a Sabbath song."

"I think we could both do with a little bit of Sabbath right now."

René rubbed his chin for a moment, then cleared his throat. He sang and

Tshuri hummed along, remembering the wonder of the Sabbath service after that first day of horror. He recalled René's translation as the melody washed through him. Put on your glorious garments, my people, and pray.

Son of Jesse, if you can redeem, help me find her.

René got to his feet. "We shouldn't stop for the full song."

"What little you sang helped."

Tshuri pushed the cart to a body set out like trash at the head of the alley. They piled it on board, plowed along the length of the last barracks, then turned right down the end alley beside the wire. Slowing to a creep, Tshuri bumped past the knots of people gossiping with the Block J inmates across the way.

He spotted a short woman at the head of J's fourth lane stretching her arms up to a clothes line. The sway of her kaleidoscope skirt and the arch of her back halted him in his tracks. She stepped aside and a cloth unfurled, revealing a riot of flowers on a field of red. Springing to the wire, Tshuri gripped it with both hands and hauled himself up.

René caught him before he climbed past the first step. "You'll get yourself shot!"

Tshuri stared at him, then lowered his foot back to the ground. "Hishoro!"

She turned.

His heart caught in his throat.

She stepped to the wire. "Is it really you?"

"It is, my love. It's me." His tears obscured her and he willed them dry, not wanting to lose one moment's sight of her.

Hishoro pressed closer to her fence. "The children—"

Whistling cut through the din of the conversations between H and J blocks. People started dispersing. Tshuri tore his eyes away from Hishoro and checked up and down the wire. Guards approached from both sides. "What is your barracks number?"

She pointed with her thumb to the barracks behind her. "Number 3."

The whistles shrilled. "Be ready tonight!" He pushed off the wire, gripped the cart handles, and marched away without a backward glance. His hands slid up the rough wood and he struggled to keep his grip. Turning the corner at the midway, he parked the cart and inspected his hands. Blood oozed from multiple cuts, his prize for gripping barbed wire in his eagerness to reach Hishoro.

He tore a shirt off one of the men's corpses and ripped it into long strips. He wound the dirty cloth around his bloody hands and marshalled on.

Block A had less dead as René had hoped. Tshuri settled up with the Block E team on the ride to the cemetery. They filled the pit, then set to work on burying the evidence.

Tshuri chose a shovel this time.

He paced the mound of dirt piled alongside the trench and stopped at the predetermined number. He moved the earth with shallow scoops, tossing the dirt over his shoulder into the pit. The tip of his spade stopped short. He glanced around, checking the guards' positions.

The Citroën driver, a sergeant, was nowhere to be seen. The two from the chase vehicle were leaning against its hood, smoking. And walking along the top of the pile glaring down at them was the corporal with the broken mustache. He tapped his palm with his truncheon, yelling at the men to work faster.

Tshuri stabbed the spade deep into the dirt beside the buried package. He pulled up the shovel full, lost his balance, and fell forward, his arm slipping into the hole. Weight slammed into his low back, pressing him into the loose earth.

"Get up, swine!"

Tshuri clawed the dirt under his body. Cursing, the corporal kicked his side. His fingertips brushed the oil cloth. Gripping the pouch, he pulled it free and shoved it into the large pocket on the inside flap of his jacket. The boot struck his injured ribs. Grabbing the shovel, he pressed himself up.

The corporal's obscenity-filled tirade continued, his spittle showering the side of Tshuri's face. He kept his head down and threw dirt onto the decaying flesh below. The verbal assault tapered off as they started on the new trench. The guards ordered them out when it was done.

Tshuri eyed René as the others climbed out. "I'll help you up."

He boosted René up and scrambled after him. He pulled up over the lip and a boot plowed into his face, tumbling him back into the pit.

"Stupid pig can't keep his feet." The corporal spat down at him. "Worthless Jew!"

Tshuri rolled onto his hands and knees. Liquid iron filled his mouth. He spewed the gob out, spattering the dark earth red. He got to his feet. Head bowed, he rolled his eyes up to the guard bent over the ledge.

"Come on, you lazy dog!"

Face throbbing, Tshuri clawed up the side of the trench, digging his toes in as he neared the top. He heaved up with his right arm. The guard's boot rushed to his face. Tshuri pivoted right and the guard's foot swung high, kicking thin air. Tshuri swept his supporting foot with his left elbow as he scrambled out of the pit. The guard fell backward, bouncing his head against the ground.

Tshuri rushed to the back of the truck and the other men pulled him aboard. He turned in time to see the corporal find his feet and search for his target. They made eye contact. The corporal's lips drew tight, vibrating the scar from his lip to his cheek bone. Drawing his truncheon, he marched toward the truck.

"Enough!" The sergeant intercepted him. "You've had your fun. Get in the cab."

The man glared at Tshuri, then obeyed.

Tshuri slumped down in the front corner of the stake body and the truck rolled out. He couldn't breathe through his nose and what air he gulped stabbed his side. His left eye refused to open. Blood dripped from his nose and split lip, spattering the floorboards between his legs.

Kneeling in front of him, René thumbed Tshuri's gray eye open, then examined his right one. "I don't know if you're dying or just trying to get yourself killed, but your pupils are even. Can you see out of your left?"

"Bit blurry."

"Your nose is bloody, but doesn't look broken. The lip will heal. You may live another day if you can manage to steer clear of that madman."

"Help me up."

"Stay down. You should rest until they drop us off."

"He won't find me down when we stop. Help me up."

René pulled him to his feet.

Tshuri lurched forward and fell into René's arms. "My people delivered." He pulled back and leaned against the slats. René stared at him. Tshuri lifted his split lip into a weak smile.

Back inside Block C, Tshuri charged toward the main road.

René caught up to him. "We need to get you cleaned up."

"No time." Tshuri turned onto the wire side path of the last row and walked its length, noting the position of the camp lights and their relation to the webs of barbed steel that stood between him and freedom.

"We need to get in the food line before all the swill is gone."

Tshuri didn't spare him a glance. "You go ahead. Eat my portion, if you like. I have work to do." He paced the fence, calculating distances and timing.

René stood in front of him. "They won't give me your portion."

Tshuri studied the man's face for a moment. "I told you, I'm not leaving you in here."

"And I'm not leaving you alone. Whatever you're planning, you'll be better off with the little they give us than with nothing at all."

Tshuri broke eye contact and examined the lights one more time. "Fine, but we have to make it quick."

He followed René to the soup line. The two men snarfed their swill and marched back to their barracks. Inside, several men were laying down, not waiting for nightfall. He parked on the table bench in the center of the cabin, drew out the oil skin pouch, and plopped it on the table.

René sat across from him. "What's in the bag?"

Tshuri untied the flap, reached inside, and placed a pair of wire cutters down on the table. He put his hand back in the pouch and pulled out a fist. He opened it under René's nose.

"Bearing ball, fifteen millimeters by the look of it," René said. "You took a beating for a pair of wire cutters and a metal ball?"

"Not *a* metal ball." Tshuri shook the bag and it rattled. "A bunch of metal balls."

"And this helps us how?"

Tshuri checked on the other occupants. Nobody paid them any interest. He reached into his boot and laid the bayonet on the table.

René jumped up, screeching his bench across the floorboards. He stared at the blade like it was a snake about to bite him. "This whole time?"

"Sit. We're running out of daylight." Tshuri pulled out the silk stocking he had peeled from the dead woman. He handed the foot to René. "Hold this tight."

Tshuri stood and stretched the sheer to its limit. Keeping tension on it with his left hand, he pressed the bayonet point through the silk just past his finger tips and sliced his way toward René. He repeated the maneuver several times, then changed his grip so he could cut through the banding at the leg opening. He took the toe from René and splayed the silk out on the table. Cutting through the toe, he came away with six silk strips double the length of the original hose height.

He tied them in three pairs and knotted the ends together. Handing the knot to René, he pulled back on the strands and wove them into a tight braid, tying it off at his end. He retrieved the knot from René and stretched the cord across his chest. "Matches my wingspan. Should do the trick."

Turning his attention to the purse, he cut a section of cloth off the flap. He used the knife point to bore a hole on either side of it. He pressed a cord knot through each hole and tugged. They held. Pinching the cloth in half, he ran his index finger up to the cord's midpoint and sliced it. He tied a knot in each end, made a loop on one of them and slipped it onto his index finger.

He cradled a ball bearing in the cloth and held the other cord end between his thumb and index finger. He swung the contraption in several figure eights in front of him and the ball stayed in the pouch.

"A sling?" René asked. "Do you even know how to use one?"

"Gypsies do more than beg for food." Tshuri pocketed the sling, sheathed the bayonet, and grabbed the oil skin purse. "Come on. This must be done before the lights kick on."

He led them back to the first row of barracks along the main road. Winding up with the sling, he let fly at the first light. The ball fell short, striking the creosote pole with a resounding thwack. A guard on the outer perimeter paused in mid-step and glanced over his shoulder. Thsuri held his breath. Seconds later, the guard moved on. He waited for a ten count, wound up, and shattered the light.

He worked between the cabins, keeping as close to the sides of the buildings as aiming would allow. One after the other, the bulbs gave way under his onslaught of steel. The lights kicked on as the last shards of glass hit the ground. Tshuri hugged the side of a barracks and waited for nightfall. Pools of darkness sprouted like broken teeth along the back of Block C.

René stepped beside him. "We need to return to barracks."

"Not yet." The sky turned a darker shade of ink. Sprinkles dotted the dusty ground for a moment, then the sky let loose.

René looked up. "Not good. We'll be pushing through mud tomorrow."

"We won't be here tomorrow." Tshuri crept out from between the barracks into the first of the shadows he had created. He glanced back at René. The man eyed the guard tower, then nodded. Tshuri darted to the next shadow. Two guards patrolling the outer perimeter marched past, heads down against the rain.

Tshuri moved forward. Feet slipping in the mud, he plowed on to the block fence. Crouching at the tangled barbed wire, he cut a flap wide enough for a man to crawl through. He stared at the first perimeter wire three meters away.

With a glance at the guard tower, he folded the thorned flap out of the way and wormed through the mud on a diagonal to the next fence. He clipped through it, making another flap.

Wind roared down from the mountains, driving the rain in sheets across his back. He peered across the thirty-meter expanse to the final wire. Somehow, he had to make his way into Block J, retrieve Hishoro, Keti, and the children, lead them to here, and scramble to and through the outside wire.

Despite his tone of confidence with René, he feared tomorrow might find them pushing their carts through the mud after all.

He turned his attention to the guard tower with its sweep light. Its beam held steady; its spot short of his position. He closed his eyes and counted to twenty. He opened them and examined the ground they would have to cover to make the last fence. An oblique swarth of darkness stretched across the buffer zone, a slender ribbon of hope pointing toward freedom.

He crept back to René and they headed toward their barracks, the ground melting under their feet. They moved through empty alleyways and steered left at the latrine platform.

"Arrêtez!"

Tshuri and René froze, side by side.

The corporal stepped forward, his scowl turning into a sneer as he drew closer. "Filthy gravediggers can't keep clean even in the rain." He drew his blackjack and swung down.

Tshuri flinched backward, parrying the blow with his left hand. The corporal's follow through slammed the club into René's clavicle, dropping him like a felled tree. The club came up in a backhand to Tshuri's head. He dodged it, sliding right to open space between them.

They faced off, circling each other. "I'm going to leave your brother alive so he can pull your broken body out of the mud in the morning and load it on his cart." The sky flashed, making his scar look electric. "I'll watch as he dumps you into the pit with his own hands, then I'll send him on top you."

Tshuri cowered backward to the latrine stairs. The bayonet pressed against his calf, calling. Drawing it now could get him shot. He slipped the sling from his pocket instead, dipping his head in defeat.

The corporal swung a hammer blow to Tshuri's crown. He stepped in, sweeping his right arm up—the ends of the cord held in his hand—and blocked the guard's wrist with his forearm. The sling whipped around the back of his neck and Tshuri caught the pouch in his left hand.

Pivoting behind the guard, he pulled the garrote tight. He slipped in the mud and both men crashed onto the lower steps of the platform. They rolled to the ground, Tshuri landing on his back with the guard on top, flailing his arms. Tshuri rolled his wrists, winding the cord around his hands.

The guard thrashed. Tightening the garrote, Tshuri rose and toppled them onto the stairs. Driving his knee into the man's back, he hauled back on the cord. He kept the pressure up until his strength gave out. He let go and the guard's head bounced against the stair.

Tshuri uncoiled his hands, took a step back, and kicked the corporal's side. No response. He spotted the man's upturned kepi filling with rain. He dumped it out and slapped it on his head. The bill did little to keep the storm out of his eyes.

He waited through several breaths. The guard didn't move. He hustled over to René and helped him up. "Can you walk?"

"I must."

Tshuri supported him from the side and they shuffled over to the latrine stairs. "We have to get him stretched out on the steps. I need his uniform. Can you lift one more body?"

"His, I'm happy to drag."

They each grabbed an arm and hauled him up. Tshuri rolled him over. Bulging eyes stared at him, lifeless. Tshuri took off his muddy jacket and laid it over the man's face. He unbuckled the holster tack and cross belt and removed the gendarme's coat. He pulled off the boots and pantaloons.

Tshuri swapped outfits. The boots were loose, but not too sloppy. Adjusting the cross belt and holster harness, he noticed the truncheon was missing. Spotting it in a puddle, he picked it up and slid it into the loop.

He grabbed his bayonet and held it to René. "You'll need to take this."

René stared at it a moment, then took it. "Now what?"

Tshuri rifled through the pockets of his old coat, careful to keep the guard's face covered, and came out with the wire cutters. "We need to get him into one of the tubs."

René grabbed the ankles, Tshuri hoisted the trunk. They carried the body under the latrine platform to one of the fuller collection troughs. Bracing him on the lip, they slid his body into the raw sewage. Tshuri stifled a retch as the gasses of the day's dysentery bubbled out around the body. Swallowing his bile, he sunk his clothes in the tub.

"I'm headed to Block J."

"You plan to cut your way out from there?" René asked.

"No. We all leave from C. You need to wait for me in the barracks."

"What if you don't make it back?"

"*When* I get back, I'll reach through the barracks' wall and tap your head to let you know it's time to go."

René sighed, adding to the fatigue on his face. "You need to take me back in case there are any other guards zealous enough to brave this storm."

Tshuri pulled out the baton and tapped René's shoulder. "Move, pig!"

He kept behind the man, prodding him with the truncheon every time he floundered in the mud. Once René was safely inside, Tshuri made his way to the block gate. Stopping short of the gravel path, he squared his hat and adjusted his tunic. Standing straight as his worn body would allow, he marched down the walkway to the guard shack.

"Patrol exiting!"

A moment later, the door banged open and the night watch scampered out, shoulders hunched against the rain. He unlocked the gate and swung it out.

Tshuri plowed past him and hustled north on the midway to Block J. Headlights cut through the rain, brightening the glare wash from the street lamps. Tshuri kept his pace up and his eyes down. With half a kilometer to go, it wouldn't do to look like he didn't belong. A panel van sped past, dowsing him in its wake. He pressed on.

He banged on the Block J guard shack. "Open the gate!"

A gray hair rose in the window followed by a face in full yawn. The eyes blinked, then stared wide. The door flew open. "Get in here, you crazy fool!"

"Open the gate. I'm on orders to inspect Barracks 3."

"You can do that when the rain stops. Get in here before you drown."

"Toss me the keys if the rain scares you. It can't get me any wetter than I already am."

Another gust pushed in from the south, blowing rain into the shack. The sentry unclipped his key ring, tossed it to Tshuri and slammed the door.

Tshuri attacked the gate. The first three keys didn't fit the pad lock. The next two fit, but didn't turn. The sixth key twisted under his fingers and the lock slid down the shackle. He worked it free of the closure chain and slipped inside. He closed the gate and rewrapped the chain, but didn't click the lock shut.

He plodded on to Barracks 3, testing the ground for traction before committing to the next step. He paused at the door. He had told Hishoro to be ready, but his own preparations left much to be desired. His water-logged uniform was the only card he had to play.

He stepped across the threshold and waited for his eyes to adjust to the gloom. Rivulets ran down his back, arms, and legs. He dripped in counter beat to the rain as his heart ran away from him. Closing his eyes, he pulled air into his lungs past the pain in his ribs. He exhaled and took a look. He could make out the forms of women and children lying close together along both sides of the cabin. Two long tables with benches in the middle aisle had people curled up beneath them.

He crept deeper inside.

"Hishoro," he whispered, "Keti."

One of the forms under the table stirred, then crawled out and stood. "Tshuri?"

Her voice shattered his hesitance. He rushed forward and scooped her into his embrace. She clung to him for a moment, then let go. He put her down, held her face in his bandaged hands, and kissed her. She slipped her arms around his neck and pressed into him.

She broke their kiss and brought her hands down to his. Turning them away from her cheeks, she inspected his palms. "What happened to your hands?" she asked in Romani.

He gazed at the blood-stained bandages. The guard's death face clouded his vision. He brough his eyes back to hers. "I tried to tear my way to your through the wire this morning."

She took a step back and ran her palm down the buttons of his coat. "The uniform?"

"Got me through the gate."

She stroked his left cheek and moved his chin to the right. "By the looks of you, it didn't come without a fight."

He took her hand and kissed it. "You can nurse my wounds once we're out of here. Wake the others. We have to go."

Biting her lip, she turned to the table. Bending down, she shook one of the forms on the floor. It stirred, sat up, and rubbed its eyes. "Come, Tshompi." She slid him out from under the table and the boy got to his feet.

Tshompi gazed at his mother, then turned toward the door. At the sight of Tshuri, he recoiled into her skirts. "Don't let them take me, *Dále.*"

Crouching on one knee, Tshuri turned the boy's face to him and took off the kepi. *"Háide mánsa, murro shavorro."* Come with me, my dear son.

The boy stared wide-eyed. *"Dáda?"*

He pulled his son to him. Tshompi hugged his neck and Tshuri stood, picking him up. "Wake up the rest. We need to go before the rain stops."

Hishoro's chin dropped and she crossed her arms. "They aren't here."

Tshuri's legs trembled. He held Tshompi closer. "Alfonso and Pierre, are they—"

"Alive." She lifted her head. "But they took them."

"Took them?" She flinched and he lowered his voice. "Took them where?"

"The infirmary. They've been there for days."

"The fever?"

She leaned against the table. "No, they were well."

The infirmary a kilometer away. He could feign escort under medical orders, but would anyone believe the ruse at midnight in a rainstorm? "Wake up Keti and Nadja. I'll get you all safe and then get the twins."

She bit her lip again. Tshompi started coughing. It was wet and raspy. Tshuri patted his back. The coughing intensified, then broke with a wail.

"Dále!" Tshompi twisted in his father's arms and reached out for his mother.

"Quiet down," a woman nearby spat out in French.

Hishoro made no move to take the boy. "You have to get him out of here."

He pulled his son back to him and cooed in his ear. Swaying back and forth, he took measure of his wife. She was holding back. "Where is Keti?"

"They put her in the prison barracks."

Tshuri thought of the lone cabin situated in an empty block inside its own two-meter-high fence. *Ilot de Represailles*, René had called it when he asked him about it. The isle of reprisals, a prison inside an internment camp. It sat two kilometers from the infirmary on the other end of the camp.

He mapped the steps they would need to take in the harsh glare of the camp lights and measured them against his internal clock. Water dripped from the rafters onto the tables. Tshompi erupted into another coughing fit. Hishoro stiffened, but didn't move toward them. Tshuri suspected she had done her own math and reached her own conclusions.

"Nadja's cough began like his. Many in our block were dying of the fever. Nadja was strong, at first. Keti and I took turns feeding her our rations. She got worse. Keti gave all her food to Nadja until the child stopped eating. The roll call whistles blew. We rousted the boys, but Nadja wouldn't get up. Couldn't get up."

He moved forward. She checked him with a look. "What happened?"

"When the *choxãné* came to collect the dead, Keti wouldn't let them take her. I asked for a day, but the *gazhya* in the barracks screamed against this. I screamed back. While I argued with the women, the *choxãné* pulled Nadja out of Keti's arms."

Hishoro called the collectors *choxãné*, ghouls. What would she think of him once she knew what he had done to reach her?

"I hadn't heard her scream like that since we were little girls, when the *vurdon* ran over her arm. She fought the men. The *gazhya* whores attacked me. The guards came and took Keti away." Her eyes locked to his, her crossed arms drawing tighter like a breastplate. "Tshuri, I have to be here when they bring her back."

"Piramni," beloved, "come now. I've found you. I can rescue her."

"And you will. You will get us all. But not tonight. Not before you take our son from here and see him well."

"Hishoro," he pleaded.

"Promise me. See him safe and well."

Tshompi coughed and whimpered. Hishoro's lips tightened. Getting them all out was impossible, leaving any behind unthinkable. Tshuri set his son down and took him by the hand. "I will see him safe and well. Then I am coming for you and the twins."

Hishoro knelt down in front of her firstborn. She hugged him and kissed his cheek. "Go with *Dáda. Dále* must stay here and wait for your aunt and brothers." She rose and pulled back to the table. "Run, my love, before the rain stops or my tears start."

He took in her firm aspect, rigid stance, and raw beauty. *"Volvi tut, múrri Rrómníorri."* I love you, my dear wife.

He put on the kepi and scooped Tshompi up. For nearly six, the boy was too light. He squeezed into his father's shoulder when they stepped out into the rain. Tshuri retraced his steps to the gate and set the boy down on the gravel path. "I need you to walk until we are past the guard shack and down the road some."

Locking the gate behind them, he paused a moment at the guard shack. The old man didn't reappear. He marched south on the midway, forcing Tshompi into a trot to keep up.

As they came alongside Block F, Tshuri picked his son up and quickened his pace. No vehicles plowed the road. The empty midway stretched his nerves to breaking, exposed as it was. The wind drove the rain all the way through to his skin. Tshompi shivered in his arms.

Crossing the midway, he stepped to the Block C gate. Putting Tshompi down, he tried the key that worked on Block J. It didn't work. He tried the next key.

"Arrêtez!" The command came from behind him.

Tshompi grabbed his leg. Tshuri froze. "Inmate transfer." He tried the next key. No good. He slipped in the last key on the ring. Someone tugged his shoulder. He turned the key and the padlock slid open. The arm pulled him up. Gripping the chain, he spun. It whipped across the guard's forearm, narrowly missing his face.

"Imbécile!"

"Pardon," Tshuri said, "it came away easier than I expected."

The guard rubbed his arm. "My gate, I open it. What do you have?"

"Inmate transfer. Sooner I get out of the rain, the better."

"This is a men's block. No children allowed."

"Take it up with the lieutenant in the morning. Right now, I just want to get this urchin delivered and get back to quarters before I drown."

"Fine." He put his hand out. "Give me the chain. I'll lock up behind you."

At Barracks 19, Tshuri counted steps down René's side and shoved his hand through the tar paper. He tore a section away and stuck his head inside. He pulled it out, took two more steps, and ripped another hole in the wall near the ground. He slapped the head within reach.

René groaned, then peered through the hole at him.

"Time to go." Tshuri stepped back, expecting René the tear his way through the wall. Instead, he held a finger up and disappeared. Moments later, he came slogging down the alley. "You didn't have to use the door, you know."

"Your holes are bad enough. No need to make what little shelter they have any worse."

"Come on." They worked their way to the cut in the wire. Tshuri lifted the flap for René and Tshompi and crawled out after them. They paused at the next cut. He gazed down the shadow he had created in the thirty-meter buffer zone. "I'll cross to the outside wire first. Head to me with Tshompi the minute I reach it. I'll have it cut by the time you get to me."

He didn't wait for a response. Lifting the flap, he slid under it. He shot up and launched out. The ground gave way under his assault, pitching him forward. Recovering, he pressed on, moving like an ant through honey.

Light flared behind him, illuminating the ground ahead to his right. He slapped to the mud, hoping René had stopped as well. The spot moved, cutting across his shadow path and landing on the outside wire to the right of his blacked-out exit point.

He waited. One breath. Two breaths. Three. The light held steady. He bear crawled the last twelve meters to the fence. Snatching the cutters out of his pocket, he set to work on the tangle of thorns.

Checking over his shoulder, he spotted René and Tshompi halfway to him. Headlights from the north lit up the highway. Several vehicles cruised past and the road was empty again. He made his final cuts and lifted the flap.

A low rumble shook the air and Tshuri wondered at the lack of lightning. He motioned for René to hurry. They reached him an eternity later, René winded and Tshompi shivering. He pulled his boy to him and lifted the flap for René. "Go."

The man slipped past him. Pushing Tshompi through, he wormed out behind him and pressed the flap down. At the edge of the road, he checked both ways and led them across.

Once in the field on the other side, Tshuri carried his son piggy-back and marched south. The ground was firmer, but they were trekking against the wind. Three kilometers later, René collapsed.

"I have to rest."

"You can't, not yet. Come on, just a bit longer."

René struggled to his feet and leaned against Tshuri. "I don't think I can go any farther."

"Tshuri."

"What?"

"My name is Tshuri Velveloz. Your brother Jaques is waiting for us. He will think me an evil man if I show up without you, so come on."

With Tshompi held in one arm and René leaning against the other, they slogged on. He turned them onto a dirt road a kilometer later. Five hundred more meters found them at the back of a cottage.

He banged on the door. The window lit up and something scraped against the door. It creaked in and Anton's head craned out. Tshuri barreled past him, nearly knocking him over. Heat bathed his face and he followed it to its source. He found Eglantine beside the fireplace, the flames dancing in her wide eyes.

"You made it," she said.

He set Tshompi down in front of the fire and started stripping him. "I need a blanket and something warm for his belly."

Eglantine sent Raison after the blankets and told Marcel to heat up the chicken soup. Anton helped René into the common room and sat him down beside Tshuri.

René scanned the room. "Jaques, where is he?"

"Upstairs asleep," Eglantine said. "Rest easy and warm up. You'll have some time with him in the morning before we move out."

Raison came in with a pile of blankets and some towels. The women gave the men their privacy by the fire to disrobe and dry off. They got some food into Tshompi, rolled him up in a blanket, and laid him down to sleep on the lone couch in the cottage.

Tshuri sat cross-legged in front of the fire, a blanket wrapped around him and a steaming cup of coffee in his hand.

Eglantine snuggled in next to him. "What now?"

"I take the boy south, across the Pyrenees. Gorka Colón will be able to help us."

"And then?"

"Once the boy is better, I will come for Hishoro and the rest."

The top log fell into the coals below, showering sparks up the flue. Tshuri watched the flames dance on the timber and hoped he found more than ashes when he returned.

Chapter 24

The World Jewish Congress criticized the Reagan administration's ambivalence toward Spain's protection of former Nazi secret agents. "Francisco Franco has been dead for nearly thirteen years, but Spain continues to harbor these criminals," the WJC statement said. The WJC claims that Nazi Abwehr agents working in Spain obtained monkeys and other animals from Spain's African colonies for use in experiments aimed at manufacturing biological weapons.

The New York Times, September 23, 1988

Denver, Colorado – September 25, 1988

Shell dug through the refrigerator and came out empty-handed. "Amanda!"

Her daughter shuffled up the short hallway from their bedroom to the basement apartment's studio-sized common room. Yawning, she slumped into a dinette chair and snagged the comics section out of the newspaper. "What time is it?"

"Where did you put the milk?"

Amanda cocked her head. "Milk?"

"From yesterday."

"That was for us? I thought you picked it up for Ms. Sharon."

Shell flicked the door closed. The condiment jars clattered and Amanda's shoulders jumped. "Wake your brothers up, please."

She opened the door beside the refrigerator. Carpeted steps rose into the gloom above. As a rule, she avoided coming above ground before ten. But she couldn't bear disappointing Jakob another morning. She squared her shoulders, flipped the light on, and trudged upstairs.

The tones, Robert's conciliatory baritone against Sharon's soprano trills, reached her if not the words. Shell hesitated a beat, then pressed on.

"… because you're still infatuated with her," Sharon said.

"No," Robert said. "I'm not. She came to us for help."

"She came to you for help. Is David yours?"

Silence held her hand on the knob for an uncomfortable moment. She opened the door. They both glanced her way as she entered the kitchen.

"I need to go. I'm late enough as it is." Robert grabbed his travel mug from the breakfast counter and marched out.

Sharon watched his back as she addressed Shell. "You're up early."

I've been up for hours, b— She strangled the thought. "Didn't mean to disturb. I bought some milk yesterday and Amanda thought I got it for y'all. I'll just grab it and get out of your hair."

"Help yourself," Sharon said. "If you'll excuse me, I need to get Kyle out of bed."

Shell kept her spot while Sharon pushed through the door into the dining room. She crossed the kitchen to their fridge, grabbed her gallon of milk, and hustled downstairs.

Jakob was at the small table. David was in his high chair happily pawing at the cereal loops on his tray. Amanda was nowhere in sight.

"Manda said you got milk." Jakob eyed his brother's cereal. "I want ganola."

"I know, baby boy. That's why I got milk." She lifted the jug.

"I'm a big boy," Jakob said. "David's the baby. He eats Cheerios."

Shell took in the scene—two fresh-faced boys dressed and ready for break-fast—and tried to bask in its normalcy. But she hadn't washed their faces or dressed them. Her ten-year-old-going-on-twenty had. Shell's life had robbed her daughter's childhood. Mature as Amanda was, she could still throw a tantrum. The table was set, the newspaper was scattered on the floor. She resisted the urge to yell for her again.

Setting the milk on the table, she ruffled Jakob's hair. She kissed David's cheek, breathing in the fading hints of his baby scent.

They grow too fast.

She grabbed the box of granola from the cupboard and shook out an ample portion into Jakob's waiting bowl. She drowned it in milk and her son smiled at her with his father's lips. Her reverie in the ordinary evaporated to the crinkling of newsprint underfoot.

She had spent a week of slow travel on back roads to reach Denver and another week to work up the nerve to knock on Robert Gladstone's door. The last time they spoke was on her doorstep in Ferrisburg when he came bearing news of Gavin's death. They had both believed it then. She needed him to be-lieve it still.

In the end, she decided to play a page from her former life. Robert had known her as promiscuous and unstable teen. The role of a single mother in need of rescue wasn't a stretch for her. "Sorry to show up like this, but I couldn't think of anywhere else to go."

He stood in the doorway, slack-jawed, and swept his gaze from her to the children, to the junker she bought after stashing the motorhome at a storage yard.

"Honey, who is it?" Sharon's voiced sounded out from deeper in the house.

"You should come in before the sky lets loose," he said.

Dinner that first night was awkward. Sharon was accommodating, but nervous. Kyle, their four-year-old son, took to Jakob immediately. Sharon watched the boys' interactions between her telling glances at Shell and Robert. Toward the end of the meal, she got to the question Robert hadn't bothered to ask. "So, Michelle, how long are you in Denver for?"

Despite Gavin's urging, she had no intention of recovering any more of her former life than she had to. Her birth name was a treasure she only cared to hear from his lips. "Call me Shell, please." She gave Sharon's hand a friendly pat. "I haven't gone by Michelle in years." Her move provided a momentary distraction, a means of sidestepping the question.

Now, six weeks later, she still didn't have an answer. She gathered the strewn newspaper pages from the floor and tossed them on the stack by the trash can. Like the rest of them, this morning's issue contained no classified ads for a nineteen seventy-six Gran Torino, green or red.

She insisted on the Gran Torino when they worked out their communication plan. It was the type of car she drove when they first met. The beast had left her stranded at the grocery store. Gavin appeared at her window as if from the thin air—the exotic stranger with skilled hands—and rescued her.

Then he disappeared.

And reappeared, months after they lowered his casket into the ground.

She knew him much better now. But he was still exotic. And strange. And gone.

One ad for a red Gran Torino and she would be gone too. One in green meant he was on his way. Nothing meant any number of things, all of which she would rather not think about.

David slapped his tray with both hands and chortled when his sippy cup bounced up and tumbled to the floor.

"Gwavity checg," Jakob said around a mouthful of granola.

"It's still working." Shell picked up the cup and set it in front of David. "Finish your 'ohs and I'll get you a banana."

The one-year-old smiled and grabbed his cup with both hands.

Shell knew he'd perform another gravity check the minute her back was turned, but she didn't have time to play the game with him. She needed to check on Amanda.

The cup clunked against floor before she was halfway to the back bedroom. "Keep your eye on your brother," she shot over her shoulder at Jakob. She stepped into the bedroom she shared with her daughter and sucked in a tight breath against the chill air. The drapes over the sliding glass door billowed into the room.

"Amanda?"

She slid the drapes out of the way and the morning breeze bathed her in promises of colder things to come. Stepping out into the back yard, she scanned the sloping garden and along its chain-link fence. Heartrate climbing, she moved down to the English oak that dominated the Gladstone's green space. "Amanda?"

She widened her focus, taking in the scramble of trees and knee-high grass outside the fence. No movement. As she neared the base of the oak, an acorn tinked off a galvanized fence post. She rounded the trunk and squatted next to her daughter.

"You okay?"

Amanda sat cross-legged, her back against the tree, her eyes on the pile of acorns in her lap. She plucked one and flicked it toward the fence.

Tink.

"Come inside so we can eat breakfast together."

Tink.

"Amanda." She brushed the girl's chin with her fingertips.

Tight-lipped, her daughter glared at her with watery eyes. She shifted her chin away toward the back fence. "Mr. Robert calls me Amy."

Tink.

Shell's gaze was drawn to the fence pole several yards downslope. An acorn arced into view, sailed down, and bounced against the center of the galvanized pipe. Tink.

"It's what he's used to, sweetie."

"I don't like it." Tink.

"I'll get him to stop." Another acorn took flight. Shell tracked it, wishing it to miss. Tink. "Come inside. It's cold out here."

"I thought the milk was for her."

"I know, honey. Sorry for slamming the refrigerator. I was upset, but not at you."

The watery eyes met hers and welled over. "I want to go home."

Sinking next to her, Shell pulled the girl into her arms. She let Amanda cry for a few minutes, then stood, bringing her up on her feet. She wiped the tears from her cheeks. "I left your brothers at the table."

Amanda brushed the seat of her pants and strolled back into the house.

Shell eyes traveled from the acorn pile to the post and back. She grabbed an acorn, took one-eyed aim, and flicked. It shot up and dropped to the ground yards short and wide right. Shaking her head, she marched back inside.

Kyle was at the table with her boys. Sharon stood behind him, flush-faced with car keys in her trembling hand. "Something's happened to Robert. You mind watching Kyle for me?"

"Is he…" Shell's voice faltered as she shot a glance at the billowing drapes in her bedroom, then turned to survey the stairs leading to the kitchen. "Is he okay?"

"His office called. Can you watch Kyle or not?"

Shell hesitated. Sharon bit her lip, unwilling or unable to say more. "Sure."

"Thanks." Sharon shot upstairs.

Shell jumped at the slam of the front door. She waited two full breaths before returning to her room. She closed the sliding glass door and dropped the security dowel into the threshold. She stopped at the closed bathroom door. "Amanda?"

"Be out in a minute."

"I need you to eat as soon as you get out."

"Yes, ma'am."

Back at the kitchenette, she peeled a banana and gave David and Kyle each a half. She caught Jakob's eye. "Play nice. I'll be right back down."

She hurtled up the stairs and ran to the front door. She threw the deadbolt, locked the knob, then peered through the fish-eye peep hole. Stoop, driveway, and street were empty.

She exited the foyer, cut through the dining room, crossed the kitchen, and secured the garage door. Working clockwise through the first floor, she checked window locks and lowered the shades. She was near to top of the front stairs when the doorbell rang.

She froze.

She strained her hearing past the blood hammering in her ears. *Stay in the basement, children.* The bell rang again, its volume obscene to her adrenaline-soaked senses. She crept down the stairs.

Hugging the wall, she spied the front door. A man's silhouette moved in the frosted sidelight. The bell rang. The kitchen door swung into the dining room and Amanda stepped through. They made eye contact. Shell held her palm out and Amanda stopped. She signed, "Downstairs. Boys."

Amanda disappeared.

The door knob twisted. The shadow shifted in the sidelight. The lock whispered with the scratch of metal on metal. Shell spun clockwise into the formal sitting room. She padded through the family room and entered the kitchen from the other side.

She kept her pace quiet and even, resisting the urge to run. She slipped through the basement door and pulled it shut, chagrined it had no lock.

The front door creaked on its hinges.

She dashed down the steps. Amanda was pulling David out of his highchair. Jakob and Kyle were throwing granola at each other. She locked the downstairs door and snapped her fingers.

Amanda turned to her. Jakob's arm froze in mid-throw. Kyle checked over his shoulder and she held him still with a look. She tapped her tight lips with a finger, waved a circle, and pointed to the entrance to the apartment on the other side of the common room. The children nodded.

She took in the room, calculating. The stove was off, the wet cereal probably at room temperature. They'd been up long enough for the beds to grow cold.

She grabbed her set of keys off the hook by the door, opened it, and waved the kids out. They filed past her, Amanda carrying David. Shell slipped out behind them and locked the door. She beelined it to the oak tree and ushered them around to the other side of the trunk. She studied the house for a beat, then joined them.

"We're going on an adventure hike," she whispered. "But it's secret, okay?" Their eyes widened. David reached for her. She took him and chin pointed at the back fence.

Amanda led the way. The boys followed in single file.

Shell peeked around the tree. No shadows in the windows. She moved to the fence. Amanda was in the tall grass lifting Jakob over. Shell handed David over as soon as Amanda put Jakob down. She carried Kyle over the fence with her and they scrambled down through the scrub grass to the bottom of the dry gulch.

The temperature dropped with their descent. Too late, Shell realized none of the kids had jackets on. She looked up. The ceiling hung low over the Mile

High City, obscuring the heights of the Front Range.

The motorhome beckoned eight miles away. She put it out of her mind, and hiked her troop west, praying for the sky to hold.

◈

Shell couldn't stay away and was afraid to return. An hour later, the dropping mercury forced her hand. They climbed out of the gulch into a city park. She took the kids to the playground and let them work up some body heat while she thought things through.

Whoever came inside the house hadn't broken their way in. She knew common thieves didn't ring doorbells. The Gladstones would come home. She couldn't run away with their son.

She broke up the play party and walked them south from West 10th Avenue at a brisk pace until she felt comfortable enough to head east. The move put their backs to the mounting breeze and eased the chill some. Amanda held Jakob's hand. Shell held Kyle's and carried David on her hip.

"I wanna go home," Kyle said.

She squeezed his hand. "We'll be there before you know it." His drooping lower lip said he didn't believe her. She couldn't blame him. She had her own doubts.

Kyle started whining two blocks later. Jakob caught his cousin's mood, dragging his feet and letting his chin tremble. Shell quickened her pace, pulling them along.

The house came in view a mile after her patience died. The driveway was empty.

"Are we going back in?" Amanda asked.

Shell put David down. "Can you hold them together a little bit longer?"

Amanda grabbed David's hand and scooped the other two boys to her.

"You're awesome, you know that?" She kissed the top of Amanda's head. Her hair was sweaty and smelled of fear. "I'll be right back."

She cut across the tree-lined lane on a diagonal and approached the front door outside the angle of the fish-eye. Stopping near the edge of the landing, she inspected the door. It was shut tight. She listened for a moment but only caught the breeze. Backing up a couple of steps to a window, she tried to peek around the edge of the blind. The window kept its secrets.

She eyed her junker at the curb. She could start it, grab the kids, and bolt. She turned her head to the clutch of innocents shivering across the street. Something happened to Robert. Sharon left Kyle in her care.

224

Kyle was crying.

No other vehicles, door shut. Odds were in favor of an empty house. Appearances favored a trap. Faced with bad options, she counted indecision the worst of all.

She tried the door. Locked. She dug her cold fingers into her pants' pocket and fished out her keys. She unlocked the deadbolt, then the knob. She pushed the door open. "Anybody home?" Her voice filled the foyer and faded away into the house.

She waved to Amanda, then held up a finger. Just a minute longer. She stepped inside.

⊕

The sun was long down, the kids in bed. Keys rattled in the lock and the door blew open.

"They didn't tell you why?" Sharon asked.

"For the hundredth time, no." Robert's tired voice was tinged with anger.

Shell clicked on the lamp she had set beside her on the shredded couch. Robert and Sharon froze in the glare of the naked bulb and stared at their destroyed formal sitting room.

"I think it's time for me leave," Shell said.

Chapter 25

FCA Campus, West Virginia – September 26, 1988

Drom turned his head to the glowing red numbers. 2:30 a.m. He'd slept for three hours. If they kept to their routine, he had a four hour wait before they came for him.

For a man who wanted to get ahead of a West German intelligence operation on U.S. soil, Stockton's actions lacked any sense of urgency. From the moment the helicopter delivered him to the grounds of the Foundation for Controlled Anarchy, Drom had been subjected to a continual barrage of medical and psychological examinations.

They drew his blood every day for the first five days. On the sixth day, when the nurse set the phlebotomy kit beside him, he crossed his arms and stared at her. "Enough."

Stepping back from the exam table, she pushed the red call button beside the metal door. It clicked and two of Stockton's goons in white scrubs crowded into the room. Drom noted their earpieces.

Smiling, he splayed his arms and looked her in the eye. "You pick."

She tied the rubber tourniquet around his right biceps. "Make a fist, please."

He curled his fingers in, eyeing the orderlies on either side behind her. Propping his left heel on the top-drawer handle of the exam table, he leaned forward and wrapped his left arm around his knee. "Your hair smells nice." His lips were close to her ear as she swabbed the crook of his arm with an alcohol wipe. "Is it store bought or something you pick up at your stylist?"

A flush bloomed above her collar bone and traveled up her neck. She picked up the needle, its tube and vacuum vial dangling, and slipped off the protective cap.

He leaned forward a fraction more, his breath moving her hair. "Citrus?"

The flush reached her ear. The needle trembled.

He glanced at the orderly on the right. "Twenty-one gauge. It's going to hurt."

The goon pressed a hand to his earpiece. Eyes widening, he stepped forward. Too late.

Pushing down with his heel, Drom launched from the drawer handle. Vaulting over the nurse, he snatched the needle with his left hand and buried it under the orderly's ear, impaling his mandibular nerve just below the sensory root. Spinning in mid-flight, he crushed the other orderly's nose with a heel strike.

Landing on his feet behind the nurse, he bound her wrists behind her back with his tourniquet and swept her into his lap as he hopped back on to the end of the exam table facing the door. The second orderly crumpled to the ground as the first one's howl split the air.

Drom stared straight into the camera. "I asked nicely."

The door blew open. Muscle in proper security uniforms jumped in, pistols drawn. He pulled the woman closer to him, the side of her head against his cheek.

Stockton appeared between the guards. "Let her go, Gavin." Though weary, his voice carried a tinge of amusement.

"Glad to, so long as she's going on vacation," he said. "I've given you enough of my blood."

"After this, I'm sure she could use a couple of days off." Stockton laid a hand on each guard. "Holster your weapons, gentlemen, and see to your colleagues."

They led the injured out—one wobbling, the other mewling.

Drom untied her wrists and dropped his restraining arm.

She stepped away, turned, and locked her hazel eyes on him. "Orange blossom." Head down, she darted out the door.

Stockton's impassive face studied him.

"Boston?" Drom asked.

"In time," Stockton said.

Days passed. No one drew his blood. No one briefed him on Boston either.

2:35 a.m.

He flipped a coin in his mind's eye. Heads, he got up. Tails, he pretended to still be asleep. It was no use. His coin flips were never subject to chance.

He got up.

✦

Stockton leaned toward the CRT as the video moved frame by frame. The sequence played like the final movement in a musical comedy dance number. But the woman being swept off her feet was his staff hematologist, Dr. Janice King, and her impromptu dance partner was Stockton's only hope. And his worst nightmare.

The security officer turned from the room monitors. "Sir, he's up."

"Play it again at regular speed," Stockton said to the video technician.

Gavin's face rose over Dr. King's shoulder. "Twenty-one gauge. It's going to hurt."

The time stamp read 08:59:57. At 09:00:00, Gavin had Dr. King in his lap and two of his men down. Three seconds. Four days of analysis and Stockton still couldn't wrap his head around it.

How did you get deadlier?

He made a circle in the air with his finger. The video rewound. "What's he doing now?"

"His pushups," the security officer said.

Stockton turned to the thermal image on the room monitor. A triangular red glow with a yellow center moved up and down the screen on red and pink sticks. Gavin's pushups were invariably of the headstand type.

"Give me audio."

The speakers popped to life. Electronic crackle gave way to an explosive exhale. Stockton's shoulders drew up. The breath was intimate, too close.

"Diez," Gavin said. *"Los leoncillos necesitan, y tienen hambre; pero los que buscan a Jehová no tendrán falta de ningún bien."*

Phew.

"Once." The radiating trunk paused up screen. *"Venid, hijos, oidme; el temor de Jehová os enseñare."*

"What happened to you in Spain?" Stockton asked.

The security officer turned to him. "Sir?"

It dawned on Stockton he had spoken the question out loud. "Kill the audio. Send the recording over for translation and transcription once he's done."

The phone rang. The video tech picked up. "Observation." He listened a moment, then turned to Stockton. "It's Dr. King. She would like to speak with you."

He glanced at the wall clock. Almost three. He stepped back to the video display. "Frame by frame." He took the receiver. "Janice, last I checked you were on compulsory R&R. You shouldn't be up this early."

"And you shouldn't be up this late, Director."

"What's on your mind?"

"The report the lab just faxed me."

"They finished running the last batch?"

"Yes, sir. They must have worked around the clock."

On screen, Gavin uncoiled like a viper and for several frames appeared suspended in mid-air, his body an arrow moving parallel to the floor. Microsecond by microsecond, he buried the hypodermic needle below the orderly's ear. Gavin's body corkscrewed left. Stockton quelled the urge to warn the second man. It hadn't helped the first time, it certainly wasn't going to help now.

"When can you get here?"

"Give me an hour," she said.

"Take two. I need to wake the others."

Stockton poured himself another mug of coffee and returned to his seat. He decided to command the conference table from the middle, giving the heads to his competing poles: Dr. Frederick "Steve" Morrison, the FCA's resident psychiatrist, to his right and Dr. Janice King to his left. She was flanked on either side by a member of her lab team. FCA's chief physician, security chief, and neurologist rounded out the assembly.

Stockton rubbed his eyes with thumb and forefinger, then took a sip from his mug. "I appreciate everyone getting here on such short notice. Dr. King, the floor is yours."

"I know some here had doubts regarding our preliminary test results," her eyes were fixed at the other end of the table, "but the latest results confirm them. Same blood type, same genetic finger print as the benchmark sample."

Stockton turned to Dr. Morrison. "Satisfied?"

"Mystified is more like it." Steve scratched his beard, then pushed his glasses back up on his nose. "Was Dr. King's team given our original sample, the morgue sample, or both?"

She glanced at Stockton. "Morgue sample?"

"You've observed him for ten days, Steve," Stockton said.

"I also read his postmortem. Victoria witnessed the autopsy, for goodness' sake."

"Steve, it's Gavin." Stockton leaned into the table. "Janice and her team ran the blood work five times. It's him."

"Which sample, Director?" Steve asked.

Stockton broke eye contact and spoke across the table to his security chief. "How are your men?"

"Crowder has a broken nose. Hernandez was fine once we removed the needle." He cleared his throat. "I know you have history with the asset. From where I sit, he's more of a security risk than a benefit, sir."

Stockton turned back to Steve. "You watch the video?"

Steve faced Janice. "It was an impressive maneuver."

Her neck flushed. She took a sip of water from her glass and turned to the biochemist seated next to her, taking the stack of papers from his hand. "I didn't doubt my first findings, Director. You asked for confirmation and now you have it. But that's not why I called you earlier." Placing the first set of stapled pages in front of her, she passed the rest to her left. The copies made their way around the table.

Stockton skimmed the first couple of pages. "What are we looking at?"

"A unicorn." Her face held no trace of humor.

"Who prescribed the supplements?" Dr. Roger Alcott, FCA's chief physician, flipped back and forth between the first and second pages. "I did not authorize any nutritional supplements or performance enhancing drugs." He tossed the report into the center of the table, crossed his arms, and leaned back in his chair. "I cannot properly oversee the patient's health if your specialists don't read me in, Director."

Stockton took another sip of coffee. It was getting cold. He slid it to the side. "We've only fed him our normal food, so you can relax, Roger."

Some of the pinch drained from the doctor's face, but his arms remained crossed.

"Same results each time?" Dr. Chandan Mammen, the neurologist, asked.

"Yes," Janice said. "We ran the battery on all the new samples."

Stockton glanced at his mug. No amount of caffeine would make up for his lack of medical degree. "Break it down for us, Janice."

"The patient's cellular biology is unique in many aspects," she said. "For starters, his leucine metabolism level is extraordinary. The body metabolizes leucine to produce β-hydroxy β-methylbutyric acid."

"That's a mouthful," Sam Gerber, the security chief, said.

"On page two of the report, the beta-hy beta-meth is referred to as HMB. The graph shows the patient's levels against the mean."

Sam whistled. "Okay, the asset is way above average. What does that mean?"

"It means someone's been doping him." Roger's protruding lower lip punctuated his accusation.

"Or…?" Stockton hung the question over the table.

"Definitely 'or,' Director." Janice tapped the report. "He hasn't been supplemented or doped. Healthy adults produce about a third of a gram of HMB per day. He's producing at least an order of magnitude more."

"Three grams a day?" Steve asked.

"At least," Janice said.

"What does HMB do?" Stockton asked her.

"Body builders supplement with it to increase exercise-induced gains in muscle mass and strength. It promotes wound healing and reduces skeletal muscle damage. With elevated HMB levels, his muscle cells breathe better and recover faster."

The video played in Stockton's mind. Gavin was fast before. He was faster now. "How much would aging influence the process?"

"What was the age of the base draw?" Janice countered.

"Never mind the baseline for now," Stockton said. "Does metabolism increase with age?"

"Depends on the age," Roger cut in. "Our patient is twenty, twenty-one at the most."

Janice's eyes narrowed. Bending sideways, she reached into her soft leather briefcase and extracted another file. She leafed through the report, then addressed Stockton. "Puberty is a hormonal onslaught for both sexes. Increased testosterone levels could have influenced the upward shift of HMB from the base levels."

He studied her pale face and blood-shot eyes. She hadn't slept much during her enforced hiatus. Even so, she avoided accusing him of having had the patient in custody while a minor. *Good for her.*

"And this elevated HMB classifies him as a unicorn for you?" Stockton asked.

"If that were all, I would have called him a red wolf or an Amur leopard. Lord knows there are precious few of those left in the wild, but at least they exist."

Stockton checked the wall clock. Gavin's room would light up in a half hour. "What else did you find?"

"Dr. Blau, if you would." Janice stretched out of her chair and filled her glass at the refreshment counter.

"If you *vill* give your attention to page four." The biochemist's German tongue whittled down the double-u to a vee. "Please note *ze* creatine levels. *Ze* serum samples indicate *ze* subject may *haf* as much as one hundred and eighty millimoles of stored creatine per kilogram of dry muscle mass. *Dis* is beyond any upper stored limit in *ze* literature and fifty percent above average."

Chandan's Punjab-spiced, boarding school British rang in. "Any elevated levels in his urine, Dr. Alcott?"

Unfolding his arms, Roger leaned closer to the table. "No, nothing abnormal."

"Odd," Chandan said. "If his system is synthesizing that much creatine…" His eyes wandered to the ceiling for a beat, then he turned to the German. "Pardon the interruption, Dr. Blau."

"*Ve* are here to discuss, yes?"

"Yes," Stockton said. "If I am recalling my very undergrad biochemistry days, creatine helps with the body's energy production?"

"It helps recycle adenosine triphosphate, ATP," Dr. Blau said.

"Cellular energy." Stockton pressed his sleep-deprived mind to chew through the implications.

"Cellular energy, exactly." Janice landed back in her seat. "ATP is produced in the mitochondria."

"Mitochondria!" Chandan slapped his briefcase flat on the table and sprung the brass clasps. He hinged it open, reached inside, and came out with a thick stack of green-bar computer paper, its punch-hole edges still attached. He fanned through the pages and stopped a third of the way down the stack. He grabbed the hematology report, flipped to the next to last page and compared the two. He faced Janice. "The neurological report showed a high mitochondrial mass fraction per cell. I thought it was an artifact from the testing, not a true result. But your findings corroborate it."

"High mitochondrial mass fraction?" Steve asked. "What's that?"

"I can explain it in non-specialist terms, if it helps," Janice said.

"By all means," Stockton said.

"Let's suppose there was an average number of mitochondria per cell in a normal, healthy human being. Let's further suppose that average was between a thousand to two thousand mitochondria per cell. Our patient's mitochondrial mass fraction is indicative of four to six thousand mitochondria per cell."

"Let me get this straight," Stockton said. "You're telling me the asset can grow, strengthen, maintain, and repair muscle mass at artificially enhanced levels, produces an extraordinary amount of ATP, and has over twice the average power plants per cell than most human beings?"

"I would venture to guess he has more than any human being. And he's not rusting out. We expected to find elevated reactive oxygen species based on his ATP turnover rate, but he's detoxifying somehow." Janice took a deep breath, pushed her fingers through her hair, and wrapped it into a pony tail with a band she slipped from her wrist. "He's not a rare specimen of an endangered species you could find in the wild. If you don't like unicorn, then call him a manticore or a gryphon. His type simply doesn't exist."

Stockton eyed the clock. "His official day started a few minutes ago."

"He's been awake for hours," Gerber said.

"I am aware." Stockton tilted his chair back. "Steve, have you or Dr. Mammen gotten to the root of his insomnia yet?"

"There is no root," Chandan said. Coming from Dr. Blau, it would have sounded like a rude interruption. From Chandan, it sounded like the opening lyrics to a song.

"No neurological cause?" Stockton pivoted his chair to the right, his fingers steepled at his chin. "So it's in your wheelhouse, Steve."

Steve's mouth opened, but Chandan's voice sang in Stockton's ear. "There is no root because there is no insomnia."

Steve's hands shot up and he turned to the neurologist. "He hasn't slept more than three hours a night since he got here, Chandan! Your imaging doesn't change the clockface."

"And your emotions are clouding your science."

"Gentlemen." Stockton stayed reclined, elbows resting on chair arms.

Steve's hands came down. He remained squared off with the neurologist for a second, then turned to face him. "It's a lot to process, Stockton." His abandonment of formal address in deference to the boss was more telling of his exasperation than his outburst had been.

Stockton brought his chair upright and placed his elbows on the table. "I could use a good three hours of sleep about now." He stretched his arms out front, the palm of his right hand pressing against the back of his left, and brought them over his head as he arched his back. He brought them back down and gave in to a satisfying yawn. He rolled his shoulders and noticed the others' postures had relaxed. "Dr. Mammen, you have the floor."

"As I was trying to explain to Dr. Morrison before the meeting began," Chandan said, "the subject is not short on sleep, he's a short-sleeper."

"I assume you mean that as a diagnosis and not a pun," Stockton said.

Chandan's face went blank for a second, then his head wobbled. "No, no pun, Director. I took Dr. Morrison's concerns seriously. The patient's brain scans are not consistent with a diagnosis of insomnia or poor sleep hygiene. All his tests show him to be in prime health. The patient rarely sleeps more than three hours a night because three hours is all he needs. We call such people short-sleepers."

"Even if—and in my book, it's a big if—three hours is all he needs," Steve said, "he's had nights with much less than that, and several when he's woken himself screaming. We need more time."

"I'm afraid we've already used more than we had." Stockton came to his feet and strolled over to the coffee pot. The room remained quiet behind him as he poured the hot Colombian roast into a fresh mug. He turned to face the room, leaned against the refreshment counter, and took a sip as the steam bathed his sore eyes. "Sam, is the facility ready?"

The security chief checked his watch. "Echo team should be done with their run through. They'll need another twenty minutes to reset the systems."

Stockton took another swallow of hot coffee, trying to loosen the cold knot in his stomach. "Perfect. Dr. Morrison, time to get our boy."

Chapter 26

O korro kaj phenel ke chudela barr pe tute, lesko punrro musaj vuzhe t'azbal barr.

The blind man who threatens to stone you, his foot must already be touching a stone.

Romani proverb

FCA Campus, West Virginia – September 26, 1988

Drom waited in the chair at the foot of his bed, legs outstretched and ankles crossed. He glanced at the clockface reflection in the mirror above his dresser. 7:00 a.m. They were late. Or they were doing something new.

The room's electronic lock released with a click. The door swung in, the hand pushing it pale and dusted with freckles. Something new, then. And old.

"Come to finally see for yourself," Drom said.

Dr. Fredrick "you can call me Steve" Morrison stepped into the room like an underdressed man late for a funeral. Atlantic green eyes, framed in equal parts doubt and concern, measured him for a long moment. "I've been watching you since you got here." His eyes flicked toward the mirror. "But we were overdue for a face to face."

"Stockton and I worked out an arrangement, then he benched me. That your doing?"

"Not entirely," Steve said. "You know the Director. He has his processes and keeps his own counsel."

"And you, what's your counsel?"

"To not repeat the mistakes of the past." He palmed the beads of sweat off his high forehead, mopped his hand through the bush of his sandy-brown hair, and parked it at the back of his neck. "Do you remember what I told you my role was the first time we met?"

"You said you were here to help me."

"You didn't believe you needed help back then."

Drom rose. "If I still believed that, I wouldn't be here."

Steve's hand unhooked from the back of his neck and gave a thoughtful tug at the hair on his chin before dropping to his side. "It's been my experience that the help people say they want is seldom the type of help they really need."

Drom wondered if the doctor was probing him or warning him. "Well, Doc, my prison suite doesn't have a couch and you came without a notepad. I'm guessing you're not here for a psychotherapy session."

"Perceptive as always. I'm here to escort you to your next evaluation." He stuffed his hands in his pockets and his head tilted to the door as if his neck had tired of holding its weight.

Drom stared into the mirror and the surveillance equipment he suspected it concealed. "I take it you're still not happy with how the last blood test went." He turned back to Steve and stretched his hand toward the door. "Escort away, Doc."

The last time Drom was in FCA's custody, they housed him on the bottom floor of the main administration building. He woke up in an oversized hospital room with luxury furnishings and Dr. Morrison served him breakfast in bed. They worked to mend his mind and body. Then they set him loose on a blood-soaked rampage.

His current quarters sat in the Human Behavioral Sciences building of the Foundation's campus. The grounds—graced with manicured lawns and tree-lined walkways—had the feel of a small, private institution of higher learning. The feel was intentional, Drom knew, because the FCA was a private intelligence agency hidden inside a fully accredited university.

The university was Stockton's personal preserve of the best and the brightest. His students, curated at an early age from disadvantaged quarters and funneled into his institution after years of anonymous favor, graduated with a predisposition to his cause. They found placement in key sectors of government, military, industry, and finance becoming extensions of the Director's vast influence.

The building Steve led him to held none of the genteel charm of the university architecture it brooded over in monolithic ugliness.

If Stockton Wilson was the Wizard of Oz, the Warehouse was his curtain. Without it, influence was his only power. Drom's gaze traveled up the arch windows piercing granite walls that stretched six stories into the mountain air. The clouds above boiled in backdrop to a structure more at home near the Brooklyn dockyards than the West Virginia countryside.

"I had hoped we were past this," Drom said.

Steve's pace slowed and he glanced at Drom. "We had to come if only to find out."

The Director was waiting for them at the entrance. Beside him towered a barrel-chested man whose appearance reminded Drom of the vintage strong-man circus posters. Instead of dwarfing Stockton, the man's body-builder frame accentuated the grace of Stockton's ballet-dancer form. To Drom, the Director was the sleek, black bishop standing beside an oversized pawn.

"Gavin," Stockton said, "this is my Chief of Security, Sam Gerber."

Gerber put out a hand Drom suspected was capable of crushing lesser mortals. He left it hanging and eyed Stockton. "I burned my father's to the ground, what makes you think this one's safe?"

"Who said anything about it being safe?" Bloodshot eyes sat on their baggage in an otherwise placid face.

Gerber lowered his ignored hand. "Shall we do the briefing inside?"

Stockton glanced at Steve before responding. "After you, Gavin." He pulled the right side of the double doors open.

Neither Stockton's calm demeanor nor Steve's casual stroll managed to cloak either man's tension. The first time they brought him here didn't go well. Their apprehension was unwarranted, but he let them keep it anyway.

"Looks dark in there," Drom said. "Anyone have a lighter?"

As if in response to his veiled threat, the entrance brightened in invitation. Drom strode past Stockton with Steve close on his heels. Flood lights marched ahead of him, revealing portions of the Olympic-sized swimming pool, the target dummies on their rails, and the first band of obstacle courses. He paused, letting the lights finish their run.

The pool water sparkled under the mercury vapor lamps.

"The key," his father said, "is to not lose your sense of time. Any discomfort can be managed when you know how long it has lasted."

His father picked him up and tossed him into the deep end, the chains locked around his wrists and ankles dragging him through the chill water to the smooth cement floor three meters down. He ticked off the seconds as he worked the needle out of his thumb pad and attacked the first lock.

"Gavin." Hearing his name, he blinked the memory away. Steve was studying him intently. "Care to talk about it?"

"Nothing to say." Drom swung his gaze to where the scaffolding should have tangled up from the hardwood floors to the steel girders six stories overhead.

"We've done some remodeling," Stockton said.

"Leave it to you," Drom said, "to construct buildings inside a building."

"Pulling off an operation in a two-story restaurant you've had the run of for weeks is one thing. Infiltrating a secure facility based on an intelligence briefing is another."

He glanced at Stockton. "This is Boston?"

"No, Boston is later. You can think of this as Lexington, if you like."

"Always the revolutionary, eh, Stockton?"

The Director didn't respond. Instead, he glanced over his shoulder at the oversized pawn and sailed off to the control center, scooping Steve in his wake.

Drom eyed Gerber, his military posture and no-nonsense gaze fitting the mold of Stockton's penchant for recruiting from the special forces. "What do you have for me, Mr. Gerber?"

The security chief lifted the metal clipboard in his hand and drew a pen from the crowded vinyl sleeve in the breast pocket of his white, pinpoint Oxford shirt. He thumbed the plunger on the top of the pen and drew a red X in one of the rectangles on the diagram.

"The information you are to retrieve is in this file cabinet. The door to the office is here." He drew it in, a perpendicular line stubbing out from the larger square's border and connected to its wall with a swing-arc line. Gerber flipped the page and turned the clipboard sideways.

Drom leaned into the man's left side, craning his neck over the next diagram. "Why two buildings?"

"The five-story structure on the right is where the target office is. Fourth floor, middle office, here." He pointed to the office on the blueprint. "The shorter building across the alley is your way out."

Drom scrutinized the target building, taking in its window placements, ledges, and mortar grooves. His gaze swept across its flat roof, vaulted over the alley, and came down on the roof of the four-story. All the proportions were right. He was looking at a recreated skyline from downtown anywhere USA.

"Security?" he asked.

"In this scenario, we're granting unalarmed, front door access. Beyond that, armed security personnel will be actively patrolling both structures."

Drom spied the entrance to the five-story, then strode to poolside for a different angle. "You want me to enter a building with an armed security contingent and you expect me to go through the front door?" He turned toward the control center's bay window a stone's throw away and raised his hands to shoulder height. "Seriously?"

Through the glass, he saw Stockton lean into the microphone.

Gerber pressed a fingertip to his left ear and marched over to Drom. "I was of the understanding, Mr. Leoppard, that you have run through multiple training scenarios similar to this one in this very facility. Can you do the exercise or not?"

"Mr. Gerber, an infiltration such as you have outlined is a chess match. But you've set the board for checkers."

"I'm not following your logic."

"A real-world op like this calls for stealth. Your set up demands a brute force assault."

"You aren't being asked to assault anything. The task is to retrieve a file from the third cabinet from the left."

"Security have lethal ordnance?"

"It's an exercise, not an execution. They have marking rounds, non-lethal. You get chalked with a kill shot, it's game over."

Drom pressed into Gerber's personal space and glared up at him. "And if I kill them?"

Glowering, Gerber came nose-to-nose with him. "Game over."

Muted words spilled from Gerber's earpiece, Stockton jerking back on his dog's chain. Gerber got out of his face.

"I know a better way," Drom said. "May I see the plan again?"

Gerber handed him the clipboard. "What do you have in mind?"

Drom studied the print, then looked at the building. "Stockton's stage carpenters have done a great job on this set." He took the pen from Gerber's hand. "See the CCTV cameras they've placed near the roofline?" He pointed up with the pen, its bottom held against his thumbpad with his ring finger as he unscrewed the top barrel with his thumb and index finger.

Gerber's chin tilted up as he viewed the roofline.

Tightening his grip on the top barrel, Drom let the pen works spill from his hand. Spinning left into Gerber, he drove his elbow into the man's solar plexus, flicking the clipboard toward the control center's bay window at the same time. He thrust the pen barrel into the hollow of Gerber's throat with his right hand as the man doubled over. Air whistled as it struggled to enter the big man's lungs through the pen-point opening.

Continuing his spin, Drom swept Gerber into the pool. Water splashed to the background of shattering glass. He sprinted to the front door of the target building, Gerber's pen-filled pocket protector held firmly in his grasp.

⊕

The window shattered before Stockton registered what was happening. He threw an arm up, saving his face from the worst of the glass shrapnel. When he brought it down, Gavin and Gerber were gone.

"Son of a—"

"My eye, it's in my eye!" Steve writhed on the floor, holding his face.

Stockton jerked the handset from its cradle and stabbed one of the direct dial buttons on the phone base.

"Infirmary."

"I need EMTs in the Warehouse now." Water plumed out of the pool. He dropped the phone and ran to the pool, the crack of gun fire in his ears.

⊕

Drom hunkered behind a desk on the third floor, five disabled men scattered throughout the floors below. He would be on the fourth if they were dead. Emotional cost aside, killing unavoidable contacts was more efficient than maiming them.

He had to hand it to Stockton. He pushed his crews beyond façade building. The floors were decorated and furnished in bland governmental tones reminiscent of the FBI offices he had scoured through six weeks before. But the effect wasn't complete. The desks—devoid of accessories, tools, supplies, and personal mementos—made them ghost offices. Stockton provided form without function, leaving the space clean of any ammunition Drom could pick up along the way.

Whatever game Stockton was playing, it wasn't the scenario Gerber briefed him on. The objective was too simple, the obstacles too few. This test was about something else.

A carbine barked a double tap, tattooing the desk behind him with blue chalk. He made a mental note to talk with Gerber about his men's training. Searching shots wasted ammunition and gave the shooter's position away. He glanced at his two remaining pens, then studied the chalk patterns. He worked out the origin trajectory, chose the metal pen, and flung it as he rushed the guard. The pen impaled the man's trigger hand, severing the median nerve.

Howling, the shooter dropped the rifle and reached for his pistol with a left-handed cross draw. Drom slammed into him before he could skin it from the holster.

Stockton kneeled dripping next to Gerber while the EMTs worked on the half-drowned security chief. They extracted the pen tip, then executed a more orthodox emergency tracheotomy. Stockton stayed with them as they got the big man loaded on a gurney.

Someone dropped a beach towel across his shoulders. More shots echoed from the target building as he stumbled back to the control room. He found Steve manning the CCTV feed desk, his unbandaged eye flicking up and down as his head moved back and forth.

"You need to put a stop to this," Steve said.

"He has to play it out."

"You know how this ends." Steve turned to him, one eye pleading.

"How bad are you hurt?"

"Never mind me. What's Gerber's status?"

"He'll live."

Steve turned back to the monitors. "And Gavin?"

Stockton sank into the chair next to him, tight-lipped.

Drom dragged his latest victim into an office. Closing the door, the scanned the room for cameras. Finding none, he crept to the window and peered down. A medical team wheeled a gurney at double-time toward the exit, its payload too large to be any other than Gerber. He crawled back to the unconscious guard, removed his helmet, and grabbed his earpiece.

"—remaining."

"Hold position, Bravo." Stockton's voice, steady and commanding. "Charlie, do you have eyes on target, over?"

Silence.

"Charlie team, report. Over."

"Team—" Coughing blared in his ear. "Team down, sir."

"Sit rep."

"Charlie One and Three are unconscious. Lost visual and comms on Charlie Two."

"I have you on the feed, Charlie Four. Can you make your way out?"

Breathing. Cough. Hard swallows. "Negative. Request exfil. There's a bone sticking out below my knee and I'm losing blood."

"Bravo, retrieve Charlie Four from sector three-two-zero and exfil."

"Roger."

Stripping down the unconscious Charlie Two, Drom wished for Julia's quick-change skills. He had a minute, maybe less, to get in position.

⊕

"No fatalities," Stockton said.

"Yet." Steve's eye continued to flick across the screens.

Bravo One and Four vacated the bottom left monitor and popped onto the top middle one. Four took point in the Level Three corridor, his modified AR-15 held at the ready as he eased down the hallway. Bravo One cleared rooms behind his point man, his backward gait keeping time with Four's forward push. He disappeared from the middle top monitor and reappeared on the one next to it. Bravo One backstepped to the edge of the monitor, bounced off it, and fell forward cursing.

Four spun on heel, cheek pressed to rifle stock, then abandoned the carbine to its sling and moved off monitor. Bravo One rolled over, got to his feet, and passing through the side of the monitor, disappeared.

"Bravo Four, report."

"We have Charlie Two, sir. Says Target disabled him with a choke hold. His radio is damaged, but he's operational."

"Roger. Proceed with caution and exfil Charlie Four."

"Yes, sir."

All three guards appeared on the third top screen, Bravo Four still on point with Charlie Two flanking him. Bravo One held the rear as the team pushed down corridor to save their bleeding comrade.

⊕

"Lay him down and grab his thigh." Drom grabbed Charlie Four's ankle before the Bravo contingent could question his order. "Gentle, looks like his arm's broken too."

He groaned as they shifted him. They pressed down on his thigh and Drom jerked the ankle to him. The bone retracted with a pop. Charlie Four sat up with a scream and crashed back to the floor.

"You two need to get him out of here," Drom said.

"Where are you going?" Bravo Four asked.

"I'm pushing up to help Delta get this bastard."

The man pulled out his sidearm and handed it to Drom. "Lose the AR. Level Four is live ammo."

Drom thumbed the magazine release on the Beretta M9 and checked the load. Fifteen rounds, nine millimeter. He slapped it back into the grip and racked the slide. "Let's move."

"They're bringing him out," Steve said.

Stockton tore his eyes away from the lone figure creeping up the stairs—pistol trained on the landing above in a two-handed grip—and observed the exfiltration of Charlie Four. Bravo quickstepped from the building holding the casualty in a two-man fore-and-aft carry. EMTs rushed with a gurney to meet them.

"How many does that make?" Steve asked.

"Counting Gerber, nine."

"At the rate he's going, we're going to need a new security team."

Stockton put his hand on Steve's forearm and pivoted the doctor's chair to face him. "Those aren't our men."

Chapter 27

Men willingly believe what they wish.
Julius Caesar, *De Bello Gallico, III,* 57 BC

The Warehouse, FCA Campus – September 26, 1988

Pressing sideways against the door jamb, Drom cracked the door and peered down the deserted main corridor. Opening the door wider, he turned into it, hiding his right side from the stairwell camera. He cocked his right heel and snapped it down against the concrete floor. He spun into the door at the noise, banging it wide as he fired several rounds from the Beretta.

He kept firing as he backed into the corridor. "Intruder is armed! Take cover!" He dove sideways into the first office on his right, dragging his bleeding right calf across the carpet. He rolled clear of the doorway, sprang to his feet, and swept the room, pistol raised.

Desks and file cabinets greeted him with megalithic silence. Blood trickled down the shallow groove of the self-inflicted gunshot wound, soaking his sock. Wiping his brow with his shirtsleeve, he held his breath and listened.

Boot falls—faint, fast, and approaching.

Exhaling through pursed lips, he tucked in against the strike-side jamb and peeked down the corridor to the mahogany stairwell door pockmarked with bullet wounds. Muted jangles drifted up from behind him mixed with the rasp of boot soles against Berber carpet.

He slid out into the corridor, his back to the approaching guards, his aim on the stairwell. "Radio is down. Rest of Charlie team is out." Hugging the wall, he backstepped, his leg marking a blood trail.

Someone tapped his shoulder. A guard stepped past him on the left, his MP5 trained forward. A tug on the back of his collar directed him into another side room. A second operative came behind the first moving up the hallway, then the door closed, hiding them from view.

Drom was spun around and slammed against a wall. "The Colonel is going to vice your nuts in debrief, you stupid bastard. You guys were only supposed to carry non-lethal."

He shoved the man out of his face. "Back off, Sphincter King. Bravo jacked this op up, so shut your trap and toss me your med kit." He slid down the wall onto his buttocks and ripped the pant leg away from the wound. A black ballistic weave pouch landed between his legs.

"Take your time, numbskull. Drezic and Carter got the door covered. He won't get far."

Drom unsnapped the pouch and dumped the contents out. Grabbing the field bandage, he tore the packaging open with his teeth and wrapped his wound. "Help me up."

"Sit tight. We got this."

"You have no idea what you got. We couldn't chalk the guy, so I'm not confident Drezic or Carter can put a bullet in him. But once the firing starts, we'll both have a better chance if I'm on my feet." Drom stretched out his left arm.

The guard hesitated. He toggled his mic. "Drezic, any movement?" He listened. "Roger." He slung his submachine gun across his back. Bending forward, he grabbed Drom's arm. "You're not out of the vice yet."

"The Colonel is the least of my worries at the moment." Drom drew his left leg under him. "Just pull me up."

The guard pulled.

Drom sprang with a twist, slamming his right knee into the man's jaw. He dropped to the floor, out cold.

He grabbed the gauze roll, patch bandages, and tape from the med kit. Ripping open the bandages, he stuffed them into the guard's mouth. He pulled the helmet off and jerked the earpiece away, snapping its wire. He traced the wire to the radio unit and killed the power.

He blindfolded and gaged the man with the gauze, then taped his hands together behind his back. He unlaced his boots, rolled him over, and hogtied him with the strings.

He moved back to the door and cracked it. Drezic and Carter held their positions on either side of the corridor guarding the stairwell exit. He eased the door shut, then hurried over to the nearest desk. Tipping it up on end, he pushed it against the door. Climbing on top, he reached overhead and slid one of the ceiling tiles out of his way.

He stood up into the grid and waited for his eyes to adjust to the gloom. Darkness soon turned to pale shadows bright enough to reveal the cut corners of Stockton's set piece. The carpenters hadn't bothered with firewalls. Drom eased himself onto the top of the corridor wall and slid the ceiling tile back in place.

Stockton searched the control board again. He flipped several toggle switches and scanned the displays. He had a front angle view of the two guarding the corridor. The injured Charlie Two and the other Delta operative had ducked into an office. "You see them?"

"No," Steve said. "Can't find Gavin either."

Stockton's fingers danced across the board. "Third floor feeds. Look again."

"There." Steve pointed. A man in his underwear stumbled down a hallway.

Stockton whistled through his teeth. "Delta team is in trouble."

"You going to warn them?"

"No. They should have stopped him before he reached Level Four. They're on their own now." Stockton switched the feeds to the fourth floor and leaned back in his chair. "Keep your eyes on that corridor."

Drom wormed through the tight plenum space, keeping his weight on top of the jack walls and maneuvering around the evenly spaced king studs. He came to an intersection of hallways and checked memory of Gerber's diagram. He needed to go right.

Stretching out, he grasped a joist. Once sure of his grip, he brought his left foot up and pressed it against the face of the joist connected to the corner king stud. He moved his injured leg next and planted his right foot beside his left. He worked his way along the intersecting corridor, the joists his horizontal, upside-down ladder.

The air pulsed with the heat of the lighting fixtures. Sweat slicked his hands, forcing him to rely more and more on the tension of his undercling. His right calf screamed in protest. Salt burned his eyes. He craned his head all the way back to check behind him. Twenty joists to go.

Pushing forward a few yards more, he wedged in hard with three points of contact and pulled up a ceiling tile with his right hand. He dried his palm on his pant leg, gripped the joist, and shook his left arm out. He wiped the hand dry and clamped it back on the wood. Drawing his knees to his chest, he pivoted his body down, threading his legs through the opening in the ceiling grid. He stretched straight and let go.

The plyboard beneath him boomed like a drum.

He checked over his shoulder to the target office three doors down. Ahead, boot falls—fast, loud, and closing. Drezic and Carter pounding to him. He drew the pistol. How many Delta operatives covered Level Four? He holstered the weapon and pulled out Gerber's last pen.

"There!" Steve tapped the screen.

Stockton skated his chair over for a closer look. A body lay facedown in the target corridor. "When did that show up?"

"I just noticed it."

He spun back to take in the monitor array. Two Deltas approached the body. One stopped short and held a covering position, the other knelt to check on the fallen guard. Removing his glove, he placed two fingers on the man's neck. His head turned to his partner who nodded in acknowledgement of whatever was said.

"Do we have audio?" Steve asked.

Stockton turned the volume knob up as they rolled the body over.

"—it!" The guard sprang up, his back blocking the body from view.

The other man toggled his mic. "Delta Three to Control. Request medic ASAP."

"Delta Three, Control," Stockton said. "Need visual to assist."

The man swiveled his head and his eyes locked on the camera. "Carter, step left."

Stockton pushed on the control board's miniature joystick, zooming in on the body. Gavin's blood-soaked face came into view, a pen buried halfway into his eye socket.

"Get them out of there!" Steve made a grab for the microphone.

Stockton caught his wrist and held it firm. "It has to play out."

"He's going to—"

Gunfire erupted from the speakers.

On the monitor, two men writhed on the floor, dark stains spreading across the carpet under their knees. Gavin kicked their MP5s out of reach, then holstered his pistol. Bending down, he picked something up and faced the camera.

Eyes open in a hard gaze, he raised his hand and they could make out the back half of a pen in his hand. He flicked and static filled the screen.

Drom steeled himself against Drezic's and Carter's pleas for help. They were Stockton's responsibility, not his. He maneuvered to the target door. Four Alpha, Four Bravo, Four Charlie. Three Delta? He wasn't buying it. He waited.

No rescuers came for the screaming men.

Drawing the pistol, he dropped the magazine into his hand. Empty. He shoved it into the grip and pulled the slide back a fraction. His last round was chambered. He released the slide, pointed the pistol forward, and turned the knob with his left hand.

He slipped into the room and found himself in another world.

"Echo team, you have eyes on?" Stockton switched all views to the target room and cut the hallway audio feed.

"Subject is in sight."

"Hold for my signal."

"Copy, Control."

"Delta, you copy? Acknowledge."

"Those are my men bleeding out there."

"Subject has advanced. Your men are alive. No one moves until I say. Acknowledge."

"Copy, Control. Holding for your signal."

He closed the door, shutting out the cries of the wounded and blocking the harsh florescent light from the hallway. A row of narrow, bullet-gray, metal filing cabinets bathed in the twilight on the wall to his left. Across the room stretched floor-to-ceiling windows displaying the urban sprawl far below.

He knew the city.

He knew this place. Dark paneling covered the walls between built-in mahogany bookcases. Staining these touches of modern Spanish décor were the castaways from some government surplus warehouse. A computer terminal wired to a printer squatted on a metal and pressboard banquet table. Folding chairs peppered the space like the scattered remains of a late-night poker game.

The meanness of the cabinets was upstaged by a monstrosity of steel and Formica, the desk of the beast of this lair.

Drom holstered the pistol.

His gaze swept past the desk through the window to the dusk shrouded blocks of the city below. Somehow, Stockton had transported him to the eighteenth floor of #8 Calle Isabela, Madrid, Spain.

Third file cabinet from the left. Its contents had upended his life before. What bones lie buried there now?

⊕

Stockton leaned in toward the monitors, fingers curled around the microphone stand and his thumb hovering over the talk button.

Gavin holstered the pistol. He turned a slow three-sixty, his head sweeping up and down. He rocked the first cabinet away from the wall and walked it with twists and turns until it blocked the door. He planted himself in front of the third file cabinet. Seconds spun their way to minutes on the monitor's time display.

"He's not taking the bait," Steve said.

"He will. He doesn't have a choice." Stockton held his right hand at the ready, his left tapping out the rhythm of his tension on the desk.

⊕

The middle drawer held the only files in the cabinet. Their white labels stood out in contrast to the manila background. The names were typed in black, all caps: BOSTON, DENVER. He lifted them out, slid the drawer shut, and set the folders on top of the cabinet.

BOSTON promised to bring him closer to Bastien Frabron, to safeguarding his family.

He opened DENVER.

The first photo captured a man in profile beside a sedan in front of a house. Drom hadn't seen him since his own funeral three years' previous. Robert Gladstone, Jr.—Shane Leoppard's oldest son—bore the stamp of his father's likeness as deeply as Drom carried his talents.

Robert's face always unsettled him.

He slid the eight-by-ten to the bottom of the stack.

The next several shots gave glimpses of the Gladstones' life through the windows of their modest home. Sharon at the stove. Robert bending over a toddler bed. Kyle boosted at the table.

An outdoor shot followed, the back garden perhaps, Robert and Sharon squaring off. Her arms crossed, his open and upraised with torso tilted forward. *"What's the matter with you?"* Drom could hear his father saying. He knew the stance, the emotion on the face. He shuffled the photo down.

Michelle appeared in living color, chestnut hair framing her oval face. A slight smile played across her full lips. Gold-flecked eyes sparkled atop flushed cheeks. A teal, sleeveless knit top revealed tanned shoulders. Her hands held an earthenware mug aloft, about to drink or about to set it down.

Drom's pulse hammered in his ears. His right calf begged for attention.

A wide-angle shot came next, his wife smiling at Robert across the table. He flipped through the scenes. Robert holding David. Michelle holding Robert, her lips on his cheek. Denver held dangers he hadn't foreseen.

Everyone has a weakness.

"Why did you come here?"

Drom spun, picture in hand.

The massive bulk behind the mammoth desk rose, scalp glistening under blond stubble. "I thought we had an understanding, you and I."

Drom fought for air. His right leg trembled. His bladder threatened to void.

The man stalked out from behind the desk, all shoulders and meaty claws. Toxic green eyes glared at him over gluttonous cheeks.

"How…?"

John Swenson, his mother's murderer and Gavin Leoppard's most brutal kill, stepped closer. "What did you come here for?"

"You're not real."

Galaxies exploded in concert with the force crashing into the side of his head. He bounced off the cabinets and fell forward into a punch that lifted him off the floor, followed by another that plowed him down into it. He gasped, forcing his diaphragm to move.

A bulbous nose pushed its way through the stars of his pain. Foul breath spilled across square, yellow teeth. "Why did you come here?"

I came for revenge.

"You can't be real."

The giant lifted him and tossed him against the inset bookcases. Shelves tore loose, raining books on him as he crashed to the floor. He caught a leather-bound volume in each hand.

His opponent stomped forward and cocked his leg back like he was going for a field goal. Drom let fly with both hands. The first took out the man's supporting knee, the second slammed into the bridge of his nose as he fell forward.

Drom rolled left, narrowly escaping being crushed. He scrambled away from the wall and got to his knees.

Swenson was on his feet already. He felt his nose, then wiped his fingers on his shirtsleeve, staining it with blood. "You're nothing but Gypsy trash. You want to know why you're here? You're here so I can take you out like I did your whore mother."

Drom drew the pistol and fired the last round. The Madrid city scape behind the desk shattered in an explosion of glass and sparks. He stripped the slide off the Baretta's frame and held the pieces up in his hands. "Call your double off, Stockton. I think we've gone far enough."

The giant charged.

⊕

Stockton scrubbed his eyes. Sleep clawed at him. Shaking it off, he bent over his desk and read the after-action report again.

What happened in Spain?

The intercom button flashed. He tapped it. "Yes, Beth?"

"Sorry to disturb you, sir, but he insisted I put him through."

"He's early."

"By an hour, at least."

"Give me five, then put him through."

"Yes, sir."

Stockton reviewed the list of damages. Gerber should make a full recovery. He wouldn't be yelling at his men anytime soon, though. Steve had a lacerated cornea. Stockton shipped him out to a specialist. The cost of the control center's bay window was negligible compared to the thousands it would take to replace Echo team's high-tech projection display destroyed by Gavin's last bullet.

Gavin.

He had slipped past a quarter of the building's defenders. The rest were less fortunate. Their injuries stretched the resources of the emergency personnel and the two operating rooms of the modest hospital the FCA called the Infirmary.

"No fatalities," he said to Steve.

"Yet."

Steve's reply rang in his conscience.

A button on his phone flashed, yellow and demanding. He stabbed it down. "Wilson speaking."

"How long before the tapes get here?"

No salutation, no small talk. Straight to the chase like his hard-charging career. Stockton sank back in his chair and picked up the handset. "Good afternoon, Colonel. How's the weather in Washington?"

"Cut the crap, Wilson. Tapes, when?"

"You received the after-action report or is your fax on the fritz?"

"Spare me the sarcasm and get me more reliable evidence. Your report isn't worth blowing my nose on. You expect me to believe one man did all that?"

"I told you I had the asset you needed for the job. The after-action report confirms it. You're welcome to come down here and debrief Gerber yourself."

"Not likely. Your report says he's a week away from even trying an electrolarynx. What's the status on Haak?"

"He's in surgery."

"Still?"

"You're early."

"I'm concerned. You made a special request for him. His assignment to this exercise put several other operations on hold. I need to know his status ASAP."

"He was critical when we got him to the OR. Even if the doctors get the recoil spring and guide rod out of his neck without killing him, he won't be returning to active duty. Ever."

There was a long silence. Stockton held his tongue and waited the Colonel out. Finally, the other man cleared his throat and spoke. "Recoil spring and guide rod?"

"Yes. My asset impaled Haak with them behind the mandible under his car."

"That wasn't in the after-action."

Stockton checked his watch. "Patient men get better information."

Breathing, undergirded with shuffling paper, filled the line. "You think he'll pull through?"

"It's a complicated surgery, but the doctors are confident. If my asset intended to kill him, he wouldn't have made it out of the building, let alone onto the operating table."

"Tapes?"

"My courier leaves within the hour. I'll need the funds wired to proceed." He was cash starved and stretched thin. The capital infusion was critical.

"If I like what I see, you'll get the first installment by mid-morning. Get me an update once Haak's off the table."

"Call me in an hour. I'll make sure to be available."

With a clatter of hard plastic, and the line went dead.

Stockton hung up. He steepled his fingers and rested his chin on them, eyes closed. Shane Leoppard's son had changed. Without Stockton's trainers, his skills had improved. Without Steve's sessions, he had greater self-control. And yet … and yet, he was unpredictable.

He sat up at the knock on his door and rolled closer to his desk. "Come in."

"Sorry, sir." Beth entered, papers in hand. "This morning's transcript was sent over hours ago. With all the commotion, I forgot to put it on your desk."

Stockton took the report from her. He scanned through it and stopped where it correlated to what he had heard.

ASSET: Ten. The young lions suffer want and hunger, but those who seek the Lord lack no good thing.

[ASSET exhales, then inhales.]

ASSET: Eleven. Come, O children, listen to me: I will teach you the fear of the Lord.

Stockton glanced up at Beth. "Have you read through this?"

"Yes, sir."

"It reads like something out of the Bible. What's your take?"

"It's one of the Psalms, but I don't think he was reciting."

"What then?"

"Praying, sir. I think he was praying."

Chapter 28

In wartime, the movement of nomads—most having ethnic character specific to the Romani, bohemians, and Gypsies—who under the guise of tinsmiths, basket makers or horse dealers travel along roads without concern for hygiene or legal regulations constitutes a danger to the national defense and safeguarding of secrets. The nomads incessant displacements permit them to discover important intelligence information that they are likely to communicate to enemy agents. Accordingly, nomads are to be subject to internment or compulsory residency and are required to live under police supervision.

"Decree Regarding Nomads"
French Third Republic, April 6, 1940

Gurs, France – May 28, 1942

Volvi tut, múrri Rrómniorri. Hishoro replayed his words over and over as she chased sleep under the table. A low rumble drummed through the wind, rhythmic and mechanical. She wrapped her shawl tighter around her shoulders. *Volvi, tut, múrri ...*

Whistles, insistent and sharp. She patted around for Tshompi then recalled what she had done. Did Tshuri succeed?

The other women wandered out of in clumps, some with children, most with none. Alone, Hishoro took a moment to steel herself. She retied her headscarf, its field of flowers covering her crown and flowing down to the middle of her back. She brought her two long braids forward over her shoulders and smoothed out her skirts. Striding into the gray light of dawn, she merged with the procession streaming toward the assembly yard under the screeching blare of the gendarmes' whistles.

Quickening her pace, she marched into a swirl of bright dresses, long braids, and curses. Camouflaged in the company of other Roma, she hoped to avoid scrutiny until she was ready. As they trudged to the roll call, she fueled animosity toward their jailers with her bitter complaint.

"They've stolen my babies and won't give them back."

Others joined her refrain and their rage infected the rest. The Roma entered the assembly yard in an uproar.

"*Rassemblement! Formez les rangs!*" The guards punctuated their orders with shoves and whistle trills.

The Roma mob refused to get in line. "Give us our children! Where are our babies?" Hishoro's voice drove the rest, amplifying the shouts.

The guards closed ranks, truncheons held horizontally at chest level, and pressed against the crowd to force them into formation. The women pushed back. Hishoro stayed behind the front line, stoking the rage. "Bastards! They took our horses, burned our wagons. Now they've stolen our children!"

The woman in front of her knocked a guard down. The one beside him smashed his truncheon across the woman's shoulders. Hishoro flew at him, all teeth and nails. Bodies piled into her, smothering her in the melee. She kicked and clawed indiscriminately.

Gunfire and bugle blasts cut through the din. The press around her melted away. The shouting tapered off as the riot died. She was pulled to her feet and marched to the front with several others. She twisted in the guard's grip looking to see how many had been shot. No bodies littered the ground.

An officer approached the guards holding the singled-out offenders. "Get their names and take them to the prison barracks to await loading."

Hishoro pulled fire and fell on her knees in front of the officer. "My children." She gripped his trousers above the boot tops. "They took my boys to the infirmary. I must see them."

He swatted her hands away with his swagger stick and lashed her face with a backswing. "Get this Gypsy whore to the prison barracks now."

Rough hands jerked her to her feet. Shouted names followed her as she was led out of Block J with eight others. The women marched as ordered with a steady stream of whispered curses and insults at the guards, some in French, most in Romani.

They moved north on the midway past the cheering and jeering fence flies of Block L. As they approached the Isle of Reprisals, Hishoro spotted a train at the platform outside the main gate. Recalling the muted rumbles in the night, she wondered at the lack of commotion that usually attended the delivery of new inmates.

The gendarmes took them through the barbed wire alley into the inner yard of the prison block. She eyed the lone barracks. Unlike the rest, it had proper wood siding instead of tar paper walls. Its entry was in the middle of the long side facing the midway. The metal door was bolted shut and secured with a round padlock the size of a small dinner plate. There were no windows, just framed ventilation slots near the eves.

A guard unlocked the door and swung it open. "Let's go! Move! Move! Move!"

Hishoro needed to go inside, had instigated a riot to do so. Now, facing the open door, she hesitated. What if she went in only to find Keti's corpse? What if she went in never to come out again? The other women filed past. A sharp poke in her back made her jump forward.

"Inside, move," the guard said.

She turned on him. "My children, when do I see my boys?"

"Get inside before I drag you inside!"

She stepped into the darkness. Fetid air enveloped her like a wet blanket— an overwhelming assault of urine, excrement, menstrual rags, and stale sweat. Gagging, she shuffled behind the others through the central corridor. A guard opened a door on the left. They filed through and it banged shut behind them.

Light from the ventilation slots left the interior in shades of gray. She sipped the air in shallow breaths. Three-tiered bunks crowded either side, leaving a claustrophobic aisle between them. The aisle soon clogged with women spilling into it from the bunks and spaces in between. A cacophony of questions and jeers surrounded the new inmates as they plowed forward.

"Keti! Keti!" Hishoro pushed through the packed women, searching the bunks tier by tier. Empty platforms spurred her on, listless stares gave her pause. She clambered to a top bunk and was torn from her hold. She smacked to floor on her side, knocking the wind out of her.

"Keep your filthy Gypsy hands off my bunk!"

Hishoro got to her hands and knees and fought the foul air into her lungs. A blow to her rear sprawled her on the floor. She rolled onto her back and kicked out with both feet. The woman standing over her stumbled back with a yelp. Hishoro got her legs under her. The woman moved forward. Hishoro held her palms out. "I'm looking for Keti."

The woman tipped her head to the right. "*Gitanes* are in the back with the piss buckets."

Hishoro slipped past her. "Keti! Keti!"

The stench worsened with each step forward. A makeshift curtain of blankets, slips, and dresses hung at eye level across the back wall. A woman stepped out, pinch-faced and frail.

"Keti!"

Her sister looked up, squinting. "Hishoro?"

"Keti, I'm here." She squirmed through the last knot of women and embraced her twin.

Keti hooked her left arm around her waist. "Help me to my bunk."

Hishoro took a half-step back and examined her. Keti was bent forward and swaying, her lame arm keeping time like a broken pendulum. "Where?"

"Hold me up, I'll drag us there."

Hishoro moved to her side and slipped an arm around her waist. Keti leaned into her and shuffled forward. At the second row of bunks, Keti chin-pointed right. Hishoro took them in. "Which one?"

"Bottom."

She backed them to the bunk and lowered them down with a slow squat. Seated, she turned to her sister. "What's wrong?"

"Why are you here?"

One of the new internees stepped into the row. "Wicked *gazhe* accuse us of kidnapping babies and then rob us of our children." Others in earshot affirmed the woman's complaint, their clamor filling the barracks. The coals of the morning's fury flared into flame. The Roma beat on the walls with their fists. Their pounding settled into a rhythm, their cries into a melodic wail.

At first, the other women shouted against them. But Roma fists turned the wooden prison into a drum. French Jews, Spanish expatriates, and petty criminals abandoned their dissonance and joined the beat. The walls shook.

Keti leaned into her. "Tshompi and the twins, where are they?"

"The nurses took the twins."

Keti pushed away from her. "How could you let them?"

Keti's scowl hit her like a slap. Her cheeks grew hot and she dropped her gaze. "Tshompi needed me." Her response evaporated in the shouting.

Keti shook her shoulder until she looked at her. "Where is Tshompi?"

"Tshuri came. I made him take Tshompi."

A crash broke through the clamor, followed by shouts louder than the screams. Glancing toward the door, Hishoro spotted dark blue uniforms breaking through the prints and polka dots.

Hishoro rose. "Can you stand? They'll be on us soon."

Keti took Hishoro's hand and pulled herself up. "I'm weak, but I'll manage."

She reached the aisle and was ripped away from Keti. She pulled against the hands holding her, twisting back to keep her sister in sight.

Keti staggered after her. "Don't fight. Go."

Pushing and prodding, they forced her outside. All was shouts, whistles, and confusion. Squinting in the mid-morning sun, she tried to get her bearings. Spinning about, she spotted Keti and lunged toward her. Blinding pain exploded across the left side of her head. She hit the ground dazed.

Rolling onto her side, she could make out legs forming lines. The cries of the women faded away. Baritone words, measured and thin-edged, filled the void.

"I should punish the lot of you. We are a civilized camp. Such outbursts cannot be allowed. Sergeant!"

They pulled her to her feet. Her pulse hammered in her head and she feared her skull would crack, if it wasn't already. Her stomach twisted with the pain, splashing her throat with bile. Sparks danced in the air as she scanned the lines for Keti.

She was spun away from the formation and frog-marched toward the barracks. As she drew near, she spotted a pillory to the left of the door she hadn't noticed before. They locked her into the device. She stood on tiptoe to keep from choking against the bottom brace.

"Many of you will be moving to a work camp today. But we must have order on the train. We must have order here."

Fire broke across her back. She flinched up, striking the nape of her neck against the rough wood holding her down. Before she could recover, a second lash crossed the first and her legs gave out. Choking, she struggled through two more blows to prop herself on tiptoe and catch a breath. The lashes rained down and she thrashed against the pillory, screeching like a wounded animal.

The torture stopped.

Hishoro pressed into the pillory for support. Sobs racked her lungs as tears, snot, and spittle dripped from her face. Her legs shook and she fought to keep her feet under her. Her back was in flames, her agony still rising despite the lack of additional blows.

"Ten lashes is light punishment for all the trouble this *gitane* sow caused today. Anyone stepping out of line on the train will receive twice as many. France has been generous to you. She has given you food and housing and now, work. We will not put up with any demonstrations of ingratitude."

The pillory unlocked and she spilled to the ground.

"Get in line," a guard said.

She struggled to her feet and staggered to the formation. She made her way down the file, subtle hands supportively guiding her into the center of the grid. Names barked out and inmates answered. Keti's calico dress caught her eye and she headed to her side.

"*Shingale,*" Keti said, devils. "Someone should punish them."

Swaying beside her sister, Hishoro thought of Tshuri's swollen face and bloody hands. "Somebody already has."

Alfonso and Pierre stirred in her arms and she buried her face in their hair, fighting against the pain pulling her from the beautiful dream. The pain won, forcing her eyes open. It was a dream, and not. Her boys were in her lap. She was awake on the train, awake in her nightmare.

It was midday before the guards led the inmates out of the Isle of Reprisals. They joined the column streaming toward the main gate. Hundreds of people marched ahead of them, hundreds more flowed behind. The train rolled forward, pulling another coach car in line with the platform. Gendarmes herded people inside.

Hishoro and Keti helped each other onto the platform. Through the windows of the German coaches, Hishoro made out the sparse interior furnished with plain, wooden benches. She needed to get them inside before they collapsed.

She tugged on Keti's arm. "*Háide!*" Come on! She shoved through the line. Some cursed in protest, none moved to stop them. The coach door loomed within reach. A gendarme stepped in their way.

He pointed his baton down the line of the train. "Gypsies go in the last car."

Turning left, Hishoro squinted toward the horizon. The train bent around a curve, no end in sight. Men, women, and some children trekked down the line stumbling in the castoff track ballast. Gendarmes kept vigil along the siding, threatening and shouting whenever anyone stopped or fell. Hishoro turned back to the guard.

"Move along," he said.

Head pounding, back burning, legs shaking, she moved, pulling Keti with her. They hobbled like uncoordinated Siamese twins toward the end of the train. It slipped forward, overwhelming Hishoro with vertigo. She clung tighter to her sister.

"Careful," Keti said in full older-sister tone, "or you'll knock us both down."

Hishoro stared at the train wheels, hearing Keti's screams as their father's wagon rolled over her arm. "I didn't mean to."

"Of course, you didn't."

"We should run away, hide until they leave."

"Run how? Hide where? Keep moving. I can't bear seeing you whipped again."

"The boys …"

"You're no good to them dead. Come on."

The last coach was a cattle car.

Hands reached out and helped them in. Keti's face twisted in on itself as two men hauled her up by the arms. Hishoro yelped as they lifted her up. Biting her lip, she caught the rough floorboards with her knee and pressed down to leverage herself in. Scrambling to her feet, she thanked the men.

"*Dále!*"

The boys ran into her with such force she almost toppled back out of the car. Pain forgotten, she bent down and wrapped them in her arms. "Alfonso! Pierre!" She kissed them, her tears cutting tracks on their dirty faces. "You are here. *Nayis le Devléske.*" Thanks be to God!

She clung to them as the flow of humanity forced them deeper into the boxcar. Keti captured her somehow, anchoring them in a space she had carved out by the back wall. Hishoro sunk to the floor beside her sister and wept, her sobs pouring out in waves she couldn't restrain.

The boys piled in atop her skirts. Keti's soft lullaby filtered through Hishoro's sobs and built a dam against her fear, pain, and loss. The train slipped forward and gained speed. Under the soothing melody and over the rhythmic tracks, she fell away into darkness.

Awake now, she filled her lungs with suffocating air. The train was stopped. Through the slot high on the side wall, she could make out a few stars. She swallowed on a dry throat.

Keti tugged on her arm. "Stand up, the air is better up here."

She did her best to slip out from under the boys without waking them. Pierre whimpered, Alfonso coughed, then they settled back down. Stretching her numb legs, she took a deep breath. The air was better, but not by much. "How long?"

"Long enough to make me worry."

"Where are we?"

"I don't know. We've been heading northeast all day. Can you stand for a while? I'll sit with the boys."

"Water?"

Keti squeezed her hand and squatted to the floorboards.

The train lurched forward, the press of those around her all that held her up. She listened to the night noises of this enforced *kumpániya*. Coughs, cries, and whispered conversations reminded her that she wasn't alone, her suffering not unique or new. They were Roma.

Movement brought the breeze with it, its freshness reviving. Dawn stabbed through the air slots. The train rolled on. By midday, the heat offset the benefit of the breeze. Her boys woke up, begging for food with the tenacity of four-year-olds.

Keti slept.

The boys whined. Hishoro shooshed them. They whined louder. A different wail cut across their complaint, rose a half tone, then bounced through a measure of notes. The twins quieted. The violin played on, picking up tempo and flow. She couldn't see the source and marveled at the wonder of it. Farther away, a guitar joined in. Soon after, feet stomped in counterpoint to the click clack of the rails.

Someone took up the song and other voices joined in. Keti stirred, then rose to her feet. With no quarter and short of air, the Roma danced with minced steps. Compressed humanity moved as one, circulating in the confines of their fouled space. Hishoro lost herself in the music, choosing the moment and movement over pain and fear.

The *gazhe* stole their horses and burned their wagons. They split their families and robbed their freedom. But they couldn't take their hearts.

Sometime after sundown, the wail of the locomotive whistle drifted to them. The train slowed, then stopped. Minutes later, it lurched forward and stopped again. The intermittent motion took on a predictable pattern. The chatter in the boxcar intensified, filled with questions and speculations.

"I hope they have food," Keti said.

"I'd be glad for some water." She stroked her boys' heads, trying to remember the last time they had a drink.

After another lurch and stop, the doors rolled open. Roma poured out into the shouts of the gendarmes.

Hishoro gripped her boys' hands and stuck behind Keti. They were herded off the platform, down a cordoned path, and through a double set of gates. Sulfur lights splashed their harsh glare on the bare ground of the deep courtyard before them. At the edges, walls with evenly spaced windows rose into the night.

"Where are we?" Keti asked.

Hishoro shrugged her shoulders and instantly regretted it.

A man in front of them turned around, removed his hat with a short bow, and swept the view with it. "Welcome to Paris, the City of Light."

Chapter 29

1976 FORD GRAN TORINO – 2-door hardtop. AM-FM stereo, AC, power steering. Red paint, no rust. Runs great. $700 or best offer. Phone 555-1288

Classified Ads, *Rocky Mountain News*, September 28, 1988

Colorado Foothills – October 5, 1988

Shell stepped into the morning, taking a moment to admire the Rockies towering over the aspen. If she ever made it back to the Ozarks, she knew would never see them as mountains again. Stuffing her hands into her coat pockets, she turned away from the scenery and walked over to the cabin.

Jakob begged his way into a sleepover with Kyle the night before. His antics would have normally earned him a resounding no. But the circumstances were far from normal. Fighting on many fronts, Shell lacked the energy to deny him his fun and gave in. And overslept.

Leaves crunched underfoot, the sound seeming irreverent in the quiet mountain air. Lightening her gait, she tiptoed onto the porch. She raised her hand to knock on the cedar door, then didn't.

Muffled conversation spiked with laughter vibrated through the wood. Robert and Sharon were up with all the kids. Oversleeping made her uneasy. Waking up to an empty motorhome didn't help. Amanda got out with David while she snored. What if it had been somebody else?

She turned to the wilderness surrounding them. Somebody else would have to know they were here. Pizza man assured them no one did.

"Leaving so soon?" Robert asked.

She jumped. "For goodness' sake, didn't Hazel teach you not to sneak up on people?"

"No, but mom did teach me to knock." He posed in signature Hazel. "Robert, it's impolite to step on someone's porch and just stand there."

"She did not." Shell smacked his shoulder. "Don't scare me like that."

His smile faded. "Sorry, I didn't mean to …" He cleared his throat. "Brunch is ready. Why don't you come in and eat?"

The door stood open behind him and she could see to the kitchen in the back. The kids were packed around the table and Sharon was dishing out scrambled eggs from a cast iron skillet. "Any coffee left?"

"For you? Always."

She followed him inside. Sharon glanced up at their approach. The skillet clanged down onto the stovetop.

"Mama, painpanks!" David stabbed the short stack on his plate with glee.

"You should have some," Robert said. "Sharon's blueberry pancakes are the best."

"I'm sure they're great," Shell said, "but I'm still waking up. Coffee will do for now."

"Pot's fresh, help yourself." Sharon sat down between Jakob and Kyle. "Eat up, boys, before your eggs get cold."

Shell made eye contact with Amanda. Her daughter swallowed a mouthful of food with a healthy dose of milk. "I wanted to let you rest."

Shell left it there. She was irritated and had no right to be, which irritated her even more. She grabbed a mug from the cupboard, then a second. She filled them both and handed one to Robert. "I take mine black. Not sure how you like yours." Squeezing in between David and Amanda, she contented herself with watching her children eat.

Sharon wouldn't look at her. She busied herself with Kyle and Jakob as if they were the only ones at the table.

Robert ate in silence, his eyes on his plate, his expression miles away.

Shell lied. She knew how he liked his coffee. And his eggs. They grew up together, went to school together, worked together. She knew that look. He was lost in thought, trying to work it out. And he was hiding something. Still.

⊕

The Gladstones returned that night to a ransacked house. "I think it's time for me to leave," she said.

Sharon stood wide-eyed, taking in the destroyed living room. "What the—"

264

Robert's hand clapped over her mouth. Tapping a finger over his closed lips, he lowered his hand. He pointed at the couch and left the room.

Sharon turned to her, eyes welling up and hands trembling.

Shell sat frozen on the couch, too worn from the day to give comfort, too shocked to move. Robert's footfalls traveled upstairs. Moments later, his steps echoed in the kitchen and tapered off. Checking the basement apartment, probably. Things there weren't as bad as upstairs. She had spent the rest of the day straightening up her living quarters.

She was packed. The children were asleep in their street clothes. She had waited in the dark, wanting to catch them and leave before Robert could call the police.

Hugging herself, Sharon plopped down on the shredded cushion next to Shell. She leaned into her and Shell leaned back in a rare show of support.

A door click followed by steps on linoleum. The plastic rattle of the kitchen handset coming off the cradle. Shell sat up, ready to bolt.

"I'd like a large Italian sausage with onions, olives, and peppers. No anchovies. How long? Thank you."

He came into the living room and collapsed into the crippled arm chair on their right.

"Robert Gladstone, Jr., what in heaven's name is going on?" Shell's voice touched the edge of shrill.

He ran his hands through his hair and laid his head back on the chair. "Pizza will be here in a half-hour. We can talk after that."

Sharon pushed herself off the couch. "I'm going to check on Kyle."

Robert stared at the ceiling, ignoring her as she passed.

"Robert," Shell said, "what happened to you today?"

He faced her for a long moment, a sad half-smile on his face so reminiscent of Drom that her heart ached. "The pizza is worth the wait."

The pizza was mediocre. The pizza man wasn't.

He walked straight into the kitchen, opened his thermal pouch, and pulled out a black plastic case with stainless trim and latches. The pizza came out next. "Cash or credit?"

"Cash only," Robert said.

The man opened the plastic case and lifted out a piece of electronic gear that looked like a portable cassette recorder. He plugged in a set of earphones and something resembling a small microphone and waived it around the kitchen.

The pizza was down to two slices by the time the delivery man finished going through the house. Shell had had no appetite until she took the first bite. After that, it was difficult to stop, mediocre or not.

"You're clean." The man shot a glance at Shell and Sharon, then turned back to Robert. "They find it?"

Robert shook his head.

"Good. Stay put until you hear from us." He packed up and left.

Sharon's chin trembled. "Babe, what have you gotten us into?"

"I work for some dangerous people."

"Dangerous people? You're a computer programmer, Robert. I had to bail you out of jail and my house is destroyed." Her tears flowed unabated now. Her shuddering said she was scared. Her tone and face broadcast anger. "What's she got to do with this?" Her arms stayed crossed, but she might as well have pointed a finger.

"No need to worry about me," Shell said. "Let my babies sleep tonight. We'll be out of your lives in the morning." She marched across the kitchen to the basement door.

"Michelle—" Sharon's explosion cut off Robert's plea.

Shell closed the door.

⊕

"Can we, Mommy?" Jakob's voice brought her back to the present. He was leaning toward her, his belly pressed against the table.

"I'm sorry, honey, can we what?"

"Hike with Miss Sharon and Kyle to the lake."

"Can we?" Amanda said. "I want to climb that wall."

Shell locked eyes with Sharon across the table. The other woman looked away. Shell helped herself to a bite of pancakes from Amanda's plate. "I don't know. After all that food, David's going to weigh a ton."

"The hike's not that bad, Mommy. He can walk." Amanda snatched her fork back.

She drained her mug and set it down. "We should clean this mess up first."

Sharon got up. "Knock yourself out. Grab your coats, boys, in case it gets cold."

Kyle and Jakob scurried from the table and followed Sharon outside. A moment later, she came back in and grabbed their jackets off the hooks in the entry and left.

Shell pushed away from the table. "I'll clean up. You two run along. I'll bring David to the lake once I'm done."

"Thanks, Mommy." Amanda bolted out the door.

"Amanda, your coat!" Too late, her daughter was gone.

Robert stacked the dirty plates. "If we work together, we can get these done in no time."

"Too much time alone. Go. I've got this."

He lingered a moment, his hands cradling the plates. She broke eye contact and wiped David's face.

"At least let me take David for you."

"You want to go with Mr. Robert?" Shell asked.

David scooched out of his seat and ran to Robert who promptly scooped him up in his arms. "I'll take Amanda's coat."

"Thanks." She rose and poured herself another cup of coffee. When she turned around, he was still there, staring at her.

"You will join us?"

"Yes. Now git, before Amanda freezes out there."

She took her time cleaning the kitchen, the task's mundaneness comforting even as it heightened the surreal sense of her circumstances. Isolated with Robert Gladstone was the last place either of them needed her to be.

Sunrise the morning after the break in should have found her on the road to somewhere, anywhere. But where? Arkansas was too obvious, Canada out of the question, and they had been found in Philly. It left her with the rest of the country to choose from and no place to go. It took her a couple of hours to decide leaving was the thing. She would figure out the going later.

"Amanda, help me get the bags upstairs." Shell slung one of the duffle bags onto her shoulder and lifted the large suit case with both hands. She trudged upstairs, Amanda heeling her with another duffle and a backpack.

The luggage never made it to the car.

Robert blocked her path to the foyer. "You can't go."

"Watch me." She pushed forward.

He stood his ground. "Please. I can't let you go."

"I was never yours to keep." She held his eyes, but he wouldn't turn.

"Michelle." Sharon's voice caught her off guard. What had she heard?

Shell turned her shoulder to Robert and spotted Sharon sitting on the stairs, swollen-eyed and red-faced. "Listen, Sharon, you don't have to worry about me. Soon as we load these up, I'll grab the boys and head out."

Sharon walked over to Amanda, took the duffle bag out of her hands, and drew her into a hug. "You're a good girl, you know that?" She bent down to Amanda's eye level. "Your mommy is lucky to have you." She kissed her forehead. "Why don't you leave your backpack here and mind your brothers for a minute?"

"Go ahead, honey." Shell put the suitcase down but kept the duffle slung on her shoulder. She glanced at Robert, then faced Sharon. "I know what you're going to say and—"

"You can't leave."

It was the last thing she expected to hear from Robert's wife.

⊕

Shell pressed her aching thighs upward, her eyes on the crest of the climb still half a football field away. The hike was steeper than she remembered. That, or she was more tired than she thought. Good thing Robert had David. She was struggling enough on her own.

She powered through the last two steps and the saddle opened before her. She picked her way down the rocky trail, her legs relieved to be on a down slope. She glimpsed Sharon near the lake shore before the trees blocked her view.

She kept to the trail, the glint of the lake pulling her forward even as her nerves knit her gut. She had had her fill of Sharon already and the day was barely half done.

⊕

"You're better off without us here." Shell grabbed the suitcase double-fisted and spun on Robert. "Open the door."

"They planted drugs on him at work," Sharon said.

"What is she talking about?"

"The police searched my office on a tip. They found cocaine in my briefcase."

"How much?"

"Enough for an intent-to-distribute charge."

The heavy case thunked on the floor. "Robert, that's crazy."

"It might get crazier," he said. "I'm afraid the house won't be the worst of it."

"All the more reason for me to leave," Shell said.

"I can't risk it. If they hurt you, I—"

"They. They who?"

"People I work for. Or with. I'm not sure. Pizza Man is working on it. We stay put until I hear from him."

She glanced back at Sharon, unsure how she wound up being the grand prize winner in the crazy life lottery. "You okay with this?"

Her shoulders stiffened. "No, not entirely. But the alternative is worse. If you leave now, it puts us all in danger."

The duffle hit the floor. She locked eyes with Robert. "Who is the pizza guy?"

"He's DCIS, Defense Criminal Investigative Service."

⊕

The pines gave way to pebbled shore. Shell followed it north until the coast bent in on itself, forcing her northwest. She came to the narrow trail leading over a finger of land scratching the lake. Once on top, she spotted Sharon near the water with Jakob and Kyle. Robert stood several feet behind them with David on his shoulders holding on to his forehead.

She scrambled down the scree to join them.

Sharon plucked a stone from the shore. She cocked her arm and hooked the missile across the water. It skipped twice and sunk.

"Woohoo!" Kyle jumped up and down.

"My turn, my turn!" Jakob scratched around underfoot and came up with a smooth stone a size smaller than his fist. He stretched upright, then flowed into a sideways arch as his right arm whipped out. The first splash sprayed up fifteen feet out, then the stone skipped and kept going.

Shell counted as the rock bounced farther and farther from shore. One, two, three, four—*sink already*—five, six, seven, eight—*dear God*—nine, ten—

"Jakob!" Running in, she scooped him up and spun, his laughter covering her tears.

⊕

Shell kept her brood in the basement the day after her failed departure. The fridge was stocked and the rain made keeping the kids inside easier. By the following morning, she was at war with herself again. Leaving could jeopardize Robert. Staying could compromise Drom.

She repacked their bags just to have something to do. A day's wait had generated its requisite laundry. Burning the clothes would have been Drom's move, but the Gladstones were jumpy enough without her starting bonfires in the backyard.

She grabbed the hamper and trudged upstairs.

Pizza Man was back.

"I thought you could fix it." Robert paced between the center island and the sink counter.

"It doesn't work like that." Pizza Man removed his ball cap and scratched his scalp.

"So what? I'm supposed to wait here until they arrest me?"

"I know it's not ideal—" Pizza Man clammed up at the sight of her.

"Decided to come up for air?" Robert asked.

She raised the hamper. "Children equals laundry. Y'all having pizza for lunch?"

Pizza Man eyed Robert. "We need to talk this through."

Robert crossed his arms. "Talk away. She's part of this now."

"A part of what?" Sharon made her way to the center island. Leaning her hip against it, she turned her back to Shell and faced Robert.

"The charge still stands," Robert said.

"Shouldn't matter since you're innocent, right?"

Shell would have sworn the woman's foot was tapping. She dropped the hamper. Everyone stared at her. She looked Sharon in the eye. "I have dirty laundry to wash. That okay with you?"

Sharon's head dropped and Shell regretted her tone. None of this was Sharon's fault. She should have never come here.

"Washer's free," Sharon said. "Our stuff will be out of the dryer soon."

"Thanks." She picked up the hamper and cut past Pizza Man on her way to the small laundry room that connected the kitchen to the garage.

She tossed the clothes in, spun the water selector to cold, and pulled the knob. Water splashed into the tub. Robert's voice carried through the noise.

"When I came to you guys, you said you could protect me."

"And we can. Just not here."

Shell closed the lid and checked the timer on the dryer. The day's issue of the *Rocky Mountain News* was strewn over its top. Picking through the paper, she kept her ears tuned to the kitchen.

"Not here?" Sharon sounded incredulous. "You work for the Defense Department. Aren't you guys responsible for keeping the whole country safe?"

"Sharon." Robert's calming tone. It didn't work.

"No, Robert, I'm not out of line here." Sharon's volume rose a notch. "If Mr. DCIS can't protect us in our own home, what am I supposed to think?"

"We have a plan, Ma'am."

"I'm listening." It was Sharon's foot-tapping voice.

"There's a safe house in the mountains."

Robert coughed, his nervous-tick throat clearing. "Safe house? I'm out on bail. The detectives told me not to leave town."

"And I'm telling you it's unsafe to stay."

"I have to run away from the law to protect my family?"

There was silence for a beat, then Pizza Man spoke up. "If it helps, don't think of it as running away. Think of it as hiding under a higher authority."

"How big of a safe house?" Sharon asked.

"A bit of a squeeze for a small family."

Shell found the classifieds and started leafing through them.

"Robert, I'm really trying here, but you've got to help me."

"Babe, you know we can't leave them behind."

Shell located the automobile listings and ran her finger down the columns.

"We need to get you out with none being the wiser," Pizza Man said.

GRAN TORINO. Red paint. Runs great.

"I think I can help." All eyes were on her. "If you want it, that is."

"No offense, Shell, but you came to us for help, remember?" Sharon said.

She faced her for a beat, then turned to the Pizza Man. "How about I spell it out and you tell me if I've got it right?"

Pizza Man nodded. "Be my guest."

"You're running Robert as an informant and he's come across something higher than your paygrade. You keep saying 'we,' but I've only seen you; which has me wondering how worried you really are about Robert's find. You secured a place to hide him, just. And you still haven't worked out making him disappear without raising any eyebrows until it's too late for them to do anything about it. How am I doing?"

"He said you two grew up together."

"We did."

"He also said you cut your education short."

"What of it?"

"He was wrong about one of them."

"Some things can't be taught in a classroom."

"Where did you learn it, then?"

"We can leave their vehicles here," Shell said. "Sharon can dump a bunch of clothing and essentials into trash bags. Robert can take them out with the garbage. I figure you're resourceful enough to retrieve them from the trash man before they get to the dump."

"Go on," Pizza Man said.

"Forecast is calling for rain within the hour. I'll make a show of packing my car and demanding the garage to finish the job."

"Slow down, Shell." Robert raised his hands. "Trash bags? Your car? I'm not sure I'm comfortable with where this is going."

"I know I'm not," Sharon said. "Who are you?"

Shell withstood her gaze. *Good question.* "My car has a large trunk. Anyone watching the house will only see me and my kids leaving."

Sharon's brow furrowed. "You expect us to ride into the mountains in your trunk?"

Robert stepped beside his wife. "Shell?"

"Only eight miles," Shell said. "Then we switch vehicles."

She stopped spinning and set Jakob down.

"Do it again, Mommy!"

"Maybe later, honey. Mommy's made herself dizzy." Shell ruffled his hair. "Where's your sister?"

"Manda went climbing."

She turned to Robert. "Where is Amanda?"

He put David down. "She said something about climbing the rocks farther up shore."

Her pent-up irritation exploded on him. "And you let her go?"

"What's going on?" Sharon came over with Kyle in tow.

"Which way did Amanda go?" She tried to keep her voice down, but Sharon's flinch told her she was still yelling.

"That way, Mommy." Jakob pointed uphill into the woods.

Amanda's breakfast banter caught up to her. "The wall. She said something this morning about a wall."

Robert's eyes opened wide. "Oh, no. When she said rocks …" He scooped David up and handed him to Sharon. "This way." He ran. Shell sprinted after him.

"What's going on?" Sharon's question died in the woods, unanswered.

Robert hustled uphill through the pines. Shell followed, feeling like she was in a dream trying to run away from danger on legs of sludge and molasses. The harder she pushed, the slower she felt.

Robert rounded a curve and she lost sight of him. She dug into her pace, only the balls of her feet striking the ground as she pressed another drop of speed into her exhausted legs.

Coming around the bend, the trail opened up. Red sandstone framed in evergreen filled her view. High on the outcrop face—too high—hung a dash of violet. At least she has her coat on, Shell thought, then panicked as she realized she was clutching for any comfort, however useless.

The ground leveled out some and she widened her stride. The air cut into the furnace of her lungs as she charged the rock face. "Amanda!" It came out a croaked exhalation, far from the yell she intended.

She caught up to Robert and they sprinted side-by-side. She kept her eyes on her daughter as the girl pulled herself another foot toward the sky. She scanned down the bluff, working out the vertical distance, anger pressing against fear as Drom's voice filled her head.

"Find a seam about your height, then use it as your measurement perspective."

Climbing lessons from her lover. Survival techniques from an assassin in hiding—her daughter's step-father.

Amanda was two stories above ground and climbing.

The sight of her—close enough now to make out her hands and hair, too far to reach and rescue—squeezed Shell's adrenals for one last rush. She surged ahead of Robert, her legs now forgotten as she picked out which handholds she would use first.

Her foot struck stone and Amanda slid from view as the world tilted up to meet her. She landed hard on her side, her head smacking the unforgiving scree.

She rolled right, getting her hands under her, and pressed onto her feet. Robert crashed into her, knocking the wind out of her. She tumbled and came to rest on top of him.

She fought for air. His chest rose beneath her, his heart hammering into her ear. She blinked her eyes clear and the tree line came into view. She was facing downhill. She rolled off Robert's body—larger than Drom's and less firm, but not soft—and knelt, gulping air.

Her head throbbed. Her face stung. Her shoulders ached.

Lifting her gaze, she zeroed in on her daughter.

"Amy!" Her cry pierced the mountain air in full-throated anguish.

The name, Amanda's birth name, echoed back to her as her daughter's dangling frame broke free of the ledge and shot down the rock face. Shell fought her way up the gravel incline, her heart cracking as the girl's feet caught on a jut, her legs folding into a violent crouch, then slipping straight as she continued to fall.

Shell despaired of catching her, her own legs slower than gravity even though time seemed frozen.

With deepening horror, she scrambled across the loose stones underfoot, transfixed on her daughter's fall. In slow motion, they rushed to one another. Shell's adrenalin-spiked mind translated Amanda's trajectory to its landing zone. Everything around her brightened and she could make out the individual rocks her daughter's body would splatter over. Her feet found solid ground and she sprang forward, pain forgotten. She had ten feet to go.

Amanda only had five.

Shell fell to her knees as her daughter's body struck the ground feet first and collapsed into itself. Her legs folded. Her buttocks rushed to ground—and reversed course. Legs recoiling, her body shot up and arched back.

For an instant, Amanda hung upside down in midair facing her. Then the legs came around. She landed on her feet, fell forward, and slid down beside her.

Shell dove to her and rolled her over. Amanda's eyes popped open. Her lips stretched into a feral grin. "Did you see it, Mommy? Did you see it? I told Daddy I could do it!"

Her heart beat its way into her throat and stuck there. Relief, regret, rage, and wonder flooded through her simultaneously in competing streams that washed away all of adrenalin's favors. She drew Amanda into her arms, unable to speak.

Robert's shadow fell across her. "Who is she calling Daddy?"

Chapter 30

No person employed by or acting on behalf of the United States
Government shall engage in, or conspire to engage in, assassination.
Executive Order 12333, § 2.11, December 4, 1981

Washington, D.C. – October 7, 1988

Rick Cannon doublechecked the spreadsheet's embedded formulas. He
stared at the results, looking for the empty spots in the puzzle. CIA appropriated
funds through Congress like every other federal department, his included. The
smoke and mirrors came downstream, after budgets were approved. Where
listed expenditures fell outside of reasonable tolerances, his formulas raised flags
and tracked the slush.

His process led him to an operation spending far more than its official profile
warranted. The line-item expenditures had the mundane feel of a field office:
catering, waste removal, janitorial services, building maintenance, office supplies. Scattered among these were others with names so general, they could be
anything: professional services, training, personnel improvement, capital expenditures.

Titles hid, money talked. The dollar pieces framed the shape of a high-secu-
rity containment facility. CIA blacksite detention centers peppered the globe.
This one sat where it wasn't allowed.

He reviewed his notes on the compartmentalized SL/OMEGA information
against all he had on his person of interest. His stomach growled. He checked
his watch. He was pushing his luck, busy cutting bait when he should be fishing.

He dialed the number.

"Special Agent Cannon, to what do I owe the pleasure?" The Senator's nasal
twang signaled anything but pleasure.

"Sir, I've gone through it time and again, like you asked. The facility is there. I'm
sure of it." Static hung on the line. He shifted in his seat, loosening his tie. "Sir?"

"You a sports fan, Agent?"

"Uh, no, not really."

"I'm a big fan of the Army-Navy rivalry. Other institutions buy their players. And who really knows what goes on with the pros, am I right?"

"I'm not sure I—"

"What I mean is, our academy boys are patriots. They play against each other, but they're on the same team. They'll smash helmets on the gridiron, call each other names. But it's a game, right? Comes down to the oath, it's all about the red, white, and blue."

Rick checked his watch again. He was going to be late for dinner. "Red, white, and blue is what we're all about, sir."

"Be nice if everyone thought so." The line hissed for a long moment. "Patriotic or not, every team has its share of sore losers."

Rick propped himself on the edge of his desk. "I'm aware of the risks, sir."

"Are you? You pulled warrants already."

"Some teams still play by the rules."

"Once an eagle scout, always an eagle scout."

"Sir?"

"Your world view blinds you to its reality, I'm afraid. The warrants are legal, but not smart. You packed?"

"Packed?"

"Too late to get a flight and I know you're not up to driving there tonight."

Rick stifled an involuntary yawn. "I'm wrapping up here and heading home, Senator. If you could do your magic, I hope to serve the warrants early next week."

"Your warrants will be pointless next week. You think I'm the only one who knows you pulled them?"

Rick rubbed his eyes. "Can you get me in?"

"Last train leaves the station in a couple of hours. Be on it."

The off-hook tone bled into Rick's pondering. He stared at the receiver, unsure of how much time had elapsed since the senator hung up. He leaned over the desk, tapped the switch hook, and dialed Union Station.

The train left in ninety minutes, not enough time to pack, let alone to see his family.

He dialed the safe house. "Hey, Sarah. It's Rick. Put my wife on, will you?" Cradling the receiver between his ear and shoulder, he moved around the desk and opened the credenza.

"Hello." His wife's full French vowels arrested him. He ached to be with her, to bring them all back home.

"Adelaide." Her full name broke past his lips like a prayer.

She gasped. "Richard." She breathed his name out in French, *Reeshaar.* "Are you okay?"

"Yeah. I'm … I'm fine, honey. Something's come up. I won't make it for dinner."

"Oh. The children will be disappointed. Should I leave some out for you?"

He pulled his just-in-case bag out of the cabinet and tossed it on his desk. "Don't bother. I've got to go out of town."

"How long?"

He unzipped the duffle and checked the contents. "A couple of days, at least."

"Do I get to know where?"

Rick picked up the family photo stroked his wife's profile with his thumb. "Someday," he said. "I hope."

⊕

Something tapped Rick's foot. Sleep-slick eyes opened to the dim-lit train car. Shifting his weight in the generous, coach-class seat, he stared out the window. Darkness greeted him.

Something tapped his foot again. His glanced down and traced the offending boot up the braced leg to the man seated across from him.

"Tired, *mon ami?*" The man leaned back into his seat. Even relaxed, he looked menacing.

The train rocked, steel wheels clacking out the tempo of its travel. Pulling himself from its hypnotic seduction, Rick willed his mind to full-alert status. "Where have you been, Bastien?"

The older man scratched his scalp through his close-cropped hair. "Hunting, my dear Cannon, hunting."

Rick glanced at the leg brace. "All these years we've know each other and you never mentioned your love of softball. How's your batting average?"

"Better than yours, I think. How is my niece? She had quite the scare, I hear."

"Ada's fine, no thanks to you. You could have warned me."

Bastien waved his hand over the brace covering his left leg from thigh to ankle. "My broken leg wasn't warning enough?"

Rick had to concede the point. Fifteen years his senior, Bastien Frabron still carried his Legionnaire's physique. His effectiveness in the French Foreign

Legion was only overshadowed by his ruthlessness in the DGSE. "You could have told me what you needed from Karoly."

"Yes, well." Bastien settled back into his seat and stared out into the night. "I thought you might find some of the money you were looking for."

"And you? Who is Drom Reiziger to you?"

Bastien faced him. "I am as you are, a humble servant of my nation. France wants him found. That's enough for me."

"You owe me more than that. I got you Karoly."

"No, you did not. Karoly, I gave you. You are still catching up to me. Perhaps after this trip, you will have information to trade, no?"

"Fill in the gaps and the trip becomes more productive for us both."

Bastien grunted a chuckle. He pushed up from the seat and moved into the aisle. "Do you believe in ghosts, Cannon?"

"It wasn't a ghost that invaded my home."

"Yes, well, tell me how you feel after your visit." Bastien limped away.

Rick spun in his seat. The man was already at the gangway. "How do I contact you?"

Bastien didn't turn. "I'll be in touch." The door closed behind him.

Rick quickened his pace through the drizzle, regretting his decision to walk the seven blocks from the hotel. Four hours of horizontal sleep in a warm bed loosened most of the knots the train tied in his back. He figured a good walk would do the same for his legs. He hadn't counted on the rain. Or the cold. His taped fingers ached. Switching his briefcase to his left hand, he shoved his right into his coat pocket and pressed on.

Two blocks later, he caught sight of the brownstone high rise huddled against its neighbors. He adjusted his bearing south one block and stepped into the service alley on the brownstone's southwest side. He hustled past the large trash compactor and loading dock, both overkill for what the operation pretended to be. The alley dumped him out onto a two-lane, one-way street. Turning left against traffic, he trudged uphill to the building's main entrance.

It was locked.

He inspected the elevator lobby through the glass double doors. Its cracked paint and chipped tile floor bore witness of neglect and age. A roach darted up a wall and into an air duct. Nothing else stirred.

He studied the entrance alcove. A tarnished bronze plate with a vertical row of yellowing buttons clung to the east wall. He ran his thumb down all the buzzers. No sound came from the entry intercom, not even static.

Glancing up, he caught a glint in the mortar. He stepped up for a closer look and found himself eye-to-eye with a miniature camera lens. Stepping back, he held up his credentials. "FBI, open the door."

The door buzzed. He pulled it open and walked in.

He marched to the elevator bank. The arrival light winked on over the left elevator. Painted metal doors slid open, revealing a freight car in gleaming stainless steel. He entered the cavernous lift and the doors shut him in. Expecting to go up, he was forced to grab a handrail when the car shot down.

He checked the operating panel. It had buttons from ground to the sixteenth floor. It offered no choices for sublevels.

The elevator stopped. The doors parted, revealing two T-framed men in uniforms straining against their muscle mass. Tweedledee and Tweedledum.

"Special Agent Cannon, I believe you know the drill," Tweedledee said.

Rick let go of the handrail and tightened his grip on his briefcase. "Better than that. I know the law." He pulled a warrant from his breast pocket and slapped it against Tweedledee's chest. "The Agency is served. Take me to my witness."

Tweedledum kept quiet as Tweedledee opened the warrant. Rick waited as the man's eyes flicked across the document. He faced Rick. "Special Agent Cannon, I am to inform you that you stand in apparent breech of your non-disclosure agreement. Should you press ahead, your exit from this facility stands in question."

Squaring his shoulders, Rick edged closer to the man. "I'm not the one on thin ice here. We've all sworn to support and defend the Constitution. This facility violates it under the pretext of defending it. So, you can take me to my witness and let me get on with my business or you can take me to the chief of station where my other warrants will put an end to yours."

Tweedledee glanced at Tweedledum. The taller man nodded. "You'll need to locker your weapon and submit to a search."

"Of course," Rick said.

Weaponless but shod and in full possession of his briefcase, Rick followed Tweedledee down a concrete hallway, Tweedledum bringing up the rear. Florescent fixtures dangled from the ceiling, casting cold light on the bare walls' only artwork. The yellow, triple triangles on the fallout shelter signs reminded Rick of fangs. They gnashed at him from black circles, sinister reminders of the precarious state of the world they were serving their nation in.

Near the end of the corridor, Tweedledee opened a door on the left. Following him through, Rick was surprised at the slope and direction of the passageway. "We're going down and back?"

"And they say you Bureau boys aren't observant," Tweedledum said.

The corridor ended at a set of fire doors. The floor leveled out on the other side. Tweedledee increased his pace, widening the space between them. Several yards later, he squatted and pulled a floor hatch open. "After you, Agent. It's a rung ladder. Sure you don't want me to hold your briefcase for you?"

Rick stopped short, déjà vu holding him in place as the bared teeth of the shelter signs nipped at his composure. Sweat trickled down his sides despite the chill air. "I can handle my case."

He stepped down, chest pressed close to the ladder, his left hand gripping the rungs, and the unbroken fingers of his right hand curled around the briefcase handle. He reached the floor, pivoted away from the ladder, and came face-to-face with a guard in full tactical gear pointing a submachine gun at him.

"Please await your escort, sir."

The hatch creaked shut. Tweedledee glided past him. "Taking guest to Sector Twelve."

"Hatch secured?"

Tweedledum came beside Rick. "Locked and bolted."

It locks from the inside?

Spinning on his heel, the guard led them to the next security door. He swiped a keycard through a reader and pulled the door open. Rick followed Tweedledee into a wide passageway with metal doors set in the walls every fifteen feet. Rick counted ten in all, each with its own guard.

"How bad do you have to screw up to pull duty down here?" Rick asked.

Tweedledee glared at him. "Only the best of the best pull duty down here."

"Everyone else gets escorted," Tweedledum said.

They marched single file to the end of the corridor. Tweedledee presented the warrant to the guard at the last door on the right. She examined it for a minute and handed it back. "Step to the middle of the corridor, please."

Tweedledum tugged on his right elbow. Rick shrugged his hand off and took a step back.

The guard slid a panel on the metal door and peered through the observation window. She toggled the mic clipped to her shoulder strap. "Prisoner 69742, face the back wall and assume the position."

She maintained her stance a moment, then pulled a key from the metal reel on her belt and plunged it into the lock. She turned the key, gaze fixed on the observation window. She pulled up on the center lever, drawing the lock tabs from their holding slots in the top and side jambs.

All the other guards leveled their weapons on the cell door as she swung it open. She charged into the cell toward the orange clad inmate facing the back wall, his hands held overhead and his feet shoulder width apart.

"Palms on the wall."

The prisoner complied. Rick noted the knobbed thumbs and thin wrists. The officer patted him down, then led him to a chair at the steel table in the middle of the cell, left of the doorway. Dropping his wiry frame into the seat, the prisoner plopped his hands on the table. The officer cuffed him and zip-tied the cuff chain to the eyebolt welded on the tabletop.

She took her post at the door's edge. "He's all yours, sir."

Rick entered the cell.

The prisoner leaned back in his chair, taking Rick in. His seamed forehead furrowed, pushed up by dark brows shading inquisitive hazel eyes. "Well, what brings you down the rabbit hole, Alice?"

The cell door banged shut and the lock tabs slapped into place.

"Special Agent Rick Cannon." He parked himself in the chair opposite and plopped his briefcase on the table. He popped the latches, dug out the files, then set the attaché on the concrete floor.

"Will wonders never cease," the prisoner said. "Lady Justice is blind, but the Bureau still has a nose."

Rick slid out a folder from the middle of the stack, flipped through the photos, and chose three. He set them in a line across the center of the table. "These bring back any memories?"

The prisoner leaned forward, rubbed the side of his crooked nose, and sat back. "Only bad ones."

Rick pushed the photo on the left—a headshot of a man's bloated face with bulging eyes—closer to the inmate. "Alvarez Colón Zamora, assassinated on his wedding day." He pushed the next one forward, a coin-encrusted corpse with a knife handle protruding from its chest. "Michel Jugaro Carrero, tortured and murdered in his office." He pressed his palm on the last one—three men face down on a wide sidewalk—and slid it under the prisoner's restrained arm. "Juaquin Morreno Zapato and his security detail. All victims of your treachery, Mr. Drake."

Charles Drake lifted his arms as high as the zip-tie allowed, bent forward, and blew across the table's edge. The photos flitted like scattering leaves and floated to the floor. He settled back into his seat and eyed Rick. "I haven't seen daylight in four years, Agent. If you're here for your pound of flesh, you're a bit late."

Rick broke eye contact and examined the room. Though spacious by solitary confinement standards, the white-washed cell lacked any amenities. A concrete shelf on the wall behind Drake served as bedframe to the thin mattress convalescing on it. A stainless steel sink-and-toilet unit squatted against the wall to his left. The table and chairs were the only furnishings.

He rose and gathered up the scattered photos. Stepping behind Drake, he laid them back out in a row in front of him. He resumed his seat and faced the prisoner. "If I am to believe the official report, you recruited an asset to kill Shane Leoppard then used the same asset to sabotage SL/OMEGA at the direction of your Soviet handlers."

"And how is your faith holding up, Agent? You believe the official report?"

"The Government of the United States backchanneled a substantial amount of funds to Spanish officials to facilitate your extradition. You boarded a plane in Barcelona four years ago and vanished. It only took me four weeks to locate you, Mr. Drake, which tells me that nobody else is bothering to look. But arranging this interview took a minor act of Congress, which means no one wants you talking. So, no. I don't believe the report."

"Then you're here for my version of the events?"

Rick propped his elbows on the table. "I'm not interested in versions, Mr. Drake. I'm here about a body."

Drake tilted his head. "I'm guessing not any of the ones you've shown me so far."

Rick reached into his stack and pulled out two more photos. He slid the first over, a night shot of an open grave with Gavin Leoppard's headstone in the spotlight.

Drake danced it closer to him with his fingertips. Edging to the table, he studied the image for a moment. "Where was this taken?"

"You know the name?"

Drake's eyes flicked up. "We're both familiar with the surname, Agent. Where?"

"Northwest Arkansas in a centuries old community graveyard." He slid the next shot over, a body on a slab. He focused on the prisoner's face as he pulled the body on top of the open grave. Drake's upper lip twitched under flared nostrils. "Anyone you know?"

Drake skated the pictures back to him. "You should let that Basque bastard rot. Better yet, toss him on a trash heap and let the rats and ravens tear apart whatever is left of him."

"Any idea how he wound up buried in Arkansas?" Rick asked.

"None. So, he was the Leoppard's son. I figured as much. Doesn't matter now. What matters is that both of them are dead. The world is better for it, believe me."

"And this is the man you shot dead in Castellón, Spain?"

"Man? More of a boy, really. Killing him was the best move in my entire career. CIA may keep me in purgatory for the rest of my life. I don't care. It was worth it. Putting that animal down was a favor to humanity."

"Says the man who supplied terrorist organizations to undermine European governments. How is he any worse than you?"

Drake's eyes narrowed. Shifting back in his seat, he rested his hands flat on the table with a clatter of handcuffs. "Tell me, Special Agent, how many years have you given to the Bureau?"

"Fast approaching thirteen, why?"

Drake leaned forward, grim-lipped and dead serious. "At thirteen, this 'Gavin Leoppard' had killed more men than you've probably arrested in your entire career."

"I've been read into SL/OMEGA, Mr. Drake. I know what the file says."

"Phfft." The dismissive exhale came at Rick like a jab. "If all you know is the file, you don't know the half of it. He wasn't just an assassin. That monster was a sadist. He lived for blood and suffering."

Crossing his arms, Rick rested against the seat back. "Which, I presume, is why you contracted him."

"I contracted him in spite of it. It was a mistake."

"Four years without sunshine and Gavin Leoppard is the only mistake you're owning? What of the entire operation itself? You lost officers and agents in an illegal operation designed to undermine governments we are aligned with."

"Necessary evils. Carlos Parada, Rat-gêló, Gavin Leoppard—whatever name you choose to use for that Basque scum—he was an evil too far."

"You considered him a threat even after your operation collapsed. Why?"

"Would the FBI let a known serial killer roam free?"

"No, we would arrest him and bring him to justice."

"Spoken like a true law enforcement officer. You boys run around like the planet isn't run by criminals. I've been an intelligence officer most of my adult life, Agent Cannon. There are problems the courts can't touch. SL/OMEGA was launched to deal with a symptom, like throwing aspirin at a fever. We had other operations aimed at dealing with the root. He was a threat to those as well."

"Other operations? Such as?"

A shadow of a smile played across Drake's lips. "You said you were here about a body. What is it you really want, Agent Cannon?"

"Gavin Leoppard's origins and demise were known to the CIA. The Inspector General's initial report had the background history, the medical examiner's report, and location of burial. His whereabouts were no mystery. How he gained control of and subsequently hid a substantial amount of the funds allocated for SL/OMEGA is."

Drake laughed. "The Bureau discovers an extrajudicial confinement facility operated by CIA on US soil and they send an accountant. Classic. What's next, you going to ask me about my tax returns?"

"Do you know where they are?"

"The returns? I mailed last year's in. You didn't get it?"

Rick pulled out a notepad and wrote, *Bugs?* He showed it to Drake. The man shook his head. He scanned the room again. They could have microphones buried in the walls. He would never find them. He stepped over to the sink and cut both taps on.

"I doubt they put any in there," Drake said. "No one wants to listen to that."

Rick splashed water on his face and combed his wet hands through his hair. He glanced at the towel wadded on the floor, then unrolled some toilet paper and dried his face.

Careful, Rick. You only know as much as they let you know.

He leaned back against the wall and stacked the man in the orange jumpsuit against his file. Charles Drake had given nearly twenty-five years of his life to his country, much of it in harm's way, before his supposed defection. A promising Army officer, CIA recruited him in the early years of the Vietnam War. His service record was exemplary and his financial records displayed the modest earnings of a civil servant.

If justice was what the Government wanted, Drake wouldn't be here.

Rick returned to his seat. He bent forward and held the prisoner's eyes with his gaze. "I can't make sense of why they had me exhume the body. I am missing something in the Leoppard legacy. I was hoping you could fill it in."

"In exchange for what?"

"Much better accommodations."

Drake eyed the cell, then leaned over his bound hands and rubbed his bent nose. He came back up with a couple of loud sniffs. "The air is dry in here. Can't remember a time when my nose didn't itch."

"What's not in the file?"

"We provided training for Shane Leoppard to be a particular type of an assassin. Most targeted killing operations require extensive manpower and resources to execute after months and sometimes years of intelligence gathering. Shane was CIA's attempt to make the process more efficient."

"None of this is new, Mr. Drake. The Senate Intelligence Committee's investigation dug all that out in the opening months of the SL/OMEGA review."

"Did the investigation uncover what Shane specialized in once we lost him?"

"Specialized? You said yourself what his specialty was."

The shadow smile darkened Drake's lips again. Rick dug in the briefcase and came out with his compartmentalized notes. He flipped through the pages, focusing on every mention of Shane Leoppard. They all detailed the who and how—those killed and methods of dispatch—but not the what and why. He looked up.

"We've all been guilty of it at some point," Drake said. "We are presented with consistent evidence that fits a logical scenario and we buy into it, blinding us to other possibilities."

"What became his intelligence specialty?"

"Science and technology. He acquired state and military secrets along the way, but they weren't his focus."

"How did this make Gavin Leoppard a danger to your other operations? We're you trying to stop the leaks to the Soviets or open them wider?"

"If you believed I was a traitor, you wouldn't have risked coming here."

"You were trying to stop the leaks."

"Stop them, yes. But it wasn't the Soviets we were worried about."

"No? Then why play the double-agent at all?"

"By then, Swenson hadn't left me much choice. Regardless, the Basque had to go. If he kept digging at his father's wells, the damage would be irreparable."

"Damage to what? National security? Corporate interests?"

"The human race, Agent Cannon. The human race."

Rick weighed this out, shifting the array of information in his mind. "What type of science and technology?"

"Ask yourself," Drake said, "what type of sci-tech would drive them to make an accountant dig up a body?"

Rick pulled out his Penticton folder. Choosing two photos, he placed them in front of Drake. "What do you make of these?"

Drake plucked one up, a tortured mannequin with multiple impalings. His lips stretched thin. The eight-by-ten jittered in his grip. "Where was this?"

"Penticton, British Columbia. I found several like these on property recently vacated by one Drom Reiziger. The name mean anything to you?"

"How sure are you that it was Gavin Leoppard's body you dug out of the grave?"

"DNA sure, why?"

"Drom is a Romani word."

"Romani?"

"Gypsy," Drake said. "Drom Reiziger is a Gypsy name."

Chapter 31

The Reich Criminal Police Office (via responsible Criminal Police and local offices) is hereby ordered to transfer all Gypsy mixed-bloods, Róm Gypsies, and Balkan Gypsies to Konzentrationslager (Zieguner-lager) Auschwitz.

Heinrich Himmler
Reichsführer – SS
16 December 1942

Drancy Internment Camp, Paris, France – March 1943

Hishoro climbed the stairs, worming her toes through the filth-laden straw in search of firm purchase with each step. Eyes down, she kept her shoulder close to the stairwell wall. The ground-floor guard had given her no trouble. She hoped to cross the rest with similar success.

Women flowed past her, most likely returnees from the *Chateau rouge*, the camp latrine. Others plodded behind her, their work passes—like hers—pinned to their chests.

"Get moving, you lazy sows!" The gendarme's order echoed down the well.

The tempo of muffled heels on concrete increased. The skirts in front of her widened their lead. Hishoro pressed on, the dead rat stuffed in her dress pocket bouncing against her thigh.

The next ration distribution was a week away and they only had two days of food left. The rat would help, scrawny as it was. With the meat, bones, and remaining flour she could make a thin stew to sustain the four of them a few more days.

Scrambling past the guard, she hurried her pace and reached the fourth floor winded. She slowed down, thankful for the level ground. She entered their apartment, an open room furnished with bunks and little else. At times packed with as many as sixty women, it was a beehive of body odor and discontent. A convoy marched out of the camp two days previous, freeing up some bunk space and leaving more air. Safe in her prison cell, Hishoro approached their bunks by the window and stopped short.

A black man perched on the edge of her bed, a parcel in his lap. Pierre and Alfonso clung to either side of Keti on the bunk opposite. Thronging them were several other children Hishoro did not recognize.

"Kon si kako?" she asked Keti, who is this man?

Rising, he faced her. "Andre Bakhoum at your service, madame. You are Tshuri's woman, no?"

She studied his face, from its wide brows above intelligent eyes perched on prominent cheek bones to its sharp chin. *Too many here approve of Herr Hitler.* His warning to Tshuri rang like a fulfilled prophecy in her mind. "I am his wife. You have news?"

"I have gifts. This is for you." He extended the package to her.

She crossed her arms. "What has happened to Tshuri?"

"He is well, madame. Tshompi, you son, has recovered and is living with Gorka Colón's family. Tshuri said the boy and Gorka's son, Alvarez, have become inseparable."

"If Tshompi is well, why is Tshuri not here?"

"Locating you has been difficult. The cost of the information has him detained in the south."

"And Mateo? What news of Mateo?" Keti asked.

Andre's gaze dropped. "Tshuri promised to send more and is sorry this took so long to find you." He extended the box again.

The weight of it surprised Hishoro. Hugging it against her hip, she turned and set it on the bunk near Keti.

"What of Mateo?" Her sister asked again.

She held Keti's hand and faced Andre. "You remember Mateo, my sister's husband?"

His eyebrow raised. "You have noticed the work in the courtyard?"

"Who hasn't? We were already cramped before they closed that area off."

"The work hides other work. Members of the Résistance are digging a tunnel."

"Jews are doing that work under their own supervisors. If they're digging a tunnel, it won't be for Roma."

"Tshuri has secured your passage." He eyed the package. "I must take my leave. We will meet again." He gave them a slight bow and hurried out the door.

She slumped onto her bunk, fatigue assaulting her with a vengeance. "Sister, feeding us is difficult enough. Who are these children?"

"The train came and out poured hundreds of children, crying and lost. The gendarmes drove them into the yard and left them there. No adults came off the train. I had to help."

"How are we to care for so many?"

"I could not save Nadja. I could not bear all those lost children. I begged God for a miracle and the black man came."

"His name is Andre." The children's eyes were on her, round and pleading. Hishoro slid off the bunk and kneeled in front of the package.

Digging into the hidden pocket of her skirt, she pushed the rat aside and grabbed her bread knife. She cut the twine and opened the box flaps. Canned fruits and vegetables crowded against a sizeable ham. Lifting these out, she found bags of sugar, flour, and a crystal salt shaker. A bit of paper stuck out of the sparkling grains.

She unscrewed the cap and pulled out a rolled piece of paper. She unfurled it, revealing Tshuri's elegant cursive with its tight loops and precise stems.

Ma chérie,

I apologize that you have to read this in French instead of hearing Romani from my lips. How I long to be with you! Soon, very soon, my darling. I promise.

Our last time together was too hurried. I should have told you then, but could not. Mateo died during our escape in Nantes. You must protect Keti. We are all she has now.

The Pyrenees! Some of our people say we were Jews once, long ago. I am not convinced. Regardless, the Sabbath Lord gave us strength for the crossing. Gorka took us in without question. His son Alvarez promises to be a fine man one day. He has made Tshompi his personal charge. When I left him, our son was well on his way to becoming a shepherd.

My messenger could not get the supplies to Monsieur Blum directly. Forgive me for saying so, but you, my dear, are less obvious. Get them to him as soon as possible. The Résistance has promised to get you out.

I know you will want to keep these words. You must not. Know that I love you, am fighting my way to you.

Burn the note.

Tshuri

"What does he say?" Keti asked.

Hishoro hefted a bag of flour out of the box. Below it sat tan cylinders emblazoned with the Reich's eagle swastika and the word **DYNAMIT**. She lowered the flour back in the box.

"The ham will keep, this will not." Hishoro plopped the dead rat onto Keti's lap. The children scampered off the bunk. "I'll get a fire going. You skin dinner."

It took several days for Hishoro to find out where her contact was. After her morning shift in the camp kitchen, she pressed through the throng idling in the walkway bordering the courtyard. The *Union Générale des Israelite de France* had a corner office on the ground floor. A Jewish organization, the UGIF was responsible for the camp's internal management. It decided who got what, who was housed where, who worked, who stayed, and who got sent to Pichipoi. The man in charge was Monsieur Blum.

The milling crowd coalesced into a firm line in front of the UGIF office. She plowed into the queue spitting and cursing. Resistance stiffened momentarily, then gave way under her determined onslaught.

A kapos caught her arm as she reached for the door. "Back of the line, you!"

He dragged her back several steps before she twisted her arm loose. She dashed through the door, the kapo on her heels. "I demand to see Monsieur Blum!"

The men seated in the anteroom looked up in surprise. She was spun around and a stinging slap sent her crashing into a desk. A vice clamped on her biceps and hauled her up. "Outside, *gitane* witch!"

The kapo's scowling face filled her vision. She worked up a glob of phlegm and spewed it into his glaring eye. She bit his hand and slammed her heel down on the bridge of his foot. Howling, he hopped back a couple of paces.

"I need to speak with Monsieur Blum."

The kapo wiped his eye and cleaned his fingers on his trouser leg. Reaching down with his bloody hand, he pulled out his truncheon. "You won't be able to chew, let alone speak, when I get through with you." He raised the club.

"Evry, what is all this commotion?" A man not much taller than Hishoro stood in the doorway of the back office. His round face and sharp eyes seemed to hold the kapo in place by force of will alone.

"This *gitane* filth barged past the line demanding to see you, sir. I'll get her out of here so you can go back to your work undisturbed."

The short man peered at her through wire-rimmed glasses. "My work is disturbing enough. See her in." He turned his back to them and disappeared into his office.

Evry pointed at her with his baton. "When he's done, you're all mine."

Hishoro pulled a kerchief out of her blouse sleeve and wiped Evry's blood off her lips. Tucking it away, she smoothed her skirts and straightened her head scarf.

She forced her left eye to stay open against the swelling. Ignoring the burning sting on her cheek, she marched into the director's office and closed the door behind her.

Blum looked up from the file in his hands and he waved to the wooden chair in front of his desk. "Sit, please."

Hishoro stood, hands on hips. "What are you doing about the children?"

"Which children?"

"The train dumped a thousand of them out into the courtyard days ago. No one has assigned them a block or stair. You can't just leave them out there in the dirt on their own."

"The apartments are crowded and the food shipment is late. I have spoken to the authorities about this."

"Where are their parents?"

"They were supposed to be on the train with the food."

"My sister and I have taken in six of them. We need more rations."

"Did you not receive a food parcel several days ago?" He remained slouched in his chair, his features relaxed as if he were discussing the weather.

She glanced over her shoulder to make sure the door was still closed. "It was intended for our passage out."

"Not only yours." Placing his elbows on the desk, he leaned toward her.

She drew a stick of dynamite from her skirt pocket and laid it on the desk. He rolled it in his fingertips, sniffed it, and stuck in a desk drawer.

"And the rest?"

"In time," she said. "The children?"

"Where are you housed?"

"Stair eighteen, apartment forty-three."

"I'll make sure more supplies reach you."

"And Evry?"

"I'll deal with him."

"I'll get the rest to you as I can. How long will the project take?"

"Too long, I fear. But this will help."

Her swelling eye was winning the battle against her will to hold it open. She wanted to be gone before Evry could enjoy the fruits of his brutality. "We will be ready when the time comes."

Blum walked her out and waved Evry in.

Ignoring the kapo's glare, she marched out onto the walkway. Taking a deep breath, she soaked her eyes with the blue sky. They had avoided deportation for months. Escape, if not close, was at least now a hope.

The rumors spoke highly of the place the internees called Pitchipoi. People taken there found ample food, spacious lodging, and meaningful work.

Hishoro wanted nothing less than Tshuri and freedom.

Chapter 32

The courts disallow evidence gathered without a warrant and disregard confessions beaten out of the accused. Why should the medical establishment hold to lesser standards? Some argue that the experiment findings could save lives and should therefore be used. But Nazi "medical" data was obtained through mass enslavement, intentional torture, and cruel deaths. The information is poisoned from its source. Any parties using it make themselves participants in the torture and murder of countless Jews and Gypsies.

Henry P. Killough, M.D.
Letter to the Editor, *New York Times*, April 19, 1988

Boston, Massachusetts – Sunrise, October 8, 1988

Drom's first view of the Boston skyline was as familiar as a memory. He crept to the ledge and inspected the target area, a patch of sandstone bricks between two windows on the thirteenth floor of the building across the alley. A gust of wind pressed him against the parapet, driving the morning drizzle through the back of his black turtleneck. He glanced at the gray sky and hoped the full rain would hold off for a few more minutes.

He crab-walked back to the gear stashed next to the air chillers and picked up both fanny packs. He opened them in turn, counting their contents. Eight rubber balls in each, sixteen in all. Fifteen wouldn't be enough, seventeen was one too many. He snapped the packs around his waist so they hung at his hips. He buckled their bottom straps around his thighs and he swiveled his hips. The packs stayed in place.

Moving over to the knapsack, he unzipped the main compartment. Changes of clothes were tightly packed beneath the smoke grenades. Satisfied, he zipped it shut and unsnapped the front compartment. Plastic explosives with caps, wires, and detonator snuggled together in their foam bed. He snapped the flap shut, threaded his arms through the shoulder straps, and buckled the chest and waist straps.

Street noise, the yawns and scratches of a city coming awake, rattled up to him. He glanced at the buildings north and west, both taller than his launching pad, and breathed easier at the absence of lights. Someone could still be watching, but the dark windows helped him believe they weren't.

He grabbed his armor.

Stockton had implored him to wear a bullet-proof vest. Drom laughed at the idea. "I'm carrying too much weight as it is. Besides, if I miss, they won't. A vest isn't going to keep my head from being blown off."

Stockton took his hand off the tactical helmet next to the vest. He picked up the knee and elbow pads—fabricated from high-density polymers so dark they seemed to absorb the light—and handed them to Drom. "Won't these impair your movement?"

"Not if your techs made them right."

He pulled them on now and performed several mock throws and a ten-set of squats. Stockton's fabricators had outdone themselves. The hard-shelled pads articulated with his joints, their undersides pillow soft. Affixed to elastane tubes, they clung to his arms and legs without cutting off his circulation.

Another gust brought larger drops with it, hitting his last pieces of equipment in a staccato stutter. If his father was to be believed—and that was always questionable—when Hashim al-Muttalib al-Askari ad-Din, the missionary assassin of Alamut, arrived in Iberia, he fell in love with the Saunion. Though it didn't lend itself to the juggling acts al-Askari was bending to deadly deeds, as a soldier, he immediately appreciated their simple design and devastating use.

The Saunion was a javelin. Unlike those used by the Romans and Greeks, the Iberians made theirs entirely of iron. Their rods of death would launch from well-trained arms and rain down on enemies up to ninety feet away, slamming through shield and armor, flesh and bone.

al-Askari ad-Din insisted his disciples train with them, even as Drom's father—centuries later—insisted with him. "I'll never use these," his Carlos-self had protested.

"It's not the point," Shane Leoppard said. "It's tradition. Besides, you never know. It might come in handy someday."

Handy, indeed.

Slipping on his gloves, Drom hefted a metal shaft in each hand. The weight was right despite his tweaks to the ancient design that cut them from six feet to four and a half. He made up for the loss in shaft weight with the extra payload in the head. When it all came apart, the heads would vaporize and the shafts would be two more pieces of rebar in the debris.

"Where did you get this design?" Stockton's engineer asked him when he showed him the explosives plan. "It's brilliant. Incredibly robust, but elegant. Simple, even. I'm surprised it hasn't been used before. You must tell me where you got it."

In a dream. Out loud he said, "You wouldn't believe me if I told you."

Marching to the ledge, he eyed the target once more. He took five steps back and hurled the javelins. They shot up, twin flyers, then dove out of sight.

One, two, three—

CHINK.

He backstepped ten more paces and spring-loaded into a runner's starting crouch, a black figure on a field of gray.

A rumble in crescendo, like an approaching thunderstorm, stirred his stomach and vibrated his bones. It climaxed in an ear-splitting boom with a flash of fire and billow of smoke. The floor beneath him lurched and he ran instead of standing his ground. Launching off the ledge in a parallel parabellum of the javelins' flight, he pierced through the smoke ring two stories down on the building across the street.

Landing hard on unyielding concrete, he rolled, absorbing the shock. He sprang to his feet, unable to see through the smoke. It didn't matter. In two bounds, he was through the stairwell door. He turned right and jumped. His boots hit the landing below, sounding it off like a giant drum. He spun left, flexed his knees, and jumped again. Jump, land, and repeat; three turns per story.

He was five floors down from his entry point when the klaxons wailed.

Dear God, keep me from murder.

Ten floors to go.

His footfalls echoed in the concrete hallway as he sped to the intersection. Unzipping his pouches halfway, he loaded both hands with four balls each. Five feet from the hallway's mouth, he launched a curve ball. It arced into the passageway and thumped against the facing wall. The light winked out with a shattering of glass.

Men shouted. Machine gun fire erupted.

He charged toward it.

Launching the remaining balls out of his hands, he zipped the packs and cartwheeled into the melee. Flashlights cut through the darkness. Red dots danced on the walls. Muzzle flashes revealed focused faces behind riot visors. Drom danced to the beat of the bouncing balls, slapping and kicking them into their debilitating ricochets.

He captured his last ball after its final bounce. Stowing it in the pack at his hip, he stepped over to the guard splayed in front of the door. A carbine lay across his chest, its undermounted tactical light casting a garish hue on the shattered visor and bleeding face. Squatting, he removed a glove and pressed his fingers against the man's carotid.

Alive. Thank you, Lord!

He dragged the guard away from the door, cracked it open, and peered down the hall even though he knew what he would see. The fire doors at the other end of the corridor banged open and guards in full tactical gear poured through. Putting his back against the cold steel, he reached inside his pouches.

One, two, three, four.

He exploded into the hallway with a barrage of vulcanized rubber. Powdered glass from shattered fluorescent tubes rained down amid the winking flashes of dying light fixtures. His mad dance traced a horizontal tornado as he charged into the defenders. They fell like wheat to a hail storm, some before they could fire a shot.

He took a ten count to steady his breathing, then pulled the left-hand door open. He sailed a sacrificial ball through and dove in after it.

Shots fired, chasing the ball. Landing on his stomach, he rolled to the opposite wall. Back against the floor, head pointed at his next targets, he threw the balls against the ceiling and kept them flying through a series of back handsprings. He landed beside a round metal hatch set in the floor. The last guard standing spun around, his rifle light playing across his fallen comrades littering a field of shattered glass.

Drom fired a direct assault. The first two balls disarmed the man. The next one struck his right knee, careening him into the final three that in sequence turned off his higher brain functions. He crashed to the floor, comatose.

Drom unsnapped the front pouch of the backpack and pulled out the explosives. He shaped the plastique charges around the hatch edge, set the blasting caps, and wired them to the detonator. He unclipped a flashlight from one of the submachine guns and inspected the corridor. On the floor near his entrance lay the scattered remains of his first ball. These operators were better shots than the first ones he encountered. The guards under the hatch would be better still.

He took count of the fallen. Seven bodies, thirty feet for each plus the double-back. Eight minutes would give him a comfortable margin of safety to clear the area. The detonator was hardwired for five. He thumbed the switch and jumped to work at the wink of the green light.

His mental clock registered forty-five seconds left before the hatch blew. His dream told him reinforcements from upstairs would arrive within the minute. He had three bodies to go: his, the doorstop, and the last guard. Grabbing the man's wrists, he dragged him up the hallway, through the door, and on top of his fallen comrades.

The stomp of approaching boots bled through the metal door of the middle corridor. Drom yanked the doorstop through and lay on top the man's limp form. The fire door's closing slam was followed by the deafening peal of hyper-expanding air, ripping concrete, and crashing metal.

The shockwave reverberated through the floor. Drom pushed himself up on all fours and barreled into the corridor. He sliced through the cloud of concrete dust, burnt motor oil and ground teeth registering on his taste buds, and raced to the hatch. Reaching into the main compartment of the backpack, he extracted two grenades and pulled the pins. He lobbed one down the hole and chucked the other one toward the doors behind him.

He reloaded balls into his hands and jumped feet first through the torn opening. He landed in a crouch and spun to the right before the machine gun fire could splatter him against the wall. He couldn't see through the smoke, but his heart and hands knew where the targets were. All was memory. Trusting the dream, he slapped his missiles home.

Creeping forward, he searched the body left of the door and unclipped the card key from the breast pocket flap. A dim red glow shone through the smoke. He reached into his hip packs for his remaining handballs. Four rounds, ten targets, seven hundred square feet of battleground.

In the face of insurmountable odds, the Romani response often resolved to dance and disregard. The beat of *palmatas* clapping out a flamenco rhythm flared in his mind, raising his heartbeat another notch. His heels tapped against the concrete floor in response, setting his timing. He slid the card through the reader. Red turned to green. He yanked the door open, hiding behind its protective plate steel.

Concrete shards set free by the fire pouring through the doorway peppered his face. The shower paused. He spun, firing the balls out from his waist, and vaulted through the opening. Darkness ate its way down the corridor as balls shattered lights out of their moorings. His mental clock informed him his right arm only had a few seconds of operational use left, so he made the most of it.

Reaching the first guard on the left wall, he slammed his elbow into the side of his head with a cross and slapped an inbound ball down range with the follow up backhand. He thrust his knee up, clipping the guard's falling head, finishing the job his elbow had started. As he spun away from the wall, a bullet tore through his biceps, rendering his right arm useless with searing pain.

Three limbs kept four balls in play. He pressed his attack, using his knee and elbow pads to devastating effect each time he got within range of a guard. Increasing his tempo, he beat down the last guard, then concentrated his wall bounce juggle on one spot in the end wall until his balls went through it. Light spilled out of the hole, dispersing the darkness.

Yanking off his right elbow pad, he lifted the injured arm to his mouth with his left hand and tore a hole through the sleeve cuff with his eye teeth. He ripped the sleeve past the elbow, repeated the process on the opposite side and used the resulting tethers to wrap the wound. Using his mouth as an adjunct hand, he tied it off and pulled the elbow pad over it for compression.

Stepping to the back, he kicked the wall below the hole he had made until it gave way in chunks. It was a chink in the scales of the dragon's dungeon, a section of false wall for easy access to a utility maintenance shaft.

Time to get what he came for.

If Stockton was to be believed—and that was always questionable—the asset he was extracting had intel on Bastien Frabron, the Butcher, the Throat-slitter of Abéché.

Drom padded to the fallen figure in front of the last cell door on the right-hand wall and unclipped the key ring from her utility belt.

He slipped the key into the lock, turned it, then pulled the central lever up. He swung the door open, revealing a brightly lit cell occupied by a man in an orange jumpsuit seated at a metal table with his hands cuffed and zip-tied to an eyebolt on the table top.

Drom froze.

Drake? Prisoner 69742 is Charles Drake?

The prisoner's eyes widened, furrowing his brow. Blood drained out of his face. "How in the ..."

Drom detected motion on his right. In his mind, his right arm shot up to block the incoming chair. The limb was too injured to respond. The blow caught him from brow to breast, driving him to the floor.

Chapter 33

The Nazis have, to a certain extent, succeeded in convincing the peoples of the world that the Nazi system, although ruthless, was absolutely efficient; that although savage, it was completely scientific ... The evidence which this Tribunal will hear will explode this myth ... These experiments revealed nothing which civilized medicine can use ... the experiments were not only criminal but a scientific failure. It is indeed as if a just deity had shrouded the solutions which they attempted to reach with murderous means.

Opening Statement in the Doctors Trial
Brig. General Telford Taylor
Nuremburg, Germany, December 9, 1949

Boston, Massachusetts – Morning, October 8, 1988

Drom rolled out of the path of the second blow and slammed his heel against the inside of his attacker's knee. It folded out with a thrust of shattered bone and blood spray. The man crashed to the floor and the metal chair bounced out of his hands.

Drom sprang to his feet. Rick Cannon's eyes popped wide. Drom kicked his head, knocking him out.

Someone slammed into his back. He toppled forward and manacled hands snapped back against his throat. He careened backward into the cell, driving a flurry of elbow strikes into his assailant.

They crashed onto the table, Drake beneath him, increasing his throttle on Drom's throat. Reaching over his head, he found Drake's ears and latched on. He yanked, folding himself in a crunch, and popped them both off the table.

Sparks danced in his eyes as his vision tunneled. He focused on the wall ahead, tucked his chin, and charged it like a bull. Drake's head smacked the wall and his hold went slack. Drom dipped out from his arms, sweeping sideways with another elbow strike as he sprang clear. Drake bounced against the wall and fell to the floor.

Drom coughed his throat open and drew in several ragged breaths. His vision cleared and the ringing in his ears tapered down a couple of decibels.

Groaning, Drake got to his feet. With a shake of his head, he took a fighter's stance, bound fists up ready to box.

"Stop." Drom held his hand up. "We don't have time for that."

Drake's face was several shades paler than his hands, the blood seeping out of his forehead taking on a vivid hue in contrast. "Jesus, Joseph, and Mary! How are you still alive?"

"Joseph and Mary had nothing to do with it." Drom raised the set of keys he took from the female guard. "I'm here to get you out, unless you would rather stay."

Drake chin-pointed at doorway. "I was brokering a legitimate release when you showed up, thank you very much."

Drom glanced left. A pool of blood was spreading beneath Cannon's destroyed leg. He could avoid using lethal force. Maiming attackers was too ingrained to counteract. Someone's leg usually paid the price. "I need to take care of him. Don't do anything stupid."

Drake blocked his path. "You think I'll just stand here while you finish him off?"

"He's bleeding out. I need to fix it so he doesn't die."

Drake checked over his shoulder, then stepped out of the way. "We're not done."

"Not by a long shot," Drom said.

Dashing out of the cell, Drom shifted his brain from assault gear to EMT drive. He rolled Cannon onto his back. Bone jabbed through the soaked pant leg below his knee. He couldn't set it, but he could slow the bleeding.

He grabbed a submachine gun, slipped the sling under the thigh, and twisted it tight. He wedged the rifle between Cannon's legs to keep tension on the torniquet and unclipped the tactical light.

Drom breathed out, fatigue assaulting his soul with unbearable weariness. "I warned you it would get ugly."

He returned to the cell, his gaze flitting over the scattered photos and documents on the floor. He should take Cannon's file. He should gather the intel and find out what the FBI knew. No time.

Drake sat on the floor, his back to the wall, eyes shut and mouth agape. He held his left arm tight to his side. With every expansion of his chest, his face twisted tighter.

"We need to move," Drom said.

"You know," Drake said, "I was perfectly content with the idea of never getting beat up by you again. Were you born brutal or did you go to a special school for that?"

"You moving or do I need to carry you?"

Drake's eyes opened. Using the wall for support, he got his legs under him. "I'll manage." He held his hands up. "What about these?"

Drom unlocked the cuffs and tossed them to the floor. "We're two minutes behind clock. Slowing me down won't do, understand?"

Drake pushed off the wall. "You're the conductor. Which way?"

"Out the door, turn right. You'll find a hole in the wall. Go through it."

The pair made their way out, Drake in the lead. They stepped over the fallen guards and wriggled through the jagged hole. Drom reached into his backpack and grabbed the last two smoke grenades. He reran his calculations for the secondary timetable.

"Where to?" Drake asked.

"Hold. Fifteen seconds." Thirteen seconds later, he pulled the pins and rolled the grenades down the center of the cellblock. He shone the flashlight down the narrow utility crawl and landed it on the rung ladder fifteen feet ahead. "Reach that, go up."

He cut the light and shoved Drake forward. Footfalls echoed in the cellblock. Keeping his hand on Drake's back, he duck-walked at double time. They made the ladder. Voices reached them from behind, words with no meaning except that reinforcements had come. Drake climbed up. Drom gave him enough lead to be out of reach of a kick, then followed behind.

"How far?" Drake hissed several minutes later.

Drom shot a beam overhead, lighting up a square hatch thirty feet above Drake. "Two more floors, old man. Move."

Drom's right arm throbbed, his left was on fire. He pumped his legs rung by rung, ignoring their complaint. Pull, step, step. Pull, step, step. His useless hand grew cold and he worried that he had tied the bandage too tightly. His shock-induced nausea had him wondering if he had failed to tie it tight enough.

Light spilled down the shaft. He craned his neck back in time to catch Drake pulling himself through the hatch. Drom covered the distance between them with a hard heave followed by a vertical jump with his head tucked. His right shoulder caught the hatch, preventing it from slamming shut. He lashed out with his left arm, caught Drake's ankle, and yanked him off his feet. Springing out of the shaft, he kicked Drake's side as the man tried to rise.

Drake writhed on the floor, coughing. "If my ribs weren't broken before, they are now."

"I told you we don't have time for this. Getting away from me buys you nothing. Quit your whimpering and get up."

Drake struggled to his feet. "Had to try."

Drom glared at him for a beat, then checked their surroundings. They were in a mechanical room not much larger than a walk-in closet. Water and steam hissed through an array of pipes, breaker boxes hummed with energy. Tracing the electrical conduits with his eyes, he moved to the box nearest the door and flipped all the switches off.

The room went dark.

Cracking the door, he peered out. Emergency lights cast their harsh glare in the passageway. Nuclear shelter signs with directional arrows pointed the way to safety should humanity lose faith in itself. Drom slipped out and moved in the opposite direction, tugging Drake along with him.

They pushed through a set of double doors and left the world of bare concrete behind for the drab gypsum board walls of a service corridor. Drom guided them through it to the trash room. A commercial truck backup alarm beeped through the outside wall.

Drom rushed to the trash compactor controls. He punched the FORWARD button, counting in his head as the compression sequence cycled through. He climbed up the side of the hopper and jumped in. Crawling forward into the body of the self-contained compactor, he slid his hand across the slimed floor until he found a recessed metal ring. He hooked his fingers in it and pulled up. A section of the floor flapped open.

"Drake, get in here!"

The Drake peered over the hopper's edge, shaking his head. "A trash compactor? Gypsy bastard! This the best you could do?"

The container shuttered.

"Driver's lined up. This can leaves in twelve seconds."

Drake pulled himself over and dropped to the hopper floor. Drom watched as he squeezed head first through the opening in the false floor. Drom slid through behind him, feet first, and pulled the flap of metal back down.

The container lurched forward, tilted sharply, and began to climb.

Drake slid into Drom, smashing his injured arm against the plate steel. Grunting with pain, he shoved him off.

"You could have warned me they were going to lift it," Drake said.

"How else did you figure it was getting on the truck?"

Hydraulics whined and the container panned down to level. Another lurch forward was followed by constant motion. They were on their way. Sirens wailed, near and approaching.

"Move forward. There's more space up front," Drom said.

They slid under the false floor to the compartment behind the fake bulkhead in the nose of the compactor. There was enough room to sit up. Drom unbuckled the chest and waist straps of the backpack and shrugged it off. He thumbed the flashlight on and held it in his mouth as he dug through the pack.

He tossed a set of clothes to Drake, then took the light out of his mouth. "Change."

He killed the light and worked himself into a brown hoodie, biting his lip as he pulled the sleeve over his right arm. He leaned back against the cold steel and rested a moment, waiting for the throbbing in his arm to subside. Ducking his head through the neck hole, he settled it into the large hood and sleeved his left arm.

"Where are you taking me?" Drake sounded as winded as Drom felt.

"The grave if I don't get some answers." Drom unclipped the fanny packs, skinned the kneepads, and shimmied out of his trousers. He donned a pair of blue jeans and slipped into an oversized jean jacket. "What can you tell me about Bastien Frabron?"

"Bastien who?"

Drom blared the light into Drake's eyes. The man blinked several times, then turned away. "You're locked in a metal box with me. You saw what I did to Swenson. You know what I did to you even after you shot me the first time. You sure this is how you want to play it?"

Drake's eyes came back to him. "I've been in a hole since you've been dead, boy. Anything I know is irrelevant, ancient history."

"Ancient history is what I'm after."

"Frabron. Phfft. Bad enough you show up, ghost of failures past, you want to throw the Boogey Man into the mix too? How are you even here? What business does a dead man have with the Butcher?"

"He was in Madrid."

"Is that where you've been hiding? Who did the coroner carve up?"

"Madrid, four years ago. He approached Gregory Miles before I got to him."

"Your last death was too quick. I hope next time they burn you alive in an acid bath. Miles was a good man, a good intelligence officer."

"He was."

"You broke him all the way to his core."

"I know. But he's improving. Little by little, but he's getting better."

A bump bounced them both, interrupting their conversation. Drom kept quiet a moment, hoping the memory of violence coupled with the threat of it would be enough. Stockton said Boston had answers for them both. If Drake was the answer, then Stockton hadn't moved on much since Drom burned Shane Leoppard's Warehouse to the ground.

"You're not him," Drake said. "You look like him, you sound like him, you even move like him. But the Basque dog I put down would have killed Cannon and made me watch. And he sure wouldn't be checking in on former victims to see if they were getting better."

"Old dogs can learn new tricks."

"I suppose. But you're still a kid, so save it. What did Miles say?"

"Frabron knew CIA was hunting down a weapon."

"Velhoussen's fabric, the sun filter."

"The world's most devilish weapon of mass destruction. CIA wanted it, KGB wanted it, my father had it. I destroyed it."

"The fire?"

"The fire."

"So why the interest in Frabron now?" Drake asked.

"He told Miles that CIA was looking for the wrong weapon."

Drake whistled.

Another bump rattled the can. The truck changed directions, pressing Drom against the sidewall. He shone the light above Drake's shoulder. "I had them weld a handle. Best hold on." Clicking the light off, he grabbed the metal bar beside his head.

With a hiss of airbrakes, the truck stopped. The container rose to the beat of the hoist-up alarm. They came up a few degrees shy of vertical, then the container rolled down and landed with a jolt and a deafening crash.

"Frabron was DGSE." Drake's voice cut through the din. "He was also Mormon royalty who found a new religion."

The floor lowered to level. They were off the truck. Clicking gears reverberated in the dark and light cracked through the bulkhead, then widened.

"A Mormon in the DGSE?"

"Don't sound so shocked," Drake said. "You couldn't sneeze in an FBI office or CIA station without hearing one of them say, 'Bless you.' Why should the French be immune?"

The bulkhead swung away, a massive steel door. Grabbing his bag, Drom stepped out of the container. Once Drake was clear, Drom pulled back on the eyebolt. The angled false bulkhead dropped down with a bang and trash spilled down, filling the space in.

Drom tossed the backpack on top of the refuse and turned to the driver. "It all burns." The driver nodded. Drom marched to the door under the unlit exit sign. He shot a glance at Drake. The man hesitated a beat, then followed him out into the rain.

"What was Frabron doing in Madrid?" Drom asked.

"What are you doing in … where are we, exactly?"

"Boston. I was hired to extract Prisoner 69742."

They walked through narrow streets in silence. Drom lifted his hand into his jacket pocket for a sling. His sweatshirt sleeve was wet. He hoped it was the rain.

They crossed into a residential street with crammed rowhouses and cars parked bumper-to-bumper. He approached a purple Cadillac that hadn't seen the inside of a paint booth since leaving the factory in the early nineteen-seventies and reached under the back bumper. He pulled the hide-a-key tin loose, unlocked the car, and motioned for Drake to get in.

"Classy," Drake said. "Murderer and thief, I had you down for, but pimp? You're full of surprises today." They were on the interstate heading south before Drake spoke again. "Prisoner 69742. You didn't know it was me."

"No, I didn't. But since you are, whatever Frabron was after—is after—is somehow connected to my father."

Drake chuckled.

"What's so funny about that?" Drom asked.

"Ancient history, it has a way of haunting us."

"You said Frabron found a new religion. What's that about?"

"You know what, figure it out yourself. I shot Gavin Leoppard center mass. Agent Cannon had the body exhumed and showed me the photos and reports.

So you—Carlos, Sergio, Gavin, Drom, or whatever else you want to call your-self—are just a middleman. I'll play my cards for the man in charge."

"Suit yourself."

Drom drove another mile, then took the exit toward the inner harbor. He navigated through decaying waterfront neighborhoods that used to house mid-dle-class longshoremen. The tenements crumbled away, revealing bare docks and weathered concrete pilings. Pointing the hood at the waterline, Drom floored the accelerator. The Cadillac roared and the speedometer arced past sixty miles per hour and kept climbing.

Drake glared at him. "Hey, cut the—"

The car leapt from the pier and dove into the bay. Drake smacked into the dashboard, bounced back into the seat, and fell forward again. He pressed away from the dashboard and Drom kicked him into the passenger door. The Cadillac continued its dive, the engine pointing the way.

"You have three minutes of air. Use the time wisely and I'll make sure you don't drown. Keep fighting me and you can find your own way to the surface. Frabron's new religion?"

"*La Société des Cinq Cornes*. Best we could piece together, they recruited him when he was in the Legion."

"That sounds more like a social club than a religion."

"I take it you haven't been to church much," Drake said.

Water pressed its way past the door gaskets and through the air vents, nee-dling Drom's legs to mid-calf and rising. He clenched his jaw to keep it from rattling against the artic grip of the harbor. "Enlighten me."

"Frabron comes from a prominent Mormon family generations deep in the faith. He signed up for the Legion months into his mission. Not long after, he was associating with known members of Cinq Cornes. His rise in the Legion after that is the stuff of legends and guaranteed his placement in the intelligence services."

"What's the significance of Cinq Cornes. Five horns. Five horns of what?"

Waist deep in water, their air bubble was shrinking fast.

"Mérovée, the progenitor of the Merovigian dynasty, was supposedly fa-thered by a quinotaur."

"Not familiar."

"The quinotaur is a mythical five-horned sea creature, half bull, half fish. Mérovée became the touchstone for French nationalism and hegemony.

Mormons preach the promise of being god-like in the afterlife. La Société wasn't keen on waiting."

"How does this connect to Shane Leoppard?"

"We're twenty feet under water. How about you tell me your plan for not drowning."

The water engulfed their shoulders. "Shane Leoppard?"

"The French weren't the only ones with dreams of god-like hegemony. Their German cousins believed it to be their birthright. The Nazis tried to make the dream a reality. Men like Frabron and Shane believed they had found a way to make the dream come true."

"Frabron was in Madrid chasing my father?"

"Chasing whatever Shane was chasing. We dying together or are you a fish?"

Drom unbuckled his seatbelt and swam up to the back seat. He forced the stiffening fingers of his left hand to work the concealed latch on the back dashboard. The back of the bench seat dropped forward. Reaching into the trunk, he unclipped the metal springs from the first bottle, cracked the valve open, then donned the attached face mask.

He unclipped the second bottle, swam down to Drake, and shook his shoulder to stop him from beating against the glass with his fists. Bulged eyes stared at him over puffed cheeks. Drom handed him the rig and Drake slipped the air mask on.

Drom reached back into the trunk and grabbed the waterproof lantern and an ice ax. Gripping the shaft near the bottom, he drove the shaft spike against the back window. The glass spiderwebbed, then rushed into the cab as the water pressures equalized. He kicked through the opening, dropped the ax to the depths and turned in time to see Drake's shadowy form swim out of the car.

Drom turned the lantern on and shone the beam in Drake's face to get his attention. He swung the light toward shore and kept it on the mouth of a large drainage pipe stabbing out of the seawall.

They swam into it side by side. Handing the lantern to Drake, Drom took the lead with a one-armed front stroke. Spotting debris caught in cross current, Drom swam out of the main shaft. The light followed, glinting across the metal rungs running up the vertical pipe. He pulled himself up until his head broke water. Heaving his body out into the dank storm drain, he pulled the mask off. Drake splashed out moments later.

"Drop your bottle down the hole."

Drake ripped his mask off, coughed, then took a couple of deep breaths. "You give me a change of clothes and bring me to a sewer?"

Drom dropped his air bottle down the shaft after Drake's, then pointed. "That way. Not much farther now."

They scrambled along the drain, hunched over and shivering. A quarter mile later, they reached another set of rungs. Drom motioned for Drake to climb up, then followed him at a safe distance.

"Manhole cover," Drake said.

"Lighter than it looks. Out you go."

Metal scraped against concrete and light spilled down their well. Drake dropped the twelve-volt lantern, bouncing it off Drom's shoulder before he could get out of the way. "Payback."

Drom rose out of the hole into a bright pump room. Stockton was there, nurse orange blossom at his side. Drake was on a stool surrounded by other members of Stockton's medical team checking his vitals.

"You made it," Stockton said.

"You had doubts?"

"I had well educated reservations."

"This the big man?" Drake broke in.

Stockton turned toward him. "No, Mr. Drake. I'm just the broker."

The door behind Stockton swung open and a burly man in Army fatigues ducked through and towered beside him. "I'm the Big Man of this operation, Charles."

Drake eyed Drom then faced the Army man. "This day just keeps getting better. First, the FBI. Next, the ghost here wants to talk to me about the Boogey Man. And now the Scum. Tell me, Colonel, what would the Pond need from the likes of me?"

PART THREE

Rat-gêló

Chapter 34

We have devoted five years trying to narrow a dangerous gap born of illusion and neglect, and we've made important gains. Yet the threat from Soviet forces, conventional and strategic, from the Soviet drive for domination, from the increase in espionage and state terror remains great. This is reality. Closing our eyes will not make reality disappear.

State of the Union Address
President Ronald Reagan
February 4, 1986

Colorado Foothills – October 24, 1988

Shell basked in the heat from the fire pit, focusing on the flames in an attempt to forget all else, if only for a moment.

Robert stirred the coal bed with the poker and sparks danced up on the thermals, a galaxy in miniature expanding against the night sky. He slumped into the lawn chair next to her, his gaze fixed on the fire. "We ever going to discuss it?"

She stole a glance at his profile, at once reminiscent of Drom and totally different. Anger warred with longing. She picked a tongue of yellow with flares of blue and kept her eyes on it. "Nothing to discuss."

He caught her hand in a gentle grip. "Don't do this, Michelle. Don't shut me out."

Glaring at him, she jerked her hand away before his warmth could travel to places best ignored. With Drom gone, Robert was the one left she could hurt. "Don't call me Michelle. I haven't been that girl in a long time."

Robert kept his eyes locked with hers, his ice-gray stare chilling the heat of his opening overture. "Fine, *Shell*. We still need to talk about it."

"Talking about it will only make it worse."

"Talk about what?" Sharon stepped into the glow of the fire, an Indian blanket draped over her shoulders.

Robert leaned back in his seat, his eyes back on the flames. "I asked Shell to level with me about Amanda's father."

"Why do you want to dredge that up?" Sharon asked. "You know how traumatic that was for her, Sammy escaping prison and abducting her. Your brother killed the man, for pity's sake. Why would you…" Her voice faltering, she panned her gaze from Robert to Shell and back again. "Oh, dear God, no. You told me you never … You said you didn't…" Sharon spun, the draft of her blanket driving smoke and ashes into Shell, and ran into the house.

"Great!" Robert's glower pressed the air out of her. "We are going to talk this through."

She wasn't ready to retract her claws. "Best tend to your wife. We can wait."

"Not for much longer." He strode to the cabin.

Shell hunted for another flame she could hide in and failed. The present was too present. She pushed herself out of the lawn chair and shuffled to the light of the porch, her soles crunching on the frost-crusted leaves.

She soft-shoed up the steps, then hesitated at the door. Robert's voice vibrated through the wood, low and pleading. Sharon's tone scratched behind it, high and accusing.

She stared at the lit bedroom window of her motorhome. Amanda reading, no doubt. She was tempted to join her, to let Robert dangle on the hook of his own question. He wanted answers. Well, so did she.

Pings on a fence pole, rocks skipping across a lake from the hand of a four-year-old, Amanda's drop from the cliff. She hugged herself wondering why God let her have children. Why did she fall for dangerous men?

Drom, what have you done? What am I going to do?

Sharon's sobs poured through the door, drowning out Robert's consoling voice. They were suffering, mostly because of her. She shouldn't have come. And mad as she was, she knew she was wrong to take her anger out on them.

She eased inside and shut the door behind her. Sharon hunched at the table, face buried in her hands. Robert knelt beside her, his hand on her shoulder.

"What did you tell her?" Shell asked.

Sharon's face came up. She shrugged Robert's hand away. "He denies it. Are you going to deny it too?"

Shell looked from Sharon to Robert. "What have you told her?"

Steadying himself with the table, he pressed to his feet. "The day Shell and I ran after Amanda—"

"I don't want details," she glared at Shell, "from either of you. I just want to know it's over." She turned her face up to Robert. "Are you still in love with her?"

"Amanda was thirty feet up the rock face and climbing," Shell said.

Sharon looked at her. "What are you talking about?"

"She wanted to climb," Shell said. "She always wants to climb because…" The tears came and she tried restrain them, to shut down longing and loneliness with fear and anger. She crossed her arms and grit her teeth.

"She reached a ledge and Shell called her name," he said. "And Amanda let go."

"Let go? What you mean she let go?" Sharon's eyes darted between the two of them.

"It, uh, it …" Robert plunked down into the kitchen chair. "She … fell, kept bouncing off the juts of the cliff face, her body folding in on itself." He looked at her. "Shell?"

She bit her lip, not trusting herself to speak.

"Robert Gladstone, Jr.," Sharon said, "you stop this nonsense. Spinning tall tales is worse than silent denial."

"She flipped away from the rock face," Shell said, "and landed on her feet beside me."

"But that's …" She looked at them. "You're serious, both of you?"

"I watched it happen and still can't believe it," Robert said.

Sharon moved to the chair next to him. "Okay, I'm not going to pretend to get it. You two were acting weird when you got back with her and I thought …" She rubbed her eyes. "You two were talking about her father. What's this got to do with that?"

Robert took her hand. Sharon let him keep it. "Amanda was euphoric. She said she told her daddy she could do it. I want to know who daddy is."

Both of their eyes were on her now. "I tried to leave. You two were against it. I'm only here because you asked me."

"I wanted to protect you," Robert said. "But I need to know what's going on. We have our own drama, but who are you running from?"

Shell stood her ground, refusing to bolt and not moving closer. "No, you first. Drama doesn't cover what you're putting your family through. Who are we hiding from out here? What did you stumble into, Robert?"

He leaned back and ran his fingers through his hair. His head stayed on the chair back, his eyes on the ceiling. "A couple of years ago, President Reagan called for a new Orient Express during his State of the Union Address."

"Orient Express, like the train?" Shell asked.

"Only in name. The project had already started. He made it part of the speech because of the Challenger disaster. I guess he wanted to reassure us that America was still in the space business."

Ronald Reagan and space reminded Shell of the Strategic Defense Initiative the President proposed during his first term. The press dubbed it Star Wars. Scientists and senators worked for and debated against its development. And shadow warriors like Gavin Leoppard—Drom to her and Daddy to her children—had hunted an apparatus that made the entire concept obsolete.

Drom carried scars from the underground war resulting from Reagan's first-term dream. Now Robert was caught in the weave of this one. She took a seat across the table from him. "What was the Orient Express supposed to be?"

"A spaceliner capable of accelerating up to twenty-five times the speed of sound. Dulles Airport to Tokyo in two hours. Rockwell International calls it the X-30."

"You don't work for Rockwell," Sharon said.

"I don't, but my company does. The X-30 is a massive project requiring expertise from multiple industries. We were brought in to program flight control, specifically the GUI design."

"Gooey?" Sharon said. "English, Robert, please."

"Sorry. It's an acronym, not a word. It stands for graphical user interface. The NASA specs called for advanced graphic interfaces, an order of magnitude upgrade to current touch screens and attendant software."

"So they hired a video game company." Sharon sat straighter and wiped her eyes, clearing away some of her streaked mascara. "What happened?"

"The GUI did better than expected. Early on, I argued for look screen instead of touch screen, a means for the firmware and software to register the operator's eye position. It took some doing, but we worked it out. We ran the prototype through a hundred different tests, then called Rockwell and their military liaisons in for a demonstration."

"They bought it." Sharon rose from the table, filled a glass of water from the tap, and drank half of it in a single gulp. "You got promoted. You said you couldn't share the details because of the non-disclosure clause in your employment contract. But that was it, wasn't it?"

"Yes. I got promoted to Director of Research and Development."

"Why was your home ransacked?" Shell asked.

"The demonstration worked beyond Rockwell's expectations. They were ecstatic, as were the officers with them. But the equipment functioned below benchmark. If I hadn't been involved as I was, if I'd just stuck to my programming lane, I wouldn't have noticed."

"But it was off, so you had to look," Shell said. He was Shane Leoppard's son no less than Drom. Of course, he had to look.

"It's how it started. By the time I contacted DCIS, I felt I had enough evidence for them to act on. Someone built doorways into my code, a means of overriding pilot commands. They ran their demo in tandem with ours. It's what caused the minor glitches. I showed them what I had, but he said they needed more."

"That's when he asked you to spy on your own company," Sharon said. "That whole time, all those late nights. Why didn't you tell me?"

"I was afraid," Robert said.

"Afraid of what, Babe?"

"That you would talk me out of it."

Sharon drained her glass and set it on the counter. She made eye contact with Shell, then swept her gaze across the cramped quarters of their cabin. "I wish you had given me the chance."

"They compromised the integrity of the operating system of what promises to be one of America's most advanced weapons platforms. I couldn't let it go."

Sharon returned to her seat. She put her hand on Robert's and gave it a squeeze. "And this thing with Amanda really happened? You weren't worried you might be her father?"

"No chance, hun. Michelle and I never, you know." He turned away from Sharon and faced her. "Who was she trying to impress? Who is she calling Daddy?"

"Robert, please—" The door banged open. Shell spun in her seat.

Pizza Man was backing through the doorway. He made a slow turn, bringing into view a square-shouldered man in a wheelchair, his left leg held out straight on an elevated rest.

"Sorry to barge in at this hour," Pizza Man said. "I recruited an old childhood friend to help us. You can trust him."

The injured man removed his gray stocking cap and brushed a thick lock of mouse-brown hair away from his high brow. Shell noted the therapeutic tape binding his index and ring fingers together. The side of his face was green-hued with yellow highlights. The fading bruise ran from his temple to the bottom of his lantern jaw.

It must have been quite the accident, Shell thought.

The man reached inside his down jacket and came out with a wallet. He flipped it open, displaying a badge and identity card. "Special Agent Richard Cannon at your service."

Chapter 35

Sources close to the Winthrop Tower project claim faulty workmanship in the gas lines led to the explosion that destroyed a portion of the exterior wall on the thirteenth floor and shattered numerous windows in the surrounding buildings. No injuries were reported. Europlan Urbanlife has been renovating the former office building into upscale apartments.

The Boston Globe, October 12, 1988

Colorado Foothills – October 24, 1988

Rick closed his credentials wallet and stuffed it back into his coat pocket. "James, care to make the introductions?"

His comment was calculated. According to James, only the informant knew his name. To the women, he was Pizza Man. Using his name could ease the tension and buy him some trust with the near thirty-year-olds huddled at the table.

He studied Robert Gladstone. *"Do you believe in ghosts, Cannon?"* Bastien's voice haunted his head. Being assaulted by a man he'd dug out of the grave was its own brand of horror, staring at a copy of Shane Leoppard's face was another. He longed for the simplicity of spreadsheets.

"You have a last name, James, and a fancy wallet like your FBI buddy?" The brunette's cherrywood eyes were on his friend.

James displayed his credentials. "James D. Cooper. The D is for David, like your youngest." Returning the leather fold to his pocket, he made the introductions. "The gentleman at the table is Robert Gladstone, my informant. The blonde lady beside him is his wife, Sharon. And this is their friend, Michelle Lane. Do I have that right, Ms. Lane?"

The woman made as if to speak, then bit her lip. She scooped a stray lock of thick hair with her thumb and tucked it behind her ear. "It's late. You folks obviously have lots to discuss, so if you'll excuse me." She rose.

Rick put out his hand. "Please stay, Ms. Lane. This matter involves you as much as the Gladstones now."

"Actually," she said, "I've been more involved than any of us likes. I'll leave y'all to it. I have children to look after."

Rick noted the southern slip in her otherwise non-regionalized speech. She took a step toward the door. Pulling back on his left wheel, he moved his elevated leg in her path. "Stay. I insist."

She moved a half-step closer, then looked over her shoulder at the Gladstones. "You two don't need me here, right?"

The couple exchanged a look, then the Shane look-alike spoke. "The kids are fine, Shell. Amanda would get you if there was a problem. Let's see what Agent Cannon has to say."

Her polished irises landed back on him. "You look like you've been in a car wreck."

"I feel like I was hit by a bulldozer. Would you mind rolling me to the table? The chill is no friend to these broken bones." He lifted his right hand with its taped fingers to strengthen his plea. If he could get her sympathy now, she might be more cooperative later.

"Pizza Man delivered you through the door just fine. I'm sure he can manage getting you to the table." She turned her back on him and headed to the coffee maker on the counter. She pulled the carafe from under the drip basket and faced the room. "I need a cup. Anyone else?"

"Might as well make a full pot." James rolled him to the table. "This could take a while."

Rick watched her as she prepared the pot, then turned to the Gladstones across the table. Sharon's eyes were red and swollen, her mascara smeared. Robert perched on the edge of his seat, tight-jawed, his eyes drifting between the two women.

Something going on there.

James stashed these people in his grandfather's cabin at the end of September. A lot could happen in a month. Mrs. Gladstone was easy on the eyes, but the Lane woman was a breath taker.

"I take it you've reviewed the evidence?" Gladstone asked him.

He tore his gaze from Ms. Lane and addressed him. "I have. I won't pull any punches here, Mr. Gladstone. It doesn't look good for you. The search was clean and the drug packs had your prints on them. On top of that, you've jumped bail. I think the best an excellent lawyer could get for you is a reduced sentence in a plea bargain."

The man's jaw muscle twitched. Rick expected to hear teeth grinding next. His leg throbbed all the way to the center of his brain. He skipped his morphine dose in favor of a clearer head for this meeting. But the pain made him edgy. He feared he was coming on too strong. He didn't need Robert Gladstone blowing up on him.

To his surprise, the man blew out a long breath through pursed lips and leaned back in his chair. "The folks in Denver consider me a fugitive?"

"I'm afraid so. Your arraignment was three weeks ago."

Gladstone rose and moved toward the coffee maker. Ms. Lane met him halfway with a steaming mug. He took a sip, nodded appreciatively, then settled back into his seat. "They're not aware of the DCIS involvement?"

"The locals? No."

"Thank God."

Not the reaction Rick was aiming for. He wanted Gladstone to feel isolated, make him need what Rick had to offer. "You aren't worried about the charges?"

"I know powerful people are working against me. It doesn't change the truth."

"How do you and Pizza Man know each other?" Ms. Lane leaned against the counter, her coffee mug held in both hands. The mug rose to her full lips and she took a sip, a long lock of chestnut hair spilling away from the confinement of her ear.

Sweat rolled down his sides. He resisted the urge to pull his jacket it off. "James and I grew up in the same church."

Gladstone leaned forward, the corners of his mouth up a tick. "You're believers?"

Faith mattered to Gladstone. It could be an in. "Yes. We're Latter-day Saints. You?"

The smile died and he looked away. "Uh, Christian. My wife and I are." He glanced over at Ms. Lane. "And Shell." He didn't sound so sure. "I asked if you had reviewed the evidence. I meant the information I gave James, not the junk they planted on me."

"I shared it with him," James said.

"And?"

"Do you still have the hard drives?" Rick asked him.

"I know where they are."

"I vetted the code chunks you gave us with some top-notch experts in the Bureau. Without knowing the full scope, all they could tell me was that the algorithms were intelligently compromised. It wasn't programming errors. It was tight code that buried alternate functions."

Robert put his elbows on the table, one hand clenching the other. "And that's not enough?"

"The code portions …" If his leg wasn't broken, Rick would have gotten up and paced for effect. As it was, he had to content himself with spinning his knit cap on his finger to fill the pause. "You wouldn't have any way of knowing this. Here's the thing, Robert, may I call you Robert?" Gladstone nodded. "The buried code is proprietary, U.S. military grade."

"What's that supposed to mean?" Robert exploded away from the table, arms raised. His chair clattered to the floor. His wife slid hers to the side, giving him space.

Ms. Lane laid a hand on his wrist like a woman soothing her lover. "Breathe, Robert." Her voice was soft and hypnotic.

Rick relaxed into his seat sling, unaware of his body tension until it released. James told him Ms. Lane came up with the get-away plan from Denver. Now her voice was calming the room. He was forced to raise his initial estimation of the woman.

Robert did as instructed. After two breaths, his arms hung at his sides. After a third, he righted the chair and sat down. "My apologies. I'm a bit stressed, as you can imagine."

"Understandable," Rick said.

"You'll have to be clearer about the code. You say 'military grade' like it's something special. All due respect, I was writing next generation military programs. The program languages are the program languages. You might as well have said, 'the guys on the recording were speaking military grade English.'"

"Fair enough." Rick raised his hands palms out and instantly regretted it. The move sent a bolt of agony from his broken fingers to his elbow. "Listen, the tech stuff is way over my head. I'm a glorified accountant. I'll try my best, though, to explain what my folks told me. Your company was developing new technology, hardware and software, correct?"

"Yes. We've invented completely new interfaces."

"What processors did you use?"

"State of the art, best the market had to offer."

"The Department of Defense has processors better than the market can offer. They talk in a different language, the type of language the compromising code packs were written in."

Robert scrubbed his face. "Help me, Jesus! I'm deep in the pile, aren't I?"

"Yes," Rick said. "But exactly how deep depends on a couple of things."

"Like?"

"How forthcoming you decide to be with me, for starters."

"For starters? I'm the one that brought this to James."

"But you didn't give him all you had. I'm going to need a bit more access."

"I'm not handing over the drives without assurances. I want the false charges cleared and help getting a job when this is done."

Rick gave a slight turn on his wheels and parked at an angle against the table's edge. "I can work something out, but I need information from you first."

"I'm an open book. Ask away."

"What is your relationship with Gavin Leoppard?"

Earthenware shattered across the floor. Sharon sprang out of her seat, her pant leg spattered with coffee. Ms. Lane stood pale-faced, hands trembling.

Now we're getting somewhere.

"Shell, you okay?" Sharon asked.

Ms. Lane stared at him for a beat, then turned and grabbed a dish towel. "Sorry, the mug slipped." She knelt to clean up the mess.

"What does Gavin Leoppard have to do with any of this?" Robert's jawline twitched.

"So, you know him," Rick said.

Robert rose, glaring at Cooper. "Jim, what is this? What game is your friend playing?"

"Hear him out, Robert. We need his help. He needs yours."

Sharon moved to the sink, wet a towel, and spot cleaned her pant leg. She came behind her husband and whispered in his ear. He turned his head toward Ms. Lane as she dumped the mug shards in the trash bin, parked her back against the wall, and crossed her arms.

What did Gladstone read there? Permission? Resignation? Whatever it was, the man sank in his chair with a sigh and faced him. "What is it you want to know?"

"You mind if I get some coffee first?" He glanced at James. "Would you be so kind? Cream, no sugar. Ms. Lane, another cup?"

She shook her head.

James poured them each a mug and returned to the table. Sharon came around, moved her chair closer to her husband, and settled in. Ms. Lane stood her ground, odd woman out.

Rick took a sip and set the mug down. "What was your relationship to Gavin Leoppard?"

"My mother was his guardian," Robert said.

"She was fostering him?"

"No. He showed up on her doorstep one day needing help and she took him in."

"Just like that?"

"Just like that."

"Your mother in the habit of taking in strays?"

"She was a social worker for years. She's always had a soft spot for troubled teens." Robert glanced at Ms. Lane. She stared at the floor.

"When did he show up?" Rick asked.

"It was …" Robert's eyes went up to the left, then reconnected with his. "Around five years ago."

"I've been to the grave," Rick said. "What happened to him?"

"Honestly, I have no idea. He was with my mother for six or seven months, then disappeared. Spring of eighty-four, I think. About a year later, he came back to my mother in a casket."

"Someone must have known he was important to her."

"Your guess is as good as mine. Or, maybe better? What's your interest in him?"

"Like your case, his is a matter of national security. But his presents the greater danger."

"How can that be?" Robert asked. "You've seen his grave. We buried Gavin. I can't see him posing any national security risk. Meanwhile, I'm holed up here with my family because James can't trust his own agency."

These people kept surprising him. That, or he seriously needed to take his pain meds and damn the consequences. He had to get them back on track. "I not only saw the grave, I exhumed the body." He gave his wheel a slight tug so he could face Ms. Lane. Her expression was blank. "Ms. Lane, I know some of that missing year. I can show you where Gavin was, if you care to join us at the table."

His comment turned all eyes on her. She glanced at Robert. Looking for what? Strength? Help? She dropped her arms and faced him. "You know?"

"That you and he were lovers? Yes. James tells me you have an older girl, Amanda?"

She nodded.

"And two young boys," Rick continued. "David and …?"

"Jakob," she said.

"Gavin's son?"

"Yes."

"Ms. Lane, I've read the police reports about Amy's … sorry, Amanda's father. I don't blame you. If that had happened to me, I would want a new start. I would leave town, change my name, and never look back."

She put her hands in her pockets and stared out the dark window over the sink. "Sammy was a monster."

"And he died a monster's death. You were in love with Gavin Leoppard, were pregnant with his child when he saved your life. He disappeared only to come back in a coffin a year later. Don't you want to know what happened?"

Her shoulders hunched, like she was wrestling with herself. Her face came up and she tucked her beguiling lock behind her shapely ear. Brushing her nose with the back of her hand, she peeled away from the wall. Robert pulled a chair out for her and she joined them at the table.

Rick reached behind him and hefted his leather satchel off the wheelchair handles. Setting in his lap, he unbuckled the flap and pulled the folder out. He placed it on the table and dropped the satchel on the floor beside him.

He examined their faces a moment, then leaned as far forward as he could. "Folks, I am truly here to help you, all of you. It is not my intention to barge in and open old wounds. Unfortunately, I need to share some things with you." He patted the file. "Difficult things. Let me start with a baseline."

His first photo was from John Swenson's collection, one of the many pieces of evidence gathered during his murder investigation. He handed the black-and-white headshot to Robert. "Recognize that boy?"

Robert stared at it for a couple of seconds, then handed it back. "Looks like Gavin, a bit younger than when we met him."

"Ms. Lane?" Rick skated the picture to her.

She looked down, but didn't touch it. "That's Gavin."

"That picture comes from a CIA file. At the time, Gavin was a contract agent the Madrid station referred to as 'the Basque.'"

No one spoke. He studied their expressions. None of them seemed surprised. They knew more than they were willing to say. So be it.

Reaching back into the folder, he slipped out another eight-by-ten glossy, leaving it face down on the table. "I am sorry to have to do this, but I need to make sure." He slid the photo over to Robert. "Please take a look. The embalmer did an excellent job. The decay is minimal for a body that's been buried for four years."

Taking a deep breath, Robert turned the picture over. Sharon glanced away from the color print. He slid it back. "It's him."

Rick picked it up and handed it to James. Just as they had planned it, James walked the photo over to Ms. Lane, and placed it in front of her on the table.

She kept her eyes forward.

"Ms. Lane, I know this is difficult," Rick said. "I need confirmation from you before I proceed."

She turned to Robert. His eyes softened. She bit her lip and bent over the photo. Her eyes sprang wide with her gasp. She sat up, her posture rigid. "It's … it's Gavin."

"When he left you," Rick laid his hand on the sheaf of photos, "he went back to Europe, to his old job. These are pictures of some of his handiwork." He delt them to her at a measured pace, slow enough to see and register, too quick for her to recover before the next shock.

A man sprawled on a discotheque floor, a dagger through his throat. A bloody figure crumpled on a racquetball court, the walls pockmarked with blood splatter. Swenson's cannibalized face in close up.

She brought her hand to her mouth, shoulders trembling. She caught him in her wet gaze and pushed the stack back. "I don't need to see any more."

Locking eyes with her, he gave himself a four count before leaning forward and retrieving the prints. "Ms. Lane, you suggested I might have been in a car wreck." He tapped the photos on the table top, straightening the stack. "The actual cause and circumstances surrounding my injuries are classified top secret, which leaves us in a pickle."

Her eyes narrowed. "Us? I'm sorry you're hurt, but it's got nothing to do with me."

He filed away the SL/OMEGA shots and pulled another set from the folder. He held up two of them. "I took these pictures myself on a burned-out lot near

Penticton, British Columbia." Once again, he handed them to James who stepped behind her and laid them out.

Her head turned from one to the other, then she closed her eyes and held her forehead in the grip of her right hand. Her lips moved and a word whispered out.

"I'm sorry," Rick said. "I didn't catch that."

Her face came up, her fist pressed against her lips. Tears spilled down her cheeks. "The mannequins. Dear God!" She flattened her hand across her mouth and sprang away from the table. She crossed to the sink, bent over it, and heaved through a choking sob.

Gladstone got halfway out of his seat and his wife tugged on his forearm. He swept his gaze from Ms. Lane to his wife, then plopped down. He grabbed the pictures of the tortured mannequins. "What is this about?"

"It's what I am here to find out." Rick waited while Ms. Lane rinsed her mouth and splashed water on her face. She dried it with the dish towel and faced the room. Her lock was loose again, her eyes red, but hard. Her jaw was set, her shoulders back. She looked shocked, harried, caged, defensive, determined, and disarmingly beautiful.

"I need to go," she said. "I've left my children alone long enough."

Rick swallowed on a dry throat. "Just a few more minutes, Ms. Lane, please. I can't help Robert without your cooperation."

She tucked the lock. "I can't help you."

"You've already helped me more than you know. Please, sit."

Robert glanced over his shoulder and they exchanged a look. She pushed off from the sink and took her seat, avoiding Rick's attempt to maintain eye contact.

He pinched several pictures from the stack and held them against his chest. "These images are from CCTV footage in a maximum security facility. By law, I am not allowed to show them to you. That's my pickle."

She finally met his eyes. "And mine?"

"That depends on what you do after I break the law." He sailed three of the photos across the table. Each showed groups of armed guards sprawled on the floor, eyes open and mouths agape.

"Are they …" Her hand covered her mouth for a second. "What happened to them?"

"Not what, Ms. Lane, who. An operative broke into the facility. Twenty-five guards, Ms. Lane. One man did this to twenty-five of the CIA's best trained special operations personnel."

Robert craned over to get a better look. "One man?"

"I was in the facility interrogating a witness. The intruder opened the cell and I managed to hit him with a chair."

"Good for you." Mrs. Gladstone's tone was sincere.

"Not good for me. This is the man entering the cell." He handed the photo to James who placed it between Robert and Ms. Lane. The cell doorway backlit a man in silhouette. "I knocked him to the ground and stepped forward for a follow through."

He laid out the next shot. The imaging wizards had performed their magic on the dark footage from the CCTV feed, coaxing enough light onto Rick's grimacing features so that he was recognizable. The intruder was on the floor on his side, back to the camera. His leg was extended, foot flat against the inside of Rick's knee. The unnatural bend in Rick's leg was unmistakable.

He kept his eyes on Ms. Lane as she picked up the photo. She winced, then traveled her gaze up his braced leg. "How bad?"

"Compound tibial fracture. It took a couple of metal plates and a bunch of screws to piece it back together." He didn't bother to mention that someone had applied first aid before they found him. "I'm in the wheelchair for another month or so, and then it's on to crutches. They tell me that maybe by summer, I can start putting a little weight on it."

"I'm sorry," she said. She was looking at him but seemed to be seeing something else.

"Ma'am, in my career I've encountered world class criminals and men expert in violence. I have never seen anything like this. In a facility with more cameras than Rockefeller Plaza, he got in and out without once showing his face. Well, almost once."

He slid his last picture to her, the intruder leaving the cell. She held it up, then dropped it like it burned her fingers. Bracing her arms around her midriff, she rocked herself to low-pitched keening.

"Shell?" Robert came out of his chair, disregarding his wife's hold. He knelt beside her. "Shell, what is it?"

She didn't acknowledge him and kept folding into herself. "How could you? Dear God, how could you?"

Robert picked up the photo, then faced Rick. "It can't be. This is some sort of mistake."

"I'm afraid not," Rick said. He leaned in toward her. "Ms. Lane?" Then louder, "Ms. Lane."

She looked at him, but wouldn't speak, lost in her own turmoil and pain.

"Ms. Lane, or should I call you Mrs. Reiziger? I don't know why monsters seek you out." He had a good idea why and unfocused his eyes. "But you don't have to protect them. Years ago, you were brave and put a murderer behind bars. I'm asking you to be brave again. Help me bring him in."

She shook her head. "It's too much." She bolted from the table and was out the door before Robert could gain his feet.

"Let her go," Mrs. Gladstone said.

He handed her the photo ran after Ms. Lane.

"James, help me." Rick spun his chair around and they rolled out in pursuit.

James lowered the chair down the steps. Turning left, he set off in a trot. Rick couldn't make out anything beyond the cast of the porch light in the starless night. Snow flurried past, small and sharp.

"Amanda!" Ms. Lane's cry cut through the darkness. "Oh my, God! Baby, talk to me."

Floodlights came on, their sudden flare hurting Rick's eyes. The camper came in view, its side door hanging by a hinge. Michelle Lane, a.k.a. Shell Reiziger, sat cross-legged on the ground, cradling a girl.

"Jakob! David! JAKOB!" Robert's calls boomed out of the motorhome.

"Call it in, James. Get help out here." Rick rolled forward and stopped beside Ms. Lane.

Robert flew out of the motorhome and raced up a trailhead. "Jakob! David!"

The girl groaned and looked at her mother. Her lip was split, her nose bloody. "I tried, Mommy." Her voice was thin. She moved to sit up, but her mother cradled her again.

"Shh, honey. You're safe now." She rocked her, stroking the child's back.

Amanda pushed away and scrambled to her feet. "We have to catch them." She took two steps and collapsed.

Ms. Lane crawled over and gathered her up. "You're hurt, honey. Help's coming. Mommy's here."

"I tried to stop them. I couldn't, Mommy. They were too big."

"Who, baby? Who was too big?"

"The bad men. They took the boys."

"Jakob! David!" Robert's voice was working its way back to them.

"Ambulance is on the way," James said.

"Law enforcement?" Rick asked.

Ms. Lane spun into him. "You did this!" She pounded his braced shin with her fist and he howled with the shock of it. "You brought this!" She kept punishing his injured leg.

James restrained her after a brief struggle. "Ms. Lane, Ms. Lane, we need to look after your daughter."

Rick took a series of short breaths to ride out the crest of the pain. Robert replaced James at Ms. Lane's side, then scooped Amanda up. "Let's get her inside, Shell." He headed to the cabin and she followed.

Rick faced the motorhome. "I need to get in there."

"I can't get your wheelchair through that door," James said. "And you're not supposed to put any weight on that leg."

"Can't hurt it worse than she just did. Get me inside."

James rolled him to the stoop. Rick swung the leg rest out of the way and with James's help, got on his good leg. Leaning on his friend, he hopped up the steps one at a time. He held onto the doorframe and pulled himself in.

The motorhome was ransacked.

Dragging his injured leg, Rick stumbled to the galley. There was blood on the floor and smears of it on the cabinets, more than Amanda's nose and lip could account for. *I tried to stop them.* What had the little girl done?

He made it to the back bedroom and peered inside. Cabinets over and beside the bed were smashed open. Broken doors and trim littered the comforter. Hopping forward, he landed wrong and fell down.

"For pity's sake!"

"You all right in there?" James called from behind him.

"Fine! Took a spill, that's all." He slid his buttocks under him, his leg dragging a toddler's boot toward him. He grabbed it to toss it out of the way, then noticed the broken heel. Pulling it the rest of the way off, he found a key hiding in its hollow.

Using the bed for support, he pressed onto his good leg. Scanning the damaged cabinets, he spotted gray metal behind some of the broken trim. He got on the bed, scooched across it, and clawed the rest of the wood away. He stared at the built-in lock box a moment, then slipped in the key he had found.

He reached inside the box and came out with a stack of Canadian passports. The first three belonged to the children. The next one pictured Michelle Lane and identified her as Shell Reiziger. The last one belonged to the dead man not dead, Drom Reiziger, a.k.a. Gavin Leoppard.

Rick kissed the passport. "Gotcha!"

Rolling over, he sat up. On the wall beside the door, someone had painted a black hexagon, the five horns of the quinotaur drawn in its center. "Joseph, Mary, and Brigham!"

Chapter 36

Drink the sea and know the Supreme Intelligence drew you from bitter waters. Eat the grass and be reminded man is not a beast. Taste the honey and embrace wisdom's sweetness. Grasp the Third Horn with your left hand and raise your right hand to the Mayor of the Palace and declare: I swear to give my all for the continual evolution of man.

Lecture on the Rite of the Third Horn
Alfred Phélypeaux, conte de Saint-Exupéry
La Société des Cinq Cornes
Lyon, France, June 21, 1895

Drancy Internment Camp, Paris, France – April 1943

Hefting the last pot, Hishoro carried it to the serving line of Block 14. Eyes fixed on the steaming broth, she minced her steps to keep the thin soup from sloshing. Her stomach growled. Serve first, eat later; that was the rule. She glanced up. Five meters to go. She tripped, tried to regain her balance, and fell, splashing the boiling liquid over her hands.

"Stupid, clumsy *gitane* whore!"

The kick caught her midriff, knocking the wind out of her. She balled up in the puddle of scalding soup as a flurry of kicks followed the first, each salted with insults of increasing debasement.

Whistling broke through the ringing in her head. Opening an eye, she saw two gendarmes restraining Evry, the UGIF kapo. He was far from his post. Willing her body to move, she pressed her hands against the rough concrete, got on all fours, then rose on trembling legs.

One of the gendarmes pointed at the pot with his baton. "Pick it up and get back to the kitchen."

The gendarmes frog-marched Evry toward the camp office. She bent over, head and ribs screaming, and lifted the pot. Fire flared through both hands. The pot bounced on the sidewalk, ringing. Stitching sense to sound and sight, her mind forced her to inspect her hands. Blisters covered both of them.

"Let me help you." A woman's voice, foreign and kind. A hand grasped her elbow and pulled. Hishoro followed. She lifted her head to see her helper and the world spun. She dropped her gaze. The calves beside her were sheathed in silk, the feet shod in brown leather lace-up heels.

Hishoro's feet were bare.

"That brute tripped you. As if we don't have enough trouble with the Germans and their Vichy lapdogs." Her French held German overtones. Her sentiment contrasted with her accent, adding to Hishoro's disorientation.

She concentrated on breathing. Her soles struck dirt and the world brightened as they came out of the shadow of the covered walkway into the open courtyard. Hishoro registered the thumps and clinks of the work crew digging up the grounds in their attempt to realize the architect's original vision for the *Cité de la Muette*, as if beautifying the prison camp would make it less cruel.

"Laughter," the woman said. "That's good. You might survive this."

Hishoro didn't realize she had laughed. Had Evry kicked her head? He must have.

"What is your name?" The woman asked.

"Hishoro." Her mind wandered to the work below ground. How long before she could crawl out with her family? The curb on the other side of the courtyard caught her by surprise and she stumbled.

"Careful." The woman pulled her along to a door painted with a square, red cross. Hishoro stopped. "No."

The woman leaned down to her, ruby-lipped and light-skinned. Compassionate brown eyes held hers. "You are badly burned and probably concussed. I know the doctor. Let's get you looked at, shall we?" She opened the door and pulled Hishoro in.

The astringent air turned her shallow breathing into a mercy. She risked a turn of her head and took in the clinic. It was about the size of her apartment with half as many beds. Several sections were cordoned off with white curtains. Men, women, and children were scattered on the beds in no discernable pattern. Incessant coughing drummed backbeat to moans and pleas.

Other smells wormed through the chlorine. Pungent iron from blood-soaked bandages mingled with sour vomit and putrid dysentery. She shifted toward the door, but the woman tugged her back.

A nurse in a blue dress with a white apron, her golden hair stuffed in a bleached bonnet decorated with a red cross, sailed to them. "Hélène, I just shooed you out of here! You cannot keep working like this."

"I couldn't leave her." She lifted Hishoro's elbow, bringing her hand in view.

"You must have passed a dozen others with worse problems. Why bother bringing a *gitane* here?"

"Help me wrap her up and I promise to get some rest."

They led her behind one of the curtains and sat her on the examining table. Hélène stepped out while the nurse gathered her information. "How did you burn them?"

"The soup spilled."

"You should be more careful. The camp doesn't have food to waste."

"It wasn't her fault, Gisele." Hélène set a basin of water down next to Hishoro. "One of the kapos tripped her on the way to the serving line."

Gisele's face hardened. "I thought your people would be more compassionate."

"I thought you were less bigoted."

The two women stared at each other for a moment, their tension adding to Hishoro's discomfort. She started scooching off the table.

Gisele placed a hand on her thigh. "We need to treat those burns."

Hélène lowered her hands into the cool water in the basin. The relief was immediate. Using a soft cloth, Hélène swabbed days of grime away from her sore fingers, calloused palms, and blistered skin.

"Do you think Karl could examine her?" Hélène asked.

"He left shortly after you did. We can handle this. No need to bother the doctor." Gisele dried Hishoro's hands, her touch lacking Hélène's feathered grace. She refused to wince as several of the blisters tore away.

Hélène winced for her. She dabbed jelly from the cobalt jar onto the burns, then wrapped the hands in gauze. She faced Gisele. "I am no less an inmate than she is. Not long ago, you and I were like sisters. Both of us are here now, but you can still go home. I could be sent to the train station tomorrow."

"Nonsense," Gisele said. "Monsieur Blum wouldn't put you on the list."

"You still believe he has a say? His office is just a nicer prison cell. They mean to have us all out of France."

Gisele glanced about, then stepped closer to Hélène and lowered her voice. "It cannot last. Like a bad fever, this Nazi madness will break."

"Would that it was only the Nazis."

"That isn't fair, Hélène. I'm here. I'm helping. All of France isn't poisoned."

Hélène hugged her friend. "You are right." Taking a half-step back, she palmed Gisele's face. "Help me save as many as we can."

"Let's finish with this one, then you take the rest you promised."

They turned their attention back on her. Hélène helped her remove her blouse and they inspected her for other injuries. Hélène wrung the cloth out and gave Hishoro a sponge bath after which Gisele bandaged her ribcage.

"This will help a little bit with the pain," Gisele said. "Broken or bruised, time is the only cure for injured ribs."

Hélène helped her off the examination table and led her out of the ward.

"Come by day after tomorrow and I'll change the dressing," Gisele called after her.

Hishoro looked over her shoulder. *"Merci."*

Back in the courtyard, Hélène quickened her step, Hishoro's elbow still in her guiding hand. Their angle led to Stair Ten.

Hishoro stopped. "I need to get back to the kitchen."

Hélène gave her a sad smile. "Not today, you don't. Those burns will heal so long as you keep your hands clean and dry. You are too hurt to carry pots and are certainly in no condition to wash them."

Hishoro didn't move. "Thank you for your help, *mademoiselle,* but I'm afraid it's work or the apartment for me. I don't need any more attention from the kapos or gendarmes."

"When did you last eat?"

Hishoro kicked the dirt with her toes. "Yesterday or the day before, maybe."

"Come. No one will bother you so long as you are with me."

Hélène strode on. Hishoro hesitated a moment, then let her stomach lead her feet. Hélène turned left at the entrance to Stair Ten and opened the door to an apartment on the ground floor. Hishoro envied her easy access to her quarters even though she recoiled at the thought of the floors of filth over her head.

Hélène led them toward the back, ignoring the complaints of the other women about Hishoro's presence. She stopped at a bunk by a barred window and invited Hishoro to sit down.

"I've been saving this." She pulled a bundle from under her pillow. "Gisele baked *challah* for me. I'm certain it wasn't done in a kosher kitchen, but the blessing has to be greater than any contamination, don't you think?"

She untied the checkered tea towel, exposing the browned bread with its shining glaze. She held the loaf up in both hands, looked up at the ceiling, and chanted words Hishoro didn't understand. She broke the bread and handed Hishoro half. Hélène took a bite of hers and chewed it as if savoring every crumb.

Hishoro followed suit and was surprised at the bread's lightness and hint of sweetness. She tried to match Hélène's respectful pace, but found her stomach too demanding. By the time Hélène swallowed her first bite, Hishoro's half roll was gone.

"My, you were hungry. I can't blame you for wolfing it down. Gisele outdid herself. I suppose she tasted my mother's *challa* enough that she figured a way to replicate it."

"You two are friends, but you chanted a spell in case the bread was bad."

"A spell? No, something more powerful. It was a prayer, a blessing of thanks for the bread."

Something more powerful than a spell?

She made the sign against *beng* and pain shot through her fingers. Maybe blessings were better. "What are the words?"

Hélène's eyes widened. "What use does a Roma woman have for a Jewish prayer?"

"If it's stronger than a spell as you say, it could change my luck."

"That's not how prayers work, but I'll teach it to you. *Baruch atah Adonai Elohainu,* Blessed are You, Lord our God. You try."

Hishoro repeated the words. "That's it?"

"No, that's just the first part. But you got it right. You have an ear for language."

"I am Roma."

The woman looked at her as if unsure why that should explain it. "The next part is *Melech Haolam, hamotzi lechem min haaretz,* King of the Universe, who brings forth bread from the earth."

"King of the Universe? Who is he?"

"*Adonai Elohainu,* the Lord our God."

"Oh, it's another title for your god."

"No, it is the title of the God most high, the Creator of the heavens and the earth Who gave us the Sabbath."

"The Sabbath?" Hishoro thought of Tshuri's letter. "Is he the Lord of the Sabbath?"

"I've never heard it phrased that way, but it would be right to call Him that."

"*Baruch atah Adonai Elohainu, Melech Haolam, hamotzi lechem min haaretz.*"

Hishoro kept her eyes on the woman instead of the ceiling as she said the prayer.

"That's it. You've got it."

"Thank you for the bread and your help. You remind me that not all *gazhe* are bad."

"*Gazhe?* Is that the Roma word for Jews?"

"No, it's what we call anyone who isn't Roma."

Hélène laughed. "We have a similar word for all non-Jews. We call them *goyim*."

"Perhaps we are cousins."

"Don't tell the Nazis I said so, but we're all related, Hishoro. Let me walk you to your stair." She rose, brushing the crumbs off her skirt.

"No, you have done enough already. I'll manage. Your friend was right. Even I can see you need rest."

Hélène sunk back onto her bunk, her face losing its brave smile. "I am weary. Be careful. And do return to the infirmary. Ask for Gisele. She will take care of you."

Hishoro left, sad for the departure and anxious for the smells of her own apartment. She stepped off the sidewalk into the dirt of the courtyard and marched with her head down.

Teams of gendarmes charged past her. She turned to see what the commotion was about. The guards poured up Stair Ten while others banged on the ground floor apartments. Whistles blared and the command shouted out. "Pack it up! Pack it up! Twenty minutes! You have twenty minutes!"

Inmates stumbling out of the stair were herded into the courtyard. Hishoro stood transfixed until she caught sight of Hélène being hauled out of her apartment. They shoved her into one of the lines, a battered valise in her hand.

Stair Ten was being deported to Pichipoi.

What if Stair Eighteen was being marched out? If she got separated from Keti and the boys, how would she find them?

Her ran, her skirts flying. Darting into the entrance, she charged up the stairs. Trauma and exhaustion caught up with her on the second floor. Her hands screamed. Her legs trembled. Her lungs burned. Eyeing the second-floor guard, she resisted the urge to stop and catch her breath.

Stumbling onto the fourth floor, she pressed her back to the wall and slid to the floor. She let the din of packed humanity wash over her, comforting her with its presence. Finding silence would have been terrifying. She fought air into her lungs and waited until the sparks stopped dancing in front of her eyes.

Blum had all her dynamite. He gave them extra food until the additional children were gathered up and sent elsewhere. Since then, he had proven an unreliable benefactor. His inability—or unwillingness—to restrain Evry was further evidence of that. She supplemented their rations with scraps she snuck out of the kitchen. Even so, she skipped meals to make sure Keti and the boys were fed.

She looked at her bandaged hands and refused to cry.

She pressed herself up and trudged into Apartment 43.

"Yoi! *Bibi*, that hurts!"

"Lie still, Pierre. Alfonso didn't make such a fuss." It was Keti's stern I'm-the-one-in-charge voice.

Hishoro cut through the aisle and found Keti on her bunk. Pierre lay shirtless on his stomach across her lap. Keti dipped a needle into her cup, then pricked Pierre's right shoulder blade with it. The boy squirmed.

"I can't make this as nice as Alfonso's if you keep moving like that."

"What are you doing?" Wounded and exhausted, Hishoro lacked the energy to intervene.

Keti's focus stayed on the boy's shoulder. "They took those children away. They could take our boys."

"Ouch, Auntie! I don't like it!"

"Stop being a baby," Keti said.

"Keti, what are you doing to my child?"

She glanced up. "Making sure we can always find them." Setting the needle down beside her cup, she grabbed a cloth and wiped his shoulder. A red blotch the size of an angry pimple had several legs growing from it. It looked like a flattened spider.

"Keti, stop."

She picked up the needle, dipped it in the cup, and continued jabbing Pierre's shoulder.

Hishoro kicked her shin. "I said stop."

"You made me mess up the line. Where is Alfonso?" She panned the room. "Alfonso!"

The boy appeared a moment later. *"Dále!"* He hugged Hishoro around the knees. *"Bibi* decorated me." He pulled his ragged shirt off and turned his back to her. "Do you like it?"

"What's it supposed to be?" Hishoro asked.

"A wagon wheel. Half of one, anyway." Keti bent to her task. "What happened to your hands?"

"Evry." Hishoro sank onto her bunk. "I don't understand."

"He hates you. People have hated us all our lives. What's hard to understand about that? Alfonso, show me your back."

Keti was playing with her. She was too tired for games. "Why are tattooing my boys?"

Keti studied Alfonso's tattoo. "You messed me up, so the marks won't be exactly the same. Maybe that's for the best. Even twins have differences."

"I'm exhausted, Keti. Please answer me."

"They dumped those children by the hundreds into the courtyard. No parents, no adults, no papers. Babies without identity thrown out like garbage."

"My boys know who they are."

"Now. But if they're taken? If Nadja could see me now, would she recognize me? If you didn't see your boys for years, would you know them on sight?"

"They emptied out Stair Ten."

"More will come. How bad are you hurt?"

Hishoro told her what happened. "I think he broke my ribs."

"You should stay with the boys. I'll volunteer for cleaning duty. I doubt they left anything valuable behind, but you never know. I might get lucky."

"They won't pick you because of your arm."

"I have a better chance than you do with those hands." Keti pressed the cloth against Pierre's shoulder blade and held it there a moment. She lifted the rag and inspected her work. "All done. Put your shirts on, boys, and play in the hallway."

The twins scampered off, children in hell thinking ashes were toys.

Keti held her eyes with her gaze. "You made a deal with Blum. We'll crawl out of here yet, you'll see."

⊕

The memory of Hélène's kindness drove Hishoro back to the infirmary. Her burns no longer hurt, making room for the demands of the other insults to her body. The air of the clinic assaulted her nose and her resolve wavered. Before it shattered, a nurse approached her.

"You shouldn't be in here."

Hishoro lifted her bandaged hands. "I was told to ask for Mademoiselle Gisele."

The nurse gave her a suspicious eye. "Wait here."

Gisele came for her minutes later. "You came back." She sounded more surprised than pleased.

"Hélène insisted I should. It seemed wrong not to honor her wish."

Gisele's countenance softened at the mention of her friend. "Follow me."

She took her into an exam area. Hishoro perched on the table and Gisele unwound the gauze from her hand. Frowning, she wiped the salve away. "I don't understand. It's only been two days. Let me see your other hand." She removed the bandage and wiped the skin clean. She brushed her fingertip across the red skin on the back of her hand. "Does that hurt?"

"No."

Gisele rinsed Hishoro's hands in the basin. She dried them off and kept running her fingers on the new skin. "This is incredible."

"Can I go back to work in the kitchen?"

"The doctor needs to see this."

Moans and cries seeped through the curtain. "He has enough work out there."

"He'll want to see you. Please, it won't take long. For Hélène."

"For Hélène," Hishoro said.

Gisele disappeared. Hishoro inspected the backs of her hands and wondered how many days it would take for her deep walnut tone to reappear.

A man in suit and tie and a white smock stepped through the curtain, Gisele on his heels. "Tell me again, slower this time." The two faced each other as if Hishoro wasn't there.

"Hélène brought this woman in for treatment a couple of days ago. A kapo had beaten her and her hands were burned, second degree."

The doctor turned to her and raised his eyebrow as if seeing her for the first time. "You knew her?"

His tone unsettled Hishoro. It was the kind of question one asked about the dead. "No, monsieur. She helped me get up after the beating and brought me here." Their bread and prayers were none of the doctor's business.

"When we were children, she had the habit of rescuing stray dogs, not matter how hopeless. Let's have a look at these hands, shall we?"

Hishoro held them up for inspection. The man peered at them over his aquiline nose. He reached into his breast pocket and pulled out a pair of glasses. Donning them, he took a closer look. "She's been burned, but it wasn't a couple of days ago. You have your dates confused."

Gisele handed him her clipboard. "I assure you, Doctor, two days ago this woman's hands were covered with blisters. It was a bad, scalding burn."

He read the chart. "What is your name?"

"Hishoro Velveloz."

"Number?"

She gave it.

Handing the clipboard back to Gisele, he took Hishoro's hands in his. Their warmth surprised her. His skin was soft, the nails manicured. He had a wide gold band on his left ring finger. Set in its center was a large, honey-yellow sapphire cut in hexagon. The engraving on its face was painted with black enamel and reminded Hishoro of Tshuri's elegant cursive script, like one of his Ys hanging inverted below one of his Ws.

"That is an unusual wedding band," she said.

"I'm a bachelor, thank God. The ring is a family heirloom." He turned to Gisele. "How did you treat the burn?"

"The usual salve, Dr. Phélypeaux."

"Incredible. Take her to my office in the staff clinic. I'll meet you there momentarily." He dropped Hishoro's hands and slipped through the curtains.

"I knew he would be impressed," Gisele said. "Come with me."

"Why? My hands are fine."

"Better than fine. Those burns should have taken weeks to heal."

"Wounds never linger on me," Hishoro said.

Gisele's head tilted right and she eyed her a second. "Come again?"

"Wounds never linger on me. I've always been a fast healer."

Gisele wrote on her chart. "If Dr. Phélypeaux could determine why that is, it would help a lot of people. Wounds are never in short supply in wartime. Hélène must have seen something in you."

"Hélène sees the world through a kind heart. I am nothing special, just a Gypsy woman."

"The Doctor disagrees. Come, I must get you to him."

She followed Gisele through the ward. She unlocked the door on the south wall and motioned her through. Gisele followed, locking the door behind them. She took her down the hall and unlocked another door. "This is the clinic where we treat the government administrators and the gendarmes."

Hishoro followed her in and was struck by the immediate improvement in air quality. Human waste and chlorine gave way to fresh-cut flowers, alcohol, and a hint of aromatic cigars.

Gisele ushered her into the middle office on the east wall. Clinical equipment dominated the room. A plain oak desk with a single set of drawers sat in a corner like an afterthought. She pulled a towel and a linen gown from a shelf by a narrow door near the desk. "Wash up in the shower and put this on when you're done. The ties go in the back."

Gisele opened the narrow door to the private bathroom. Compared the *Chateaux rouge*, its simple plumbing and plain white porcelain were gleaming luxury.

"You washed my hands already." Familiar only with buckets and tubs, she knew nothing of showers.

"He'll want to see more than your hands. He's a doctor, there is nothing to be afraid of." Gisele pulled the curtain aside and Hishoro saw the vertical pipe with the wide nozzle pointing down like the end of a watering pot. The nurse turned on the tap. "It's like standing in the rain with your clothes off."

Hishoro's last full washing had been in the *vurdon* the Nazi's had burned. Since then, she had only been able to take half measures. "You will be here when I'm done?"

"Yes."

She emerged refreshed and covered in the gown.

"See, that didn't hurt, did it?" Gisele waved her to the examination table, this one padded unlike the bare metal one in the infirmary.

Dr. Phélypeaux came in and headed straight to the bathroom. He whistled a complex melody to the undercurrent of running water and came out drying his hands. "I'll need to do a full examination." He stood in front of her, his brown eyes sparkling. "This means I'll be drawing some blood. Do you have any children?"

"Yes, three boys."

"I'll need to perform a gynecological inspection. It's purely clinical, you understand."

Hishoro didn't, but she was too dumbstruck to ask what he meant.

Gisele busied herself at the foot of the table. She lifted two metal poles with curved rests on the top and tightened their knobs to hold them in place.

The doctor brought the stethoscope to his ears and placed its cold medallion above her breast. He stared at his watch as he listened, then jotted a note on the chart. He glanced at Gisele. "Bring me the phlebotomy kit and plug in the cauterizing iron."

⊕

Hishoro fidgeted with the bandage on her arm. April was hanging on, but the May rains were already here. She eyed the morass of the courtyard below, dreading her walk to the clinic and the horrors awaiting her there.

Keti put her hand on her shoulder. "This is insanity. Don't go back."

"He'll just send the gendarmes to drag me there if I don't show up."

"He's cut you, burned you, and poured acid on you." Keti turned her so they faced each other. "What's next, Hishoro?"

She reached up and stroked Keti's cheek. Her face was fuller than it had been since their arrest in Nantes. "We have food and my boys are clothed. It is enough for now."

"I would rather starve that see you suffer like this."

"Don't. I couldn't bear it. We just need to hold on for a bit longer."

Keti leaned her forehead on Hishoro's brow. They stood like that for a long moment, adding strength to each other. Taking a deep breath, she broke away from the sisterly embrace.

Stepping into the hallway, she found Pierre and Alfonso kicking the ball Dr. Phélypeaux had given them. "Boys, go inside and stay with *Bibi*." Hugging them both, she kissed their heads. Alfonso scooped up the ball and the twins scampered into the apartment, the heels of their new shoes clicking against the concrete.

Hishoro braved the stairs, the wounds and sores on her thighs and abdomen reminders of what lay ahead. Each time one of her injuries healed, the doctor inflicted a new one of greater severity. He assured her it was all in the interest of science. His bright eyes and flushed face made her think otherwise.

She should have resisted, run away somehow. But Blum was inaccessible and Tshuri silent. Camp rations kept them starving and her family wasted away before her eyes. Dr. Phélypeaux promised food and made good on his promise.

Whistles echoed up the stairwell. Startled, she missed her step and tumbled to the third-floor landing.

"Pack it up! Pack it up! You have twenty minutes!"

Chapter 37

1976 FORD GRAN TORINO – 2-door hardtop. AM-FM stereo, power steering. Black paint, some rust. Dependable. $500 or best offer. Phone 555-0001

Classified Ads, *Rocky Mountain News*, October 30, 1988

Denver, Colorado – November 4, 1988

Rick Cannon stared out of the third story window of his command center. The crowd on this stretch of the parade route kept growing, pressing up against the police barricades at the edges of the wide sidewalks, their faces bright under the trellis of Christmas lights. He checked his watch. 8:05 p.m.

He toggled the radio mic. "Sarah, they leave the Civic Center yet?"

"Not yet, Boss. Floats and horses are still lining up." Sarah's voice was tight and high. "Those poor kids are going to freeze."

"What kids?"

"The first marching band. Their majorettes are out here in leotards. Crazy!"

"Radio me when they set out."

He could spot Shell easily. Her bright red coat stood out in the field of blues, grays, and blacks of the bundled throng. He grabbed his binoculars anyway. Training them on her, he brought her face breath close. Her cable knit cap hung loosely on her head, its hunter green hues complementing her chestnut hair. Her eyes were on the street. She drew her full bottom lip between her teeth for a moment or two, then blew out a cloud of steam that framed her in mystery.

He needed to call his wife.

Sarah's voice crackled out of the radio. "First float is out, Boss."

Rick raised the walkie-talkie. "Everybody copy?"

All the agents on the route confirmed.

They heard his speech before taking their posts. *Stay alert. Heads on a swivel. Expect the unexpected.* No need to repeat himself now. He didn't know how Gavin

Leoppard, a.k.a. Drom Reiziger, would make his way in. But there was only one way he was coming out.

Shell swept her gaze up and down the street. Her lip was stuck between her teeth again, her shoulders shivering. He had debated giving her an earpiece, finally deciding against it. Getting her to agree to the wire was difficult enough. And he knew she was right. Regardless how small the earpiece, Drom Reiziger would spot it.

Aside from the symbol drawn on the camper wall, Bastien Frabron had left no trace of himself. Michael Blackmore, his Paris missionary partner, had warned him about the family the first time he saw Ada. It was at a Christmas program in the chapel. Ada sang in the choir. Rick couldn't keep his eyes off her.

"Steer clear, my friend," Michael said. "We have a year to go and her family is in trouble with Salt Lake. Her uncle's been excommunicated."

"A Frabron excommunicated? Doesn't seem likely."

"Trust me, Rick. She's more trouble than she's worth."

He might have listened to Michael if his friend hadn't been ogling Ada as he spoke. He knew the two had been pen pals since the Blackmores met the Frabrons while vacationing in France years previous.

Rick still had no doubts that Ada was worth it. Bastien, however, was costing him dear. The Frenchman had played him, had used him to find his quarry. It grated on him even though he worked it in his favor.

Shell and the children were under Cooper's care. Their abduction was a mark against DCIS, not the FBI. He lobbied and called in favors to jumpstart James's stalled investigation and work out a deal for Robert Gladstone. Once he got the Gladstones in the clear, Shell became more cooperative.

Through multiple interviews, gaps in the afterlife of Gavin Leoppard started filling in. He made contact with her after the burial. She found her way to Canada. Amanda embraced their new life. Jakob met his father. David was born. Shell homeschooled the children. Drom sold firewood and volunteered on the rescue squad. They attended an evangelical church in Penticton.

"Sounds ideal," Rick told her.

"It was. Best years of my life."

"Why run?"

The softball game. Her hands trembled and she wouldn't look him in the eye as she recounted the event. The batter's leg snapping. Drom's charge to home plate. The bleeding woman, Drom's cleat imbedded in her face. The inferno of their property, the only home her children had known.

Holding her hand, he told her of the night Drom invaded his home. "My fingers still aren't right. I honestly don't know if my leg will ever be."

She squeezed his hand back. They had a common fear. He kept playing on hers. She was sick with worry. He transformed it to anger. "I hate to say this, but what if it was Drom who took the boys?"

Reasonable doubt worked both ways. He swung it at her until he spotted an opening.

They sat in the Gladstone's restored living room. Rick took a sip of his coffee and set it down on the end table. "I can't see him sending you off without a communication plan."

The classified ad for the black Gran Torino garnered a response within days. Their method of communication didn't allow for Shell to specify the meeting place or time. Drom set these, which made the parade route his game board.

Drums drew him out of his reverie. He brought the binoculars back up, not sure of when he lowered them. He scanned the sidewalk. She was still there, her head turned to the parade's vanguard. He checked his watch. 8:13 p.m.

The marching band banged out their rendition of George Michael's "Faith." On their heels came several floats, each more intricately lit than the last. The Cattlemen's Association clattered behind on thoroughbreds, quarter horses, and ponies. A small gap in the line appeared, the following group giving the manure crew time to clear the path.

Fire department chiefs marched into view followed by two ladder company trucks strung with enough lights to be a fire hazard unto themselves.

A ringmaster, built like two stacked barrels, waved his top hat to the watchers. Elephants lumbered behind him followed by clowns with colorful snow shovels. One made a pass on the pavement with his shovel and flung out to the crowd. People cowered away from what turned out to be a shower of confetti and candy.

Caged lions and leopards came next, followed by acrobats on horseback. More clowns fanned out from the parade body and worked their way through the packed sidewalks on either side. The police half-heartedly tried to bring them back in line. Their efforts only added to the hilarity as the clowns tripped each other, sprayed silly string, scattered glitter, and handed out sweets.

Rick panned back to red coat and focused on the face.

It wasn't her.

His sphincter tightened. He scanned farther up the street and spotted another red coat. Wrong face. He dropped the binoculars and the tether slapped the back of his neck. Pain shot up from the back of his head to his right temple and parked there with persistent throbbing. Across the street, red coats multiplied. After twelve, he stopped counting.

He radioed the nearest check points. "California! Stout! Anybody have eyes on Shell?"

"I've got her, Boss. Red coat dead ahead." The man on California and Seventeenth sounded confident, then his voice jumped a half step. "Negative, not her."

Below, red coats kept blooming and dispersing. The parade pressed on.

"Arrest them!"

"Arrest who, Boss?" the agent at Stout asked.

"Anyone in a red coat!"

He flinched at the boom, hyper-extending his elevated leg and bouncing his forehead off the window pane. Strings of fireworks rattled off, filling the street with smoke.

Chapter 38

Learn from the acrobat, the magician, and the jester. Do not neglect the apothecary or the alchemist. Bewilder. Enchant. Amaze. Entertain. Above all, juggle. Juggle and kill.

Al-Askari ad-Din, *Juggler's Creed,* c. 1240 AD

Denver, Colorado – November 4, 1988

Drom held his post beside the other police officers as the circus came into view. Denver's finest were out in full force for the annual Parade of Lights. No one questioned his presence. The department was large enough for strangers to hide in.

The clowns pushed into the crowd. Julia's makeup and moves were unmistakable. He caught her in his peripheral vision as she collided into Shell. Other clowns swarmed past. He counted to three, then gave chase.

Julia stood where Shell had been, greasepaint gone and costume nowhere to be seen. Squaring her shoulders under the red coat, she adjusted the knit cap on her head. Drom grabbed Shell—now wearing a blue puffer jacket and a burgundy beret—by the elbow and led her northwest on 17th Street.

"Keep your head up, eyes forward."

"Hello to you, too." She kept pace with him, but her arm was stiff. "Where are we going?"

He didn't respond.

The air shook with a boom. He increased their pace. Firecrackers exploded up and down the street, filling the sidewalks with smoke. Pushing a door open, he pulled her in. He brought her past the display counters and through the beaded curtain at the back.

"What is this place?" Her voice was louder than the situation called for.

He stopped at the foot of the stairs and pressed her back against the wall. She stared up at him, eyes wide. Before she could say another word, he kissed her and wouldn't let up. She turned her head. His lips stayed glued to hers, his left hand worming inside her jacket and under her blouse.

She pushed. He wrapped his right arm around her waist and drew her closer. His left hand snaked up the warm skin of her tone side, slid across her smooth back, and rose to her bra clasp.

She wrenched her lips away from his. "Stop! We need to talk." Her beret tumbled from her head and her hair cascaded down.

He re-engaged, his mouth smothering hers. His hand came around the inside of her bra. His fingers brushed the wire. She fought him, trying to break out of his embrace. Twisting the wire around his fingers, he yanked down. He brought his hand out and stepped away.

He held the miniature microphone up, its frayed wire dangling. "Now we can talk."

She glared at him, thin-lipped and breathless. Scooping her hair back with both of her hands, she sank against the wall and slid down into a squat. Her tears came, heavy and unforgiving. "You're a first-class bastard, you know that."

He knelt down eye-to-eye with her. "Technically, I'm an orphan. We need to take this upstairs. We don't have a lot of time."

"Who are you?" The swoops and swirls of her burlwood irises pinned him in place.

"You know who I am, Michelle."

"Where have you taken them?"

"Them? Them who?"

"The boys. Where are my boys?"

Pulling her to her feet, he spun her to the stairs. "Up, now!" He pressed on the small of her back and she moved. Tearing his gaze from her ascending form, he checked his six. The jewelry shop was quiet.

Taking the steps two at a time, he came alongside Shell and grabbed her hand. He wheeled them around at the top of the staircase and guided her to the back bedroom of the jeweler's living quarters. He set her down at the foot of the queen-sized bed. "What happened?"

It tumbled out of her in fits and starts; out of order, incomplete, and chopped with sobs. He redirected her, coaxing her to focus. Gaining some composure, she told of the Gladstone's break in, their escape to the cabin.

She flew at him, punching his arm.

"Shell, stop." Pinning her arms, he tossed her on the bed. "I haven't seen you this angry since ..." He let it go. His wound hurt enough, no need to pick at hers.

"She fell down the cliff! I stood there helpless, sure I would see her splattered on the rocks and she did a back flip. A back flip! Where do you get off? What gives you the right?"

"Slow down, honey. You lost me again."

"My daughter, Drom. You've been training *my* daughter. And Jakob. I don't want this for them. What were you thinking?"

That the world is a dangerous place, especially for Leoppard cubs.

He kept the thought to himself.

He knelt in front of her. "Michelle, what happened to the boys?"

"They're gone." She filled him in: Robert's dilemma, Agent Cooper's ineptness, Rick Cannon's appearance, the boys' abduction.

"Cannon was on the other side of that wire?"

She nodded, avoiding his eyes. "He showed me pictures. I saw your body on a slab. I saw the bodies you left behind."

"You know what I was. Sammy's death should have made that clear."

"Who did Hazel bury?"

"I'll tell you one day, promise. But not now. When did they take the boys?"

"On the twenty-fourth, last month."

"It took you six days to buy the ad?" Rising, he paced the room. "Six days! For the love of God."

Her jaw trembled. Her hands were shaking. "Rick was convinced you took them." She hooked her bra, then fiddled with her front shirt tail. She wouldn't meet his eyes.

His radio squawked, a sergeant asking clarification on the red-coat arrest order.

"Michelle, look at me." Her eyes came up, guarded under a vail of bangs. "After all we've been through, how could you possibly think I would ever do anything like that to you?"

Her face hardened. "Jakob skipped a stone halfway across a lake. Amanda sat in your brother's back yard and pinged the fencepost with acorns from yards away like it was the most natural thing in the world. Rick showed me the mannequins, Drom. Your work or theirs? Aren't your nightmares enough?"

"I wasn't teaching them to kill."

"No?" She came off the bed and got in his face. "You know how to do anything else?"

He met her glare. "I know how to survive. I was giving them basic skills in case someone came after them and I wasn't there."

"You weren't there!" She pounded on his arm again.

He drew her into a bear hug and pressed his lips to her ear. "I know, I know. I took too long. It's my fault."

Her rage shuddered out of her. He walked her back to the bed and sat them down. The radio barked from his shoulder tab, a lieutenant cancelling the general arrest order. "I didn't expect Robert to be mixed up in anything. I thought he was a safe bet."

"You thought wrong."

He didn't argue the point. "What did Cannon tell you?"

"They caught you on camera breaking his leg." She pushed him away. "All those guards! You told me you were done with killing." She was shaking.

"He told you I killed the guards?"

"He said you went through twenty-five of the CIA's best."

"Went through, yeah, but kill? We talked about this, Shell, after I performed the Box. Remember?"

"He showed us pictures. They were all over the floor, mowed down."

"You saw pictures of me on a slab and I'm sitting here talking to you."

She scooped a lock back and tucked it behind her ear. "Turn yourself in. Work with the FBI to find our boys."

"If Cannon convinced you I had them, what makes you think they can find them? No, all this is leftover business from my father. Tell me again what Amanda said."

"She was on our bed, reading. David cried, then she heard a man's voice. She came out and two men were hauling the boys off the bunk. She screamed and one of the men came after her. She said that's when she threw the butcher knife."

Drom suppressed a smile. "Butcher knife?"

"Yes, she thought she missed because he kept coming and punched her in the face. When she came to, they were gone. She ran out of the camper to get me, but passed out again. I found her outside on the ground."

"You said she thought she missed. Did she?"

"No. There was blood all over the galley."

"What else?"

"They were after more than just the boys. They ransacked the camper."

"The passports."

"They didn't find them, but Rick did. He brought me into the camper and confronted me with the safe and David's special boot."

"The passports are legitimate, Shell, yours and the kids. He can't charge you with anything." It was another reason why he left, to keep her innocent. "Anything else? Did the FBI check the blood, process the scene?"

"They kept us holed up in the cabin a couple of days. A forensics team came out. Rick didn't share anything with us, but by the time he got us back into your brother's house, he was fairly convinced that you had them. I started worrying that all that blood was yours."

"I've bled my share since we parted, but not there. How is Amanda?"

"How do you think? She blames herself. She's worried sick about the boys. And she's angry with you."

Just like her mother. Out loud, he said, "She thinks I have them."

"What else was I supposed to tell her?"

The radio blared, an all-points bulletin describing Shell. "They're getting serious."

"Did you buy the uniform or knock off a policeman for it?"

He ignored the jab. "Think, Shell. Was there anything else? Did Amanda get a good look at them? Did they leave anything behind?"

"Aside from the drawing, no."

"What drawing?"

"The one in the bedroom. I told you about that."

"No, you didn't. What kind of drawing?"

"It was weird. Rick kept saying one of the kids must have done it. But Amanda said no."

He lifter her chin with his finger. "Love, what was it?"

"A hexagon. It was drawn with a black marker on the wall beside the door. It had a weird design in the center, like a curly capital double-u with a handlebar mustache under it."

"Frabron."

"What?"

A bang on the door made them both jump. Drom put his finger to his lips.

"Leo, it's me. Open up."

Shell glared at him. "You roped Julia into this mess?"

She banged again. He sprang up and opened it. Julia stepped in and eyed them both. "If you two love birds are done playing cop and criminal, we need to go." She tossed Drom a duffle bag.

He set the bag on the bed and faced Shell. "Robert's house was vacant for a month. The ad worried me. I needed help in case it was a trap. László and Julia came to the rescue."

Unhooking the mic from his shoulder tab, he unbuckled the duty belt and dropped the gear next to the duffle. He unbuttoned his cuffs and collar and pulled uniform and undershirt off over his head.

"You have a tattoo?" Julia said.

He glanced at her over his shoulder. "Present from my grandmother."

Leaning forward, Shell brushed her fingers across the puckered wound on his arm. The heat of her touch squeezed his lungs. He fell into the grain of her irises, his pulse quickening. "What happened?"

"A lot."

Her hand trailed down to his, leaving gooseflesh in its wake. "Where else?"

"My leg, but I did that one myself. Just a flesh wound."

Julia stood beside Shell and inspected the topic of discussion. Her eyes traveled across the rest of him. "What happened to you? You're covered in scars."

The radio squawked again, jarring all of them.

He let Shell's hand go, shed his pants, and donned the street clothes Julia brought him. "You have to go. Switch jackets with Julia and head back out onto the street."

"That's it? I don't get to know what happened or where you're going?"

"I was in Boston. D.C. and West Virginia before that."

"West Virginia? Oh, Drom, you didn't."

"I had to. I can't do this on my own. He was my only option."

She bit her lip and hugged herself. "He sent you to Boston."

"We made a deal. He needed someone extracted. He said that someone had information on Frabron."

"That's the second time you've said that name. Who is this Frabron?"

"The Frenchman, the batter at the softball game. He's the one who took our boys. Cannon is married to his niece."

The blood drained out of her face. "Rick ... Rick knew?"

"He knew." Drom buckled the belt around his blue jeans and pulled the sweatshirt hood onto his head. "It's time."

Stepping to him, she pulled his head down and crushed his lips with hers. He buried his fingers in her thick hair, bergamot and clove engulfing his brain. Her arms wrapped around his waist and held him tight. She came up for air all too soon, her eyes searching and watery. "I …"

He kissed her again, then broke their embrace. "I know."

"Where will you go?"

"I have to return to Spain."

Shell's eyes widened. She opened her mouth, but Julia's voice filled his ears. "Spain? I thought you were Romanian, Leo. And what's this 'Drom' business?"

Shell had made him forget that Julia was in the room. He turned to her. "Actually, I'm Romani, which is what we Gypsies call ourselves. Drom is one of my Gypsy names."

"Gypsy names?" She stared at him a moment. "Was any of it real?"

"Julia—"

"You know what, save it." She took off the knit cap and red coat and handed them to Shell. "Give me the puffer. Where's the beret? It's one of my favorites."

"I think it fell off downstairs," Shell said.

"Where you two should be headed," Drom said.

"What about you?" Shell asked.

"I have another way out."

"Rick will pick me up. What am I supposed to tell him?"

"Tell him I got frisky and found the wire while trying to rip your bra off."

"Drom, seriously. He'll want to know what you told me. He'll want to know how it is you're alive."

He thought of his time in Cannon's house and all the pressures the agent was shouldering. He remembered the children sleeping in their beds, the picture of innocence. He smiled at the memory of the little one's eyes fluttering open at the touch of his hand on her chest and how her heart took on a steady beat.

"Drom?"

"Tell him his fears shouldn't keep Jewel from her checkup. Tell him miracles still happen."

Chapter 39

Phabol lampa maskar o logori,
Voi svetil amare Romange.
De man, Devla, dui bare phakora
Te urav Nemso te mudarav.

A lamp is burning in the camp,
It shines on our Roma.
O God, give me two big wings
So I can fly and kill a German.

from "Phabol Lampa," a Romani
song of the *Porrajmos*

Pitchipoi ("the place beyond") – May 2, 1943

Hishoro huddled with her family in the cattle car. Unlike their journey from Gurs to Drancy, they were packed in with Jews as well as other Gypsies. Not long into their trip, a recently interned Jewish woman told her that Pitchipoi was in Poland.

"Don't believe the newspapers," she said. "Poland is worse than France."

Now, five days later, the stench and heat of the packed humanity pressed in on her from all sides. She needed air. Worming her way to the wall, she stood under the ventilation slot and drew a couple of breaths before being pushed out of the way by others seeking the same relief.

"There's a sign up ahead," a man who displaced her said.

"Can you read it?" another man asked.

"Almost. There, Birkenau."

"Never heard of it. You?"

"No, but we're five kilometers from it."

Hishoro slipped back to Keti and the boys. They drank the last of their water yesterday and their last meal had been the thin soup of Drancy. The twins were cried out. Keti was too tired to complain. The train clacked on. Leaning against Keti, she dozed off, the press of the other passengers keeping her on her numb feet.

The throng lurched, shaking her awake. The door rattled open and those nearest it tumbled out.

"Schnell! Schnell! Schnell! Schnell!"

Guards barking. Passengers falling, jumping, being hauled out and dragged. Hishoro scrambled out with her boys into a storm of blows, insults, shouted commands, and terrifying confusion. She gripped them both by the hand and held her ground until Keti was beside her. "Stay together."

People poured out of cattle cars up and down the siding, as far as the eye could see. German guards in high boots and gray uniforms with lightning bolt insignias beat the arrivals into massive columns. The river of humanity moved, carrying Hishoro and her family with it.

She filled her lungs, glad for the air's lightness, free as it was of excrement, urine, and sweat. The freshness soon gave way to the oppressive taint of burnt hair and flesh. Ahead, dark gray smoke belched out of towering brick chimneys, smudging the brilliant blue sky. She tightened her grip on the boys' hands.

They flowed toward the smoke clouds on the horizon. The river split into two streams around an officer holding a pair of white gloves. Were it not for the SS uniform, Hishoro would have taken him for a Gypsy. His broad face, dark hair, and brown eyes reminded her of her uncle.

The officer shone in the rabble, a slight smile on his generous lips, his high boots gleaming. People moved to the left or right depending on the flick of his gloves. As she came abreast of him, his heavy-lidded eyes opened a margin wider. He uttered a single word, *"Zwillinge."* He flicked his gloves and a man in striped pajamas shoved her into the column on the officer's right. She carried the boys and Keti in her wake.

The column shuffled forward. Marshal music blared from overhead speakers. At the sides, barking dogs struggled against the chain leashes of their snarling masters. *"Schnell! Schnell! Schnell!"*

The column stopped alongside a brick building. Groups were herded in. The line surged forward, filling in the gaps.

Hishoro stepped inside, blind in the gloom. The boys were ripped away from her hands. Someone shoved her onto a wooden chair. Rough hands jerked her left arm across the table and pushed her sleeve up.

"Don't move. This won't take long," a man said in French. Her eyes adjusted and his skeletal frame came in view. His skull was topped with dark stubble. His filthy striped shirt was several sizes too large.

A man with a clipboard stepped next to him. "Name?"

"Hishoro Velveloz. Ouch!" She jerked her arm but the prisoner's grip held firm.

"Be still. It will be ugly enough without you moving the canvass." The man continued pricking the outside of her forearm, making her blood flow.

"Papers," the record keeper demanded.

Hishoro dug into her skirt pocket and handed the family packet to him. He opened it and glanced right. Tracking his gaze, she spotted Keti seated at the next table, followed by Pierre and Alfonso. The man jotted notes. He kept her papers. The skeleton rubbed ink on her arm.

Rising as one, the group was driven into the courtyard. "Get undressed! All clothing in the bins!" All around her men, women, and children disrobed. One woman pulled off her dress, but kept her shoes and underwear on. A guard prodded her with his submachine gun, shouting orders. Arms crossed, she shook her head. His gun burped and she fell backwards, awash in blood.

Hishoro tore her clothes off, then stripped the boys.

They stood bare, baking under the hot sun. The mass moved forward again. She was prodded onto a low stool and told to hold her arms out at her sides. Electric clippers buzzed like angry bees as the crew of men made the arrivals bald from head to toe. Hishoro stared at the rafters, unable to face her own shame.

They were pressed into a room. Hishoro held onto her boys. She squeezed her eyes shut, not wanting to know whose skin pressed against her naked flesh. Water crashed down, hot and scalding. Someone screamed. She opened her mouth and gulped, not caring if she burned her mouth or worrying about the water's metallic taste. Doors opened and they splashed out. Groups formed; Jewish men separated from the women, Gypsies herded off to themselves.

The Jews were issued striped pajamas. The Gypsies dug through the bins for their clothes. Hishoro spotted a riot of flowers on a field of red. She pulled the kerchief out, put it on her shaved head, and tied it under her chin. It smelled of pesticide. Digging out a blouse and long skirt, she threw them on and dressed the twins.

Her eyes met Keti's. The sorrow there was beyond tears. She pressed her forehead against her sister's brow for a moment's comfort.

"Look, *Dále*, they decorated my arm." Alfonso lifted his arm, the dark Z with its string of numbers standing out on his raw, red skin.

Chapter 40

The serious espionage cases that came to light in 1987 and 1988, added to the celebrated cases of 1985 ... make the 1980s the "Decade of the Spy." The Committee's concerns about the threat to the nation's security from espionage, expressed in previous annual reports and in a 1986 report on the counterintelligence challenge, remain unassuaged.

Report 101-219
Select Committee on Intelligence
United States Senate

Madrid, Spain – November 7, 1988

Drom clutched his shoulder straps as the C-130 leveled out on the runway with a shudder, engines roaring to slow the troop transport.

The giant seated next to him laughed. "Still worried, I see."

Drom eyed him a moment, then leaned forward to check on Drake. The man was fast asleep; head back, mouth open, and drool trickling. "Not fond of planes." Sitting back into the webbing, he unwound his fingers from the straps. "Or international airports."

"O ye of little faith! I told you, when you hop the puddle with the Pond, no one checks your passport." Unclipping his safety belts, Colonel Russell McAbee unfolded his massive form out of the web seat. His body seemed impervious to the movements of the taxiing plane. He kicked Drake's foot. "Wake up!" His voice cowed the engines' roar.

Drake straightened his neck, wiped the drool off his cheek, and glared at the Colonel with the same disdain that had painted his face in the Boston pump room four weeks previous.

⊕

"This day just keeps getting better. First, the FBI. Next, the ghost here wants to talk to me about the Boogey Man. And now the Scum. Tell me, Colonel, what would the Pond need from the likes of me?"

"Is that anyway to thank the man who just got you out of purgatory?"

"That bleeding boy over there got me out. If I had known he was bringing me to you, I would have stayed put."

"Bleeding?" Stockton looked him over. "Are you hurt?"

"I told you up front there was no way of doing this without getting shot at least once." Drom shrugged out of his sopping jean jacket and ventured a glance at his arm. The blood stain on his hoodie sleeve was plain to see.

"Dr. King, if you would." Stockton nose pointed at the wound.

Orange blossoms bloomed in his nose as she bent in front of him with a pair of scissors and cut the shirt sleeve away. "All this time, I thought you were a nurse."

"And I thought you were a patient. Take a seat." She prodded him over to a stool, then cut away the elbow pad and makeshift bandage.

"It's an in-and-out. No bone, no fragmentation. Irrigate it and wrap me up."

Hazel eyes flashed at him through auburn bangs. "I was an ER doc before I specialized in hematology. I've treated my share of gunshot wounds. You've done your job, let me do mine." She held eye contact for a moment, then set to work on the wound.

"What's this about?" Drake asked the Colonel.

"It's about CIA holding its cards too close to its chest. You're the last man left tied to SL/OMEGA. Why did they bury you?"

Drake shrugged. "Vindictiveness? You know the drill. Brass issues orders and grunts follow them. When everything goes sideways, the grunts always get the blame, never HQ."

"Still gnawing on the bones of Khe Sanh, I see. We gave up on Vietnam years ago, Chuck. It's high time you did the same."

"Tell that to the bones, Colonel, on your way to hell."

Drom picked the scissors out of Dr. King's breast pocket and flicked them at Drake. The finger loops popped him between the eyes and the scissors flipped over and stuck into the stool between his legs.

"Ow!" Drake rubbed his face.

"That's for the lantern," Drom said. "Now, would someone please explain to me exactly what the Pond is?"

No one spoke. Dr. King finished wrapping his arm, ran tape around it, then reached into her breast pocket for the scissors. She looked at Drom, then stared over her shoulder at Drake.

He pulled the scissors out of the stool cushion and handed them to her. "The Pond is the dictionary definition of an oxymoron."

"I don't follow." Drom fingered the bandage and Dr. King swatted his hand away.

"Look it up," Drake said. "Oxymoron. First example: military intelligence."

⊕

Drake climbed out of his seat. "You clear it with the locals?"

"This operation is need-to-know and the locals don't need to know," McAbee said.

The underside of the C-130's tail peeled down. Drom unclipped his restrains and stretched in the cavernous center aisle. "Let's hope they don't find out."

The men weaved around the cargo and traveled down the tail ramp. A soldier on a forklift saluted. Drake and the Colonel saluted back. Old habits die hard, Drom thought. He knew Drake had been out of the Army for decades. The Army wasn't out of him, though.

McAbee was in civilian clothes, which meant the forklift driver knew him. It made Drom wonder how many people were in the need-to-know loop. He and Drake were both were wanted men in Spain. Spanish memory didn't fade and wounded pride was seldom forgiven.

The trio approached a two-door, red Fiat parked in the hangar.

"What are we, a circus act?" Drake asked. "I'll have to sit in the back seat to drive that thing. And there's no way you're getting in, Russ."

The Colonel pulled a set of keys out of his pocket and tossed them to Drom. "I'm not getting in and you're not driving. And I strongly advise against trying to lose your partner. The Cortes would love to have you back in their clutches, Chuck. As I recall, the last time they had you, they strung you up by your thumbs."

Drake scowled. He hadn't been happy about Spain from the start.

⊕

"Spain? You're out of your mind!" Drake sprang up from the sofa in their New York hotel suite. He paced the room, massaging his thumbs. "We're after Frabron, the Butcher of Abéché, who you said was here in the States, remember?"

Boston was three weeks in their rearview. Drom's bruises had faded, but the gunshot wound still hurt like an abscessed tooth. "You think I'm anxious to go back there?"

"Why Spain?" The Colonel's bass voice boomed from the dining room. The man was deaf to his own volume.

Drom returned to the table and its scattered printouts from CIA's WALNUT files, America's treasure trove of captured Nazi documents catalogued and duplicated on microfilm. He plucked two sheets from his working pile and added a third from his father's files. He handed them to the Colonel one by one.

"What am I looking at?"

"Ratline logistics. Former SS and Gestapo who couldn't get hired by the American military or the OSS found other ways to hide."

"You think the Soviets didn't hire their fair share?" Drake's upper lip twitched. "You're a fine one to moralize, Rat-gêló. I've seen your handiwork first hand. You would've fit right in with those death's head *Schutzstaffel* monsters."

"Mahk & hurjal ande muj phanglo."

Drake glared at him. "Flies in my mouth are the least of my worries, so I won't shut it. I'll take a black site cell over an Inquisition dungeon, hands down. Spain is out of the question."

"Spain looks like the right move to me. I'll get the ball rolling." The Colonel snagged the handset off its cradle and tapped out the number. "Send the car." Hanging up the phone, he faced them. "It'll take me several days to set up. Get Chuck up to speed and keep to sanctioned exercises. The doc will be by tomorrow to check on you."

McAbee blew out of the room. Drom and Drake squared off on either side of the document-strewn table.

"Run me through it," Drake said.

"Once you cooperated and told McAbee what you knew, I finally knew where to look."

Drake dragged a chair out and sank into it. "You didn't need me to tell you where you stashed Shane's files. You could have bypassed Boston and come straight to New York."

"I discovered those records a long time ago. Back then, all I looked for were targets. Targets and revenge. I was convinced my father was an assassin for hire, that the only way I could flush out his ... flush you out was to keep killing."

"And my full disclosure changed our mind?"

"It widened my scope. I thought my father was just an assassin. You and Swenson knew my father was gathering a biological arsenal. Stockton thought he was on board with keeping the superpowers in balance."

"We were convinced Shane had gone over to the Soviets."

"He had us all fooled." Drom grabbed a bottle of water from the minibar. Eyeing the clock, he snagged an airplane bottle of Chivas Regal and flicked over his shoulder. It tumbled through the air and landed on its top in front of Drake.

"Losing your touch?"

"No great feat landing it on its base."

Shaking his head, Drake twisted off the cap and took a deep draft. Blowing out a contented sigh, he grabbed the papers Drom had shown McAbee. "Franz Liesau Zacharias. Why go after him?"

"He was an Abwehr agent operating in Spain during the war. They called him *der Affenmann*."

"The Monkey Man? Odd code name for a spy."

"In his case, the handle couldn't be more fitting."

"How so?"

"Zacharias procured monkeys for the Reich from Spanish colonies in Africa."

"And now?"

"No idea. But eight years ago, he was a professor at the Biological Research Center of Complutense University."

"Madrid." Drake drained the bottle.

The next morning, Dr. Janice King appeared as promised, medical kit in hand and sports bag on her shoulder.

Drom stood in the doorway eyeing her bag. "Planning on staying a while?"

She shook a bang away from her eye, releasing a hint of her scent. "No, thank you. You're dangerous company."

He restrained his urge to lean into her. "You're not exactly safe yourself."

Drake crowded in from behind. "Got anything for a headache, Doc?"

She kept her eyes on Drom. "Headaches are easy. Hangovers require behavioral modification. You letting me in or am I treating you in the hallway?"

"Sorry." He slid to the side and she stepped past him, her shoulder brushing his chest. Orange blossoms clouded his thinking, rooting him to the spot.

Drake pulled the door from his hand and shut it. "Afraid she'll bite?"

"Not exactly," Drom said.

She pushed their papers to one end of the dining table and tossed the sports bag on the cleared spot. "We're doing a dressing change and a strength evaluation today." She unzipped the bag and pulled out a handful of colored rubber hoses.

He joined her at the table. "Looks like you're setting up for an interrogation."

She slipped out of her coat and laid it across the chair back. She selected one of the quarter-inch hoses and faced him. "These are resistance bands." Holding it in both hands, she stretched it in front of her chest. Her emerald green, silk wrap top shimmered against her skin and made her eyes glow. "We need to exercise your arm without exacerbating your injury. How's it feeling?"

Form fitting up top, the blouse draped over generous hips from which flowed toned legs covered to the knees with a white skirt. Drom snapped his head up when he caught himself staring at her calves. "It's …" He cleared his throat and bent the arm. "It's feeling better."

She waved him to a chair. She took the bandage off and inspected the wound. "It's healing better than I expected." Her touch, though professionally clinical, was also warm, welcome, and distracting.

"How did you wind up working for Stockton?"

"I'm sure you can imagine. The details are unimportant." She held a square pad on each side of his biceps with finger and thumb until she wrapped enough gauze around to secure them. "The swelling is almost gone and the hole has closed well. We'll keep bandaging it as a precaution. Flex the muscle for me."

He curled his arm, tightening the muscle into the ache. She squeezed, increasing the pressure gradually. "Tell me when it hurts."

The heat of her hand bled through the bandage. He shifted his knees away from her. "It's uncomfortable."

"You can relax it." She loosened her grip, but didn't let him go.

He straightened the arm. "What's next?"

She ran her fingers down his arm, probing. "We see how much you can take."

"By the looks of him, Doc, not much more." Drake parked himself at the table with a steaming mug of coffee. "He's young and full of Gypsy blood. I'd be careful if I were you."

Janice turned away, but not before Drom caught the flush rising on her pale neck. She snagged the yellow band, tied one end into a screw clamp, and sauntered over to the bedroom doors. "Which one is yours?"

Ignoring Drake's snicker, he pointed to the left one. She fixed the clamp around the jamb. "Well, come on. It's not like you can pull it from over there."

After a series of trials, they settled on the red band. Its light resistance fooled him at first. But as she ran him through the exercises, he was amazed at his own weakness.

"How long before it's back to normal?"

"Hard to say, especially since your normal isn't." She led him back to the table. "Stick to the red one for the next three days. After that, stand on this while you do it." She pulled a wobble board out of the bag. "It will make the exercise more functional. I put a couple of light hand weights in the bag as well. Don't overdo it. Exercise until it starts hurting, then rest it. Understood?"

"Understood, Dr. King."

"Janice, please. I think you and I are past formalities at this point." She pulled her stethoscope out and checked his pulse. A slight smile played across her lips.

"What?"

"Twenty-nine beats per minute. It's a wonder to listen to." She checked his other vitals and jotted her findings in her notebook. "I need one more thing from you." She produced a leather fold from the medical kit and laid it out between them.

"Blood?"

"Only if you let me."

Looking into her eyes, he splayed his left arm on the table. "Better take it from this one. The right's bled enough."

Drake was in fine form the next morning. He tossed his napkin onto his breakfast plate and eyed Drom. "What's with you and the doc?"

Drom ignored the question just as he had the night before. He stacked Drake's dishes on his and set the room service tray out in the corridor.

Drake was waiting for him in the entryway. "Come on, you can level with me. You two have a lover's tiff, or was it something else?"

"Something else. I'm a married man, Drake."

"You sure about that? I bet if you chased her, she wouldn't run real fast."

Drom pushed past him. "You've been in solitary too long. How about you use that imagination of yours for something useful."

"Like what?"

"Intelligence gathering. Get dressed. We're going to the library."

"Which one?"

"Main branch."

"Midtown? Russ would have a fit if we ran down to Fifth Avenue. I'll be ready in two."

They left the hotel through the restaurant's service entrance. Hours later— after multiple double-backs, roundabouts, taxi trips, and subway shifts—they arrived on the steps of the Main Branch somewhat sure they had lost all tails.

Navigating away from the central revolving door of the portico, Drom shot through the left-side swing door. The vaulted white marble of Astor Hall gave him pause, quieting him like a cathedral. He soaked in the palatial atmosphere for a moment, then made for the south corridor.

Drake marched beside him. "Where are we going?"

"Periodical room. We need updated information on *der Affenmann*."

Past the door to Room 108, white marble gave way to carved walnut walls that reached from the terracotta tiled floor to the chandelier lit, crafted walnut ceiling. Long wooden tables with shaded, golden lamps invited readers to absorb current news from home and abroad.

"How's your Spanish?" Drom asked.

"Better than my Russian. What do you have in mind?"

"Check out recent issues of *El País* for anything useful on Computense University."

"Why don't I ask that cute librarian over there to fetch me the latest *Who's Who* for the University of Madrid?"

"That's why you're an intelligence officer and I'm just a spy," Drom said. "Knock yourself out. I've got a couple of other things I need to check on."

Drake shuffled off to the help desk and spoke with the young woman. Smiling, she picked up a handset and dialed. Drake turned to him and winked, his wolfish grin displaying his square, yellow teeth. He had definitely been in solitary too long.

Drom located the Denver newspapers on the rack and grabbed a week's worth of issues. He picked a table near the arched windows and dug into the classifieds. Half an hour later, forearms streaked with ink, he found a nineteen seventy-six, black Gran Torino for sale. His stomach knotted like a sour muscle cramp.

Black: life-threatening. No AC listed: situation hot. Some rust: damage done. Dependable, $500: this is Michelle, not a coincidence. 555-0001: come now.

Jumping from his seat, he scanned to room for Drake. The spook was gone. He charged into the corridor and almost knocked Drake over.

"What's gotten into you?"

"We need to go."

Drake shrugged and turned back to poster on the easel by the door. "How's your Hebrew?"

Drom looked the poster. A dark modernist jumble in blue hues with dashes of yellow depicted Jewish distress. On the left was a man knocked off his feet.

Flying in the air above him was another holding a scroll. The moon shone yellow; or perhaps it was the sun unable to dispel the darkness. On the right, a woman held her child, her back turned on a crucified man. Roman letters in a Hebraic font advertised a lecture on the *Malach ha-Mavet* the following evening.

"What's it about, I wonder," Drake said.

"Don't know and won't be here to find out. We need to go now." He grabbed Drake by the elbow and headed to the main hall exit.

Drake pulled his elbow loose. "Where's the fire?"

"Denver."

⊕

Drake rubbed the base of his left thumb. "You've been keeping tabs on me, Russ?"

The Colonel eyed Drake, then turned to Drom. "Let me tell you about these CIA cowboys, son. You see, they're supposed to be America's first line of defense against foreign threats. They are tasked with gathering intelligence and forestalling calamity. But somehow, their mission never appealed to their management, past or present. They put the lion's share of their resources into coups and conspiracies, trying to export democracy by rigging ballot boxes and killing candidates. My people—the Pond—we've never lost focus on our true mission." McAbee handed him a Spanish passport. "Happy hunting. Let's get some real enemies." He spun on his heel and marched away.

Drom opened the passport and caught the driver's license that fell out of it. Tucking it inside his back pocket, he scanned the identity McAbee had set up for him. The photo was recent, a headshot captured while he was at the FCA, no doubt. His full name was in all caps, each one in its appropriate place. He shook his head in disbelief.

Carlos Javier de Leon Velveloz got in the Fiat and cranked the engine to life.

Chapter 41

"There is no man who lives and,
seeing the angel of death,
can deliver his soul from his hand."
Targum, Psalm 89:48

Konzentrationslager Auschwitz-Birkenau – May 16, 1943

Hishoro lay on her side, the four of them huddled together with six others on a middle-tier bunk. She scratched at the stubble beneath her headscarf, hoping it was growing hair causing the itch and not the vermin crawling and biting everywhere.

Her eyelids grew heavy and exhaustion nearly took her. *"Alle antreten!"* broke into the barracks from the loud speakers, snapping her awake. She shook Keti's shoulder. Her sister rose with a groan and Hishoro caught the glint of her eyes in the gloom. "Help me get the boys down."

Hishoro clambered out and sunk to her ankles in the quagmire floor. Pierre came out first, then Alfonso. Keti used her good arm to hold herself against the bunk as she swung her legs out. Hishoro set Alfonso down and wrapped her arms around Keti's knees. "I've got you, let go." Keti slid off the bunk and she set her down.

They slogged out of the barracks with the hundreds of others herding to roll call. Hishoro turned her eyes away from the dead being dragged out.

Her bare feet found new purchase on the bricked pathway. She followed the people in front of her, their way lit by the chimney flares that still outshone the gloom of early dawn.

All hope of Pitchipoi being better than Drancy died within hours of their arrival. Their camp, reserved exclusively for Gypsies, was bordered north and south by the massive brick chimneys of the human ovens. Their barracks sat no more than a soccer field away from their billowing stench.

Pushing up her sleeve, she took her place in the formation. She eyed the tattoo, recommitting it to memory. They were all numbers now, their names not used or recognized.

During their second muster, a number was barked out and no one responded. The guards hauled a man out of the line, tore his shirt off, and tied him to a post. "This is what will happen to you if you do not respond when your number is called," the SS sergeant said. He whipped the man until his kidneys fell out. He called the number again. A woman responded, sobbing hysterically. One of the female guards attacked her, slapping her repeatedly while informing everybody else that crying was forbidden.

Hishoro checked the boys' arms again. She stood on trembling legs and waited for the guards to begin.

It was midday before the SS marched up to their formation and started barking numbers. They had a different officer with them this time, resplendent in his immaculate uniform and gleaming boots. He held a pair of white gloves in his hand. The guards moved along her left pulling children out of the line.

She gripped Alfonso's hand and bent toward a woman beside her. "What is happening?"

"Uncle Mengele is collecting more twins," she said.

"What for?"

The woman glanced at her boys. "He's a doctor. You can see his children, Jews and Gypsies, playing in the field in front of his clinic on the other side of our wire. They're clothed and well fed. Your boys would be better off with him than rotting in the barracks with us."

"Present!" Keti said.

Hishoro suffered a moment's panic, then heard her number. "Present!"

Dr. Mengele swaggered down their column. Prisoners left and right gave way without prompting. He stopped in front of Hishoro. She kept her eyes on the toes of his boots. Soft leather stroked the underside of her chin.

She lifted her head and met his eyes. Her knees wobbled and heat rose from her bosom to her face.

His generous lips formed a handsome smile. "*Zwillinge,* you and your sister?"

"*Ja, und meine Söhne auch.*"

His gaze shifted down to Pierre and Alfonso. "They are not identical like you and your sister. No matter. Follow me."

She returned from the clinic clean and feeling dirty. Keti wouldn't speak with her.

Dr. Mengele's assistant had spirited the boys away. She and Keti were stripped and ordered to shower. They were led naked to an open examination area where they waited with other twins, male and female, of various ages. Her sister avoided eye contact and covered herself as best as she could.

She was weighed, measured, then placed on a cold metal table for gynecological inspection. After taking her blood, they returned her clothes and handed her a loaf of bread. When she asked about the boys, she was told all the young twins were being housed in Barracks 14 of Camp F.

Walking back to their barracks in Camp E, she told herself she wouldn't eat the bread. Her boys could not be bought for such. Her dignity was worth more. But her hunger overpowered her pride. Half the loaf was gone before they reached their bunk.

She lay on her back, the cramped space seeming empty without the boys. She glanced at Keti, but her sister kept her back to her. Closing her eyes, she thought of her last encounter with Tshuri. She remembered the sopping gendarme uniform and the rigid kepi. But when she tried to fill in the face beneath the bill, it was Mengele who smiled.

Someone rapped against the bunk posts. All around were whispers of "Stay awake." People climbed out of their bunks and moved to the middle of the barracks.

"Keti, something is happening." Her sister didn't respond. She reached her hand over and met a stiff shoulder. "We have to survive, Keti. The woman told me Dr. Mengele makes sure his children get food. I would rather they ate than see them fed to the ovens."

Keti remained quiet. She climbed over her and got down. She pushed her way through to the center of the barracks where several men were holding court.

"We must arm ourselves," one of them said. "I'm told they're coming for us tonight. We've had a lot of typhus cases and many of the barracks are overcrowded."

"They have machine guns," someone protested.

"Not enough to shoot us all. Sharpen your bread knives, break chairs and pull planks from the bunks. Those of you on the road commandos, get your pick axes and shovels. If they come in, we'll pounce on them."

"That's right! Beat those Nazi bastards!" Others shouted similar sentiments.

Wood cracked and knives scraped up and down the barracks. Hishoro checked on Keti. Her sister wouldn't look her in the eye. She risked a quick sortie outside. The camp lights cut on, holding dusk at bay. Men slipped out of the barracks all around, makeshift clubs in their hands.

Men from her barracks filed past her and took up posts by the door, ready to do violence. Reaching into her skirt pocket, she gripped the handle of her bread knife. Bile burned at the back of her throat. The smoky air made her eyes water.

She trudged back inside and climbed in next to Keti. She wrapped her arm over the stiff shoulder and held her close. "I won't let them take you."

"Alle antreten! Alle antreten!"

Hishoro woke up with no memory of falling asleep. Keti's frame was stiff under her embrace. "Keti, we must go."

Her sister rolled over, a plank of wood in the grip of her left hand. Her eyes were puffy and red-rimmed. "They didn't come."

"You should have slept."

Roll call began at sunrise. She was at the point of collapse when they were dismissed. A guard stopped as they left the assembly yard. "You two, to the clinic. *Schnell!*"

Hishoro was torn between fear and famine. Her legs, shaky during roll call, demanded her full attention to keep moving. They entered the clinic and to Hishoro's relief, were led away from the examination area. She passed through an internal door into a ward with hospital beds lining the walls and two steel tables commanding the center.

At one of them, his back toward her, stood Mengele in a bleach-white smock. He turned and smiled at her. Her breath caught in her throat, then her stomach tried to charge past it when she saw what was on the other table.

"Your boys are over there." He pointed.

Tearing her gaze away from the dissected girl on the table, she panned it across the beds along the wall. Her boys were side by side, Alfonso rosy-cheeked and Pierre thrashing. She moved toward them.

Mengele caught her arm. "You must get them through the fever." He let her go.

She dove to their bedsides, then looked back for Keti.

Her sister was gone.

Chapter 42

The FBI raided the headquarters of Gamma Tech International in Denver on Tuesday as part of a joint operation with the Defense Criminal Investigation Service. The raid resulted from whistleblower testimony. Multiple hard drives were confiscated from the software company. The company's chief operating officer was arrested as well as several high-ranking Air Force officers connected with Rockwell's X-30 project. The case is yet another espionage scandal for the Reagan administration.

New York Times, November 2, 1988

Madrid, Spain – November 7, 1988

Drom maneuvered the Fiat through the post-siesta traffic. North Americans would call it a rush hour. But this was Spain. No one was rushing.

"I don't get it." Drake was pressed against the passenger door like he was ready to bail.

"Get what?"

"McAbee tells me Frabron snatched your boys from a hideout in the Rockies. I get the thread we're following. I don't get Rat-gêló straying thousands of miles away from his quarry or his cubs."

"Would it make you feel better if I killed someone?"

"You wouldn't have to kill them. A little bit of torture would do the trick."

"Day's still young." Drom kept his eyes on the road and his face placid. Truth was, he feared killing someone might make him feel better, if only for a moment.

His decision to chase instead of run was a mistake, a burst of ego that pulled the pin on his fragile family. Michelle was angry enough to play the bait in Cannon's trap. Amanda thought he had abandoned them and taken the boys. And the boys ...

Dear God, the boys.

He told himself that Frabron and his masters needed them alive, that if it was vengeance they were after, Amanda and Michelle wouldn't have been spared. But what if he was wrong? If the boys were dead, he would lose his girls too. He would lose himself.

He parked on Calle de Gabriel de Lobo and stepped out into the crisp bluster of the November air.

Drake slammed his door and faced him. "What's the play here? We going to his office or crashing his lab?"

"Neither," Drom said. "We're going for *tapas*."

He strolled down to Calle de Joaquin Costa and paused at the corner a moment to take in the east wing of the Center of Biological Research, Spain's crown jewel of cellular science. Eight years ago, Dr. Zacharias was one of their microbiology professors. Now he was the head of the entire institution. Considering the man's history, it was enough to make one want a drink.

Want, but not have. Drom could no more afford alcohol than he could murder.

He turned right and headed north, Drake on his heels. A short block later, they stepped down through the dark green doorway of the Bar Velázquez, a narrow hole-in-the-wall bistro with a bar facing the grill and a scattering of four-tops in the dining room.

"Cover the door and get what you like. My contact should be here soon." Drom took the farthest seat at the bar. He ordered mineral water and some *pulpo a la gallega.* She stepped through the door just as the plate of sizzling octopus in olive oil slid under his nose.

Her legs, as toned and tanned as he remembered them, carried her down the four steps to the restaurant floor. She paused a beat at Drake's table, signaling her awareness of his presence.

Drom popped another tentacle into his mouth and savored it, working to appear calmer than he felt. He pulled a swallow from his bottle of sparkling water, set it back down on its condensation ring, and rose to face her.

Removing her oversized, square sunglasses, she brushed a rich lock of chestnut hair over her shoulder with the stem. Her eyes widened, the sunglasses trembling in her hand.

"Hola, Doctora Bohorquez."

Recovering quickly, she glided across the room looking more like a model on a catwalk than a chemistry PhD in a college bar. Warm arms encircled his waist. Soft lips pressed against his for a half-second longer than a friendly hello. Jasmine with vanilla notes infused his brain and he breathed her scent in deeper.

She stepped back to arm's length and trained her emerald irises with their central sunbursts of gold on him. "For a dead man, you look positively gorgeous."

"It's good to see you too, Victoria. Hungry?"

She glanced at his plate. "It's bad luck to drink water with *pulpo a la gallega.* They're called *tapas* for a reason."

"Thirsty, then. Wine, beer, or—"

"Cerveza."

The bartender poured her a glass of Mahou from the tap and Drom ordered ham croquettes and a couple of *tortillas de patata.* She stared at him. He shrugged. "I'm hungry." He took another bite of octopus and offered her the plate.

She joined him in the nibble, then dabbed her full lips with a cocktail napkin. "You've grown."

"A little," he said.

She stroked his cheek, then smoothed his brow with her thumb. "A lot. I used to be taller than you."

He smiled. "You're still prettier."

"That's sweet, but it's not why you brought me here." She sipped her beer without taking her eyes off him. "I watched them carry your body out of that fire."

"You saw what you needed to."

"Stockton could have warned me."

"He didn't?" It came out more accusatory than questioning. He attacked another tentacle, then carved into a tortilla with his fork.

"I didn't believe him."

"He was a bit shocked himself, though not as much as I had hoped. He tell you what I needed?"

"You should let the old man be." Her lips narrowed, draining some of the red out of them.

"I know letting sleeping Nazis lie is official Spanish policy, but I'm not Spanish."

"No, Carlos? Your choice of *tapas* says otherwise. Zacharias is harmless."

"Then he should be safe with me."

"Oh, my dear boy, you're a lot of things. Safe isn't one of them." She stroked her neck and he thought back to the time when his hands were wrapped around it.

"They've taken my sons, Victoria." His voice cracked. He focused on the bartender's movements while he fought for composure.

"Children? You have grown up. Who's the lucky woman?"

"I'm no woman's luck."

She placed her hand on his forearm and kept it there until he looked at her. "You didn't kill Isabela, Carlos. And this woman chose to make a family with you. That's not a small thing."

"I thought as a dead man, I could leave my ghosts behind."

"You are the ghost, my dear. And a nightmare to some, still. What does the old man have to do with your children?"

"That's what I'm here to find out. My father had contact with him."

"That's it? That's all you have?"

"No. I have you." He patted her hand and she took his. Her fingers were warm, her grip strong.

"Witnessing your autopsy was the last job I did for Stockton."

"Still, you came."

"How could I not? If only to see for myself."

"I just want to talk with him, Victoria."

Her eyes hardened. "Then invite him for *tapas* if talk is all you want."

He turned back to the octopus and chewed through his thoughts before voicing them. "I may need to do more than talk, but I promise not to hurt him."

She laughed, but it had no mirth in it. "Your appearance alone might give him a heart attack."

"It's genetics," he said.

"You are your father's son."

"No, you misunderstand. Zacharias is a geneticist. The French have my sons. He knows something Nuremburg never uncovered."

"You think those Nazi pseudo-science sadists actually discovered something of value? Come on, Carlos. The nineteen-forties might as well have been the stone age compared to where microbiology is today."

"My boys weren't kidnapped in the forties."

She considered him a moment, then took a deep swallow of her beer. "Zacharias and others like him, they're all protected."

"You say that like it's a problem."

"Only if you plan on killing more Guardia Civil."

He scratched at the burn scar on his chest. "I told you years ago I was done with killing."

"Yes, you did." She lifted the fork from her tortilla plate and took a bite from his.

She chewed through it slowly, then chased it with another sip of beer. "He lives close by on Calle Gómez Ortega."

"Walking distance."

"He likes to keep in shape."

"His office?"

"Fourth floor of the west wing."

"He takes the stairs." It wasn't a question.

"How old are your sons?" she asked.

"Jakob turns four soon. David is on the edge of the terrible twos."

She finished her beer, then brushed his hair back with her manicured fingers. "You shouldn't have come."

"What choice did I have?"

"Life is nothing but choices, *cariño*, one after the other." She slid off the bar stool. "If it goes wrong, this will be our last meeting as friends."

"I'm glad we had this, at least. I'll be out of your country as fast as I can."

She gripped his hand and he palmed the piece of paper. Her eyes welled up. She threw her arms around him, then kissed him again. "Don't count on me to claim your body from the morgue."

He wiped the tear from the corner of her eye. "You said he was harmless."

She pressed his palm to her cheek. *"Adios, cariño."*

He sat entranced as she floated out of the bar. Jasmine and vanilla lingered in the air as he weighed her words.

Drake took her place, breaking the spell. "You must have hit puberty with a vengeance. Care to tell me where that one fits in?"

"It's not what you think."

"No? You forget I'm an experienced intelligence officer with a keen eye for habits and patterns. You, boy, definitely have a habit pattern."

Drom held up the folded napkin between his fingers. "I have an address. That's the only intelligence you need to concern yourself with right now."

Had it been in a meadow surrounded by olive groves, Drom would have called it a villa. Close in to Madrid's central district, it had the feel of a compound instead. Concrete walls, painted sage green to match the house, rose above his head. They were topped with wrought iron fencing painted black as coal. The black steel driveway gates were ornamented with corn flower rosettes clinging to Euler spirals serving as handles. They were the only German touches on the quintessential Spanish exterior aside from the electrified barbed wire strung across spear-pointed, sloping protrusions along the fence's top rail.

The two-story mini-mansion, set well back from its protective walls, peered down at the street through multiple security cameras tucked against the white eves. The terracotta-tiled roof presented a treacherous landing zone for any jumper intrepid enough to assault the house from above had there been taller structures near enough to jump from. There weren't.

He had to navigate the fence.

Afternoon turned to early evening while he sipped espresso at the sidewalk café and searched for blind spots.

The stakeout dragged him back to a time in his former life when, filled with rage and vengeance, he had hunkered down in a holly hedge and studied the sweep of the CCTV cameras on his target building looking for a hole to run through. An old man with walnut skin and shock-white hair had barged into his hideout. He remembered wanting to bolt, but the stranger turned a piercing eye on him and froze him in place. The old man unrolled a bundle of handmade flutes and after selecting one, breathed out music so pure it pacified his soul.

"We doing this tonight or are you just enjoying the coffee?" Drake asked.

He drained his cup. "Now is as good a time as any."

"Been nice if you had said that a couple of hours ago before my butt went numb."

"A couple of hours ago, I was still thinking like a spy." Drom ambled across the street and made his way to the sidewalk gate.

"You figure a way over the wire?" Drake asked.

"Now you're thinking like a spy." Drom pressed the intercom button.

Drake tucked against the wall beside him. "What are you doing?"

"Ask, and it will be given you; seek, and you will find; knock, and it will be opened to you." He mashed the button again. "I'm knocking."

"*¿Quién es?*" Two words, polite, precise, and laced with a Germanic s.

"*Doctor Zacharias, yo soy Carlos Velveloz,*" Drom said, then switched to German. "*Ich glaube du hast meinen Vater gekannt, Shane Leoppard?*"

"*Willkommen.*" The electric lock buzzed and Drom pulled the gate open. He glanced at Drake and waved him in.

They walked under the branches of the poplar trees standing guard on either side of the flagstone path to a spacious arcade on the south face of the house. One side of a set of distressed oak doors ornamented with iron swung in, revealing the erect frame of *der Affenmann.*

"Gentlemen, come in, come in," he said, sticking with German.

Drom followed him across the red-tiled foyer, up two steps, and through the arched entrance of the marble-floored salon. The body guards who had escorted the doctor home were nowhere to be seen. Either Zacharias was confident in their abilities or unconcerned for his safety.

"Thank you for inviting us in, Dr. Zacharias," Drom said.

"Have a seat, gentlemen." He waved his arm toward the easy chairs huddled against an oval end table. "I was just about to indulge in a cognac nightcap." He busied himself with the decanter and snifters at the sidebar behind the sofa.

"None for me, thanks," Drom said.

Zacharias came back around with the drinks and handed one to Drake. He moved an armchair in closer to the two of them and folded himself into it. Even seated, he towered over Drom. The professor examined him over a sip of brandy. "You have his eyes. I always found them fascinating. They reminded me of how clouds glow when lightning flashes. How is your father? I haven't heard from him in years."

Drom coughed to clear the sudden lump in his throat. "I am sorry to inform that he is dead, *mein Herr*."

"Dead? Tragic, simply tragic. Recently?"

"No. He passed eight years ago."

"How awful for you, young man. What was the cause, if you don't mind my asking?"

An open train car. Spits of suppressed gun fire. His father bleeding out in his arms, the light fading from his electric eyes.

"Kidney failure," Drom said. "He went fast. Didn't suffer much."

"My condolences. Your father was intriguing company. I shall miss the expectation of seeing him again." He raised his glass in salute. "Your colleague, I don't believe we've been introduced."

"James Alderson," Drake said. "I was an associate of Shane Leoppard's back in the day. The kid and I have been working on a couple of projects together."

"I see." Zacharias set his snifter down on his side table and leaned forward, his hands clasped in front. "And these projects involve me how, exactly?"

Drom had come to question only to find himself in front of an interrogator. He wasn't sure the professor's command of the conversation resulted from his Abwehr training, his years of teaching graduate students, or Drom's own lack of focus.

He trained his eyes on the bookcases lining the wall on the far side of the room. Heavy tomes squeezed against each other along all the shelves except the central ones of the array. These held photos, awards, and mementos. They gave a sketch of the professor's life, past and present. The two-toned gray Maltese cross with a black swastika embossed in its center said he wasn't hiding.

"The Iron Cross," Drom said, "was that for your work as *der Affenmann* or your combat experience?"

"Funny, your father asked me the same thing the first time we met. Some spies can avoid combat, but not all of us, *jah* gentlemen?"

"What type of biological research were your monkeys being used for?" Drake asked.

"What type weren't they being used for." He shifted in his seat, leaving himself more exposed to Drake than to Drom. Maybe Zacharias knew more about his father than Drom first thought.

"It doesn't bother you in retrospect that you were helping Hitler?"

"It was the Führer himself who awarded me the medal. I was a soldier fighting for the Fatherland. Herr Alderman here understands that. As a *Zigeuner*, I wouldn't expect you to. You have no country." Unapologetic, he said it matter-of-factly without disdain.

Drom was struck by the ordinary humanness of the man. He and hundreds of thousands of his generation had marched to the orders of a madman and succeeded in giving mankind its darkest blot in recent memory. He wanted to despise Zacharias and instead was struggling not to like him.

He pointed to the medal. "May I? I've only seen them in pictures."

"By all means." Zacharias turned his gaze on Drake. "More cognac?"

"I won't say no." Drake handed him his glass.

The professor moved to the sidebar as Drom approached the display on the wall behind him. "I must admit it was a clever idea Berlin concocted. Disease slows armies down as much as artillery and rifle rounds, sometimes even more." He refilled the snifters. "They wanted to find a way to exacerbate the usual afflictions that accompanied armies on the move."

"How is that any more clever than the Mongols catapulting plague-infested corpses over the walls of Caffa?" Drom kept his back to them, his eyes soaking in the silver-framed photos on the shelf.

"Kahn Janibeg's Mongols were desperate, not clever. Decimated by the plague, they flung their dead into Caffa as they pulled the siege away. They were securing their retreat, not planning for victory. Besides, the Christians in Caffa would have avoided the corpses if they could. It's what humans instinctively do, avoid the sick and putrefying. Berlin had a better idea. They wanted to produce healthy carriers."

"Healthy carriers?" Drake asked.

"*Jah*," Zacharias said, "people who could spread infection while being unaffected by the disease."

"And your monkeys fed this research." Drom lifted a photo off the shelf, a young Franz Zacharias holding a green monkey in a Spanish Sahara setting.

"For a time. But in the face of Beppo's thousands, what were a few hundred of my monkeys?"

Drom put the picture down and grabbed another that caught his eye.

"Beppo?" Drake asked.

Drom carried the picture back to his seat and examined it while Zacharias spoke.

"He and I studied underneath Professor Otmar von Verschuer, head of the Reich's Institute for Health, Biology, and Racial Purity. During the war, my monkeys and Beppo's findings from his human studies all supplied von Verschuer's program."

"Is he someone we could speak with?" Drom asked.

Drake shook his head. "That snake died in sixty-nine. How about this Beppo character, where did he wind up?"

Zacharias leaned back in his arm chair, took a sip of his cognac and contemplated Drake with an amused look. "You and much of the Western world would like to know the answer to that question." His eyes shifted to the picture in Drom's hand.

Drake looked at him. "What am I missing?"

Drom handed him the picture of three men in their prime: a young Zacharias in regular German army uniform with a man on either side of him in the uniform of the Waffen-SS. He pointed to the man on the right.

"Mengele? Dr. Josef Mengele, the Angel of Death, is Beppo?" Drake said.

"*Jah.*" Zacharias affirmed it like it was common knowledge.

Drom took the picture back. He studied the other figure in the black-and-white photo, a man with the distinctive ring on his left hand. He stepped to Zacharias and tapped his finger on the image. "And this man, who is he?"

Chapter 43

The necessity to expand all available forces to highest efficiency in the interest of the state requires, not only in peace but also, and especially, in wartime, the concentrated effort of scientific research and its channelization toward the goal to be aspired ... Leading men of science above all are to make research fruitful for warfare by working together in their special fields.

Führer Decree Concerning the Reich Research Council
Adolf Hitler
Führer Headquarters – June 9, 1942

Konzentrationslager Auschwitz-Birkenau – May 25, 1943

Tshuri never thought about hell before. Now, he fueled its furnaces.

His luck ran out in a Corréze forest, his arrest the final act in a tragedy of errors. He was operating with a band of the Marquis in Clermont-Ferrand surveilling the Michelin plant. A British agent supplied them with plans of the tire factory and promised delivery of explosives to sabotage it. So, they watched and waited, waited some more, and grew bored.

Another Marquis cell south of them sent news of reinforcements heading for Clermont-Ferrand. Disrupting the Michelin plant was the job he owed for his family's passage out of Drancy. Reinforcements would make that job harder, if not impossible. Thinning out their ranks in the forest made sense. Tshuri left three men behind to watch the plant and took the rest south.

His misgivings began when they joined the Corréze cell. They were deserters from a conscripted logging crew. Of the eight men, only one had been in a skirmish. Between them, they had three grenades, two pistols, and seven bullets.

Tshuri's crew, five including himself, had two hunting rifles, an MP40 submachine gun, three Lugers, and only enough ammunition for a hit-and-run action. A sustained fire fight was out of the question.

"How large of a convoy?" Tshuri asked.

"An infantry company," one-skirmish man said.

He considered pulling out then. One hundred and forty German soldiers were marching their way. Along with the command troop and the baggage train, there would be three platoons with riflemen, machine gunners, and grenadiers. Thirteen lightly armed guerrillas against a disciplined company of the Blitzkrieg. Insanity.

"Your men have their axes?" Tshuri asked.

One-skirmish man smiled. "There are large pines on either side of the road a kilometer north of here."

"The road is straight there."

"East side of the road is the high ground. West is all downhill."

They hiked north. Tshuri chose five trees to set the trap, three on the southern approach and two several hundred meters north. They hacked the trunks within a couple of ax swings of falling.

Tshuri took the high ground with two of his men. Once the convoy passed the southern set of trees, the loggers would drop the north roadblock. Momentum would press a good number of the soldiers into the kill box before the convoy came to a halt. They would drop the southern trees, blocking retreat, pour all their fire on them, and run.

The wait stretched to late afternoon. The sharp putter of motorcycles rattled through the trees. Two scouts rolled into view on the straightaway and flew past the traps unmolested. The vanguard appeared minutes later, the command car crawling beside the baggage train wagons. Tshuri did a final check on his submachine gun as they moved through the south gate.

The baggage train lumbered past the north gate. No trees fell. Tshuri glanced at his two men and berated himself for splitting his team up. Had the rest been near him, he would have pulled out then and left the Corréze cell to their fate. Movement in the northwest tree tops caught his eye. The pine snapped like a rifle shot and the tree fell downhill, away from the road.

The teamsters whipped their draft horses into a trot, then a cantor. Half of the forward platoon surged with the baggage train and cleared the roadway before the northeast tree crashed behind them. A grenade exploded in the woods near the roadside followed by two others that detonated among the soldiers.

Tshuri and his men opened fire for a furious minute and retreated. The trees at the south end of the straightaway crashed down and grenadiers manned their mortars. The explosions knocked him off his feet, leaving him dazed and half buried in dirt.

Clawing his way out, he scrambled uphill. He dove behind a rock outcropping on the hillcrest and spied the troop movements below. The last of the vanguard disappeared around a road curve. Rifle squads pressed out on both sides of the road, hunting for ambushers.

Tshuri ran.

He found sanctuary in a village. Two days later, the Germans cleared the entire village out. On the march to the railhead, he learned that their action had wounded seven and killed five. In reprisal, the Nazis shot one hundred and twenty civilians.

The train vomited him out onto the wasted ground of Auschwitz where he was beat into the line of able-bodied men. Hot from the showers, tattoo bleeding, he was impressed into the Sonderkommando.

Compared to the tarpaper barracks of Gurs, his accommodations were palatial. The two hundred prisoners housed in the Krematorioum IV complex were supplied from the vast warehouses of goods stolen from arrivals. Tshuri's bunk was cushioned with eiderdown bedspreads and he rested his head on a silk pillow. Their dining table sported tinned delicacies, liquor, and fine wines. They lived behind brick walls and walked on concrete floors.

Slaving at the ovens made him long for the better days of burying bodies in Gurs. There, he cleared out the dead so others could live. Here, he was a line worker in a death factory, his job the final obliteration of the targets of Nazi hatred.

The lift from the basement gas chamber brought another load of corpses. He moved with his squad to clear the it. They dragged the bodies to their sorted piles: well-fed men, women, children, and the skin-covered skeletons they called *Muselmämmer.*

He cycled out with those charging the muffles. He and his partner loaded a large man face up on the charger, feet to the furnace door. They loaded the next man on top in the opposite direction. To these they added two *Muselmämmer* and rolled the iron cart forward to feed the flames.

The horror of it bludgeoned him to numbness within a fortnight of his arrival. Most of the bodies were undamaged, fresh from the trains, their flesh and fat still on them. He tried to comfort himself with the thought that their early end was better than the cruel wasting and deadly labor in the camp. It was a crumb of solace in a feast of sorrow.

He mopped his brow with his sleeve and pushed the cart forward. "How long, Henryk?"

"Soon. We've been at it a couple of hours." Henryk pulled back on the cart. They shuffled over to the bodies to reload. "Kapo has to call it soon, I can't bear the heat much longer."

"Feed the fire or be the fuel," Tshuri said. It was their motto, the phrase that kept them alive day by day, sometimes hour by hour. He pressed forward with Henryk and the bodies rolled into the roaring oven.

The lift bell rang. The kapo bellowed. "Time!"

Tshuri pulled the cart back and trudged over to the lift. The bodies there, dark-skinned with Z tattoos, broke through his numb stupor. *Zigeuner*, Gypsies and not new arrivals.

Henryk stepped past him, grabbed a woman's arms, and hauled her body out onto the concrete floor. Tshuri stared at her. It wasn't Hishoro or anybody he knew.

Someone struck the back of his head, pounding him down atop her warm body.

"Move, scum!" The kapo kicked him.

Tshuri rose. Blood trickled over his ear and down his neck. Scrambling to the lift, he grabbed a wrist in each hand and pulled. Head throbbing, he dragged the load. They were halfway out of the lift before he realized he had ahold of two bodies.

Letting go of one, he concentrated his efforts on the other, hauling it like his life depended on it because it did. Feed the fire or be the fuel.

They sorted load after load. Tshuri willed himself to keep moving. Another blow to the head would land him on the floor for good. Snag, heave, drag, stack. Repeat.

He scanned the slack-jawed faces, searching to not find. Snag, look, heave. Scan, drag, stack. Snag—

"Time!"

Tshuri dragged the body around to the third furnace. Henryk came over with a fatter corpse. They loaded it on the rails first, then stacked the other one on top.

⊕

Gypsy bodies were still coming up from the basement when the dayshift took over. Tshuri gathered bits of information from the men coming on duty. The SS moved into the Gypsy camp in the middle of the night with their lists and pulled the condemned out of their barracks. They led a column a thousand strong into the fake showers with the timed precision of an assembly line.

The Sonderkommando barracks showers were real, one of the mandatory perks of the job. Only the healthiest worked in the crematoriums. They were made to shower to help keep them that way until the day of their execution. He stood under the hot stream, scrubbing the night's work away. He toweled off, still feeling unclean. He knew they were all here to die. Somehow, turning all those Roma to ash made it more personal.

He ran a finger along the lump at the back of his head, thankful the bleeding had stopped.

He filled his plate though he had no appetite. He couldn't allow his body to shrink like his soul. He spotted Henryk in the dining hall. He squeezed in between two men who had opted for distilled potatoes instead of boiled ones and pointed across the table at the branch in Henryk's hands.

"Doesn't look too appetizing," he said.

Henryk's brow raised, giving the corner of his mouth a slight lift. "The road builders found a stand of elder bushes."

"And they brought you a branch instead of berries?"

"The branch cost me a pack of cigarettes. I couldn't afford the berries." His hand slipped under the table and reappeared with an open pocket knife. He scraped the blade down the branch, peeling away a long strip of bark.

"You should eat," Tshuri said. "You'll need your strength."

"There is more to strength than food, my friend."

Henryk's fingers worked the wood with the intimacy of seasoned practice, his movements sure and efficient. While Tshuri chewed through his potatoes, Henryk shaved the branch down to blond wood. As he cut into a piece of cured ham, his friend produced a length of stiff wire and a dowel the size of his thumb. By the time Tshuri finished his cabbage, Henryk had cleared out the soft center of the elder wood with the wire.

The man on Tshuri's right poured vodka into a glass and slid it in front of him. He tapped the yellow star sown over his heart. "Every day, it is us." He tapped the black triangle sown onto Tshuri's shirt. "Today, it wasn't you." He lifted his glass. "Drink."

Tshuri tossed it down. The vodka burned his throat and warmed his belly. He set the glass down and the man refilled it. Sawdust gathered around its base like a miniature snow drift. He looked across at Henryk and the red triangle on his shirt marking him a political prisoner.

"You never told me what you did to make the Nazis not like you." He sipped of the vodka, then drained the glass. The heat in his belly grew. The throbbing in his head persisted.

Henryk blew through the hollowed tube of elder wood, scattering more sawdust on the table. Setting it down, he twisted the knife point in its side. "For a Jew, being born is enough. Right, Yzak?"

The man next to Tshuri lifted his vodka glass in agreement.

"Same goes for Gypsies," Tshuri said. "But you are neither Jew nor Roma."

"No, I'm Polish, which in their eyes puts me half a step above you two and a full boot under them."

"Were you in the government?" Yzak asked.

"I am in the kingdom." Henryk used the wire to smooth out the two holes he had bored. He switched back to the knife and twisted it to make third.

Yzak grunted. "What kingdom? Poland's last king died over a hundred years ago. Talk sense, man."

The corner of Henryk's mouth ticked up again. He started a new hole, his eyes on Yzak. "That yellow star on your breast, what is it?"

"You know what it is. The star of David."

"David, yes." Henryk blew the hole clear and smoothed the edges with the wire. "The giant slayer, the shepherd king of Israel. The son of Jesse, David."

The phrase tugged at Tshuri like a taste he couldn't name. He contemplated his glass, then turned his attention back to Henryk. The elder wood sat at his elbow, six evenly spaced holes drilled into it. Henryk took the dowel and whittled the end, his forearms rippling as his fingers worked. His cheeks hung loose, dragging his eyes into a sad droop at odds with their lively sparkle.

"You should eat," Tshuri said again.

Henryk shaved a flat spot onto the dowel, then pressed it against the knife edge and turned it, scoring a circle a centimeter back from the end. "I am. And I will." Snapping the piece of dowel off, he used it to plug one end of the elder wood. Holding the branch in his left hand, plug end toward him, he drew the knife to him and a chip of wood fell to the table. He put his creation to his mouth and blew through the end. It gave a low whistle, like the headwind of a thunderstorm far away.

"So, Yzak," Henryk said, "you and I are both here because of the kingdom. You because long ago, David was your king. Me because my king told me to hide your people in my church basement."

He brought the wood back to his lips and breathed it to life, his fingers dancing over the holes. The music touched Tshuri's aching head in places the vodka couldn't reach. He recognized the tune and relaxed into it.

Yzak brushed a tear from his eye. "The Lecha Dodi. How comes a priest to know the Sabbath song?"

Henryk tapered off the measure with a flourish, then set the flute down. "I know the Sabbath song because my king is the Sabbath Lord."

"Who is your king?" Tshuri asked.

Henryk glanced at Tshuri, then turned his focus on Yzak. "My king is Jesus the Messiah, the son of David, the son of Abraham."

Yzak's eyes widened and his shoulders rolled forward. Henryk reached across the table and clasped the big man's hands. They stared at each other, both nodding. Tshuri understood Henryk's words, but Yzak's response told him he had missed their meaning.

He leaned toward Henryk for clarification. Before he could voice his question, a guard called his number.

⊕

He marched with four other prisoners, struggling to keep up. The vodka wasn't helping. They came out of the crematorium compound and headed east on the camp's main road. The early sun shone on the green tarpaper warehouses where all the confiscated goods were stored. To the Germans, it was Section D. To Tshuri and the rest of the Sonderkommandos, it was Kanada, the land of plenty.

They turned south on a side road. The high voltage warning signs on the wire were less alarming than the sector sign. Coming through the gate of BIIf, Tshuri's stomach tightened and the vodka turned sour in his gut.

Just east of him on the other side of the wire was BIIe, the Gypsy Camp. Over fifteen thousand Roma and Sinti were stuffed into thirty barracks that in saner times had housed horses. He peered through the wire hoping to see and dreading to find a red kerchief with a riot of flowers.

"Halt!"

They stopped in front of the only brick building in BIIf. Its lack of chimneys gave him heart until he saw the building number. No one came out of Number Ten unchanged, if they came out at all.

The guard pulled the door open. *"Hinein, schnell!"*

Tshuri ran up the steps and through the doorway. The medical staff directed them to the central stairway and led them to the second floor. They came into a cavernous room on the north side of the building. Wide windows north and east poured sunlight on the whitewashed walls and bare plank floor. A wooden trough, rectangular and twice as wide as a coffin, commanded the center of the room.

They were ordered to strip.

A sandy-haired man, his SS uniform covered with a lab coat, approached Tshuri. His pale blue eyes shifted up and down, left and right, never pausing to meet Tshuri's. He jotted notes on his clipboard, then checked Tshuri's pulse.

"Today, I give your life meaning," the man said. "Open your mouth."

Tshuri complied. The doctor jammed a thermometer under his tongue and he closed his mouth reflexively.

"My colleagues in Dachau have been doing experiments for the Luftwaffe. I've been tasked with verifying their findings. Your efforts today may save the lives of brave German airmen in the future." He pulled the thermometer out, checked it, and made another notation.

Tshuri peered over the man's shoulder. Other inmates serving as orderlies were dumping buckets of ice into the trough. Water splashed over the rim and rained on the floor. Metal boxes with knobs and dials like those on radios were wheeled closer to the tub, their electrical cords stretching back to the wall like devils' tails.

A man in a lab coat with a yellow star sewn on the breast unspooled a wire from one of the machines and lowered its weighted end into the tub. He flipped a switch and fiddled with a knob. The needle bounced to life on the dial, swinging left to right, then arced left in a steady creep. "Reading is eight degrees Celsius, Doctor."

"Add more ice. I want it at three degrees." The doctor looked Tshuri in the eye. "I think my colleagues' methods are flawed. The Luftwaffe does not have *Muselmämmer*." He swept his gaze over to Tshuri's fellow Sonderkommandos. "I've asked for the healthiest specimens for my experiments. We shall see how their science holds up."

He waved Tshuri over to the conscripted Jewish doctor. Tshuri trudged toward the humming machines. The wet floor chilled his feet and the hair on his arms bristled. The Jewish doctor uncoiled another wire and asked Tshuri to turn around. Something ripped. Warm hands pressed a cold wire against his back and smoothed tape over it.

"This will monitor your external temperature," the man said. "I need you to bend over and spread your buttocks for me."

Tshuri hesitated, sure he didn't want to suffer whatever indignity came next. He eyed the two armed guards and the four burly orderlies. Resistance wasn't much of an option. He bent forward.

"I need to monitor your internal temperature," the Jewish doctor said. "I am very sorry for this. Try to relax."

Tshuri didn't know how much of the wire the doctor inserted before taping it in place, only that it was too much.

"The tank is at three degrees, Dr. Schilling," the Jewish doctor said.

"Please begin."

The orderlies were on him before he could flinch. They lifted him off the floor and tossed him in the trough. His breath caught in his throat at the shock of the freezing water.

"*Versuchperson* is at thirty-seven degrees internal, *Herr Doktor.*"

Tshuri put his first breath behind a scream. He splashed to his feet and the orderlies pushed him back down.

"You stay in until we pull you out," one of them said. The guards pointed their rifles at him, reinforcing the order.

"Thirty-five degrees, *Herr Doktor.*"

Tshuri's teeth chattered. His whole body trembled, splashing water out of the tub. Another bucket of ice was poured in. He scanned the room like a caged animal looking for a way out. He spotted a clock on the wall behind the Jewish doctor. Five past nine.

He fixed his gaze on the sweeping second hand and tried to still his limbs.

Five minutes. I can last five minutes.

"Thirty-four degrees."

The stinging in his hands and feet faded. His fingers stiffened, his toes petrified. The second hand swept past twelve.

Five more minutes. I can stand five more minutes.

Something pricked his neck. He became aware of Dr. Schilling at his side, a blood-filled syringe in his hand. He found the clock. A quarter to ten. He gulped air, struggling to breathe

"Thirty-two degrees."

"I … I need … please." His joints were coming apart. He shook violently, cascading water and ice all around. He found the white clock face, but couldn't read it.

A prick in his neck. Pale blue eyes filled his vision. "His blood is still warm."

"Rectal thermometer reads thirty degrees, *Herr Doktor.*"

Sweat stung his eyes. *Why am I sweating?* He needed to rub them. His arms wouldn't move. His knees wouldn't bend. He searched for the clock.

"Twenty-eight—"

⊕

He came to shaking uncontrollably. His first realization was that he was dry, his second that he wasn't alone.

Heat pressed into his frozen skin, thawing his nerves. Heavy blankets itched, soft mattress yielded. An arm crossed his chest and held him tight. A familiar voice cooed in his ear and he knew he was dreaming.

And didn't care. It was a warm, skin-on-skin dream and he responded to it as he would in the waking world. His temperature rose, his blood surged.

Rolling over, he drew her in, warming his chest with her bosom. Her features came into view, still beautiful, but aged and etched with pain and sorrow. *"Rrómniorri."*

"Shh, shh." Her summer whisper warmed his cheeks.

He rolled on top of her, aware now that he was awake, unsure of how it was they were together. But together they were. Cold forgotten, his heat all consuming, he buried himself in her embrace until he was spent.

He flopped onto his back, his breaths deep and filling. *"Rrómniorri,* how—"

A withered arm wrapped across his belly, cutting him off. "Shh, shh."

Chapter 44

Konzentrationslager Auschwitz-Birkenau – June 4, 1943

Hishoro hovered near the wire—close enough to see, far enough to not get shot—and watched the boys kicking the ball around the field. Hers chased it as the older boys replicated the semblance of a soccer game. Alfonso's fluid movements and high-pitched squeals highlighted Pierre's shuffling run and pinched face. Behind them rose the giant chimneys, their fiery tongues licking the smoke clouds red.

The fever gripped them for a week, during which time Hishoro had a front row seat in Dr. Mengele's shop of horrors. Wash cloths and clean water were the only tools he gave her to save the boys' lives. Her dread deepened with each dissection in the clinic. If the boys died, they would take their turn on his table.

Another set of twins, girls twice her boys' age, arrived during her first day of vigil. One of the nurses gave them each an injection, then sat them on stools against the wall. Within minutes, they started twitching, then convulsed violently enough to throw them off the stools.

No one tended them.

Sometime after their thrashing and mewling stopped, Dr. Mengele strolled over and helped them up. He sat them back on the stools, wiped the spittle and sweat from their faces with a wet cloth, and gave them water. He spoke to them, his voice warm and kind. The girls smiled. Eyes sparking, he handed them candies in bright wrappers.

"Danke, Onkel Mengele," the girls said in unison. They hugged his neck and kissed his cheeks. He took them by the hand and led them out of the laboratory, a doting uncle spoiling his nieces.

The girls were back two days later. This time, only one was injected. The spared twin kept her seat, her gaze occasionally drifting down to her sister writhing on the floor. When her convulsions stopped, Mengele had both the girls stripped and strapped onto the metal tables. He took a syringe with a long needle and filled it from a large vile on the counter. He placed his left index finger on the traumatized girl's chest. She stared at him, her hair matted with sweat. He placed the needle on the left side of her chest and pushed it in slowly.

The girl screamed. Her sister cried. Mengele's thumb pressed the plunger. Scream turned to screech, then died. He pulled the needle out and repeated the process on the other girl. He checked for a pulse with his stethoscope, then wrote "Z.S." on their chests with chalk.

He turned to a woman in a smock that might have been white at one time. "Get the coffin commando to carry these two to the morgue." He spun on his heel and sauntered away.

Surviving, she learned, was its own penalty.

Across the way, Pierre tripped and crashed to the ground. Alfonso stopped his forward rush and crossed to his brother. He pulled Pierre up and brushed the dirt off his pantaloons. Like the rest of Mengele's children, hers were well dressed and fed. Squeals and laughter wafted to her, the universal sounds of happy, healthy children.

It was an illusion.

Her focus shifted to the fence sign. *"VORSICHT"* it warned in red, followed by *"Hochspannung Lebensgefahr"* in black. "Caution! High voltage. Danger to life." A red lightning bolt, reminiscent of the insignia adorning the collars of the camp's stalking predators, sought to add emphasis to the warning. Some took it as an invitation, hugging it in suicide if they reached it before being shot.

Hishoro had to find a way through it.

Once again, she revisited her last moments with Tshuri and her fateful decisions of that night. He had escaped with Tshompi. If she had only gone with them …

The twins would be lost to her like Keti.

The boys were back at play. She tracked the ball for a while and pretended she was watching a game that could end with a winner. Mengele appeared at the edge of the playground, his cap perched at a jaunty angle, hands clasped at the small of his back. He stood like a general observing his troops on parade.

A little boy in a white suit ran up to him from behind and tugged at his elbow. Mengele bent down and the child pointed north to the road. The doctor turned toward the gate. He ruffled the child's hair and the pair headed to the road; Mengele's stride long and smooth, the little boy running to keep up.

Curious, Hishoro shadowed them on her side of the fence. The pair stopped short of the guard post and the gates swung open.

A gray sedan rolled through and braked in front of Mengele. A uniformed driver stepped out and opened the rear passenger door. An officer emerged. Mengele popped to attention with a stiff-armed salute. The salute was returned, if not so formally, and the two men shook hands.

The other rear door opened. Another officer climbed out and approached the other two. They saluted each other, then relaxed as Mengele offered cigarettes all around. The men lit up and chatted like old friends at a picnic. The mannerisms of the last officer haunted Hishoro. His left hand brought the cigarette to his mouth and his ring flashed in the sun.

Her heart sank.

⊕

After two sleepless nights spent waiting for guards to drag her to the clinic, the summoner came in broad daylight wearing a dingy lab coat.

She inspected the number on Hishoro's forearm and checked it against the paper in her hand. "Hishoro Velveloz?"

The use of her name set her back. She hadn't heard it spoken by anyone in authority since Drancy. "That is my name, yes."

"I am Dr. Lörinc Etel." She pulled up her left sleeve, exposing her own tattoo. "I am truly sorry, but they've ordered me to bring you to his laboratory."

Laboratory, not clinic. She was honest at least, Hishoro thought. "They?"

"We best get going. My pass is time stamped."

Dr. Etel set an even pace, purposeful but unhurried. She was taller than Hishoro—most people were—but not by much. She was broad-framed for her height. Her headscarf, wrapped tight to her forehead and tied under her chin, left no strands of hair exposed. If she had any. Dark brows arched over warm brown eyes, at once inquisitive and kind.

"You are a Jew," Hishoro said. "How can you bear to work for him?"

Her escort paused. "Look around, Hishoro. Do you imagine you can save all these people?" Her tone was more chiding than cynical, her French tinged with Balkan notes. "We can't. But to save some, we must stay alive, no?"

"You are taking me to his laboratory."

"He doesn't want to kill you." Dr. Etel resumed their stroll, her head bowed.

"Uncle Mengele would see us all dead and still smile."

"Dr. Phélypeaux is the one who requested you. He considers you worth saving."

"There are days when I think letting me die would be a kindness."

Dr. Etel glanced at her. "Dying is easy. It takes courage to survive."

"How is it that the French doctor finds himself in SS uniform?"

"He said it was necessary to get him here. Regardless of the uniform, he is a French patriot. What he does here, he does for France, not the Reich's fatherland or its Führer."

"Did you know him before the madness?"

"We were in medical school together in Montpellier."

"But you are not French."

"No. I grew up among the Romanians in Sighet. I worked hard at my studies and earned a placement at the University."

Hishoro stopped. "He hurts me."

Dr. Etel eyed the gate guard. "Karl tells me you always heal. We will do what we can to make it bearable. He is not like Mengele."

"You think not?" Hishoro turned away from her and strode to the gate. Dr. Etel followed and showed their pass to the guard. He inspected it and ushered them through.

Out of earshot from the guard, Dr. Etel put her hand on Hishoro's arm and stopped her. "All this suffering around us is senseless. We would all be dead if they could kill us faster." She held her eyes for an uncomfortable moment. "Your suffering stands the chance of actually helping others."

"You say you studied with him. There was a medical woman who helped me in Drancy who also knew the doctor. Hélène, she is called. Do you know her?"

Dr. Etel's eyes tightened, the corners of her mouth dropped. "Knew her. She was an extraordinary woman."

"Was?"

"Yes. She became ill during transport. I had her in the infirmary for a bit, but sadly, couldn't save her."

Hishoro squeezed the hand holding her arm, then let it drop. "Phélypeaux didn't even try." She turned on her bare heel and marched into the clinic.

Chapter 45

In the months following the end of World War II in Europe, many of Romania's fascist Iron Guard escaped justice with the help of their Nazi contacts. The Wiesenthal Center claimed in a recent statement that the former leader of the Iron Guard, Horia Sima, is now living in Spain.

Schenectady Gazette, August 23, 1988

Montpellier, France – November 10, 1988

Drom lifted the collar of his jean jacket and buried his hands deeper in its pockets. The gray sky hid the Mediterranean sun and threatened rain. He quickened his pace.

Up ahead, a man in a camel hair overcoat set his satchel on the sidewalk, and perched the toe of his dress shoe on the bumper of a blue Renault. He tied his lace as Drom brushed past. The man caught up to him at the intersection and they waited for the pedestrian light to give them the go ahead.

Drom kept his face forward. "If you don't speed up, we'll have to break in."

"If you wanted faster, you should have bought train tickets instead of hiring a fishing trolley." The walking man lit up and Drake stepped off the curb.

Drom matched his stride as they crossed the street. "You know I don't do trains, old man. Keep up." He pulled away, shoulders hunched, a man in a hurry trying to stay warm.

They had been at it for over an hour. The boat dropped them off at a fishing wharf in Carnon. They came over the gunwale as off-duty fishermen, Drom refreshed and Drake seasick. A block from the boat, they transformed into a college student and a businessman. The medical school, ensconced in the ancient city center of Montpellier and surrounded by medieval mansions, was a two-and-a-half hour walk from the harbor if one didn't have to worry about tails or an ageing, seasick spy.

Drom tacked north. Working his way out of the residential area, he came upon one of the major east-west corridors. His distaste for trains aside, Montpellier's trolley system offered the best solution to Drake's sluggishness. He crossed the eastbound lanes of the divided avenue and stepped up to the trolley stop. He cut across to the westbound rails and tucked into one of the wait shelters. He leaned against the glass, eyes east, an anxious commuter looking for the tram.

Shoppers burdened with bags and wrapped boxes crossed the westbound lanes in a steady stream from the retail palaces on the northside of the block and filled the platform. Drake meandered through their clusters and plopped himself on the bench to Drom's right. He pulled a newspaper out of his inside coat pocket and snapped it open.

"Rat-gélane, trades po djédjésh?" Drake's relaxed posture belied his sarcastic tone.

"I'm only riding the rails because you walk slower than my grandmother, Rebniko," Drom answered in Romani, using Drake's Gypsy alias. The man's facility with the language was an asset, giving them their own form of covert communication. Even so, it grated on him. Drake mastered Romani as a means to hunt him down and kill him.

He nearly succeeded—twice.

"My land legs are back. I'll be squared away by the time we get there."

"One could only hope. Your French going to match the ID McAbee gave you?"

"Don't you worry about my French. I can make a whore blush."

"Too bad you can't hold your own with sailors."

The three-car tram rolled into the stop. Drake slipped into the lead car. Drom chose the rear one. The electric train rolled out as the clouds let loose.

Drom reviewed the intelligence that brought him here. Bastien Frabron drew the Cinq Cornes sigil on his camper wall. Dr. Franz Zacharias knew both Josef Mengele and Dr. Karl Phélypeaux during World War II. The French doctor was a direct descendant of Alfred Phélypeaux, a former count of Saint-Exupéry. In the late nineteenth century, the count codified various rites of *La Société des Cinq Cornes*.

According to a briefing packet from McAbee, Cinq Cornes was founded in the eighteenth century as a secret fraternity catering to the French vitalists. Among their more notable members was Paul Joseph Barthez—physician, physiologist, and lawyer. A luminary of the University of Montpellier, his statue stood at the entrance of one of the oldest medical schools in Europe.

Montpellier is where Karl Phélypeaux earned his doctorate. He still held a chair there in embryology and maintained an office and research facility in the ancient enclave of the *Faculte de Medecine* despite his known association with Mengele.

L'habit ne fait pas le maine, Drom thought. The habit doesn't make the monk.

The tram stopped. Four shoppers stepped off. A young woman and an old man—bent over and shuffling on a cane—came aboard. The man chose a forward-facing seat near the center of the car. The young woman, about Shell's height and with an athletic stride, made her way to the front and sat facing the back of the car. She pulled her headscarf off and wrung the water out into the aisle. Her blond hair, dark with wet, lay plastered to her head.

Rain pelted the trolley's northside windows. Drom stared out at the passing commercial districts and studied the old man with his peripheral vision. The man scratched the gray stubble on his chin, then picked his nose with a gnarled thumb.

The tram entered the city proper. Open lots gave way to high rises pushing up through older, stone-quarried blocks. They came to a stop. The old man shuffled off behind three other passengers. Two new riders boarded. The young woman with sopping hair stayed on.

Drom checked the transit map on the wall panel. Two more stops and he would be back on foot, heading west into the city's center. He made passing glances at the new passengers, a middle-aged man and a teenage boy, then brought his focus back to the young woman.

She sat in the opposite corner of the car from Drom, her back to the direction of travel. She wore no makeup. Her face, though shy of beautiful, was attractive. Her Greek nose balanced with her defined jawline and sculpted neck. These all compensated for her pockmarked cheek, scarring from adolescent acne or some traumatic accident, perhaps.

She got off at the next stop, wet headscarf tied under her chin, light jacket zipped up to her neck. Five more passengers came on. Drom gave all of them names and crafted legends for them to pass the time. His stop came before he finished the last imaginary profile.

Stepping off into the rain, he aimed for the towers of Saint Peter's Cathedral. He purposely avoided checking on Drake. The next set of surveillance detection runs—double backs and block loops to spot tails—belonged to him. He had to trust Drake to do them.

Drom took as direct a route as paths laid down in the Middle Ages allowed. Rain tapered to drizzle. He checked the odd windshield and shop window for any dangers behind him. On a couple of occasions, he dashed across streets buzzing with traffic, heedless of horns and not bothering to look over his shoulder.

He came around the twin spired columns of Saint Peter's and strolled across the wide foot bridge to the medical school entrance. Carved marble lions anchored the ends of the engraved banner over the portal arch. He clipped his fake student ID onto his collar and stepped into their den.

Navigating through the school's airy foyer, he noted the man in the camel hair overcoat arguing with the information desk attendant, a middle-aged woman with graying hair twisted into a tight bun atop her head.

"Of course, they aren't expecting me," Drake said, his French flawless. "It is the nature of compliance inspections to be unannounced. May we now progress to the inevitable? The day is late and I do not wish to spend the night here."

Drom skirted the desk, somewhat surprised. It was possible his former nemesis had regrouped and gotten ahead of him. Or he had hailed a taxi, which was more likely.

Darting into the first stairwell he encountered, he charged up the steps to the second floor. He turned his mind's eye to the facility plans McAbee had provided and hustled down the corridor like a student late for a lecture. He crossed the hall and entered the southeast stairwell. Plastering his back against the wall, he let the door swing shut.

He counted down from twenty. At thirteen, the classroom bells rang, confirming his internal clock. 3:55 p.m. The cacophony of overlapping conversations seeped through the door as students shifted classrooms. He jumped down to the landing, spun, and jumped again. In rapid succession, he descended to the second basement level and emerged into a corridor more reminiscent of a monastery cellar than a Gothic cathedral annex.

Modern fixtures dangled from the hewn stones overhead, splashing pools of light along the corridor. Drom pressed his ear to the stairwell door for a moment. Hearing no footfalls, he headed north. The network of cellars beneath the university-cathedral complex extended beyond the buildings above like roots of a tree.

Following his mental map, he snuck into the records room Drake had accessed through deceit. He was seated at the far end of the long reference table in room's center. Its classic inlaid, walnut top and surrounding ornate chairs clashed with the modern mobile shelving banks with gleaming stainless steel crank wheels that filled the room on either side of it.

"Were you followed?" Drake asked.

"You tell me, old man. Did you tip the cabbie?"

"Not my fault you're pigheaded enough to walk in the rain. And no, I didn't. This is France. Everyone knows French cabbies overcharge."

"You find the spot?"

Drake's head dipped left. "Fourth row if Russell's intel is right."

"He's been on the mark so far."

"Yeah? Well, you don't know him like I do." Drake put his satchel on the table. "I made it past Madame Ratched. This next part is all you. Just do me a favor and don't burn the place down. It's a historical landmark."

"You going to stay there or mind the door?"

Drake stepped to the other end of the table, snagged a chair and set it near the doorway. He straddled it, facing its carved back. "Clock's ticking."

Drom cranked the first file bank up against the fixed shelving units on the wall and locked it in place. He rolled the next three over in succession, widening his working aisle. "You check any records?"

"You do the math? Single banks on the walls and nine double-sided arrays on each side of the room, both nine feet deep and five shelves high." Drake scratched the back of his head. "I figure that makes somewhere around eighteen hundred linear feet of filing. There is such a thing as too much information."

Drom snagged the satchel and cut through the aisle to the stone wall. He traced a mortar line with his finger and figured it was older than the American republic by at least a century. It showed no signs of decay. He opened the satchel and dug out a carpenter's pencil and the battery-powered hammer drill.

"You should probably do some of what you said you were here for in case they check," Drom said loud enough for Drake to hear. "You never know. You might get lucky."

"Don't flatter yourself thinking you can teach me my trade, boy. I was at this game long before you were born."

"Wonder then, that a boy like me could bring you to such ruin." Drom marked out a rectangle with dots, then connected the corners with diagonals. He put the masonry bit into the drill and tightened the chuck. "I know we are two stories underground, but this drill makes a racket. There is a chance some-one will come to investigate the noise."

"Then you best get the lead out and drill the holes quick so your hands are free when they get here," Drake said. Drom could picture the smirk on his face.

He pressed the drill point against his first mark and squeezed the trigger. The drill rattled like a miniature jack hammer, then muffled as the bit ate into the mortar. Halfway through the marks, he set the drill down and came out to check on Drake.

He was still by the door, stacks of files around his feet. He looked up from the folder in his hands. "Done?"

"Find anything interesting?"

"Found a vein of financial records. These French have a different word for everything, but they use the same numbers we do."

"And?"

"And what? The records we came for are on the other side of that wall. Keep working."

Drom eyed him a moment longer, then returned to his task. Once all the holes were made, he switched to a paddle bit. He pulled a bag of powder and a paint can out of the satchel. Using a two-franc coin, he pried the lid off. He tore open the bag of powder and poured it into the can of water. He stirred it to a slurry with the drill, then grabbed the industrial syringe out of the satchel.

He filled the syringe with slurry, then pressed the material into the holes. After they were all filled, he capped the can and put it back in the bag. He took the flashlight out and packed everything else away. He came back to the table and set the bag on it.

"McAbee said the compound takes about thirty minutes to expand enough to crack mortar and stone."

"And if he's wrong?" Drake asked.

"We wait another five. What've you got there?"

"These?" Drake lifted the papers in his hand. "Endowment records. Seems *la Faculté* has made some arrangements with Eastern Bloc nations."

"Not unusual. French academics have always kept strange bedfellows."

"True, but why send your hard currency east? What are they buying with it?"

"What countries?"

"So far, I've come across Yugoslavia and Czechoslovakia. I'm guessing there are others." He glanced down at the stack around his feet.

"Let's move to the table and see what else we can find," Drom said.

⊕

He was writing his draft analysis of the financial movements when the mortar and stones snapped, jarring him to his feet.

Drake's face came away from the file he was studying. "Half hour passed already?"

"More like an hour." He bullet-pointed the rest of his analysis and pocketed the notebook. "Let's take a look."

"I'm minding the door, remember? You go ahead. I'll tidy this mess up."

Drom returned to the wall. The hyper-expanding concrete had done its job. Cracks in mortar and stone connected his drilled dots. Kneeling on the file platform, he pushed against the rock with both hands. Nothing moved. He pried out one of the broken stones with his fingers and shined the flashlight into the hole. More stone confronted him.

I should have packed a crowbar.

Shifting onto his buttocks, hands braced on the floor, he battered the wall with the soles of his boots. The rough triangles of fused stones rocked independently, alternately moving and binding each other.

He tilted onto his left buttock and pounded against the top triangle with his right leg. The section shifted in earnest and he redoubled his efforts. His sole slammed into the stones and broke through. Part of the wall above gave way in a shower of mortar and misery, trapping his leg.

"Drake! Need a little help over here!"

The metal shelving array rang like a muffled bell under staccato blows.

"Drake!"

No response.

Placing his left foot against the wall, he grabbed his trapped leg below the knee and pulled as he pressed away with his foot. His leg inched out. The shelving rattled again, followed by a percussion of violence punctuated with cracks of splintering wood.

Drom clawed at the stones above his leg and gave it another heave. It broke free with another shower of falling debris. He jumped to his feet and his right ankle gave out, lurching him sideways. Pain shot up the leg, punching his diaphragm.

Steadying himself against the shelves, he gingerly put weight on his right leg, steeling himself against each new octave of agony. Bending at the waist, he gathered broken stones. He shuffled down the aisle, the traumatized nerves in his ankle begging him to stop at each step.

He peered around the end of the file bank. Drake was sprawled on his back surrounded by papers and the shattered remains of a chair. Eyes bulging and face purple, he flailed his legs and clawed at his neck. Drom tacked right for a better view just as Drake rolled over, exposing the wet-haired blonde throttling him.

Drom fired three chunks in rapid succession, striking the attacker's left shoulder, triceps, and elbow. With a curse, she released her grip from the wire garrote. Drake swung back with his elbow, clipping the side of her head. He scrambled free, coughing through ragged breaths.

She sprang into a fighter's stance, her back to the underside of the over-turned table. Her head swept from Drom to Drake, exposing her pockmarked cheek.

The early warnings of his brain tumbled into place: his reflex to compare her height to Shell's, the nagging itch her scars gave him—scars he had made with his softball cleat. He limped out from the aisle onto the stone floor. "We should talk."

A blade sprang open in her right hand. Her left arm dangled at her side, useless. She brought the knife up and forward. "We could have talked in Penticton. Instead, you gave me this." She turned her cheek to him.

Drom raised his hands, showing her the shards of stone held in each. "I'm all ears now. Drop the knife and I let you keep the beauty remaining."

She shifted her weight onto the balls of her feet. "There's more to me than looks." She launched, closing the distance between them before he could throw.

He sidestepped her lunge, but his ankle tilted him into her backslash. Slapping the shards against the sides of her head, he stumbled back. She pressed her attack, blood dripping down her ears. He danced to her right, smacking her biceps as she jabbed with the knife.

She lunged for his gut. Shoving her arm with his left hand, he crashed an uppercut into her chin with his right. She staggered back, shaking her head. He dug the two-franc coin out of his pocket and flicked it at her as she charged. The coin lodged sideways in her right eyebrow, cutting it in half. Blood gushed over her eye.

Behind her, Drake struggled to his feet, air rattling into his lungs through his bruised neck. She spun and plunged the knife into his side. He crumpled to the floor, taking the knife with him.

She turned, grabbed a chair leg off the floor, and held it like a club as she faced Drom. Her right eye was swollen shut and awash in blood. Her left beamed malice.

Drom brought out the rest of his pocket change and showed her the backs of his hands, a coin held between each finger. She raised her makeshift bat into a guard position and squared off with him. He sent the left-hand volley, driving the coins into the chair leg. She kept her grip on the wood, her uninjured eye widening at the half-buried coins.

"You are only alive because I haven't killed you," Drom said. "Let's talk, you and I."

"How about I talk and you listen." Crouching down, she set the chair leg on the floor and kicked it away. Rising slowly, she unzipped her running jacket, then turned her palm to him. "If I had a pistol, I would have used it already. I need to show you something. After that, you can decide how this ends." Curling her fingers over the zipper edge, she opened the jacket, unveiling the right side of her chest. There, pinned on her shirt above her breast, sat a small, plastic, U.S. Border Patrol badge. "I need you to stand down. My back up will be here soon."

Heart hammering in his ears, he pictured the strike points of his last three coins. The first would split her smirk in two, shattering her top front teeth. The second would cut in below her right ear, sending her into immediate vertigo hell. On her way down, the third coin would shut down her other eye. Permanently.

He spread his fingers. The coins clattered on the floor. Her eye sprang open, her mouth shaping an O. She toppled forward.

"French women, fun to dance with but not worth dying for." Drake's voice was all hiss and gravel. He dropped her bloody knife from his hand.

"What did you do?" Drom charged toward her and his body shed its fight-or-flight focus. His right ankle collapsed. He smacked the unyielding stone and rolled over with a groan. His chest was slick and stinging. He got to his knees and stared Drake. "Why? I had this under control."

"You think?" Drake coughed, his left arm tucked hard against his ribcage, his right fist covering his mouth. He brought it away when the fit subsided. Blood speckled his lips. "That little viper almost punched both our tickets, thank you very much. I just saved you from a costly mistake."

Drom eyed blade placement, precision stabs into the kidney. It was an assassin's move; so painful, it silenced a victim better than a cut throat. Deadly, because the victim bled out rapidly. He crawled forward and checked her neck anyway. No pulse. He rolled her over and unpinned the badge from her shirt. He held it up to Drake. "It's Jakob's. I could have questioned her, found out where they took my boys."

Drake lifted his arm away, exposing his bloody side. "Take a look at me, boy. Take a look at yourself. For goodness' sake, take a look at her! You really think you could get her to talk? No sir, she had to go."

"She get your lung?"

"Nicked it, I think. Doesn't feel collapsed. I can hold it together a bit longer."

Drom shrugged off his jacket and pulled his shirt up. A weeping cut ran from just below his left pectoral up to his sternum. Scanning the room, he located the satchel and dragged himself to it. He rooted around in the bag until he found the roll of duct tape. He held it up to Drake. "This will have to do for now."

He limped to the exit, checked the corridor, then shut the door and locked it. "You were supposed to be minding the door."

"Don't remind me," Drake wheezed out, then succumbed to another coughing fit.

Drom sat on the floor and took off his right boot. He rolled his sock off and gave his ankle a cursory examination. It was swollen, but not bleeding like his shin and chest. He tore off a section of tape, folded the cotton sock into a square, and centered it on the adhesive. He picked the tape up by both ends and faced Drake. "Deep breath, pull up your shirt, then exhale. Ready?" He gave him a moment. "Go."

Drake lifted the shirt and exhaled. Blood seeped from the wound. Drom pressed the sock against it then smoothed the tape over his ribs.

"Sit up straight and don't breathe while I set this." He wrapped tape around Drake's chest, compressing the bandage and setting it in place.

"Getting that off is going to hurt worse than the wound."

"Hopefully, you live to feel it." Drom put his fingers through the slash of his own shirt and ripped the fabric away. He mopped around the wound with the hunk of cloth while he pulled away another section of tape with his teeth. Using mouth and fingers, he ripped it into strips and laid them sticky-side-up across his thigh. He mopped the wound one last time, then pinched the bottom of it closed and stretched a piece of tape across it. He worked his way up the wound, suturing it with the tape and leaving gaps between the strips.

He moved his ankle left to right, then up and down until he found a stable position with the least amount of pain. He wound tape around his foot and over his ankle to brace it. He pulled his boot on and laced it tight. He took a couple of steps to test his work. The ankle held.

He eyed Drake. "She mentioned back up."

"I think she was bluffing. But in case she wasn't, you best get to it so we can get out of here."

Drom stepped over to the dead woman and rifled through her pockets. Coming up empty, he patted her down. She had a ceramic knife strapped to her ankle, air travel concealment. He worked up the legs, then ran the back of his hand around the inside of her waistband.

"Think you'll find something or are you just getting frisky?"

"Save your breath. I'm working here." He moved up her torso to her armpits, then over her shoulders and up her neck. He reached inside her blouse and did a cursory search with the back of his hand inside her bra. The second cup had a fold of bills. He leafed through them. Between the larger franc notes and the singles was a Romanian ten lei bill. He pocketed the wad, then took the ankle knife. He strapped it to his left shin and pulled his pant leg over it.

He glanced at Drake. "Anyone comes through, yell."

"Sure thing," he rasped.

Drom limped back to the wall and dug out the rest of the stones. Shining the flashlight through the hole, he spotted a black and white tiled marble floor on the other side tapering off in the gloom. He crawled through, head first.

The space was cooler than the file room by several degrees, the air fresh. He played the light across the checkerboard floor and discovered a hexagon of yellow Moroccan zellij. He hobbled forward and the light caught the base of an ebony pedestal. He panned it up and a gold-embossed quinotaur gleamed; its fish tail curled into a loop, its proud bull head sporting five horns. His scalp drew tight and he shrugged his shoulders against the cold at his back.

Colonel McAbee's intel had the space down as Dr. Phélypeaux's private archive room, not as the inner sanctum of a Cinq Cornes lodge. He swept the beam back toward the breached wall and shuffled along it searching for a light switch. He came to a corner where the stone wall met concrete. He turned left and five paces later, found a switch by a metal door. He flipped it on and turned around.

At first, he couldn't make sense of what he was seeing. Expecting file cabinets or regalia, he was unprepared for glass jars. He stared at their contents, his mind trying to morph them into something sensible. He made it stop and the shapes assumed familiarity, then abandoned it all together. The flashlight fell out of his hand and he heaved bile onto the polished floor.

⊕

"Drake! Drake! Wake up!" Drom gave the man's cheek another light slap.

Drake's eyelids dragged up. "Where are we?"

"Safe for the moment. I need you to sit up."

Drake gazed down at his blanket-covered form. "How did I get in bed?"

"I had help. Now, sit up. You need to take your meds."

Drake pushed up to a sitting position with a groaned obscenity. "Feels like the knife is still in my side."

"Might have been better if you had left it there."

"Don't tell me you're still upset I planted it in Frenchy's back. We make it through this, I want to know who you really are."

"You know who I am, old man. Here, take these." Drom handed him a couple of pills and a glass of water.

Drake swallowed the pills and handed the glass back. "Where in the world are we? This place smells like a brothel."

"At least your nose still works. Room's only good for another hour. After that, the Madame's liable to take someone else's money." He tossed a set of well-worn, mismatched work clothes on the bed. "Get dressed. Time for Rebniko to roam again."

"Not so fast. You need to catch me up. Last thing I remember is you dragging me out of that crypt of a file room. I don't even know what time it is."

"Forget the time. Today is the eleventh. You've been out for over twelve hours, most of it drug induced."

Drake threw his covers off and inspected his chest. It was wrapped with an elastic bandage. He played his fingers down his side. "Feels like professional work."

"It was. Get dressed."

Someone knocked on the door. Drom cracked it, whispered with a woman, then came back with a tray and set it on the bed.

Drake zipped up his pants and nose pointed at the tray. "What's this?"

"Strength." He filled a mug from the carafe and handed it to Drake. "Black coffee to help with any leftover opiate fog. The tarts are *pissaladiere*, bake flatbread with caramelized onions, olives, fresh herbs, and anchovies. I had them double up on the anchovies."

Drake sniffed at it. "I could do with a different kind of tart, preferably one that doesn't smell of fish."

"No time. Eat up. We have a long way to go."

Drake took a gulp of the steaming coffee, then worked his arms into his shirtsleeves with a grimace. "What did you find on the other side of the wall?"

"A shrine of sorts." Drom picked up a slice of the *pissaladiere* and took a substantial bite. The onions were sweet, the fish salty, the olives tangy, and the bread doughy. He worked the textures through his mouth, savoring the moment in avoidance of the horror.

"Shrine, phfft," Drake said. "Military intelligence, what did I tell you? Russ said it was a records room."

"It was that as well. McAbee had it half right."

Drake's stomach growled. He bit into a slice and mumbled through the mouthful. "Start with the shrine."

"Best I can figure, it served as a ceremonial room for Cinq Cornes. There was a pedestal decorated with golden quinotaurs and topped with a five-point bull rack."

"And the records?"

"Why did CIA kill my mother, Charles?" Drom infused the name with tones of familiarity, hoping to disarm his former enemy if only for a moment.

Drake washed his food down with another gulp of coffee. "Swenson's work. Lord knows, you made him pay for it."

"You didn't answer my question. Why did CIA target her?"

"We didn't target her. We were there for Shane and she opened the door. Swenson wasn't taking any chances. He had to pull the trigger on anyone who opened the door. A second's hesitation was all the Leoppard needed, sometimes less."

"You said, 'we.'"

"Yes, we, CIA. What did you think I meant?"

"Never mind what you meant, I know what you said. You were there. She was the target, not my father. Why?"

Drake eyed the empty the bottle of pills on the bedside table. "What did you give me?"

"A bit late to be asking now."

"Touché." Drake took another bite of tart.

Drom drained his mug and set it back on the tray, his appetite gone. "She had an older sister, name of Tshaya."

"Yeah? Was she a good aunt to you, this sister?"

"Never met her. Didn't know she existed until yesterday. I found pilfered CIA files from the early seventies, probably taken from the Madrid station. Tshaya, my mother, and a host of other Roma and Jewish women were targeted in an operation code named CHIMERA."

"First I've heard of it. You bring the files? I could take a look and see if it bumped against anything I was read into."

"You were Swenson's backup on my mother's murder and you still want to play dumb?"

"Need to know, Rat-gêló. Swenson told me we were there for Shane. That was my job, after all. I didn't need any other reasons. What are you going to do, tie me up so you can beat the same answer out of me?"

Drom pushed his rage down, souring his coffee and French pizza. He breathed through a silent prayer for strength as he maintained eye contact with Drake. "You can stay here or come with, your choice. But if you come with, you're going into no man's land. I'll be your only ally and you'll be mine."

"If I stay, do I get a shot at the other tart?"

"You'll be lucky if she doesn't shoot you."

"Not much of a choice."

"Best I got. There's only so much favor a dead man can curry."

"No man's land. You found out where they took your boys?"

"I've known all along, just didn't realize it. The final piece was on the French woman you killed."

"The assassin I saved you from, you mean. What did she have, a map with a big, red X on it?"

Drom eyed him. "You know, when you act like this, I stop regretting all the times I hurt you." He pulled a backpack and duffle bag out of the wardrobe and tossed them on the bed. "Odds and ends. McAbee got your Austrian passport reinstated."

"What good is that? Showing up as me will set every station in Europe after us."

"CIA is the least of our concerns right now. Besides, we're just passing through Austria."

"On the way to?"

"The woman had a Romanian ten lei bill stuck in a wad of franc notes stuffed in her bra. Her mistake, our gain."

"Romania? Romania's the type of place you escape from, not go to."

"That's where they took my boys. It's where all this has its center."

"Romania's a big piece of real estate."

"I have location, not just country."

"From a ten lei bill?"

"No, from something my father told me once. I was nine, ten maybe. He ran me through a new exercise and one of the hired trainers didn't survive it. He took me to a café afterward, treated me to some ice cream and talked to me about purpose and control."

"Let me get this straight. Shane pits you against some hired goons, you kill one of them, and he takes you out for ice cream. What a prince! So, what, the ice cream come from some famous communist dairy town in Ceauşescu's prison paradise?"

"Yeah, not exactly. It wasn't the ice cream. It was the admonition that came with it." Drom ran his fingers through his hair. "He put on his serious face, leaned into me, and said, 'Being from the valley of wolves doesn't destine you to become a wolf. You can choose to be a wolfhound instead.'"

"Bit cryptic. How does that help us now?"

"You knew my father. His spycraft was superb. You would've caught up to him much earlier otherwise. That said, you guys trained him. Like you, he had his grab bag of aliases. Like you, he built legends in a way that made them easy to carry, fake identities with shadows of the real person scattered throughout as touchstones. I'm like you and him, only more so. The aliases he gave me, and the names I discovered, are all real. I am Carlos de Leon and Gavin Leoppard. Rat-gêló was what my grandmother Hishoro named me on the day I was born. And then, there's Leo Moldovan."

"Leo Moldovan? Afraid you've got me there, never came across that one," Drake said.

"Never needed it before the death of Gavin Leoppard. Leo was one of the identities my father set up. I renewed the passport after the incident in Castellon and used it to return to North America." Drom reached into the backpack and handed over a Romanian passport.

Drake examined it. "Nice mug shot, comrade. What am I looking for?"

"Place of birth," Drom said.

Drake looked up, brows knit. "Valea Lupşii?"

"Valley of Wolves. It's where I was born. It's where my boys are."

Chapter 46

On 13-11-43, an inspection was made of the prisoners that were furnished to me in order to determine their suitability for the tests which have been planned for the typhus vaccines. Of the 100 prisoners, 18 died during transport. Only 12 prisoners are in such condition that they can be used for these experiments, provided their strength can first be restored. Such experiments only lead to fruitful results when they are carried out with normally nourished subjects whose physical powers are comparable to those of soldiers.

Letter to Professor Dr. Hirt, Reich University
from Dr. E. Haagan
15 November 1943

Konzentrationslager Auschwitz-Birkenau – November 22, 1943

Hishoro mopped Alfonso's brow, her ears tuned to Pierre's wheezing. Before Mengele injected her and the boys, he assured her it wasn't deadly. Assurances from the Angel of Death were like condolences from the devil.

She dunked the cloth into the basin of water—its coolness soothing her feverish hands—and wrung it out. She placed it on Alfonso's brow and shifted her attention to Pierre. Though his fever had broken hours before, he was shivering. She cocooned him in the threadbare blanket and rubbed his arms and legs.

"How is he?" Dr. Etel's voice held equal measures of compassionate and curiosity.

"Barely breathing. Can't you give him something?"

"You know they won't let me."

"They? This isn't just Mengele?"

"Mengele isn't just Mengele, Hishoro. He serves his masters. But no, this experiment isn't his."

"Phélypeaux."

"How are you feeling?"

"Burning up and achy. I've done all he's asked. How could he do this to my boys?"

The older woman gave her shoulder a gentle squeeze. "He's not doing it to them. He's doing it for them."

"Can you at least get Pierre another blanket?"

"That, I can do, right after I check his vitals." She put a thermometer in the boy's mouth and checked his pulse while the mercury moved. Minutes later, she pulled the thermometer out and eyed it. "I'll grab the blankets."

Hishoro put her hand on his brow. It was cool to the touch, but her hands were on fire. Alfonso moaned. She rewet the cloth and laid it on his forehead. His lower lip was blistered, his top one cracked. Visions of her boys cut open on Mengele's table assaulted her and she pushed them back with a lullaby hummed low between her twins.

Dr. Etel returned and piled blankets on Pierre.

"What's happening to him, Lörinc?" Hishoro asked.

"I'm not sure. If the blankets don't help, we'll wake him and get him to walk."

"Will Alfonso be like this when his fever breaks?"

"Pierre's reaction is unexpected. Neither you nor Alfonso should have this trouble."

"He'll come out of it, won't he?"

"He's not supposed to be in it. Dr. Phélypeaux is monitoring some patients in another facility. I'll have him check in when he returns."

"What was it really, this serum?"

Lörinc tilted her head, as if considering what to say or what not to say. "It's something Karl has been working on since medical school. He was fascinated with the similarities between the typhus bacteria and human mitochondria. He wondered if there was a way to modify the one to increase the other."

"I don't know what meto ... metoko—"

"Mitochondria," Lörinc said. "They are what make energy in your cells."

"Whatever they are, it sounds to me like you've injected us with typhus."

"Open wide." Lörinc stuck a thermometer in her mouth, then checked on Alfonso. She made notes on her chart, then took her temperature gauge back. "I need to make rounds. You should lie down with Pierre, add your heat to his."

Lörinc's advice made Hishoro acutely aware of her exhaustion. She had stolen bits of sleep over the past two days, the boys' needs overriding hers. If the cost of keeping Pierre alive was a couple of hours of unattended suffering for

Alfonso, it was a bargain she could live with. She wouldn't be any good to either of them much longer without rest.

She refreshed Alfonso's cloth, then laid down beside Pierre and wrapped him in her arms. His cool skin soothed her fever. She buried her nose in his hair and fell sleep.

⊕

"Dále! Dále! Wúshte! Me sim bokhalo."

Alfonso's whine pried her awake. He was hungry. She felt Pierre's cheek. The chill of it ran up her arm and froze her heart.

"Pierre!" She shook his shoulder. "Pierre, *wúshte.*"

Alfonso tugged on her blouse. *"Bokhalo, Dále!"*

Hishoro swatted his hand and turned Pierre onto his back. His eyes were open, his mouth slack, his lips blue. A wail twisted up from her gut and she choked it off at her throat. Grief was a luxury she couldn't afford. Crying was forbidden.

Pierre was dead. Mengele was certain to carve Alfonso open to see why he survived. She bundled Pierre in a blanket and lifted him off the bed. She cradled him to her bosom, his face buried between her breasts. She scanned the ward, noting the movements of the staff, and mapped a path to the door. Bending down, she caught Alfonso's eye. "I'll feed you in the barracks, but you have to keep quiet while we get out of here, understand?"

He eyed his brother, then nodded. She set out through the ward and reached the door unchallenged. Shifting Pierre's dead weight to one arm, she opened it and they slipped through into the examination area.

Several men and children were perched on stools along the wall to her left. A nurse was administering eye drops to a little girl. The child blinked, then stared off into space. One of her eyes was brown, the other blue. A wiry man was next in line, his ribs prominent under his stretched skin. His head came down. He blinked and he scanned the room. Like the girl, his eyes were different colors. The right was nearly black. The left pierced her with its moonbeam brightness. The air went out of her and Pierre started slipping from her arms.

"What are you doing out of the ward?"

Dr. Phélypeaux's voice startled her. She recovered her hold on Pierre and hugged him closer to her chest. Tearing her gaze away from Tshuri, she faced the doctor. "The boys are hungry. I'm taking them back to the barracks."

Phélypeaux studied her a moment, then bent eye-level to Alfonso. "Open your mouth and stick out your tongue." The boy complied and Phélypeaux shone a pen light in his mouth. "Mengele is sorting out arrivals." He stood, pulled a pad from his pocket, and wrote her a pass. "Get to your barracks. Lörinc will come for the body later. I'll deal with Josef when he returns."

Hishoro took the pass. "Thank you."

"Go before the boy gets stiff."

She clenched her jaw, suffocating a scream that threatened to become her whole world. Moving past him, she looked at Tshuri, willing all the sentiment she could muster through a glance across a crowded room and marched out.

⊕

Lörinc came a couple of hours later bearing bread, sausage, and a pair of *choxäné* to carry her Pierre away to the carvers. "We need to know what happened to him."

Hishoro spat on the dirt by her feet. "You are what happened to him."

"It was unexpected. None of our rats died."

"We aren't rats." Fists balled tight enough to set her arms trembling, she pressed back against the rough-hewn bunk strut to keep from flying at Lörinc and tearing her limb from limb.

Alfonso peeked over the bunk and pointed at the loaf in Lörinc's hand. *"Dále, manrro."*

Hishoro pressed down her rage with the needs of her surviving twin. "Come, Alfonso." The boy scampered out and took the food from the doctor's hand. "I laid Pierre on the bunk."

Lörinc directed the two women from the coffin brigade to take the body to Mengele's morgue. She waited until they were out of earshot before she spoke again. "I told you when we met that we cannot save them all. We don't know why Pierre had such an adverse reaction. You and Alfonso seem to have metabolized the serum well. Karl will talk sense to Mengele. He will not let him waste you two."

"Perhaps another subject could help persuade him."

"What do you mean?"

"Alfonso and Pierre are not identical twins, but my sister and I are."

"Your sister?"

"Keti. Mengele brought us both to the clinic in May soon after our arrival. He injected the boys with something. It made them both sick. He tasked me with keeping them alive. I went into the ward for my boys and I haven't seen my sister since."

"I'll see what I can find out," Lörinc said. "If she's still alive, Dr. Phélypeaux could test it on her as well. Did he know you had a twin?"

"No. In Drancy, I thought one of us was enough for him to torture."

Oh, but now! Now I sell you to save Alfonso. Forgive me, Keti.

✦

Hishoro woke up and couldn't feel Alfonso next to her on the bunk. She scrambled over the other occupants—earning slaps and shoves—and climbed down to search for him. She found him toward the back of the barracks where most of the new arrivals were stuffed. He was rifling through any pockets within reach, searching for crumbs to steal.

Prisoners killed over food.

She grabbed him by the collar, clapping her hand over his mouth. He fought her for a moment, then settled down when she hissed his name.

"I'm starving, Mommy."

"We all are. Leave these people be."

He didn't. The moment she dropped her guard, he would be gone. She would find him picking through the trash heap or searching the dead. Their daily rations only deepened his hunger.

His craving need made her more aware of her own hunger. At night, crowded into their bunk with twelve other people, she waited for the release of sleep. It came in fits.

A week passed, then two. Worry over being found gave way to fear of being forgotten. Tshuri was here. Keti may still be alive. Phélypeaux's attention brought pain, but without it she had no means or hope of salvaging what was left of her family.

The day Hishoro succumbed to foraging with Alfonso, Lörinc reappeared bearing gifts of stale bread, moldy cheese, and bruised pears. She and Alfonso devoured it without an exchange of even minimal pleasantries.

"Have you been getting your daily rations?" Lörinc asked.

"They are not enough."

"I admit, they are scant." She took Hishoro by the wrist and stared at her watch. "Your heart rate is up a bit. Have you or Alfonso had any more fevers?"

"No," Hishoro said. "But we're restless. I cannot ignore hunger like I used to."

"I should be able to help you with both of those. Dr. Phélypeaux has prevailed upon Berlin to allow him to continue the experiment. You and Alfonso are to come with me."

Hishoro tucked Alfonso behind her. "Mengele will kill my boy. I can't go there."

"You won't. Karl has his own research space now, in a different building. Arranging it is what caused the wait. That, and we had to find your sister."

"You found her?"

"She's waiting for you."

Keti alive. She hadn't dared to hope. "Is she well?"

"I'll let you be the judge."

Hishoro followed her out, leading Alfonso by the hand. They exited the Gypsy Camp and walked west on the main road. Dusty women in tattered striped smocks—a road commando by the look of them—filed past heading east. Over a hundred women marched under the eyes of a German shepherd and two female guards. One of the women stumbled and collapsed onto the dirt road. The guard released the dog. The beast was on the fallen prisoner before she could regain her feet. She struggled to rise as the dog mauled her at the guard's urging.

Hishoro walked on, not sparing a backward glance for fear of reprisal. *We cannot save them all.* Lörinc's words echoed in her head and she lowered her gaze in shame at her own cowardice.

Lörinc led them through the guard post of BIIf and they made their way toward the center of the narrow compound. A lone brick building stood out among its green tarpaper companions, at once authoritative and ominous. Hishoro paused at the steps. She had witnessed enough horrors to feed her nightmares for the rest of her life. But Mengele's shop of terror was known to her. Number Ten hid evils only whispered of and best not imagined.

Lörinc looked at her. "What is it?"

"This place, there's talk of it. I've seen women come back from here burned. Burned where they shouldn't be. Others say ..." Words failed her.

"Look at the sky, Hishoro."

She tipped her heard up to the unholy clouds pouring out of Krematorium IV and V to the west and recalled how the stench of them had overwhelmed all the other smells of the camp. She was nose blind to it now. But its scorch still branded her heart. She would risk anything not to leave the camp through its chimneys. "After you."

They filed past the door sentry and turned south into a wide corridor. Lörinc showed a slip of paper to a soldier by a metal door. He unlocked it and pulled it open. Hishoro spied a set of stairs leading down.

Lörinc's heels clicked on the concrete steps. The cold stone bit through the calloused soles of Hishoro's feet, sending chills all the way up to the nape of her neck. She tightened her grip on Alfonso's hand and followed Dr. Etel around the bend of the landing. The stairs continued deeper underground.

Lörinc's voice echoed in the concrete well. "The Germans won't speak of it, but the Allied bombing has them worried. I heard from some new arrivals that they've even bombed Berlin. Karl convinced someone that his work was important enough to keep in a shelter."

After several flights, they arrived at the head of a passageway secured with a barred gate. Lörinc showed their pass to the guard inside. He opened the gate and waved them through. They walked past several doors, then Lörinc opened one on the right. Hishoro stepped into a modest ward of eight beds, four to a side, with a clinical area in the back.

Sitting up in the last bed on the left was Keti, busily working needle and thread through a piece of fabric.

"Phéno!" Hishoro rushed to her side, dragging Alfonso behind her. "Sister, my dear sister! You're here." She had her arms around her before Keti could drop her work.

"Hishoro! How did you …" Her voice trailed away and she wrapped her arm around her twin.

"What's this?" Hishoro patted Keti's swollen belly. "Are you sick?"

"No, I am with child."

"Pregnant? In this place? How?"

"It works the same here as anywhere else," Lörinc broke in. "I'll make sure you two have some time to catch up. Right now, I need to examine you and Alfonso and take some blood samples."

Hishoro glanced at the doctor, then faced Keti. Her sister wouldn't meet her eyes. "Whatever it is, you have no reason to be ashamed. We do what me must to survive."

Keti squeezed her hand and kissed it. "I am glad you are here."

Hishoro allowed herself to be pulled into the clinical area. Lörinc gave Alfonso a piece of candy and directed him to the lone stool in the corner. Hishoro rolled up her sleeve and Lörinc chose a vein.

"Pierre had an allergic reaction to the serum. We found blisters in the back of his mouth. His lungs were inflamed. He wasn't able to get enough air." She capped the vial of blood and drew another.

"Senseless," Hishoro said.

"Tragic, not senseless. Let's get you on the table." She taped a cotton ball over the puncture site.

Hishoro slid out of her chair and hopped onto the exam table. She stole a glace at her sister. Keti was back to the needle and thread with her left hand as she held the fabric in the awkward grip of her withered right. "She the only patient?"

"There were others. There will be more. I need you to tilt your head back, open your mouth, and stick out your tongue."

Hishoro complied. Her gaze landed on the shelves high on the wall, and for the first time she noticed the glass jars arrayed on them. The first two held indistinct globs in clear fluid. The rest told what the first could have been, given the chance. Dr. Etel's tongue depressor short-circuited the scream she couldn't hold back.

"Your blood work shows that the serum elevated your metabolism temporarily," Phélypeaux said. "The effects of this next round should last longer."

Hishoro was unable to get out of bed for two days after the injection. She and Alfonso had their own room in the bunker. Lörinc or one of the nurses looked after her and Alfonso. On day three, she couldn't believe she had been sick at all. She rose full of energy and restless.

Phélypeaux's bunker clinic had no shortage of food. A small kitchen fixed meals for the staff and their subjects. After making sure Alfonso was fed and breaking her own fast, she deposited him in the play room with the other children and made her way into the ward.

The beds were full, women her age and younger each in various stages of pregnancy. They watched her as she headed to Keti, their quiet disturbingly different from the rowdiness of the barracks. She stepped through the curtain pulled around her sister's bed and knew from Keti's pallor that she wasn't well.

She sat on the bed and took her hand. It was cold as a corpse. "Keti, can you hear me?"

She opened her eyes and gripped Hishoro's hand. "Where have you been?"

"Sick. I'm better now. I won't leave you again."

Keti struggled to sit up, then sunk back down. "I must tell you, Hishoro. You need to know."

"Tell me what, Keti?"

"I've … I've been here the whole time. They brought me …" She drifted off; her eyes closed. Hishoro felt her brow with the back of her hand and was relieved to find it much warmer than her fingers. Keti opened her eyes. "I'm thirsty."

Hishoro filled the glass from the pitcher on the bedside table and helped Keti sit up. "You drink. I'll hold it for you."

Keti took a deep draft. "They put me here with others, pretty ones."

"You're wasting your energy with nonsense, *murri phen*. Of course, they brought you here with pretty ones."

"Hishoro." Weakened by her trials and only minutes older than her twin, Keti still marshalled her older-sister voice. "No need to spare my feelings. I know what I look like."

"Did they hurt you?" Had she been in Phélypeaux's grip the entire time? Was Lörinc's story just another lie?

"No, they didn't. I need more water."

Hishoro helped her with another drink, then dabbed her chin dry with the sheet. Keti stared at her, her eyes sad and apologetic. "What is it, Keti? What is bothering you?"

"Upstairs is a brothel of sorts. Animal warming, they called it."

"You should rest. You don't have to explain yourself to me."

Keti closed her eyes, seeming to heed her advice. When she opened them again, Hishoro knew she had just been gathering strength. "They brought men in and froze them."

"What do you mean, froze them?"

"They put them in a bath of ice water until they fainted from the cold, then they put them in a bed for one of us to warm them up."

"And you found yourself with child."

"I am so sorry, Hishoro."

"You have nothing to be sorry for."

"It was only the first one. After that, I would warm them, but I wouldn't … Oh, Hishoro! After losing Nadja, then hearing that Mateo was dead, and being pulled away from you, I couldn't … To find him there, so cold. He came to. He came to and I didn't resist him. You mustn't blame him."

"I blame the Nazis, Keti, as you should."

Keti sunk into her pillow and her eyes closed. "He thought it was you. He thought it was you and I ... I let him." Her head tilted to the side and her jaw went slack. Her chest rose and fell in the steady rhythm of sleep.

Hishoro watched her a while, working out the implications of Keti's confession. She laid her hand on her sister's swollen belly. As if in response, the baby kicked, overwhelming all her reserves. She buried her head next to her sister's and wept, her wails of anger, grief, and joy too intense to vocalize.

She woke up in her bed with no idea of how she had gotten there. Alfonso was next to her, fast asleep. She rose, her energy spent, her legs wobbly. The cold floor bit her feet. She shuffled to the toilets and relieved herself. She got up and the world tilted. She put a hand against the stall to steady herself.

She came out and washed her face in the basin. The freezing water pulled at the cobwebs in her mind without clearing it. Her body responded to her will grudgingly, like her arms and legs were tied to weights.

She swallowed mouthfuls of water and took several deep breaths to gather herself. She pulled down a section of the roll towel and dried her face.

She remembered sitting with Keti, promising not to leave her. And here she was, alone in the lavatory. She navigated her way to the ward. The women were sleeping in the subdued glow of the nightlights. The attending nurse looked up from her book and chin pointed toward Keti's bed. "She's been asking for you."

"How long?"

"Days."

Days? She had been out for days?

She moved down the ward, holding on to the bed end rails for support. Keti's curtains were drawn. Darkness obscured the clinical area. She stepped through the curtain and gasped at the sight of her sister.

"Keti," she said, then louder, "Keti, I'm here, *murri phen.* I'm here."

Keti shifted in her bed, then started coughing. When the fit left her, she collapsed into the mattress. *"Khini sim,"* she said, I am tired. *"Gêló."*

"No, you're not gone," Hishoro said. "You're still here. Drink." She held her sister's head and tried to get some water past her cracked lips.

Keti choked on the meager drops and shook her head. She stared up out of cavernous sockets and pulled her cover away. Her smock was bunched above her waist, the incision visible even in the low light. The sheet was soaked with blood. *"Gêló. Amáro rat gêló."*

Gone. Her blood was gone. Their blood was gone. They had taken the baby, Tshuri's baby.

"Keti!" She covered her up and moved to get the nurse.

Keti caught her hand, holding her in place. *"Volvi tut, múrri phen. Khini sim. Gêló."* Her grip slipped and her eyes closed.

Hishoro bent down and kissed her cooling forehead. *"Devlésa múrri drágostya."* Goodbye, my love.

In another world, in another time, she would tare her hair and clothes and wail her grief away. She couldn't spare the strength for it now. *Rat gêló*, her blood gone. She had to find a way out before there was no blood left them.

Chapter 47

Auschwitzate si khar baro.
Othe beshel mirro piramno,
Beshel, beshel, gindil
Tha mande pa bishtrel.

In Auschwitz there is a big house.
There sits my sweetheart,
He sits, sits and thinks
And forgets about me.

a Romani Song of Auschwitz

Konzentrationslager Auschwitz-Birkenau – January 1, 1944

Hishoro wrung the mop with her hands, the blood she rinsed out in the cloudy water a bitter reminder of Keti's horrible end. The ward hadn't lacked patients since, pregnant women who would have fared better barren.

Phélypeaux continued his Drancy experiments on her. She knew he could have done so without giving her any concessions. Nevertheless, he seemed to go out of his way to make up for the pain and suffering he caused her. She and Alfonso were given new clothes, they kept their own room, and were well fed.

He put them both through another round of serum injections not long after Keti's death. Neither of them suffered any debilitating side effects. Unable to sit still and unwilling to remain useless, she begged Phélypeaux for something to do.

She mopped her way out of the ward. The patients were fast asleep in the subdued glow of the nightlights. She preferred slipping into the ward in the early hours to avoid getting in the way of the medical staff. She backed into something and yelped. She spun around and the mop clattered on the floor.

Mengele held his hand up. *"Nicht angst."*

Hishoro stood frozen with fear and dropped her gaze. *"Herr Doktor."*

"You know," Mengele said, "the way Karl ran off with you, I thought he wanted you as his mistress. Imagine my surprise to find you here as his cleaning lady."

She kept her gaze fixed on his boots. *"Arbeit macht frei."*

His backhand caught her off guard. She managed to keep on her feet, just. The stinging slap set her ears ringing. She tasted blood and her lip was swelling.

"You are free when I say you are free." Mengele said.

She didn't dare look up. The overhead lights snapped on in a blinding flood. Groans and rustling sheets slithered through the ringing.

"Aufstehen! Aufstehen!" The head nurse's voice boomed in the ward.

"Frau," Mengele said.

"Herr Doktor."

Hishoro grabbed her mop and bucket. Not waiting for permission, she scurried past Mengele and hurried to her room. Setting the bucket and mop down, she pulled the door shut.

Alfonso sat up in bed, rubbing his eyes. *"Dále?"*

She put a finger to her lips.

He slid out of bed and darted to her skirts. She held him close, her back against the wall, heart hammering in her throat. They needed to hide, but the room had no wardrobe and the bed wouldn't do. The door, set to lock her in, opened into the corridor. She glanced at her mop and eyed the bed again.

She whispered to Alfonso. Together, they spun the wrought iron bed and pushed the head end against the doorway. She unscrewed the wingnuts from the mophead clamp and pulled the mop off the wire. Holding the clamp, she twirled the handle out of it. She bent the side wire of the clamp around the doorknob and twisted the other side around the bed's head bars.

Scooping Alfonso up, she sat cross-legged in a corner of the door wall.

The regular sounds of the rousting ward were gradually drowned out in a crescendo of arguing male voices. Hishoro recognized Mengele's voice, then Phélypeaux's. Though full sentences escaped her, the words that hammered through the door told enough.

"I ... of the Reich ... and boy ... tomorrow, Karl!"

"Not possible ... experiments ... orders ... Vershuer."

"... Berlin ... French guest ... Kommandant Hartjenstein ..."

"... week ... have her."

"Them ... tomorrow!" Mengele's final bark ended the argument.

Hishoro squeezed Alfonso to her. He squirmed, whimpering. She held him tighter, rocking side to side. The Angel of Death had come. Her only hope now was for him to kill them outright. The prospect of being kept alive in his care was too awful to contemplate.

The knob rattled, then the door shook.

Pressing into the concrete corner, she whispered the only prayer she knew. *"Baruch atah Adonai Elohainu—"*

The door boomed. "Get this door loose now or I'll send you to Josef the moment after I break it down!" Phélypeaux pounded on it the again.

"Dále, you're hurting me," Alfonso said.

She let him go and pulled herself together. "I'm doing it! I'm doing it!"

She grabbed the wire on the bed rail and untwisted it. It snapped and raked across her palm. The door flew open and she backed away to the opposite wall of the tiny room.

Red-faced, Phélypeaux shoved the bed out of his way, knocking Alfonso down in the process. "What on earth did you do? I've never seen Josef that mad."

Hishoro eyed Alfonso as he got up. Fear kept her rooted to her spot. She dropped her head and clutched at her skirts. "Nothing. I was mopping and—"

His hands—smooth, warm, and smelling of fresh soap—guided her head up until their eyes met. "Damn that man. He has no reason to strike you." He lifted her upper lip with his thumb, then her lower. "Open your mouth."

She obeyed.

"He split your lip, but all your teeth are there. Does it hurt?"

"He's going to kill us."

"No, he is not." He turned to the boy. "Alfonso, have you had your breakfast?"

Alfonso shook his head.

"Come, let's get you fed." Taking the boy's hand, he glanced at Hishoro. "I'll get him settled in with the cook. Go to the ward. Dr. Etel is sure to be there by now. Have her take care of your lip and hand."

Hand? She looked at them. A gash running across her left palm dripped blood on the floor. She made a fist and followed Phélypeaux out. Once in the corridor, she hesitated, unwilling to go in the opposite direction of her son. Phélypeaux shot her a glance over his shoulder and pointed her on her way.

He had argued with Mengele. He hadn't handed her over. She was still here. She headed to the ward.

Lörinc was in the exam area reviewing charts. Her head came up as Hishoro neared. "What happened to you?"

"Mengele." She gave her the details while Lörinc treated her hand. "I need your help."

421

Lörinc tied off the bandage. "I'm afraid wrapping you up is all I can do. Against Mengele, I can do nothing."

"There is someone I need to see before I die."

"Let us not speak of dying, Hishoro. Our job is to live and help others survive."

"You found Keti. I need you to find Tshuri."

"Who is he?"

"My husband."

"I found Keti because she was already here. The Gypsy Camp has over fifteen thousand people in it. How do you expect me to find one man among so many?"

"He's been here before, for the freezing experiments. And I saw him in Mengele's clinic the day Pierre died."

"What does he look like?"

"Taller than me, dark, and too thin."

"You've just described most of the men in the Gypsy Camp."

"His right eye is burnt mahogany."

Lörinc gave her a quizzical look. "And his left?"

"His left is the silver moon."

⊕

Hishoro forced her feet into the brown leather pumps Phélypeaux insisted she wear. The toe box was too confining for a woman who had walked barefoot her entire life. She buckled the ankle straps, stood, and took a couple of tentative steps.

"Why do you *gazhya* wear such horrible things?"

Lörinc smoothed Hishoro's skirt. "Turn around. I want to make sure you've got it all on right."

She shuffled her feet, dancing a tight circle. "These heels are impossible. What if we have to run?"

"Then we've failed and they'll strip those shoes off your corpse."

She stopped. "My legs itch. If I'm going to be shot, I'd rather do it without itching. Can't I take the hose off?"

"It is New Year's Day and we are headed to a banquet. That is what the guards need to see if they look in the car, not some barefoot *Zigeuner* with no hose."

"Is he coming?"

"Karl said he could get him. Fortunate for you, your man has different colored eyes or we would have never found him."

"When I first saw him, I thought his eye unlucky. It made my hair stand on end."

"I can imagine. When I found him, it was like he could see right through me."

422

"Does he know what we are doing?"

"Too risky. Karl found his records in Dr. Schilling's files on the freezing experiments and made his requisition on that basis."

He thought it was you and I let him.

Her sister's words floated back to her, squeezing her heart and knotting her stomach. She distracted herself with Alfonso, buttoning his coat and combing his hair with her fingers. She grabbed the wool cap off the bed and set it on his head. "Keep this on." She centered the bill on his nose, then turned to Lörinc. "Thank you."

"Don't thank me yet."

As if on cue, the door pulled open and an SS officer charged in.

Hishoro screamed.

The man grabbed her in a bear hug and lifted her off her feet.

She kicked him. Hard. The pump cut into her instep with the shock of the blow.

His lips touched her ear. "*Piramni*, it's me."

She pulled her head back to look at him. Under the visor of his cap was a black leather patch covering his gray eye. His right was set deep behind the sharp ridge of his cheek bone and wide with concern.

She kicked him. Again. "Put me down."

Tshuri set her down. "When I saw you—"

"Which time?"

He stared at her a moment, then turned toward their son. "Alfonso, come here. It's your *Dáda*. Come to me, boy."

Alfonso scurried behind Hishoro's skirts. "The uniform scares him."

Tshuri looked around the room. "Where is Pierre?"

Phélypeaux came in. "Time to go. Your man assures me he can drive."

Hishoro glanced at Tshuri. The death's head gleaming over his visor unnerved her. She faced Phélypeaux. "There isn't much Tshuri can't do."

"I trust that includes speaking German?"

Tshuri clicked his heels and shot his arm out in salute. "*Jawohl, Herr Doktor.*"

Phélypeaux waved the salute away. "The maintenance shop is closed down today. I persuaded the sergeant in charge of the motor pool to bring me the Commandant's Steyr. It's outside waiting for us."

"You're not concerned that he will raise the alarm?" Tshuri asked.

"The man is a morphine addict. I doubt he'll be raising much of anything today after what I gave him."

Phélypeaux led them out. They made their way up the concrete steps and Hishoro struggled to keep up in her low heels. She was tempted to slip them off, but doubted she could get them back on. The others pulled ahead. She shooed Alfonso forward and he caught up to them. She lost sight of the party as they turned on the landing.

She focused on her steps, unsure of her footing. The smooth leather sole slipped out from under her as she pressed to make the landing. Strong hands caught her before she smacked the concrete.

"Arakhel," Tshuri said.

She looked up at his pinched face. "You be careful. German only until we're free."

He gave her a half smile and answered in Romani. "German, yes."

She glared at him. "Go."

"After you," he said in German.

Charging past him, Hishoro attacked the next flight.

He came beside her and caught her arm in a loose grip. "If this doesn't work—"

"Careful where you hold me. Staying alive has had its price."

"Hishoro, if this doesn't work—"

"It has to, Tshuri. I refuse to die here."

"I need you to know that I love you."

Her step faltered and she stopped short of the door. He was two steps below her, which put them eye to eye. "I've never doubted it."

She stepped into corridor and hustled to catch up to Alfonso. Taking the boy's hand, she slowed her pace to match Phélypeaux's and Lörinc's. They moved through the ground floor of Number Ten unchallenged. The sentry at the exit saluted Phélypeaux. The doctor returned it with a flash of his palm and they were outside.

Hishoro gasped. She hadn't been above ground in over a fortnight. The weather, already cold when she was brought to the bunker clinic, had taken on the sharper edge of a true Polish winter. Seeing her own breath, she wrapped her coat tighter to keep the needling chill at bay. She was glad for her hose in spite of the itch.

Tshuri opened the front passenger door for Phélypeaux, then opened the back door of the sedan. Lörinc slid in followed by Alfonso. Once Hishoro was seated, Tshuri shut the door and got behind the wheel.

He cranked the engine to life, put it in gear, and pulled out into the dirt roadway. They rode west, the dying light of day yielding power to the glowing red clouds of the crematoria. The road took them between Krematorium IV and V, then angled south. Once past the warehousing compound, Hishoro could make out the gate ahead.

Spotlights on top of the guard towers on either side of the gate splashed their glare on the approaching black sedan. Hishoro hooked her arm around Alfonso and drew him to her side, heedless of the tender cuts still healing there.

Tshuri stopped several meters from the massive wood-and-wire construction and revved the Steyr's powerful engine.

A guard, rifle slung over his shoulder, hustled toward them from the gate shack. Tshuri rolled his window down and stuck his head out. "What are you running here for, you idiot! Open this gate before I run you over and have your lieutenant scrape you off my grill!"

The guard stopped. He glanced over his shoulder at the other two sentries that had spilled out of the shack, then took another step forward.

Tshuri let off the brake and stomped the accelerator. He slammed back on the brake and slid to a stop within a meter of the guard. "Are you deaf, corporal? Open the gate now!"

The young man stood wide-eyed for a second, then spun on his heel and ran to his companions. "Open the gate, *schnell!*"

⊕

Hishoro kept waiting for machine gun fire that never came. Alfonso squirmed out from under her arm. She braced herself against the dizzying speed Tshuri set since clearing the gate. They headed south, flat fields giving way to hills that rolled ever higher. As the terrain climbed, the road curved and undulated. Hishoro bit her lip and balled her skirts up in her fists.

Lörinc cracked her window. "Can you slow down some? I'm getting nauseous."

"Better nauseous than dead," Tshuri said. "Close your eyes. It'll help."

"We can stop in Wadowice for the night," Phélypeaux said. "It's not far."

"Exactly," Tshuri said. "That's why we won't be stopping there."

Phélypeaux shifted in his seat. The dashboard lights set the pistol in his hand in silhouette. He pointed the barrel at Tshuri's head. "We stop where I say we stop."

Thsuri glanced at him. Hishoro caught the flash of his teeth and slung her arm in front of Alfonso, pinning him against the seat back. The brakes squealed. Hishoro bounced against the driver's seat and dropped into the floorboard. Glass cracked with a wet smack, like meat being slapped.

"Give me that before you hurt someone," Tshuri said.

Alfonso was crying. Hishoro regained her seat and checked him over. He wasn't bleeding and none of his limbs seemed broken. "Shh." She scooped him into her lap and looked over at Lörinc. The woman was sprawled in her seat, slack-jawed and eyes rolled back.

The scene up front was worse. The windshield was spiderwebbed on the passenger side and spattered with blood. Phélypeaux held his face in his hands, groaning.

Tshuri twisted toward her. "Are you hurt?"

"No, but I don't know about Lörinc."

He stared at her slack form for a moment. "She's breathing." He turned to Phélypeaux. "You kept them alive, so I'll let you live. Cross me again, and you won't like the life I leave you with."

He jammed the shifter into gear and gunned the engine.

Hishoro woke to wood smoke and damp dirt. She struggled to orient herself, unsure of where she was. Her left shoulder throbbed, her wrist was stiff and swollen. She sat up in the dark. Pain stabbed her right side. She reached under her blouse and gingerly ran her fingers over the sutures. They came back wet. She sniffed them. Blood. Her blood.

Did he cut me again?

Her legs itched. She scratched her calf and her nail snagged the hose. It all came flooding back.

Thsuri had driven through the night into the mountains. In a remote village, he exchanged his uniform for civilian clothes. He loaded her and Alfonso into the back of a farm wagon and handed the Steyr keys to Phélypeaux. "It's not hard to drive once you get the hang of it." He jumped into the wagon beside her. The farmer snapped the reigns across the backs of his team and they rolled deeper into the forest.

How Tshuri knew the farmer or the partisans hidden in the forest, Hishoro hadn't a clue. She knew she was exhausted, wrung out with fright, and sore all over. When the offer of a bed was made, she didn't hesitate.

"Tshuri?" She scooched off the haystack bed. The cold ground shocked her stockinged feet. Hand outstretched, she shuffled in the direction she thought the opening might be. Her palm met moist earth. She moved left along the dug-out wall and found woven wool.

She tugged the blanket aside and the gray morning spilled into her hole in a hill. She moved toward the camp's central fire pit where several women were already busy. One of them addressed her. Hishoro lifted her hands and shook her head. The woman bent over the fire and came over with a steaming tin cup in her hand. *"Čaj."*

Hishoro took the cup, nodding her thanks. Its warmth thawed her hands. She took a sip. The black tea was surprisingly sweet. She finished her tea and handed the cup back to her benefactor. "Tshuri?"

The woman pointed to a forest trail at the edge of the camp.

She set off to the trail head, picking her way carefully up the rocky incline. Stones tore holes in soles of her hose in short order. Her weathered feet found purchase with each step and the exercise warmed her against the biting cold.

She found him several minutes later perched on a rock off the side of the trail. He was whittling a stick with a pocket knife, his gaze on the forest below. She studied him a while, content in that quiet moment to admire him from afar.

His gaze shifted and she caught the flash of his pale eye. A slight smile played across his lips and he waved her over.

She eased through the underbrush on the small game trail that led to his forest throne. As she drew near, he tapped the end of the stick on the stone between his legs. He brought it to his lips. His cheeks puffed out and sawdust flew out of the other end of the blond wood.

"Sleep well?" he asked.

"Must have. Didn't know where I was when I woke up. I thought I might still be—"

"Slovakia," he said.

"What?"

"Slovakia. That's where you woke up. We've escaped hell, *Rromniorri.*"

She locked eyes with him for a long moment. "Not all of us."

"No." He bent back down to his work, twirling the point of his knife in the side of the tube he had carved. "Not all of us."

She climbed up on the rock and sat next to him. She remained silent, not trusting herself to share more than proximity and body heat for the moment.

He kept his eyes on his work as continued drilling holes into the wood with his knife. "They had me manning the ovens. I searched for you there, hoping never to find you."

She took a deep breath of the freezing air and stared up at the bluing sky. Living next to the stench and glow of the chimneys was horrific enough. What had feeding those fires cost Tshuri? "It must have been awful."

"I met a man there who showed me that even in the fires of hell, the Sabbath Lord reigns." He brought the wood to his lips and breathed his life into it.

Piercing notes wormed into her heart, warming it, breaking it, and mending it all at once. She had never been so overcome by such bitter sweet beauty. His song carried her, cradled her, caressed her, consoled her.

His rough fingers brushed the tears from her cheeks, bringing her back to the forest under the blue sky and the stone upon which they sat. She didn't know how long she cried. She looked into his eyes, then kissed his hands. "My love, we need to talk."

He placed his hands on either side of her face and drew her to him. He kissed her, softly at first, and then with increasing intensity. He broke the kiss breathless moments later and put his lips to her ear. "I am so sorry, Hishoro. Sorry for it all. For Nantes. For Mateo. For Gurs. For failing you in Drancy. For Keti. Forgive me, *Rrómniorri*."

She turned her face and found his lips. She lingered there, quieting him the best way she knew how. She broke away and smoothed the brow over his silver eye. "We can talk later, my love. We have other matters that need tending."

Chapter 48

The tragic experience of two World Wars on European soil has taught that human rights are secure only when those who wield power are accountable to their fellow-citizens and when their tenure of office is subject to some form of public control.

Pope John Paul II
Address to the European Court of Human Rights
Strasburg, France, October 8, 1988

Valea Lupşii, Romania – November 23, 1988

Drom trained the binoculars on the compound across the valley. Concrete walls, stained with age and topped with razor wire, surrounded the two-story, whitewashed farm house on three sides. At its back, a limestone bluff rose to a ridge thirty meters above. Steep slopes spilled down on either side of the compound and a narrow road wound up the pine dotted foothills to the guarded double gates.

Drake squatted next to him. "One way in, one way out. You plan on ringing the doorbell like you did in Madrid?"

"I'm afraid their response wouldn't be as hospitable." Drom limped back to the shepherd's cabin. He fed a couple of logs into the potbellied stove and stoked the coals until the fresh wood caught flame. He closed the stove and rummaged in this knapsack. He pulled out a half load of cornmeal bread, a hunk of dried sausage, and a block of Telemea cheese wrapped in cloth and set it all on the low table by the stove.

The ceramic knife he took from the French woman proved adequate for bread slicing, cheese spreading, and meat cutting. He had several open-faced sandwiches laid out when Drake came back inside.

"Breakfast." Drom slipped the knife back into the ankle sheath.

Drake eyed the table with a grunt. "This morning, maybe. It's near thee o'clock."

Drom handed him a slice. "Have you eaten today?"

"No, squirrel boy, you just pulled the food out."

"Then this is breakfast. Eat. You need it."

Drake sniffed it. His nose wrinkled. "Looks like cream cheese, but sure smells worse than the bad side of Philly."

"That's some of the finest fare in the Carpathians. Stop grumbling and eat up. We have work to do." Drom bit into his slice and savored the tangy cheese and salty pork sausage as they mingled with the sour notes of the bread.

"Tasty as advertised," Drake said, "but it's a bit dry. Where's the canteen?"

"Outside, hanging on the hand pump."

Drake paused at the doorway. "Seriously, kid, how do you plan on getting into that fortress?"

Drom snagged another piece of bread. "Working on it."

Drake headed out. The pump squeaked its two notes for several measures. Coughing, convulsive and deep, replaced the squeaks and ended with a string of profanities. Drake reappeared in the shed, his coughing fit having returned some color to his face, and dropped onto the cot. "We've got company."

"How much company?"

"Hard to say. At least two, maybe as many as twenty."

"Twenty?" Drom snagged the binoculars and stepped outside. He trained them south and spotted an army-green DAC truck with a canvas-covered bed lumbering up the pasture straight toward them.

He came back inside and stoked the fire. "Two in the cab, soldiers. Hope that's all. We don't have time for twenty."

"I told you not to trust Veress."

"He's a shepherd, Drake, not an informant."

"He's Romanian. They're all informants."

"I give them two minutes, three at most. I saved the last sandwich for you. Finish it off. I'll deal with the soldiers."

Drake grabbed the slice. "You might need me out there."

"Your Romanian is awful and you're carrying an Austrian passport. Stay put. Please."

The rattle of a diesel engine grew louder, then cut off. Drom stepped outside. Two soldiers climbed out of the cab, their banter jovial. They froze when they saw Drom. The driver's hand dropped to his holster. *"Unde este Veress?"*

"Up in the high meadow," Drom said, his Romanian flawless. "Should be back in a couple of days."

"Who are you?" the driver asked.

"His cousin Leo. The wife and I had fight. He's letting me stay in the cabin while she cools off."

The other soldier laughed. "What have I been telling you, Dragoş? You're going to your funeral, not your wedding."

Dragoş turned to his comrade. "My Mara is not a shriveled turnip like your wife, Radu. You won't find me camping out in a shepherd's cabin like him or hiding in the barracks like you."

"They're all pears until you pluck them," Radu said.

Both men approached Drom. The driver's hand came off the holster, but hung beside it. "My wedding is this Sunday. I paid Veress for a lamb. I've come to pick it up."

"Of course!" Drom slapped his forehead. "Veress said someone was coming for the lamb, but I wasn't expecting soldiers. The lamb is tied up behind the cabin. Follow me."

Drom gave them his back and strode around the corner of the cabin. He increased his pace along its side and whipped around to the back. He picked up two small logs from the wood pile and sprinted around the other side of the cabin.

"La dracu," Dragoş said. "Where did he go?"

Drom came up behind them and let fly with both logs. They helicoptered in the air and crashed into the backs of their heads. The men collapsed, face down.

"Drake, get out here!" Drom jumped on Dragoş, pulled the pistol out of the holster, and jammed it into his waistband. Blood seeped from the back of the man's head. Drom shifted to the other soldier. Seeing no sidearm, he rolled him over. His lids were open, his eyes rolled back. His slack jaw exposed broken bottom teeth.

"Rat-gêló returns." Drake crouched beside him. "And here I was, afraid you were done with killing."

Drom placed his finger on the man's carotid. "He's alive."

"What about the other one?"

"Help me get them inside."

They dragged the victims around and into the cabin. Drake doubled over, coughing. He spit a gob out the door, spattering the native clay red.

"Take a rest," Drom said. "I'll strip them."

Drom checked Dragoş for a pulse and prayed a silent thanks when he found one. "Their truck has a winch on the front. We can used it to get me in the compound."

"You plan on pulling the gates down with it?"

"Not exactly."

✦

"This is nuts," Drake said. "You have a bum ankle."

"And you're coughing blood. It's our best way in."

Drom climbed out from behind the wheel and belly crawled to the cliff's edge. Hiking into Romania from Hungary had punished his ankle. Running to take the soldiers out tortured it some more. He tried to ignore its throbbing while he studied the recesses and prominences of the bluff in the light of the setting sun.

The house dominated the back third of the compound. Its rounded, cedar shingled roof reminded Drom of the traditional *vurdon* of the Roma. The walls were whitewashed, the windows deeply inset. It could have been built a hundred years ago by peasants one step above slaves using straw bales for walls and local clay for daub. Or it was built when the concrete walls were poured, making the house a fortress in its own right.

Drom crawled back to the truck and cranked it to life. He toggled the winch control, unspooling the cable.

"Half the village saw us drive up here. Someone is bound to inform them," Drake said.

Drom dragged the slack cable over to the edge. "You worry too much."

"Not worrying enough gets you killed."

Drom stared at him. "There is a chance I've got this all wrong. It's possible that little fortress in this remote village is the favorite getaway for one of Ceauşescu's cronies."

"What's your point?"

"If it's military or government, you think any of the villagers would bother to report to the military that a military truck is sitting on the hill above them?"

"And if you're right and Phélypeaux or Frabron are down there?"

"Military guards at the gate. Didn't see any security in the courtyard. I think we're safe."

"Says the limping man getting ready to free climb down a bluff at dusk."

Drom lifted the steel coil in his hands. "I have cable."

"You're insane."

"Was, once." He slung the cable over the edge. "I'll open the gates when I'm done."

"And if you fail?"

Drom handed him the pistol. "If I don't have them open by daybreak, you'll need to get back to McAbee and find another solution."

Drake eyed the pistol, then looked at him. "What makes you think I'll wait that long?"

"You've come this far. I'll take my chances." Drom moved to the edge and grasped the cable in both hands. Laying on his belly, he swung his legs over and lowered himself hand under hand.

"Hey, kid!"

Drom peered over the lip of the cliff. "What?"

"Been nice working with you," Drake said, "whoever you are."

Drom uncoiled his arms and all the world was rock.

The cable bought him a third of his descent. He had to pick his way down the remainder. He took his time, keeping as much weight off his right foot as the face allowed, his arms carrying a disproportionate amount of the work. Night came and with it, a deeper chill that soon bled the day's warmth out of the rock. He looked down.

Ten meters to go.

Hanging on by the fingertips of his right hand, he ran the palm of his left across the rock face below. It skipped over the familiar shape of a vertical pinch near his knee. He gripped the formation, his thumb on the inside, and transferred his weight down and through. His right toe tapped a ledge. He pressed onto it, gritting his teeth against the pain, and shook some life back into his right arm.

Eight meters to go.

His ankle screamed until he found another foothold and shifted his weight onto his left leg. He let his right dangle. Pawing at the rock, he found another handhold.

Feel, grip, transfer, lower. Rest. Paw, pinch, drop, plant. Pant.

Despite the cold, sweat dripped from his brow, stinging his eyes. Clinging to the face, he checked over his shoulder. Lights shone through several of the upstairs windows. Exterior floods attached to the security wall illuminated the front courtyard and several of the outbuildings. The full moon brushed the rear of the compound in silver light, making it appear two dimensional.

Holding on with his left hand, he reached down with his right. He found a slope and palmed it like a small basketball. Using it as a brace, he released his left grip, leaning down and away. The edge of his left boot caught the lip of a rock and he transferred his weight.

The limestone flaked away.

His full weight dropped like a hanged man against the grip of his right hand. He searched with his left and found only smooth rock. His fingertips slipped from the slope and he shot to the ground four meters below.

His feet struck the scree. He accordioned into a crouch, tucked and tumbled backwards, slamming his left hand against the stones stabbing out of the sharp gravel.

He lay staring the moon and stars while he caught his breath. Wind gusted above the drumming in his ears. No alarms sounded. No doors creaked open or banged shut. He rolled onto his knees. His right ankle protested. He was used to that. The pain in his left hand was new.

He stood and checked himself over. His left pant leg was torn at the thigh. He peeled it open and inspected the angry rock rash beneath. The abrasion was weeping blood, but there were no lacerations. He raised his left hand. His ring finger flopped forward. His pinky was splayed away from the palm.

He rotated the wrist. Pain flared from the joint, deafening the discomfort of his dislocated fingers. Feeling around the knuckles with his right hand, he manipulated the fingers back into place. He tried to make a fist and only managed a claw. He ripped a strip of fabric from his torn pant leg and bound his injured fingers to his middle one.

He crept to the back of the farm house and ran his hand across the cool whitewash. He pulled out the ceramic knife and twirled its point into the hardened clay. Minutes later, bits of straw flaked out of the widening hole. Not a fortress, then.

Sliding along the back, he came to a window. It was double-hung, a modern touch on the traditional house. He pushed up on the bottom sash. It didn't budge.

Gravel crunched, the sound traveling away. Metal hinges creaked followed by murmurs of distant conversation. A changing of the guard, perhaps.

He wedged the knife between the top and bottom sash and slid it toward the center. It hit the latch and he increased his pressure. The latch popped. The knife skipped, hit the window frame, and snapped, leaving him with the handle and half a blade. He stuck it back in the sheath, pushed the bottom window up, and pulled himself onto the deep sill with his good arm.

He dangled there a moment, his chest laid across the half-meter thickness of the wall, his head poking into a pitch-black room. Reaching in with both hands, he grabbed the inside sill and pulled himself across, gritting his teeth against the agony of his broken wrist. His trunk tipped over the edge and dragged his legs through the window as he fell to the floor.

He rested in the darkness as his eyes adjusted. In the spare moonlight, his surroundings took shape. Wire shelving racks stacked with boxes, bottles, and cans lined the walls and cut through the center. He grabbed a can and read the label, cockles in brine from Spain. He snagged another. French pork pâté. He inspected his way down the shelf and up the rack. He was in the pantry of a gourmet kitchen. Tins of chafing fuel hinted at large dinner parties.

His stomach grumbled. He helped himself to a can of smoked sardines in olive oil.

The dainties troubled him. In his eagerness to find his boys, he had built a narrative from circumstantial evidence and chased it with self-satisfying confidence. Ordinary Romanians spent hours in long lines for meager supplies. But elites dined on luxuries. He wasn't convinced that French physicians in hiding would do the same.

He dropped the last sardine in his mouth. It tasted like more. He wiped his fingers on his shirt. If he was wrong, he would tell the Romanian honchos that he broke in because he was starving. If he was right and Phélypeaux or Frabron were here, his killing days might not be over. He shifted to the door and cracked it open.

⊕

The house proper, with its posh treatment rooms and modern surgery, rivaled private Swiss clinics. He was on the right trail. If his boys weren't here, information on their whereabouts was close at hand.

He found the file room in the forward part of the house. The compound's flood lights seeped through the window, spilling onto a reference desk against the window wall and drawing gray edges on the hulking cabinets along the side of the room. Securing the door behind him, he moved to the desk. Drawing the curtains tight, he pulled the chain on the banker's lamp and gazed at the cabinets.

Phélypeaux's arrangement of the specimens in the Montpellier cellar spoke of a man who valued order—dates and names—over aesthetics. The aborted and miscarried fetuses were lined up by date, then number. Neither size nor nature of defect had seemed to influence the display. That fact spoke to the macabre remains being records, not trophies.

If Phélypeaux was a mad scientist, he was at least an organized one. The labels on the file drawers followed the familiar pattern. Confidence in his instincts restored, Drom followed his suspicions and sifted through the Z-series drawers first.

He expected medical records, but not of the type he found. These were documents of Nazi sins. It was several drawers before the files ventured past the barbarisms of the Third Reich, adding new chapters of indignity cloaked in respectable medical jargon.

German gave way to French, easing his comprehension some, though many of the technical terms escaped him. File by file, he composed a rough sketch of Phélypeaux's dealings. The doctor had either been in Auschwitz or appropriated records from there, perhaps from Mengele himself. This Drom knew from the Z-numbers used to identify Roma in the concentration camp and from the photos of the tattoos the files contained.

All the records were of pregnant women. Though a significant number showed loss through miscarriage, many had their pregnancies "surgically halted." The language of the records was dry and clinical and at complete variance with the halted lives floating in glass jars in Montpellier.

He encountered a new vein inside the second cabinet. The patients were giving birth. Male offspring were documented with minimal statistics: gestation period, birth date, weight, and length. Females had these vitals recorded along with cross-reference numbers.

Drom turned his eye back to the cabinet labels. He located the set with ranges matching the cross-reference schemes for the baby girls and found full jackets on daughters born to Auschwitz survivors. Returning to the Z-series files, he searched within a range familiar to him. He came one short of the number he was looking for. The next in sequence was hundreds higher.

He pulled the one closest to the number burned in his memory and dragged himself to the reference desk. He tossed the file on its top and collapsed into the chair in front of it. Closing his eyes for a moment, he inventoried his body looking for some part of it that wasn't hurting, sore, or exhausted. Giving up, he propped his right leg on the desk and opened the folder.

The black-and-white mugshot transfixed him. The woman's skeletal face was etched with suffering. He imagined her well fed and worry free. The face turned hauntingly familiar.

The sensation passed under the cold facts of the file. The subject was injected several times with a serum, the purpose of which wasn't noted. After twenty-nine weeks of observation and treatment, her pregnancy was "surgically halted."

Dr. Zacharias said the Nazi's worked on producing healthy carriers. He couldn't understand Phélypeaux's exertions to continue such a program. He had spirited away Nazi medical records, had used the university's largesse to make inroads with Ceaușescu's regime, and maintained a protected private clinic in rural, Communist Romania. To what end?

Cinq Cornes held France's concerns and benefits as its driving force and raison d'être. What benefit would they derive from a batch of healthy carriers?

He rubbed his eyes. It had to be nearing midnight. Usually, the hour wouldn't find him tired. The descent, pain, and intensive study had drained him. Floorboards creaked above, someone or something moving about. He eyed his ankle and clawed hand, then leaned his head back and stared at the ceiling.

Ready or not, here I come.

Soon as I'm ready.

He forced himself out of the chair and backtracked to the nearest treatment suite. Digging through the supply cabinets, he found bandage rolls, tape, and aspirin. He swallowed four aspirin down his dry throat and replaced the cloth strips around his fingers with tape.

He wound elastic bandage around his wrist, then carried it across his palm and over his thumb web. After several turns, he had it immobilized. The arm was useless for any deadly throws, but it would stand up for a block or parry.

He killed the light and slipped out to the stairs. A chandelier dangled from the center rafter of the hall above. Its rays glistened on the burnished wood treads and cast the risers into shadow.

He climbed, keeping to the right and using the railing for support.

The hall came into fuller view as he neared the head of the stairs. An elderly man with a full head of gray hair and wearing a red, velvet smoking jacket eyed him as he ascended. Drom took the next step up. The man bent down and rose with a small child in his arms. The toddler clung to his neck, then turned its head when the stair creaked.

It was David.

"The salmon returns for its spawn," the elderly man said in French.

Drom rushed him and pain exploded across his face, turning his world to darkness.

Chapter 49

The Church is the ally of all those who defend authentic human freedoms. For freedom is inseparable from the Truth which every human being seeks and which makes human beings truly free. In the words of the Gospel of Saint John, "You will know the truth, and the truth will make you free."

Pope John Paul II, *ibid.*

Valea Lupşii, Romania – November 24, 1988

Cold, needling and wet, pulled him up from oblivion. Searching for his last thought, Drom found David and damage. Water splashed over him, sending the chill deeper. Blinking his eyes clear, he tried to rise.

It was useless.

He was strapped to a wooden chair, his hands tied behind its back and his calves lashed to its front legs. New notes of misery played through his body's symphony of agony. Stabbing pain twisted in his low back. Air refused to enter his nose. His left eye opened with difficulty, watering profusely. His head throbbed with thought-robbing ferocity. His mouth was a blood-washed desert.

His surroundings came into focus. He was in the front courtyard, facing the house. Scanning the sky, he found the moon dipping its edge below the mountain range to the west. He had been out for hours.

A bonfire blazed off to his left, painting the men in front of him with dancing light. Bastien Frabron, his leg in a brace and holding a metal softball bat, stood next to the older man in the smoking jacket. The gentleman raised a cigarette to his lips and the tip glowed red, adding its tint to the firelight playing across his signet ring.

"Dr. Phélypeaux," Drom said, "Franz Zacharias sends his regards."

Phélypeaux tipped his chin up and blew out a long plume of smoke.

Frabron lumbered to him with a stiff limp. Propping the bat on his shoulder, he bent down and pressed his thumb into the swollen ridge of Drom's left eye. Stars burst into view and fire bloomed across his face. The pressure increased and Drom feared his eyeball would pop. He shook his head to foil the thumb, but Frabron maintained contact despite his thrashing.

"Seymour, the man you blinded with your cleat, sends his regards." The thumb came away. Drom gasped. His left eye wouldn't open. His right was awash in tears. "Christelle, who you let bleed out in Montpellier, sends her regards as well."

Anguish shot through Drom's legs. His feet twitched and shuddered against their confines. He clenched his jaw and forced the sardines to stay down.

Frabron was a shadow demon, the bonfire his backdrop. He propped the bat back on his shoulder and patted Drom's face. "You'll hear from me later."

He limped away, signaling someone in the darkness. Moments later, a couple of soldiers placed an armchair in front of him. Phélypeaux sauntered over and settled into the seat like a king taking his throne.

He crossed his legs, took another drag on the cigarette, and studied Drom as he blew out the smoke. "Your children are rather extraordinary. I have enjoyed their company."

"Jakob is here, then, along with David?"

"But, of course. I am not a cruel man, Mr. Leoppard. I wouldn't separate siblings."

"Will you let me see them before the Butcher finishes his work?"

"If you believe him to be a butcher, what must you think of yourself?"

"I haven't killed any children."

"Not for lack of trying, I am sure."

Mutilated school boys, stones lodged in their faces, played across his mind's eye. He shook his head and the pain spike cleared the horrific memory away. "Why am I still alive?"

"Why, indeed." Phélypeaux uncrossed his legs and bent forward, elbows on knees. He pointed at Drom with his cigarette. "You are ever the wrecking ball, crashing into things looking for answers to all the wrong questions."

Blood pooled at the back of his throat. He hocked his soft palate clear and spat near his captor's feet. "My apologies, Doctor. Seems something in my face is broken."

"Broken? I doubt it. You're as hardheaded as your father was."

"He brought my mother here."

Phélypeaux settled back into his chair with an amused grin. "I warned Bastien you were bright. He was convinced you were just lucky."

Drom strained against his ropes for a beat. "I wouldn't call this winning the lottery. Why go after CHIMERA?"

"The Leoppard cub awakens! At last, a worthy question. CIA was destroying my life's work. I needed to know what they knew and stop them. Bastien is good. But for that, I required someone better."

Drom dragged a feeble stream of air through his nose. He held his breath a moment, listening to the pounding in his head.

His life hurt.

"You hired someone already familiar with your work."

"If he had approached me in Montpellier, I would have dismissed him out of hand. But then, your father probably knew that. Obvious wasn't his style. I first met him there," Phélypeaux jabbed his thumb over his shoulder, "sitting behind the desk in my old study upstairs. Imagine my fright."

Drom didn't need to imagine. He had his memories. "Sounds like he recruited you."

"We became partners, of sorts." Phélypeaux flicked the ash off his cigarette. "I wasn't surprised when he showed up a couple of years later with your mother."

"And now you have me. You don't need my children. Send them back to their mother."

"You think I took them for bait? No, my dear boy. They were the quarry. You were merely an obstacle Bastien was supposed to remove."

The quarry? His boys the target all along?

Drom was missing something. He closed his eye to shut out Phélypeaux for a moment and imagined a large table in front of him. Onto it, he dropped all the intelligence he had gathered. He fanned the CHIMERA file out on his left and the medical records on his right. In quick succession, he found several names that appeared in both.

Keeping the names, he replaced the table with a map of Europe. He flared red dots on the patients' locations and searched his memory for any news items on rare outbreaks in those areas.

There were none.

He peered at Phélypeaux. "You weren't breeding for healthy carriers."

"The methodology is similar," Phélypeaux said. "Similar enough to fool the likes of Professor von Verschuer. It granted me access to their wealth of test subjects."

"Concentration camp inmates."

"It was an unparalleled opportunity."

"So, you are an opportunist."

Phélypeaux narrowed his gaze. "I am a realist. War is suffering. I became a doctor to ease it. When I was drafted into Drancy, my desires and theories came together in the person of your grandmother. Wounds never lingered on her."

"I've seen your collection," Drom said. "You didn't restrict yourself to Hishoro."

"Of course not. No study worth its salt can be based on just one patient. But she was my inspiration. I followed her to Auschwitz. Beppo didn't know what he had. He was the *Malach ha-Mavet*, after all, the Angel of Death. Hishoro was life fantastic. I needed to understand it. I wanted to improve upon it."

Drom replayed the medical records through his mind, looking for patterns. One theme continually cropped up. "Mitochondria. My mother would have inherited Hishoro's, and I, my mother's. If there is something peculiar in that line, it ends with me. I have no sisters. My boys are useless to you."

"If nature had been left to its devices, you would be right."

"You were injecting the women with something. What was it?"

"Typhus was rampant in Auschwitz-Birkenau. Whenever it got out of hand in any of the blocks, Beppo would order its extermination. The infection samples were unparalleled. A colleague of mine in medical school, a Jewish woman from a Romanian town, was there. She shared my interest in the similarities between mitochondria and Rickettsia, the bacteria that causes typhus."

"You injected pregnant women with typhus?"

"Not only pregnant women and not exactly typhus. Dr. Etel and I refined the disease vector. The original goal was to cause a kind of mitochondrial cancer that would increase their number in the patient's cells."

"Your specimen jars speak of massive failure."

"Science is trial and error, fail-fast iterations to find the right path. Many patients died. They were going to be exterminated anyway. At least in my hands, their death served a purpose."

"That's a nice fairy tale, Doctor. Tens of thousands survived Auschwitz. There would have been more but for you."

The half-smile returned to the doctor's face. "Now who's spinning fairy tales? You weren't there. You have no idea of the demands of the times we lived in. And if the specimens in my jars bother you, consider the fact that were it not for them, you wouldn't be."

Drom fought to concentrate through the pounding in his head and the throbbing of his extremities. Phélypeaux's life's work led him to abduct Jakob and David. Shane Leoppard had formed alliances with brilliant scientists in a bid to gain the upper hand on both superpowers and Stockton's Foundation. What had his father gained from Phélypeaux?

"Who am I?" he asked.

"Wrong question, *mon ami*."

The pieces tumbled in, cascading into a picture he could almost see. "What am I?"

Phélypeaux's lopsided grin blossomed into a full smile. "My success. The serum was volatile, genetically active and unpredictable. Twins given the same batch would have different reactions. Some lived, some died, few changed."

"Twins." Drom's head amplified his pulse to a higher level of torture.

"Mengele inherited his obsession from Verschuer. Twins provided an elegant way to test theories. His flaw, as well as mine, was short-sighted ambition. Once I realized I couldn't produce the type of change I was after in a single generation, I changed my approach."

"CHIMERA was launched to prevent children like me," Drom said.

"Precisely. Despite their intrigues and bumbling, the CIA is still quite formidable. They moved to stop my work, though they misunderstood it."

"Not a bio-weapon, not healthy carriers."

"Not healthy carriers, yes. But a bio-weapon of the first order, soldiers of extraordinary stamina and incredible constitutions who could also be used as studs to continue their kind, males who could pass down their mitochondrial DNA."

"My boys."

"And you. You are the first, my proof of concept. Jakob and David are the product. With them, France will once again take her rightful place at the helm of the world."

"Why settle for two when you can have three?" Drom pressed against the ropes. "Cut me loose. Let me train them."

Phélypeaux relaxed into his chair and exhaled a plume of smoke. "I'm afraid that's not possible. Soldiers is what I need. You have too much of *l'esprit gitan* to conform to anyone else's agenda. Bastien, time for the children to say good-bye to their father."

Frabron marched off from his watchdog post at Phélypeaux's side. Moments later, he returned carrying David on his hip and leading Jakob by the hand.

"Daddy!" Jackob leapt toward him and was checked by the Frenchman's grip. "Let me go! I want to see Daddy!" The little boy kicked Frabron's shin just below the leg brace. Frabron swatted him down like a fly.

Drom's body shot off the chair and hit its restraints a nanosecond later. The chair hopped, creaking as it teetered, and settled back on its four legs.

Jakob got up and wiped his nose with his sleeve. He glared at Frabron, the set of his face all too familiar to Drom.

"Jakob, stop. Daddy's okay. I'll hold you in a minute. Just do what the man asks."

His son turned to him, wiped his nose again and lowered his head. Frabron grabbed him by the collar and marched him over to Phélypeaux. The doctor took Jakob's hand and received David with his other arm. He set the toddler on his lap, facing Drom.

"I promised Bastien his due. You've cost him much in honor, pain, and personnel."

Frabron reached behind the armchair and came out with the bat. "Your boys need to know their father is human, frail like everyone else." He swung.

The bat slammed across Drom's chest, toppling him backward. His head crashed into the gravel. His hands were crushed under his own body weight. He tipped onto his side and fought for air.

Frabron's boots crunched toward him. The chair righted, then settled into a creaking tilt. The man's face filled his vision, a sheen of sweat clinging to the stubble on his chin. "We can't afford to let them hold onto your myth."

Metal collided against his shoulder, tossing the chair onto its side. Drom's face bounced against the stones. Blood and sweat burned his eye.

"Stop it! You're hurting Daddy!"

Through the fog of his injuries, Drom spotted Jakob struggling against Phélypeaux's hold. The boy broke free, tripped, and fell face down into the gravel. He pushed onto his knees.

The earth tilted back to horizontal. Drom's right leg was twisted under the seat. He pressed against the ropes and the cracked chair leg shifted. Frabron patted his cheek, then backhanded him. "Your boys will watch you die and know you will never rescue them."

The Frenchman wound up with the bat. Behind him, Drom spied Jakob moving beside Phélypeaux, a stone in each hand.

"Jakob, no!" Too late.

Jakob stretched erect, flowed into a sideways arc, and whipped his right arm out. His body pivoted like a sprinkler head and the stone in his left hand traced the one from his right.

Frabron's eyes shot wide. His coup de grâce died out in mid-swing and fell as a glancing blow across Drom's neck and collar bone. The big man toppled forward like a felled tree, landing full force on Drom. They crashed to the ground, splintering the chair under the violence of their combined mass.

Drom wormed out from under Frabron's dead weight. He straightened his legs. Circulation returned and with it, the burning ache of his wounds. Gritting his teeth, he bent double and pulled his bound wrists past his buttocks. Jack-knifing his legs, he brought his arms out in front. As he pulled them over his feet, his forearm rode over a slight rise at his ankle.

He clawed his pant leg up with numb fingers and pulled out the broken knife. Flipping the half-blade toward his wrists, he sawed against the rope.

"Guards! Guards!" Phélypeaux's voice, calm and contemptuous moments before, squawked with desperation.

As if in answer to Phélypeaux's alarm, a crash of metal ripped through the air behind Drom. Light washed across the courtyard, catching Phélypeaux in its glare. Drom craned his neck back in time to see the DAC truck bearing down on him.

His hands came free and he rolled out of the way. The truck's wheels locked up and it slid to a stop, its tires dug inches deep into the gravel. Gunfire erupted, tearing holes through the bed canvass and shattering the cab windows. Drom tucked against the tandem behind the cab and cut away the cords around his legs.

The passenger door banged open and Drake dove out. He scurried over to Drom and crouched next to him. "I tried to run you over, but it looks like someone beat me to it."

Drom glared at him with his one good eye. "I said daybreak."

"You sent smoke signals."

"Not my fire."

"How was I supposed to know?" More lead tore through the truck. Drake drew the pistol. "He ran inside with your boys. I'll keep the guards busy." He rolled under the truck and fired several rounds toward the gate. "Go!"

Drom forced his legs to run over the agony of his injuries. Bursting through the front door, he dove against the wall. Windows shattered in a rip of gunfire, raining glass on his head and down his shirt.

A scream came from the staircase. He crawled toward it. A shadow broke from the stair, rushing to him. He braced himself, ready to swing as soon as the shape drew near.

"Daddy!"

"Jakob!" Pulling the punch, he hooked the boy into his arms and lay flat on the floor as more gunfire erupted. Shouted commands, the crunch of gravel, more shots.

"Imbéciles!" Phélypeaux roared. "Stop firing on the house!"

A single crack, pistol shot. A burp of automatic fire answered. More shouts outside.

Drom pressed his lips to Jakob's ear. "Where's David?" The little boy pointed toward the stairs. Drom kissed his head and parked him against the wall. "Stay put, okay, buddy?"

He crept to the staircase. Phélypeaux sat near the top in the chandelier's glow, a hand pressed against his bleeding thigh. His other arm held David's trembling form tight to his chest.

"Stop," Phélypeaux said. "Any closer and I'll fling him head first down the stairs."

"And lose your creation?"

"I can make more."

"You're hurt. Let me help you." Drom started up the stairs on all fours.

Phélypeaux slipped his arm around Dravid's throat. "Back off before I break his neck."

In one fluid motion, Drom snagged the broken knife from its sheath, flicked it up the stairs, and scrambled after it.

The knife flipped end over end, handle outweighing blade. Its blunt grip drove through Phélypeaux's eye. His hands flew to his face and David fell to Drom. He caught his son and Phélypeaux crashed into him. All three tumbled down into a heap at the bottom of the stairs. David wailed. Drom held him closer and squirmed away from Phélypeaux.

The gunfire had stopped.

"Jakob?"

"I stayed put, Daddy!"

"Good boy. I'm coming to you." He comforted David as he worked his way to Jakob. He rounded the corner and the lights came on.

"Anybody home?" Drake asked

"Over here."

Glass crunched underfoot as Drake approached the stairs. "The good doctor, I presume?"

"We need to get out of here."

"We'll need another vehicle. Whatever I didn't break on the way in, the guards took care of during the firefight."

"Search the outbuildings. I need to check the boys over, make sure they're not hurt."

"You should check yourself over. You look like a train wreck, if you'll pardon the expression."

"Don't worry about me. Find us a ride."

"On it." Drake stared at him a second. "You sure you can manage?"

Drom squeezed David to him. Crying had given way to sniffles. His boy burrowed his head into the crook of Drom's neck. "Yeah. I'm good."

"Make it quick. It doesn't take a village to call the authorities." He spun on his heel and headed out the door.

Drom hobbled into a treatment suite and perched David on the exam table. He picked Jakob up and sat him beside his brother.

Jakob stroked his cheek. "You hurt."

"I know, baby. How about you, you hurt?"

"No, I'm hungry."

"Me hungie too," David said.

"I'll feed you in a minute. Let me look you over first." He inspected their arms and legs, making sure nothing was broken. He cleaned up Jakob's face and swabbed his split lip with antiseptic. The boy winced, but didn't complain.

Drom moved to the mirror over the sink. His face was a fright. He untucked his shirt and bits of glass dusted the floor around his feet. He unbuttoned it and took it off. His chest and shoulder were red and bruising. Frabron's blow opened Christelle's cut. Fresh blood seeped out of the gaps between the torn stitching.

He turned around and looked over his shoulder. Several pieces of glass were imbedded in his back. He grabbed a pair of tissue forceps from the implement drawer and stepped to Jakob. "Buddy, I need your help. These are like big tweezers." He demonstrated how they worked. "You have to pull the glass out of my back" He turned around.

"Gross, Daddy."

"I know, baby. Just pinch the glass with the tips until the handles click together and pull." He felt pressure against his back and then a tear.

"You bleeding."

"It will stop in a minute. You're doing great. Keep going."

Moments later, the prodding and prying stopped. "Can we eat now?"

"Soon." Drom shifted back to the sink. He washed his face, mopped his back and chest with a towel, and put his shirt back on. He stuffed his pockets with supplies to treat his wounds later.

He took the boys to the pantry. "They have some tasty sardines."

"Fish, yuck!"

"How about olives? You like olives, right?"

"Olives are yummy," Jakob said.

Drom found a jar of Spanish olives and cracked it open. "Snack on these."

Jakob plucked several out of the brine and handed a couple to David. "Look, Daddy, crackers."

Drom followed the pointing finger and found the crackers sitting by the match boxes and chafing fuel tins. He opened the cracker box, pulled out a sleeve, then remembered the pork pâté. Snagging a can, he peeled the pull tab back and scooped the pâté up with a cracker. He handed it to Jakob. "Try that."

Jakob took a nibble, chewed it a bit, then crammed the rest into his mouth.

"Me!" David said.

Drom fed him a cracker and allowed himself the joy of watching him eat it.

"Those are great," Jakob said. "I bet the girls would like them."

Drom dropped the can. "Girls?"

Jakob nodded. He took the cracker sleeve from Drom and bent down for the pâté.

Phélypeaux's boast came back to him. *I can make more.* "Jakob, show Daddy where the girls are."

Jakob led him back toward the staircase. He paused at a door fixed in its side. "In there."

Drom tried the door. Locked. "Take your brother back to the pantry. Make sure you two get your fill, okay."

448

"Okay. Come on, David." Jakob took his brother's hand and the pair scampered down the hall.

Drom limped to Phélypeaux's body. He rolled the man over and retched. The first kill of the day was always hard, the first in his new life doubly so. The broken blade pointed at him from Phélypeaux's eye socket like an accusing finger.

"You threatened my son," Drom said.

He searched the doctor's pockets and found a set of keys. He palmed them, then eyed the Cinq Cornes signet ring. He pulled it from the lifeless finger and stuck it in his pocket.

The lock gave way to the second key. He swung the door open and flipped the switch on the wall. Yellow glared against concrete steps leading below the earth. He negotiated them one step at a time, his right hand on the wall to help him balance. The basement floor was dressed with cobble stones set in swirls. Their arcs led him forward like waves to an iron manhole bolted shut.

He drew the bolt. Gripping the handle, he heaved up and the lid reluctantly gave ground. He hooked his broken arm into the opening and lifted, his wrist howling in protest. The iron cover hinged to the tipping point, then flapped to the floor with a deafening clang. He bent over the hole.

"Hello?" His call echoed down the shaft.

A girl's face, acorn shaped and smeared with dirt, appeared in the dark circle. Spacious brown eyes stared up at him under dark brows and ringlets of black hair. Her broad nose pointed down to trembling lips astride a sharp chin.

"Adjutati-ne," she pleaded. *"Adjutati-ne, va rog!"*

⊕

"Rat-gêló! Where are you, boy? I found a ride. Sun's up. We need to go."

Drom came up the hallway with his boys in the lead. He spotted Drake in the bullet-riddled front salon. "How big of a ride?"

"Sedan, large enough for us and the boys. Why?"

"We have more." Drom stepped aside and five girls streamed past him.

"There's a Mercedes van stashed in the garage. Is this everybody?"

"Yeah. Get them loaded. I'll be right out." He crouched eye level with his sons. "Go with Mr. Drake, boys."

"But, Daddy—"

"Go on, Jakob. I'm right behind you." He turned to the first girl. *"Du-te cu onul."*

She corralled her sisters and helped the boys out the door behind Drake.

Drom returned to the file room. He reviewed the profile he left on the desk. He found a reference number jotted down in the margin next to the note on her surgically halted pregnancy. Turning to the file cabinets, he located the drawer with the correct range. He pulled the relevant files and stacked them on the desk.

He attacked the cabinets again, dumping their contents in scattered heaps across the floor. Snatching the files from the desk, he tucked them under his arm. He yanked the banker's lamp, snapping the cord. Holding its neck, he hammered the walls with its heavy base. Plaster broke away in chunks, exposing the ancient straw bales beneath.

He battered his way down the hall to the pantry. He put the folders inside a plastic garbage bag, pushed the air out, he tied it shut close to the files. He twisted the long neck into a cord and tied it to his belt.

He filled two more bags with food and dragged them to the front stoop. He limped back to the pantry and grabbed a couple of flats of chafing fuel cans and a box of kitchen matches. Lighting the cans, he stuck them in the holes in the hallway walls as he shuffled back to the file room.

Kneeling on the pile of papers, he smashed several of the cans open with the lamp and splashed their contents all around. Taking the last two cans, he lit the wicks and tossed them in the middle of the room as headed out the door.

Heat bloomed behind him with a woosh.

Hefting the bags of food, he stepped off the stoop and staggered to the van. He set the bags on the floorboard between the front seats and climbed in. Through the windshield, he spotted Frabron's body beneath the front tire of the DAC.

He turned to Drake. "Drive."

Drake stared past him.

Drom looked to his right. Flames licked out of the file room window.

"Couldn't help yourself, could you?"

Drom eyed him. "I've got a reputation to maintain."

Chapter 50

We gather here today to bear witness to the past and learn from its awful example, and to make sure that we're not condemned to relive its crimes. I am today signing the Genocide Convention Implementation Act of 1987, which will permit the Unites States to become party to the International Convention on the Prevention and Punishment of the Crime of Genocide that was approved by the United Nations General Assembly in 1948.

President Ronald Reagan's Remarks
on signing the Proxmire Act
Chicago, Illinois, November 4, 1988

Perpignan, France – December 4, 1988

Drom checked his rearview mirror. Jakob, David, and the girls were all asleep. He took the Perpignan exit.

They got away clean from their action in Valea Lupşii. An hour's drive inside Hungary, Drom parleyed the Mercedes van into a smuggled ride inside a trailer of furniture bound for Austria's budget market. Drake's cough grew worse during the transit. Safely out from behind the Iron Curtain, Drom insisted on getting him some medical attention.

"I'll be fine," Drake said. "Just need to rest up in a hotel for a couple of days."

"You look worse than tired, old man."

"Yeah? You look in a mirror lately?"

He had point. Three days out of the Valley of Wolves and Drom still looked like he had been mauled by the pack.

"You're right," Drom said. "We both need doctoring. You have any markers left in Austria?"

"What do I need favors for? We have the Pond."

Drom put an arm around one of the girls. "We can't contact McAbee yet."

Drake started to reply, then fell into a coughing fit. He wiped blood from his lips and eyed Drom. "Find a phone."

It turned out that even a disgraced intelligence officer who had been incommunicado for four years still held secrets valuable enough to buy a couple of favors. Within a few hours, they were all crammed into a 1985 Volkswagen Westfalia with enough cash to carry them a week.

Drom took them to Vienna and they checked into two adjoining rooms on the top floor of an economy hotel. He got Drake bedded down and charmed one of the maids to keep an eye on the children for him. He stepped out into the night scene of the city of spies and melted into familiar haunts in search of a secure phone line.

Ten minutes in a night club owner's office cost him over half their cash reserves. Hearing Karoly's basso voice vibrate across a continent, under the Atlantic, and through half of Europe made it instantly worth it. "Only one person has this number."

"How are you, old friend?" Drom asked.

"Relieved. I feared you dead."

"I get that a lot. Listen, I don't have much time. How much did the Feds get?"

"Only what I let them find and most of that they had to give back."

"Can you move a hundred thousand in my direction?"

"How soon do you need it?"

"Check out time is in ten hours."

"Must be some hotel."

"Can you do it?"

"I won't be selling any cars today, but yeah. Where do you want it?"

Drom gave him the drop site and what the courier should wear. "One more thing."

"Name it."

"I need papers for myself and seven children."

"You've been busier than I thought. I'll need more than ten hours for that. Those contacts aren't exactly sitting by the phone."

"Understood. I can help a bit from this side if you have some first steps ready in time for the courier. I know they're still watching you. If you pull this off, I'll owe you big."

"Drom, after all you've done for me, you could never be in my debt."

Karoly came through in spades.

Drom checked Drake into a hospital the next day. Hearing the initial prognosis from the doctor, he put twenty thousand dollars down on Drake's account with instructions to return any balance to the man when he was released. After his procedure, Drom sat with him in the room until he came to.

"What time is it?" Drake asked.

"Time for me to get going. You're in good hands here."

Drake tried to sit up, grimaced, then ran his hand down his rib cage. "What did they do?"

"A little patchwork. The French viper left you with a bleeder. Doc says you have an excellent chance of recovery. He also said no smoking."

"I haven't had a smoke in four years."

"So you keep telling me." Drom stood next to the bed, his gaze fixed on Drake. "What are you going to tell McAbee?"

Drake eyed the IV tube from his arm to the bag hanging on the chrome tree. "What did you have them dope me with?"

"Amnesia-inducing drugs," Drom said.

"Seriously? They have those?"

"I wish. I don't know about you, but there's a good portion of my life I would just as soon forget."

"No kidding," Drake said. "There's a bunch of your life I would love to forget, too."

Drom rolled his eyes. "So, McAbee?"

"I'll give Russell a full report, how we tracked Phélypeaux and Frabron all the way to Romania, and how you burned him and his experiment to the ground. Pity you never made it out."

"You're going to tell him I died in Valea Lupşii?"

"Man's got a reputation to maintain."

Drom gave his shoulder a squeeze. "Take care of yourself, old man."

"Stay above ground, kid."

The new identity papers took the better part of the next two days. All the passports carried the same surname, making their familial relation official on paper.

He took his time getting to Perpignan, stopping frequently along the way and camping out overnight. As they rolled into the ancient neighborhood of Saint Jaques, he dug the piece of paper out of his pocket. Discreet inquiries during the past week had garnered him an address in the Roma enclave.

He crept west on Rue du Paradis. Despite the chill, people were out. Residents squeezed past the van on narrow sidewalks and ducked into closing shops and rousting bars. Turning right on Rue Tracy, he was forced to hop one set of wheels on the sidewalk to navigate what was little more than an alley.

The three-story buildings on either side formed the crumbling walls of the manmade crevasse. Even with his windows up, Drom could smell the poverty. Ahead, the street bulged out on the right. He pressed the van over and parked it on the asphalt, leaving the sidewalk free.

He cut the headlights, killed the engine, and sat a moment soaking in the scene. Flames danced above the rim of a steel barrel, casting a warm glow on the worn, yellow face of the narrow townhouse. Children kicked a faded soccer ball around as adults engaged in lively conversation.

In the middle of this community ruckus sat an old woman in a simple black smock and sensible, square-toed shoes. A pile of limp cabbage leaves adorned her lap and in front of her steamed a pan on a propane burner. Her bony hands were a flurry as she balled up minced meat from a bowl beside her and wrapped it up with the cabbage. She fed the stuffed cabbage into the steaming pan with one hand while she scooped more meat with the other.

His stomach grumbled.

He toggled the dome lights off and slipped out of the van. He gently pressed the door shut and let the aroma of garlic tomato sauce lead his feet. He reached the old woman—her eyes fixed on the pan—and breathed deep.

"Smells delicious," Drom said. "Did you make them *ito*?"

"My *sarmi* are always pepper-hot," she said without looking up. "These first ones are done. Would you like to try some?"

"I would love some, *Mami*."

Her head tilted up at being called grandmother. The seams in her brow deepened as her eyes widened. Irises dark enough to blend with their inky pupils swept his form head to foot and back again. *"Nipóto?"*

She rose from the chair, spilling the boiled cabbage leaves to the asphalt.

"*Mami*, I've missed you so."

She took a step back, her hand forming the sign to ward off evil. "It is a dream."

Drom reached into the steaming pan and plucked out a stuffed cabbage leaf. He juggled it between his hands several times, blowing on it. Once safe enough to hold, he took a bite. The garlic tomato sauce buoyed the minced beef and carried the rice and jalapeño across his tongue. "Better than I remembered."

"Rat-gêló, is it really you?"

"Come here, *Mami*, and see for yourself."

She came around the propane burner, each step quicker than the last. Standing in front of him, she reached her hand up and placed it on his chest.

His self-control shattered. He swept Hishoro up in his arms and held her close, allowing the scent of her to reach deep into all his wounds.

⊕

He slumped in a metal folding chair beside the fire barrel, rubbing his distended belly. "*Mami*, no. I'll burst if I take another bite."

Once he set her down, she had insisted on feeding him. Already the makings of a large family meal, Hishoro turned her cooking station into the center of a block party. He met many people, but saw none of their old *kumpániya*. His uncles were conspicuously absent.

"They say I'm too old to travel with them in the winter," Hishoro said when he asked her about it. "They'll not believe me when I tell them you were here."

"I think you'll be able to convince them."

"We were heartbroken when word reached us about Castellón. Now that I know you're alive, I'm worried. Why are you here? It is dangerous for you." She patted the cast on his arm.

"Dangerous for all of us, I fear." He rubbed his brow. It was still tender, but the swelling was gone and the bruising had dissipated considerably. "I came looking for answers."

"Answers to what, *nipóto*?"

Leaning forward, he took hold of her left hand with both of his. Turning her palm to the stars, he slid her blouse sleeve up. He brushed his fingertips across the tattooed number on her forearm, then looked into her eyes. "Tell me of the *Porrajmos, Mami*."

She jerked her arm back and pushed her sleeve down. "Ugly times, those. What do you need to know?"

"Everything, from the beginning."

Hishoro gestured to a middle-aged woman a couple of doorways down. Presently, she and Drom each had a cup of boiling-hot, black coffee. The neighbor dropped four sugar cubes in each and stepped away to give them their privacy.

Hishoro stirred her cup, blew across its top, and took a sip. "We didn't notice when it started. We are Roma. The world has always hated us. After …" Her voice trailed off. She took another sip of coffee, its spill on the saucer the only sign of her distress. "After, we didn't speak much of such things. Who believes the Gypsy anyway? We had a hard time believing it ourselves."

She tilted her head up for a moment—contemplating the stars or seeing the past, he wasn't sure—then drained her cup. Her gaze fixed on the flames of the barrel, their flicking tongues dancing in her eyes. "My father was selling his horses to the German army …"

Once it started, it ran like a stream, then turned into a torrent. Her memories, Tshuri's misadventures, the escape from Auschwitz, their ultimate arrival in the Basque country to retrieve Tshompi from Gorka Colón—father of Alvarez Colón, Basque terrorist and Carlos de Leon's first victim in his crusade of vengeance a lifetime ago.

At the end, Hishoro was dry-eyed and Drom was cried out.

"Near the end of my madness," he said, "I was hiding in some holly bushes, casing a building with murder on my mind. As I sat there, this old man came straight into my hiding place. He terrified me. I wanted to run, but he held me in place with a word. He unrolled his bundle of bamboo flutes, chose one, and charmed me with music more powerful than I had ever heard before. Or since, now that I think of it. He looked through me with that eye of his and told me of David and King Saul."

"He never spoke of it."

"All you ever told me of him was his name."

"His name seemed burden enough at the time."

"How come I never saw him in the camp?"

"We barely saw you in the camp. And Tshuri keeps his own company. The war made him averse to crowds. He checks in now and again. Mostly, he spends his time walking the byways in search of lost souls."

"Are you still married?"

"Very much so, almost sixty years now."

"I'm married, too. A little over three years. I have a stepdaughter who is ten and we have two boys, Jakob and David."

"Oh, Rat-gêló! I am so happy for you. After Isabela died, I feared you would never open your heart again. Do you have pictures?"

"Not of them. But I do have one of someone else." He pulled the snapshot out of jacket pocket and handed it to her. "*Mami*, is this Keti?"

Her hand came to her mouth. *"Murri phen."* Her eyes met his. "How?"

"It's why I've come. Keti was with child, Tshuri's child."

"Phélypeaux carved it out of her," Hishoro said.

"He did. But he didn't kill it. He preserved it somehow and reproduced it when the means became available."

"Reproduce it? I don't understand."

"Me either, *Mami*. All I know is that he did it. I want to show you something." Taking her hand, he led her to the van and opened the passenger door. "Hey, buddy, wake up."

Jakob stretched his arms and legs, then clung to Drom as he lifted him out of the seat. "Where are we, Daddy?"

"France. And this is your great-grandmother, Hishoro." He presented the boy to her. *"Mami*, this is Jakob."

"My, how handsome. He favors you, but I see another beauty at work as well."

"His mother is stunning. Can you give her a hug, Jakob?"

Never shy, Jakob ran to her skirts and wrapped his arms around her waist.

Drom slid the side door open and dug David out. The boy had no interest in letting go of his father. He rousted the girls and lined them up facing Hishoro.

She fell to her knees beside Jakob. "Nadja!"

⊕

"Are you sure you can't stay any longer?"

"I've been gone too long already, *Mami*. I need to get these boys back to their mother."

"And you back to your wife."

"If she will have me."

"She loves you, Rat-gêló."

"What makes you so sure?"

Hishoro stroked his furrowed brow and brushed her fingers through his hair. "You love her children. That carries weight with a woman, even when she's upset."

"I hope you're right."

"I know I'm right."

"I'll send you more money as soon as I can."

"You've left me enough for a couple of years, even with the extra mouths to feed."

"All their medical information is in the files, except their origins. Uncle Alfonso should be able to locate a trustworthy doctor if the need arises."

"I don't have much use for doctors," Hishoro said.

He pulled her in for one last hug and kissed the top of her head. "I have one more gift for you." Reaching into his pocket, he pulled out Phélypeaux's Cinq Cornes ring. He placed it on her palm and closed her fingers over it. "He will never hurt you or anyone else ever again."

Epilogue

1976 FORD GRAN TORINO – Wagon. AM-FM stereo, AC, power steering. Great paint, some dents. Dependable. $1,000 or best offer. Phone 555-3766

Classified Ads, *Rocky Mountain News*, December 6, 1988

Washington, D.C. – December 7, 1988

Rick limped to her desk leaning hard on his cane, a newspaper tucked under his arm. "Good morning, Carol."

Her fingers continued their tap dance on the keyboard for several beats before she looked up. "My, my, you're doing better."

"It's good to be up and walking around."

"The surgery was a success, then."

"No, she ... I'm sorry, which surgery?"

"Your leg."

"The leg, yes. Doctor said it's coming along well."

She picked up her handset and tapped the intercom button. "Sir, Special Agent Cannon is here. Yes, sir." She cradled the receiver. "He's waiting for you."

He shuffled past her desk and opened the door.

Special Agent in Charge Dale Pritchett rose from behind his desk and came around to greet him. "Come on in, Rick, have a seat." He motioned to the round table in the front space of the office.

"Thank you, sir." Rick settled into the leather chair with a sigh of relief.

Pritchett sat across from him and leaned back into his seat. "Last time we met, I was a bit rough on you. Considering what you had been through, I could've handled it differently. Not that I condone your jumping the chain of command, mind you. Just, I should have handled it better."

"You had every right to be upset, sir. I was way out of line."

"I consider the matter closed. You?"

"Yes, sir."

"It's Dale, Rick. I called you here as your friend, not your boss."

"Oh." Rick sat up a little and placed the newspaper on the table.

"You cancelled your leave of absence."

"It's not a good time to be off."

"You and Ada have been struggling with this for years. When you finally decided to have Jewel operated on, I was happy for you. But as your friend, I am asking you to not let Ada go through this alone."

"She's not, Dale."

"But your leave—"

"She's not having the operation."

"I thought you two had this thing settled. What happened?"

His daughter had dreams, is what happened. At least, that's what he told himself in the days following Drom Reiziger's invasion of his home. He was broken and distraught. Ada was frantic. Jewel, his baby girl with the defective heart, was exuberant.

"The angel said I was better." Jewel's eyes sparkled. "Watch me run, Daddy!"

And run she had, until Ada forced her to stop.

"We, uh," Rick said, "we finally got back in to see Dr. Salvesen last week."

"He gave me a message for you," Shell said when he questioned her in Denver. "He said your fears shouldn't keep Jewel from her checkup, that miracles still happen."

"Rick? You okay?"

"What? Sorry, got lost in thought for a second."

"What did the doctor say?"

"She couldn't explain how or why, but Jewel's heart is perfectly fine."

"That's great news! You should be ecstatic."

"I am. It's just a lot to take in. Has me a bit baffled, if I'm honest."

"We've both seen our fair share of the inexplicable. Some gifts just need to be accepted."

Rick leaned forward. "He's still out there, Dale." He opened the issue of the *Rocky Mountain News* to the classifieds and tapped his finger on the ad circled in red.

"1976 Gran Torino. You think it's him?"

"Has to be. Forget the rumors. I know this guy. He wouldn't abandon Michelle Lane and he wouldn't return home without his boys."

"Which means?"

"Which means Frabron is most likely dead. It also means we have a good chance to arrest Gavin Leoppard, a.k.a. Drom Reiziger."

Dale stepped to the windows that formed the east wall of his office and gazed over the city for a moment. "Rick, you certain you don't want to take that leave?"

"Positive. The ad was placed yesterday. I should be on the next flight to Denver."

Dale faced him. "Carol has your tickets already. But before you go, I need you to understand something first."

"I'm all ears, Boss."

"The Government of the United States has no interest in arresting Gavin Leoppard. We want you to recruit him."

Acknowledgements

To all who took the epic journey that is *Gypsy Spy: The Cold War Files* and asked for more, thank you. Your enthusiasm for the story encouraged me to find the next chapter in the Gavin Leoppard saga.

Nothing hones one's writing like reading your work out loud and nothing improves upon that process quite like reading it to others. While crafting this tale, I was blessed with small audiences that listened attentively as I read chapters of the first draft soon after my pencil lead scratched across the paper. Their contribution to the final product cannot be overestimated. My daughter Elizabeth and her husband Anthony listened to the entire first draft in chunks, even though it kept them up past their bedtime on multiple occasions. Their excitement kept me going.

Many thanks to Kendal Butler Durfey, Carey Huddleston, and Aland Coons for their continual encouragement throughout the project and for reading through the near-final draft for continuity and to ensure that all story promises were kept.

An international story, *Valley of Wolves* contains a fair dose of several foreign languages. Its central characters are Romanies. My endeavors to produce phrases and dialogue in Romani would have been impossible without the works of Ronald Lee (*Learn Romani* and *Romani Dictionary: English – Kalderash*) and Ian Hancock's *We Are the Romani People*. Any degree of success at the attempt is entirely to their credit. All failures are my own. Sandrine Bruce, a native French speaker, coached me on the correct French idioms and reviewed all my French uses. Gottfried Sommer, my Bavarian friend, helped with the smattering of German. Barbara Kengle, my favorite sister, kept my Spanish straight (when I asked her). What mistakes remain are mine.

Every writer needs an editor. I was blessed with two. Abl Temple, my *xanamik* (co-parent-in-law—unlike English, Romani has a word for this relationship), dove into the front pages of the near-final draft with gusto and showed me what could be done. His example and coaching allowed me to sharpen the word count down by nearly fifteen percent and deliver a crisper story to my final editor, Linda-Jean Jay. Their work made mine much better, for which I am deeply grateful.

I would not have reached this finish line without the bone of my bones, the flesh of my flesh, the love of my life, my wife, Heidi. Not only did she keep me alive, she continually encouraged me to "Get writing!" and sacrificed the time and space that allowed me to do so. She listened to each day's production until the story was done. Without her, this book wouldn't be. Thank you, Sweetheart!

About the Author

NIKOLAS LARUM is a bi-vocational minister in coastal Virginia. In addition to his thirty-five years of ministry, he has worked as a government contractor and in the recycling industry. A lifelong traveler, Larum spent his formative, pre-teen years in Francoist Spain and returned to the U.S.A. more Spaniard than American. His experiences of ever being a stranger in a strange land are a major source of inspiration to his writing. He lives with the wife of his youth in Chesapeake, Virginia.